THE HORSES OF THE NIGHT

THE HORSES OF THE NIGHT

Michael Cadnum

Carroll & Graf Publishers, Inc.
New York

First Carroll & Graf edition 1993

Carroll & Graf Publishers, Inc.
260 Fifth Avenue
New York, NY 10001

Library of Congress Cataloging-in-Publication Data

Cadnum, Michael.
    The horses of the night / Michael Cadnum. — 1st Carroll & Graf ed.
        p.   cm.
    ISBN 0-88184-930-8 : $19.95
    1. Architects—California—San Francisco—Fiction.   2. San Francisco
(Calif.)—Fiction.   3. Supernatural—Fiction.   I. title.
PS3553.A314H67   1993
813'.54—dc20   93-7977
                                                                              CIP

Manufactured in the United States of America

I would like to thank Tom Rogers,
Curator of Collections at Filoli,
for his generous help.

Special thanks, always, to Sherina.

In memory of Jose Martinez, Jr.,
1983–1991

If a lion could talk, we would not understand him.

—Ludwig Wittgenstein

Part One

1

There was the cry again, nearly beyond hearing, somewhere outside.

Sometimes I am afraid that what I am hearing is not real, that it is something from my memory, something I have all but forgotten.

Nona put a finger to her lips, smiled, cocked her head. She was ready to leave for the airport, and had stopped by simply to leave me some of the pictures her patients had drawn. The carry-on bag was under her arm.

But she waited, listening. She looked at me, questioningly. "What is that?"

I experienced a feeling like relief. "You mean, you hear it, too?" I said.

She laughed, but then was quiet. "Something's trapped."

We both listened. Our eyes met. There had been a sound for hours, a plaintive, commanding announcement of trouble, a noise that came from somewhere high above, somewhere in the wind. "I wasn't sure it was real," I said.

"An animal's in trouble."

I had been afraid to listen to it. Some part of me must have identified this frightened melody as the call of an animal, but my experience with my family—and my own fears regarding the possibilities of the mind's deceit—made me struggle to ignore the sound.

She was already late for her flight to New Orleans, yet another medical conference. She hurried through the house, and I followed her. The afternoon sun was bright, the wet grass lush, the scent of earth everywhere.

She was far ahead of me. She tossed aside her overnight bag, and ran to the source of the sound, the giant ginkgo tree in the back garden.

She kicked off her shoes. She gazed upward, into the tree. And I knew what she was going to do. I knew it, the way I knew her laugh, her voice on the phone, her handwriting on a postcard. I took a breath to cry out, to stop her.

The tree had been planted before the house was built, and the house predated the 1906 earthquake that had devastated so much of San Francisco. My grandfather and my father had both lived here, and the garden was what one horticulturist had called "handsomely mature."

The large old tree was beside the greenhouse, and I had been forestalling too long what would have to be done. The big tree was marred by caverns where broad branches had fallen in recent winters, and although the early spring greenery flushed the tree with new life, much of it was bare and would never show leaf again. I knew enough about growing things to understand that what was slowly wearing down the magnificent tree was not disease, not insects, or drought. The tree was dying, and I did not have the heart to cut it down.

Don't do that, I called to her, silently.

Don't think of it.

Nona was climbing the grand, age-weakened tree, and it was not an easy climb. At one point she had to pause and disentangle herself from her jacket. She let the jacket drop, a scrap that resembled the outstretched arms of a woman until it collapsed on the lawn.

The cat was white, far up in the branches of the old tree, and it was frightened. It called down to Nona, the source of its rescue. It knew that Nona was working her way up to help, but the cat was frightened of Nona, too, frightened of everything and yet insistent—it demanded help.

It will be all right, I reassured myself. Nona is that sort of person. I had seen her resuscitate a man at the airport, a bell captain who had collapsed and lay flailing and gasping. She had tossed aside this bag, and a jacket like this one, and saved his life.

High, I thought. Too high.

A branch creaked. Nona was lithe, but the big tree was not really a living thing anymore. Some process in it remembered life, and struggled to resemble it, but she was risking too much to be up there in its branches.

I had never seen this cat before, but, like my late father, I believed that the unseen things need our help, and I had, from time to time, put out a plate of smoked salmon or braised perch when I had seen a hungry-looking cat stalking birds under the ornamental plums.

Too high.

Nona, slight, graceful, was able to reach the cat, and the cat shrank back along a gray-scaled branch. Nona held forth her hand, supplicating, encouraging, her voice soft, as soft as I have heard it with children in pain.

This is your fault, I told myself: You should have cut down this tree years ago.

She touched the cat, and the cat cringed and clutched at her simultaneously. It scrambled, fought for balance. And failed.

The cat did not fall at once. It hooked the gray bark of the tree with one paw, and kicked there, like a creature that has been mortally hurt.

Nona cried out and reached out to seize the cat, the branch swaying.

The falling cat was a blur, twisting.

It was like something I had dreamed would happen. I knew exactly what had to be done. I stepped across the lawn, looked up into the sun, and caught the cat, easily, with a certain grace, and before its claws could dig into me, I had the cat on the grass.

It was not a young cat. It was a tom, with a bite or two taken out of its shoulders from the wars of mating. It allowed itself an instant of amazement, or simple recognition of where it was. Then it was across the grass, into the gnarls and knobs of the pruned roses, up the brick wall.

Nona called my name.

I had a big chain saw in one of the sheds, a great, red, glazed-with-oil-and-dust monster one of the gardeners had used in years past. I knew how to work the saw, and I knew how to cut down a tree, how to predict its fall, how to ease the weight down with ropes and a certain eye for how a tree is balanced.

This was all my fault.

I told myself that it would be all right. Nona is one of those people who know how to survive. And not merely survive. Nona seemed to belong here on earth.

She would be all right, I knew.

She won't fall.

But even as I tried to reassure myself, I knew.

She clung to a branch, but the dead thing sagged, the bark ripping, something deep in the pith of the tree giving way. She looked down; I was amazed at the look she gave me.

She was not afraid—she trusted me. I wanted to cry out that I was helpless.

She let go.

For a moment nothing made any sense. The breath was knocked out of my body.

I caught her, held her in my arms. There was a moment in which nothing else mattered. I had Nona in my arms, my own strength taking her in.

Then we both were on the ground, in the damp grass.

Unable to move.

And then we were laughing. We laughed, tears in our eyes.

Yes, I reassured her, I was fine. "And you were amazing!" I said. She held me, laughing, calling herself the Flying Wonder, the Flying Nona.

But then I took her hand. Her forefinger was bleeding, the nail torn. "You're hurt," I said in a low voice.

It hurt me inside, caused me real pain, to see her injured even slightly. She insisted that she was perfectly all right, but I led her into the house and found a pair of delicate scissors and carefully trimmed away the ragged nail. I dabbed antiseptic onto the finger, and, working tenderly, applied a Band-Aid. All the while she watched my work with affection and amusement.

"Do you think I'll live?" she said when I was done.

I was about to say that I thought she had a pretty good chance, when she stopped me with a kiss.

Nona called and made a reservation for a later plane and we went upstairs, through my work room, into my bedroom, and fell together. We made love, a slow, carnal waltz, grateful, knowing that it did not have to be like this. We did not have to be so happy together.

"You knew," I said much later, in a murmur. "You did it on purpose."

"Did what?"

"You let go so I could catch you."

"I knew you would. You have good hands."

I considered this with some doubt, actually holding my fingers up before my eyes. "It was dangerous."

She snuggled back against me, a way of saying that she trusted me.

After awhile she asked, "When will you know about the prize?"

I didn't like to even think about the prize. "The announcement won't be for weeks."

"But you said there's usually a leak."

"There are ways of finding out. Blake might know. DeVere knows, but he never talks to me."

I felt her breathing, and knew that in moments she would be another sort of woman, dressing quickly, hurrying down the stairs.

Maybe some day, I thought, it will always be like this. Maybe some day I will be able to keep her here.

As she took a quick look at herself in a mirror, I slipped a little paper frog into her handbag. It was a frog I had made using an Exacto knife, and I was careful to find a secure place for it, folded up in her wallet.

A secret. A little secret—a surprise.

Nona has a way of kissing me when it is time to say good-bye, once on each eyelid, once on each eyebrow, and then once on my forehead, slowly, lingering, telling me how badly she wants to stay with me.

She let her lips linger there on my forehead. This is where my
third eye would be the seat of intuition, of insight. We both could
feel ourselves wanting to delay her departure. I stepped back
from her so I could look at her. I almost said the words: *Please
don't go.*

We kissed. If we could only stay like this, I knew, nothing bad
could ever happen.

When I was alone, I paced my house. The contractor was coming the next day, and plastic dust covers were folded in the hall
waiting, but the house was as yet as I liked it, plants, books,
sturdy antique furniture.

But I was shaken. It could happen easily. So easily, so quickly.
The woman I loved could be lost. In an instant.

I studied the drawings she had left with me. The peculiar fluttering made me blink my eyes. It had been bothering me more
and more lately, and some times I thought I was hearing someone whispering.

When I blinked and shook my head it stopped. It was nothing.

I loved their work. The children's crayoned animals were big
eyed, with the matter-of-fact ungainliness that looks neither animal nor human. Children can draw like this. Adults cannot.

Nona told me that the children liked the little drawings I
added to their own, and looked forward to getting their pictures
back, and so I drew on one landscape of what looked like giraffes
—or sheep with very ambitious necks—an eagle. And on a village
of houses of peaked roofs—where do children learn to draw this
traditional, pointed-house shape?—I drew a mailman, inexplica-
bly skyborne. And on the drawing done by Stuart, the child
whose work I most enjoyed, I sketched a telephone repairman,
high above Stuart's herd of what had to be colts and mares.

Until I stopped myself. I drew an eagle because Nona was in
flight by now, and I drew a mailman and a telephone repairman
because that was how Nona and I lived. She was often absent,
and what I usually knew of her came by mail, by telephone, from
far away. Even when she was in San Francisco she was either at
the hospital or stopping for a change of clothes and a nap at her
apartment in the Sunset. In a way, Nona did not live anywhere.
She had an answering machine, and a career.

And I was late for an art exhibit, another high-profile opening on a Sutter Street gallery. I was due to play my accustomed role —the man who had everything he wanted.

2

"**Y**ou don't stand a chance, you know."

I turned and met the eyes of the woman beside me. I had that near-thrill of knowing someone well, and yet, at the same time, being surprised at her appearance.

The woman continued, "With your friend, the psychiatrist. Nona Lyle. I saw her on television. So much energy. And what you'd have to call a passion for her work. She'll never have time for you."

The room was crowded. The artist stood against the wall, his art so much more colorful than he seemed to be that he looked miscast, a fugitive from his own career. I loved attending openings, and actually tried to look at the art on such an occasion, although it was the opportunity to celebrate that I enjoyed most, the chance to show that something new was still possible, that talent had a place. I knew most of the people here, good people, lively and full of curiosity.

I had not seen my ex-wife in nearly ten years. She had been described as "perfect for Stratton Fields" by every important society commentator. The daughter of a senator, Margaret herself had understood our marriage to be foreordained. It had lasted two months, not counting a long period during which she lived with an ambassador in London near Holland Park and I had designed a private school in Humboldt County, building much of it by hand when salmon season took away some of the men. Now she was married to a former national security adviser, a man of old money and Cold War politics.

She had tried playing at marriage, and I had walked through it as though involved in an amusing dress rehearsal. Our marriage was a style that did not last, although I had gathered from the occasional magazine article that her current life as a hostess to former presidents and the occasional royalty was nearly tolerable.

I had never felt about her the way I felt about Nona. Still, it was good to see her. "I thought you were in Washington."

Margaret did not speak for a moment, giving me an extra moment or two to gauge her mood. "I am."

She had lost weight and was deeply tanned, a combination that made her look at once healthily attractive and gaunt. She had always been slow to stir in the morning, more interested in champagne than sunshine. She was dressed in something you couldn't find in the City, unless you knew a designer like DeVere personally, a confection of coffee-black crepe de chine.

When I simply smiled, she added, "Here or there. What's the difference?"

At one time I had found her dead-core irony, her boredom with all of it, attractive. "You're suffering a little lingering jealousy," I said.

"Probably."

"Nona and I are close."

"When you're together."

Despite a certain hard feeling in me, I smiled. "Politics seems to be good for you."

She closed her eyes slowly, and slowly opened them. "I love politics." Her look, combined with her tone, meant that she felt nothing but boredom.

"But you manage."

"I do all right." A cigarette appeared from her handbag, and I was relieved to see at least this trace of the old, more youthful Margaret.

"She's not your type," she said. She blew smoke, and it took its place around us.

"Describe my 'type,' " I said.

"How's your brother?" she asked.

"He had some sort of accident awhile ago. Nothing serious. It was up on Devil's Slide, on the Peninsula. Tore the bottom out of one of his vintage roadsters, I can't recall which."

"But he survived intact?"

"As far as I know."

She let her eyes linger on mine. "Anna Wick wants to talk to you."

I could see Anna through the tangle of people, in conversation. She did not glance my way.

Anna was DeVere's personal assistant. I felt a tickle of hope. *Good news,* I let myself think.

I could taste it: success.

Margaret's hand was on my arm. "You still want a career, don't you?"

I wanted to say something self-mocking, ironic. Instead I said, "Of course I do."

She drew on her cigarette. "Let the others care. The people who still believe in things. Let them try to make some kind of sense out of the world. They can't. You know it. I know it."

"You think Nona and I are mismatched."

"I think you're a decent man," she said. She said this as though uttering a complaint. "I think your psychiatrist friend is a woman with a mission." She glanced across the room, in Anna Wick's direction. "Take care of yourself, Stratton."

"You're giving me some sort of warning." I kept my tone light, but I had enough respect for Margaret to take her seriously. "As though I were in danger."

"You're looking better than ever."

"I swim."

She closed her eyes, a kind of quiet laugh. "I remember your midnight swims. It's a miracle you haven't drowned."

"Nona says I'll die of hypothermia. Apparently the hypothalamus controls body temperature. She tells me I'm overworking mine."

She gave me a weary smile. "I saw your designs. The ones for the new Golden Gate Park. Everyone admires them."

My pulse quickened. "What did *you* think?"

She flicked ash from her cigarette. "You have talent. A lot of talent. And you still want to remake the world."

I thanked her, and she used the cigarette again, flicking ash, showing her impatience with even heartfelt courtesy.

"You won't get the award," she said.

I could not ask: Did she know something?

"DeVere's the one who really decides, and you know how he feels."

My words sounded lame in my own ears. "Blake has some influence. He's chairing the jury."

She parted her lips, another silent laugh. "The gentleman's gentleman. San Francisco's chief of protocol. The kindest man in Northern California."

Blake Howard was all of those things, and a friend of my family. I could not understand her tone.

She read my eyes and drew on her cigarette. "I'm sorry, Stratton. I forgot how strong your feelings are. Most people I know stopped having serious conversations years ago."

Then she took my arm and led me over to a painting that reminded me of Cezanne, if Cezanne had painted huge, oversize canvases. The gold, the citrus-bronze, was pleasing to the eye. I was not in a position to buy art, or I would have chosen this piece.

"You don't understand, do you?" she said.

"These things have a way of working out."

"I don't think you know what you're up against. Stop caring. Just live."

"All right," I said, in mock agreement, and we both laughed.

"But it amounts to a weird sort of superstition, Stratton, this faith that things will work out. Sometimes they don't."

I had forgotten how a lick of cigarette smoke burns when it gets into your eye. "Sometimes a person gets lucky."

She looked at me in her bored, intelligent way, considering what I had intended as a fairly idle statement. "You believe in luck," she said, not asking a question.

"It's just a word, really."

She watched smoke rise around her. "If there's good luck, then there's bad luck, too."

A glass or two of bubbly later, I worked my way through the crowd, shaking hands. I complimented the artist. He looked more calm now, and said that he was pleased to meet "one of the famous Fieldses."

Just as I turned from the artist I met the eyes of Anna Wick.

Anna ran a finger along the sleeve of my jacket. "You were avoiding me," she said.

She wore one of DeVere's latest, a dress that matched the Cezanne golds of the painting I had admired. She gave me a glance that could only be described as seductive. I did meet women on occasions like this, attracted by my name, or the reputed scope of the estate. But Anna Wick could hardly be hungry for male companionship. She was blond, full-figured, brilliant, and looked equally good in photographs in both *Vogue* and the financial section.

"I was dazzled from afar," I said.

She let my own thoughts capture me for a moment. Then she smiled. "We want to see you tomorrow."

"It sounds interesting," I said, trying to keep the thrill from my voice.

"I think you'll find it fascinating," she said.

Nona called that night.

"No," I told her, in response to her question. "No further sign of the cat."

"Thanks for the frog," she said. "I'll keep him here on my nightstand. I think he looks a little like you."

"That's terrific. I can make a big one. Call it *Self-Portrait as a Frog.*"

"I didn't say *exactly* like you. Just the look in its eyes." Someone in the hotel had suffered "severe disorientation after getting robbed on Bourbon Street."

"You make it sound like good news."

"It turns out he's a vice president of Rorer, one of the big drug companies. I think he'll give a donation to the hospice."

"You amaze me." I told her about the opening, about Margaret and her tan and her outlook on life, and about Anna Wick.

They want to see me tomorrow.

"It sounds wonderful, Strater," she said.

She sounded close. It made her seem, paradoxically, so much farther away. "I'm not completely sure the news is going to be good."

"Don't worry. I'm sure something wonderful is going to happen."

3

The University of California Medical Center in San Francisco is both a place for the study of medicine, and an effective hospital. It consists of tall buildings surrounded by craggy hills and eucalyptus trees. At night there is a view of the Mission District and the bay. The sunlight is usually warm, and the air cool. When there is fog it lowers over the tall buildings, parting around them, flowing with the wind.

The men and women in white coats tend to be youthful, and most walk with a certain spirit. My family had long helped support this hospital, endowing a lecture hall and a long-since torn-down hydrotherapy wing. My father had sat on the board of trustees, and I was often consulted myself on such matters as fundraising for a new "blaster" for kidney stones, and the possibilities of a new parking lot for the staff.

In the corridors of the hospital I am greeted by people I know, and people I do not know. I feel that I am in a university I used to attend, but the truth is that, on this morning especially, I missed Nona.

Nona's ward was hard to reach. It was up several flights, and down what looked like an impossibly long corridor. The implication was that these patients needed privacy. The truth was that the medical center was satisfied to keep them out of sight. I always felt conspicuous under the gaze of all those young, wise eyes.

But their smiles always delighted me, and despite the fact that I felt robust and adult, powerful and blessed with a varied life I did not deserve, a visit with the children always warmed me, and touched me in a way that no art, and no music, ever could.

Nona had made the place more pleasant than the other wards at the medical center. There were posters on the walls, Donald Duck at the beach, and Curious George on top of a fire truck ladder. I had put a few drawings of my own on the walls, animals either driving cars or operating street-repairing machinery. I am not sure why I chose to depict animals operating heavy machinery, but somehow the subject matter seemed appropriate.

I passed back the patient's drawings. I praised the giraffes, and received compliments on my own drawing when the child cried out, "I got an eagle!"

Stuart examined the telephone worker I had drawn, a figure atop a telephone pole. "It's not an animal," he said.

I agreed that it was not. "Your horses were so good, I couldn't think of an animal I could draw well enough to go along with them."

"What's he doing?"

"He's one of those people who repair telephones."

Stuart was thin, and had dark hair, dark eyes. His hair was becoming sparse uniformly around his head, so that it seemed to be vanishing into the air. He did not have the normal amount of strength for a six-year-old, so his expressions took place slowly, and had an extra cast of seriousness as a result. "I want an animal," he said.

I selected a sheet from the art tablet on his bed stand, pulling the paper slowly, deliberately. I folded the paper, in an effort to remember origami animals from my childhood. The white paper rustled, and, as I creased it and shaped it, took on the general shape of a horse's head. Held in a certain way, the paper steed even seemed to have spirit.

I examined my handiwork. I was pleased. I could make the horse arch its neck, working the paper like a finger puppet.

I perfected the folded paper, then stretched forth my hand and offered it to Stuart.

He gazed at it, and did not move.

"What is it?" he said.

Then he took it, and sat up.

The cab ride to DeVere's Montgomery Street office was uncomplicated, except for the work being done on Clay Street, a sandy peak of earth surrounded by men in yellow hardhats. A jackhammer ripped the asphalt, punching holes in the gray pavement.

Anna Wick met me in DeVere's waiting room. She smiled,

cutting through me with her eyes, measuring me, and I heard myself murmuring idle courtesies.

"Mr. DeVere has so much looked forward to meeting with you," she said. "I think I could say that he admires your work."

So the news *must* be good, I thought.

But while the Anna Wick of the night before had been seductive, this was a different manner entirely, still sexually aware, but much more businesslike after the first glance or two.

We engaged in some professional gossip, complained about one of the newer hotels in town, and about the poor quality of the air conditioning in so many of the buildings (too many "particulates in the air," we both agreed). Then she excused herself to make a phone call, and the nature of my visit began to become clear.

No one made me wait like this. In any other office in San Francisco I would have been ushered in at once. But not in this office. DeVere was in no hurry.

I teased myself with what was left of my hope: good news.

Surely there was good news.

I crossed my legs, and looked, I knew, perfectly at ease.

But I was not. Surely now, I allowed myself to think. Surely now I will hear what I have waited to hear for so long.

His door opened, and he was there, a folder in his hand. DeVere pretended not to see me for a moment, pausing at his secretary's desk. Then he handed her the red plastic folder, and he turned to me with his fine smile.

I stood and we grasped hands, and I knew. He didn't have to say a word. I could tell.

This can't be, hissed a voice in me. He surely didn't bring me all the way to the Financial District to insult me like this. But it was in his eyes, his smile. He opened the door for me, one of those large teak slabs I associate with boardrooms. This oversize chamber was his office, or one of his offices. He had chambers like this in Milan and in Tokyo. Everything about it was too grand, including the view of the Bay Bridge and the slow progress of a tanker toward the Port of Oakland.

He offered coffee, tea, "or something a little more warming."

I was careful to show no sign of emotion. I declined, thanking him.

"I think it's cruel to let a person wait." He let me think over these words for a moment. "I wanted to tell you personally."

He settled behind his desk, and I did not help him by asking.

DeVere was craggy, long-limbed. He made his living telling people what to wear, how to decorate their homes—how to live. Outside, I recalled, on the way to the airport, his face gazed down from a billboard, the sign emblazoned with his name. That's all it took: just his name on a label.

"You're looking well," said DeVere.

I imagined that I probably did look good to him, for someone dressed in non-DeVere clothing. I thanked him, and returned the compliment.

"Don't be angry with me, Stratton. I want you to understand."

I waited.

"I admire your work. Your designs are always tasteful. Elegant. Impressive—as works of art."

I waited, knowing almost to the word what was coming. But I could not disguise from myself my bitterness. This was the most important landscape design project in eighty years. Golden Gate Park was being redesigned, and competition for the prize included the best talent from fifteen different countries. This was the project of a lifetime. I had dropped by the Palace of Fine Arts several days ago, to see the work on exhibit. My work, under even the most harsh eye, would seem the most humane, the most plausible—the most beautiful.

"I have always felt that you were wasting your time trying to make a name as a designer," said DeVere.

I did not speak.

"Despite my heavy criticism of the ethereal quality of your work—its overprettiness—your plans came in second."

He was not telling me this to allay my frustration. He was saying it in a way that told me that he personally had campaigned against me.

His father had been an artichoke grower in Castroville, not an impoverished man, but a man who made money sitting in a pickup watching the bland seasons of the Monterey coast, and supervising as workers harvested the edible thistles. It was well known that DeVere never discussed his family.

"Naturally, the decision is entirely out of my hands," I said, my voice even, certain that if someone had observed me he would have had no clue regarding my real feelings. "If you thought my ideas were implausible . . ."

"If you think you can go to the jury and persuade them, forget about it. Blake agrees with me."

This information hit hard. DeVere must have read my feelings, because he added, "Blake had to admit that once again your work simply did not seem practical."

I had always been able to count on Blake. I could not keep a certain stiffness out of my voice. "I have always appreciated his opinion."

"Your kind, Stratton, your type of person . . ." He let his voice trail off. "You have no business trying to make your way in a career like this."

"I should content myself with activities that don't matter to anyone."

He smiled. His long-dead father had bequeathed to him the wrinkles and creases of a range rider. "You should enjoy a gentleman's pursuits. And leave the creation of the real world to others."

"People like yourself."

He acknowledged my words with a half nod, toying with his reading glasses. "I know how the world works."

I let a moment, and his remark, pass. "Peterson won, didn't he?"

Again, DeVere gave me that famous smile, the manly grin that sold everything from leather jackets to fountain pens. "Peterson's plans are plausible."

"I've always admired his work," I said, truthfully. And saw just a trace of disappointment in DeVere's eyes. He had hoped for an outburst, although he should have known better. "He's a good choice."

"A gentleman knows how to lose gracefully," said DeVere, perhaps intending to mock me.

"My father felt that you would go far," I said.

"Further proof of his good judgment."

"And I have been amazed at your success. Everything you turn to manages to transform itself—"

"To gold." He ran his hands over his gray-streaked dark hair. He stood, but stayed behind the desk, as at a battle station. He flicked a switch and asked his secretary to send in Mr. Peterson.

Peterson was a man I saw only occasionally, at a reception, an art opening, or sketching the same sort of building I enjoyed, one of the pre-Earthquake Victorians off Van Ness. He was a lean, athletic man, more comfortable in jeans than the slacks and tie he now wore. The tie was a DeVere, earthy splashes of grays and browns.

He had been told already. "I'm sorry," Peterson said, through the blush of victory, and his plain distaste for DeVere. He was one of those unnaturally youthful men, anywhere from thirty to forty, with a young man's self-assurance, and a tennis player's build. Looking into each other's eyes, we understood something, unified by our dislike for the third man in the room.

There was something else in his eyes, a wariness, an unease. I assumed that he found this meeting awkward, even unethical. It was obvious that no jury had reached this decision. The decision was DeVere's.

I was managing my famous poise even now, my good manners, and my well-known lack of hard feelings, carrying me to the door. When I looked back at DeVere I looked at the son of a man who knew irrigation and frostburn. This hard man in his elegant, self-designed suit, resented me, and saw me as an embodiment of all that he himself could never possess.

Local legend explained that DeVere had friends in organized crime. A fashion critic for CNN had vanished after criticizing one of his spring lines as "a cross between the Easter Bunny and the Great Pumpkin." There were rumors of beatings, of iron-fisted retaliation against labor unions.

Well, at least I have *important* enemies, I told myself. None of those wimpy, powerless enemies for Stratton Fields.

I hurried down the hall, barely noticing the paintings on the wall, DeVere's trademark charcoal grays, adobe browns.

Anna Wick was in the downstairs lobby, fussing with a cordovan briefcase. "I was so sorry when Mr. DeVere told me last weekend," she said. "You've worked so hard, so many years." Her smile displayed her white teeth. She was good looking as a fine car can be, assembled by expensive craftsmen.

I could not utter a word.

"I say hello to your brother now and then at the race track. I'm pretty sure I'll see him at Santa Anita this weekend. You and your brother are remarkable people. Mr. DeVere wants to humiliate you." She said the last phrase as though delivering pleasant tidings.

I understood. She was not being cruel. She was one of those people who like to see the distress of others in order to learn something. She was curious. She had heard so much about me, about my family. How was I going to react?

I gave her a smile, and something changed in her eyes, in her manner. She parted her lips and was about to say something.

Outside, the bustle of the Financial District surrounded me, briefcases and dark suits in a hurry. I found myself searching for a phone before I caught myself. Nona was out of town, at a convention, trying to raise money for a new ward for her patients.

I could not help leaning against a wall for a moment, pedestrians whisking past me.

I had never had a chance.

I had means at my disposal. I could have an attorney look into the competition, or raise a question or two when I next saw the mayor. But as capable as I was, DeVere was more powerful—his name was sunlight. My name was illustrious, even aristocratic. But it lacked power. It was a name from another era, an era of quiet voices and candlelight.

As I hurried up Montgomery Street my feelings shifted from frustration to anger. I could almost forgive DeVere. The man was more a creature of ambition than a human being. But Peterson. He could have declined the award on the spot. The man *knew* my plans were better. And Blake. How could I ever forgive Blake?

That afternoon I called to see how my mother was. Another restless night, the nurse said. She tried to stab an orderly with a little piece of plastic cup, "one of our water glasses she had sharpened especially."

4

Barry Montague, my personal physician and sometime tennis partner, took my arm as I entered the Montgomery Street bar. "Congratulations, Stratton," he said.

"Thanks, Barry. For what?"

"Your plans. Your entry for the Golden Gate Park competition. Everyone's talking about it. They *have* to give you the prize."

I was about to tell Barry the truth, but he had such an open, sincere smile that I couldn't bring myself to crush his enthusiasm. "I'm glad you liked my work," I said.

"*Liked* it. Mr. Modest. The worst sort of conceit. We ought to take up tennis again. I'm getting a little out of shape."

I looked at Barry closely, and I realized that he looked tired. He had gained weight, and his eyes were hidden in shadows that had never been there before. His voice was hoarse, and he smiled as though in apology for his appearance. "I've been putting off having a medical checkup of my own," he said. "There've been a record number of murders in the Bay Area this year. And you know what that means."

I had visited the emergency room with state senators to urge them to increase spending. I had seen blood on the green linoleum, the scarlet smearing, leaving the imprint of footsteps. No matter how soon someone mopped it up, the sight of it always stayed, the memory of it and the insight: What keeps us alive is so much red ink.

To be one of Barry's friends was to feel honored. To be liked by Barry was to be endorsed by someone who knew virtue and good humor. It worried me to see him like this. "You need a vacation," I said.

Barry laughed and agreed. "Or a little more tennis. I have to be at the medical center about five minutes ago. I'm lecturing on a subject Nona suggested. Responses to pain in the cerebral cortex."

"I would have thought the brain is pretty well mapped by now."

"We take a natural interest in it. Man's best friend."

Barry grabbed a rolled-up newspaper from the bar. "Do you realize that your girlfriend is a genius? I mean a literal, actual genius?"

"She always impresses me," I said. Talking about her made her seem all-too absent. For a moment, though, I could feel her lips on mine.

"She studied with a man named Valfort," Barry was saying. "Pioneered brain mapping, refined hypnotherapy. One of those guys who's so advanced he's weird. The story is that he helped Nona Lyle a lot with personal stuff, theoretical stuff. That's not my field, really. But I hear that Nona has the finest medical mind in North America, and she chose to work in psychiatry so she could help sick kids."

Dying children, I nearly corrected him, but I knew that Barry was at ease with a kind of euphemism, his style of talk both boyish and intellectual, as though an inner censor kept this complex man from expressing complicated thoughts.

He gave me a tap with his newspaper. "Take good care of her," he said, and he was gone.

Peterson leaned against the bar, and he spent perhaps a moment longer examining his sweet vermouth than it required.

"I can't agree," I was saying. I was trying to reassure him. "Your work has that solid look. The look of reality." I said the last word with just a touch of irony. The truth was, Peterson's work had looked like weak copies of my own.

Peterson shook his head, smiling, but there was a ruefulness to his expression that I didn't entirely understand. "When I saw your work in the exhibit a few days ago I knew that I didn't have a chance."

"You'll make a name for yourself. Children will run across the open spaces you designed for them." I had a vague glimpse of myself in the polished mahogany of the counter, a tall man, lean, with tie loosened, jacket unbuttoned, my face in the indistinct gleam little more than a blur.

"I can't do what you do," Peterson was saying. "When you design a landscape you realize—this is how the world should look."

I thanked him for his kind words. This was all proper and professional, two men of talent sharing the late afternoon. There was an unsettling undercurrent, however, which was unexpressed, something that troubled Peterson deeply.

He looked away from me, leaning against the counter, running his finger over a bead of water. "You don't sound bitter."

"I am," I said, but in a way that denied the words.

"I don't blame you."

Peterson leaned like a man about to deliver bad news, or a confession. "You forgot about DeVere."

"I thought that this time . . ."

"There would be justice," said Peterson, completing my thought. Peterson paused, and gave his twist of lemon a poke with a forefinger. "I should refuse the prize," he said abruptly.

I let him continue, suddenly hopeful.

"It won't be actually awarded for a few weeks," he said. "I have plenty of time to turn it down, and the prize will be yours."

"Why would you do that?" I asked.

Peterson did not respond at once. He motioned with his head, and we stepped to a table well out of the way. The bar was filling up with architects and accountants. The lounge was a study in the sort of lighting Rembrandt would have adored, and each of the scattered couples looked both weary and aglow.

But Peterson did not look youthful just now. Something kept him from speaking. At last, he said, "Anyone could understand why he hates you."

I chuckled. "Isn't that a little strong? People don't hate each other anymore. They feel competitive. They feel a rivalry. Hatred is out of style."

"He's invented his own reputation—and everyone believes him. Designs sportscars for Nissan. Airports for Zurich, Singapore. Practically dictates to the city of San Francisco what architects they should hire and what color the mayor's suits should be. He's thinking of letting R.J. Reynolds put his name on a brand of cigarettes. He and Renman have lunch with the president. And he takes the trouble to see you as a threat."

"Yes, it's a little hard to understand," I said, with a dry laugh.

"Not really. You have taste. You have a name. And people like you."

I gave a half-embarrassed chuckle.

"But it's true. You're naturally, by birth, what DeVere would love to be. His background isn't all that glamorous. Didn't he change his name—?"

"Vernon. Tyron Vernon." I felt a little protective of DeVere for a moment. Everything about him was artificial, and therefore something like a work of art. Ty DeVere was a name with spin, I had to admit. And didn't most Americans remake themselves in one way or another, changing names, dwellings, spouses, working hard to shed the past? "His background was agricultural."

Peterson considered this. "His costumes for *Carmen* were not bad. And I suppose his line of dress shirts does something for a man with a certain build. The sort of man who looks good in anything."

Peterson seemed to consider his own words, and then continued, "Anna Wick does most of the work. She has a handshake that makes your bones ache for a hour."

"She's a remarkable woman."

"She's what you might call self-made, too, isn't she?"

"Born Annabelle Wickford in Medford, Oregon," I said. "The rumor is she never sleeps."

Peterson absorbed this, then went on, "I think that he has done more harm to you than you can possibly believe," he said.

His words made me gaze into my own drink, an untouched brandy and soda. When I looked up, he was waiting, as though he needed my permission to speak further.

"How would you describe your career?" he asked.

"I've had some interesting projects. I've designed a few roof gardens, and I've drawn up plans for a few schools. Usually donating my time, of course."

"But you wouldn't say that your career has been a success."

"Well, not exactly a success, no."

"DeVere watches your work, your bids, pays attention to what you submit, and where."

My voice remained easy. "You don't mean that he's out to ruin my career."

"Exactly."

My voice did not betray my feelings. "Perhaps he's right. I should resign myself to the pleasures of my class."

"Your work is very fine. Noble, enlightening—I admire it tremendously. You deserve fame for your designs, Stratton. But listen to me. As long as DeVere is alive, and as long as he pursues you, you'll have trouble accomplishing anything important as a designer."

I reflected, "When DeVere was starting out, designing jeans and earrings, he approached my father for an entrée into what people like DeVere call 'high society.' My father was always bored by that kind of 'society,' and told DeVere about the fund for the handicapped, one of my father's pet projects. DeVere thought my father was dismissing him."

"You don't dismiss DeVere."

"Do you want me to give you permission to accept the award?"

His voice was tight as he said, "I'd like to say I can't accept it."

"I could pursue DeVere legally, sue him. I can pull a few strings and get the award overturned."

"Why don't you?"

"Because I want to win the award honorably. Really win it, not wrestle it away from you. Because fighting a man like DeVere on his level makes me despise myself." Because, I did not say, I am a better man. So that it was pride—vanity—that kept me from fighting back. "Because, in the end, it still might not work, and I would be muddy from a struggle against a man—" I did not finish my thought: a man who was not a human being so much as an ambition-beast.

"The feeling is mutual, isn't it?" he said.

"What do you mean?"

"You hate DeVere."

I laughed. "Not at all."

"I think you do. I think you despise him, and you haven't figured out a way to express it."

Like most people, I resent accurate insight into my own personality, but I had the sense to acknowledge this. I managed to laugh again, and said, "You could be right."

"I'm going to accept the award, Stratton," he said. "Please don't try to stop me. I don't feel proud. I need the money."

There was that fluttering light again, like the beginning of a migraine. "You're honest, at least."

"Do you realize I've spent the last six months designing sandboxes for an arts school in Berkeley? My wife's been working for the phone company—"

And I myself, he did not have to say, did not need the money, as everyone knew.

Except that, in truth, I could certainly use the money. My family had a secret—many secrets.

"I've been in therapy lately," Peterson said. "I've been depressed."

"I'm sorry to hear that," I said, worried about this man I found myself liking.

"I'm just a typical emotional wreck. Bad dreams, insomnia. It's too much to expect you to understand. Your work deserves the award. But I need it."

Afterward, out on the street, North Beach was a brilliant study of colors, brakelights, shop windows. The air was cool, and scented with espresso, deisel exhaust, garlic, and the faintest tang of the Pacific.

Years of suppressed anger, years of careful good manners, were stored in me.

Margaret had been right. I had always been, in a very ordinary, unremarkable way, superstitious. I had no firm beliefs, in fact I scoffed at seers and psychics, wondering why, if they could visualize the future so clearly, they needed to earn a living reading palms. Certainly a clairvoyant could pick a winning horse, or a winning lottery ticket.

And yet I found my eyes lingering on the horoscope column of the newspaper occasionally, and I was never entirely pleased to have the path ahead of me occupied by a black cat. A sunny day cheered me, and the glimpse of a full moon made me feel in touch with something profound. I had sometimes made a wish before blowing out my birthday candles, even when the cake was on a balcony in Venice, or in a lounge in Monte Carlo. Perhaps I believed, in a way I would have been ashamed to admit to myself, that the future could be outguessed.

Now, once again, my future withered.

This anger was bad. There was only one way to exorcise it.

5

Nona had once told me that I was hoping to get caught in a riptide, hoping that I would have to fight for my life in the waves.

"You might be afraid of it, but you have to admit the truth," she had said. "It's what you want."

Suicidal: she had used the word, and asked me to stop.

I took a quick cab ride to my home, and I punched the button on my answering machine, hoping to hear word from Nona. All I heard was the hearty voice of the contractor wondering when he could come by and resume work on my house.

When indeed, I thought.

I felt disloyal to Nona. I had not actually promised her that I would never go for another night swim, but I had not gone out into the surf for weeks. I stuffed the ample robe and the goose-down vest into my carry-all and grabbed my car keys.

I drove the last remaining car I owned, the Mercedes, down Ocean Avenue through the dark. The car had been armored during the days when my cousin was kidnapped in Europe. My father had taken the precaution to soothe my mother's nerves. Now the car shifted gears with the solemn forward thrust of a rolling fortress. The interior was pleasant, the ride quiet, and I did have the dubious satisfaction of knowing that the ammunition of most firearms could penetrate neither the doors nor the windshield.

I found my way to the Great Highway and parked the car at Ocean Beach, at my favorite spot.

This was not a desire for death. Far from it. I could taste the ocean in the air. The wetsuit fit snuggly and felt delightfully peculiar as I zipped it up, and I made my way down the sandy steps in the darkness. The rubber textile moved with my body in a way that made me feel protected, insulated from all harm, but this was an illusion. Only my torso was protected, and in very cold water this would not be enough.

The scene was well lit by the glow reflected from the clouds, by the reflection of that light from the pale sand, and by the fragment of moon that kept slewing in and out of overcast. I tossed down my carry-all and the keys and sprinted toward the pale line of breakers.

I dived and surfaced, spitting water. This was what I loved, this struggle, this cold.

Sandy salt water filled my mouth. I had a flash of understanding: The horizon was a void, the sea was emptiness. And I was strong enough to survive it.

Anger was gone. I worked against the surge of water, my legs aching and the chill seeping through the rubberized fabric of my wetsuit top.

The beach was a scrawl of white suds, a dirty line of brown, a vague sprinkle of headlights. A bank of fog lofted over me, spilled over the view of the beach. The beach was gone, and I could see only the tossing water around me. The Pacific tasted of cities dissolved, aluminum and concrete and chrome stewed and then nearly frozen.

When I breathed I sucked in the cold fog. The muscles of my legs were growing slowly into stone. I was heavy, and sluggish. I dived deep, into the churning bottom. DeVere and Blake, and Peterson with his needful eyes, were far away now.

This was all that mattered. Brine burned my eyes, and I could sense the writhe of sand under my feet, the unsolid earth churning. How long had it been? Five seconds, then, as my feet plunged into the bottom sand into something nearly solid, ten.

Fifteen seconds. I felt myself laugh. It was an inward sound. I was so cold it hurt the bones of my limbs, my body aching with the cold, and I was laughing! This wasn't a game, now, I told myself. This wasn't play. People died like this.

Thirty seconds, and counting. The society columnists and the critics, the heiresses and the wealth-fatigued men of leisure would be surprised if they could see this: Stratton Fields at play. Drowning.

But it was sport, I told myself. It was fun, and nothing more. When my head broke the surface I could see nothing. The air was sweet. Sand needled me, and my lungs were shrinking into

two leaden stones. My heart contracted into a smaller and tighter
fist with each pulse. I blinked, and swam, sensing the direction of
the shore.

I let the waves lift me, buoying me toward the beach. A wave
tumbled itself, and my limbs along with it, but the danger and the
greatest part of the pleasure was past. I body surfed, catching up
with another wave that warped, angled me, and then the sand bit
my knees and I erected myself panting, out of the foam.

A wedge of water nearly cut my legs out from under me. The
risk, the salt on my lips. It was all was so delicious, so unlike the
rest of my life.

Another wave tackled me, and I staggered and stalked my way
from the sea slowly, as though reluctant to leave. I laughed at
myself, gasping, dripping. Fun, I told myself, should not be so
much work—or danger. I worked at the zipper of my wetsuit with
stiff fingers.

The fog was streaky, rolling past me, and seemingly through
me, like a second, diaphanous surf. My fingers stopped unzipping
the suit. My breath caught.

I saw something.

I told myself that I must be mistaken. No one ever swam this
surf—no one but me. It was too dangerous. But there could be
no mistake. There was something out there.

I peered, striding into the wash of the waves. The fog and
darkness obscured whatever it was, then blotted it entirely. But
my instinct could not be denied: It was a human being.

There was someone out there.

I was in the water again, swimming hard as the fog closed in. I
could see only a stroke or two ahead. I called out, but my voice
was soaked in the hiss of the surf and the mat of the fog.

I plunged ahead, swimming steadily, until I reached the place
where I was convinced I had seen—what? What had I seen?
Surely not a person, I tried to convince myself. Surely it was a
seal, or a bit of ship's spar, or a life jacket fallen from a fishing
boat. Perhaps it had been nothing, an illusion.

I called, wordlessly, my voice a universal: Are you there? Can
you hear me?

Am I alone?

I was beyond the waves, the combers breaking behind me,

somewhere beyond the fog wall. I felt the unease, the flickering anxiety that meant that the cold was even more dangerous than before. I was nearly spent.

But I couldn't abandon someone out here to drown. I called again.

And this time there was an answering cry.

It was a brief, evanescent sound, almost not a sound at all. Someone was even farther out, through the fog. Someone was calling, and it seemed in my fear for the life of this stranger that this human voice was calling my name, if indeed it was a human call and not the song of a gull somewhere beyond the ceiling of gray.

I shuddered. My own fatigue clung to me. My own confusion drove me to wrestle upward, out of the water, in an attempt to see through the mist, and then fall back again.

There was indeed a voice calling. It was a human voice, and it sounded familiar.

Then I saw her.

Far off, indistinct with distance, there was a woman in the water. Her head and one shoulder were all I could see. She called out to me again, and I could not be certain any longer that what was happening was real.

When I kicked hard, fighting the water in her direction, she receded and grew farther away. I wanted to rescue this woman, but at the same time I was growing certain that I had suffered harm through lack of oxygen, or the cold. This woman did not exist.

And now I was very far from shore.

Too far, and my thoughts were becoming disconnected. She was a source of light. She beckoned me, a pale figure, and I swam until my sinews burned. My vision grew spotty. There, I told myself. This proves it. You are having hallucinations. It's the sort of thing that happens to people when they freeze to death. You are leaving the real world, and as you depart you create one of your own.

Must save her, must not let her drown.

My hand struck something, and then I felt a hand close around mine. Close, and hang on.

*　*　*

I woke on the sand, my face buried in the wet stuff so that I spluttered and nearly choked as I inhaled sharply. I dragged myself to my feet.

WARNING, the sign announced. NO SWIMMING. SURF EXTREMELY DANGEROUS.

She was nowhere. I could not breathe. I tried to call out but I had no voice. I could feel her grip in my numb hands as though she still held my fingers.

No, I breathed. *It isn't possible.*

My security man, Fern Samuels, poured more hot coffee from the thermos. I was enrobed, fortified, by layers of terrycloth and goose down. Fern did not say what he must have been thinking. He watched me drink hot coffee and then turned to see what I was seeing, the figures of policemen at the edge of the surf in what had become drizzle. There were flashlights, beams cutting into the mist, waves glittering.

"They're not finding anything," said Fern. He was tall and wide, a former Secret Service man, a man who took things in with a glance.

"There was someone there," I said. I did not let him hear my teeth chattering.

"Then she's gone," he said. He meant: drowned.

Fern let me give him a long look.

He did not comment that my pastime was a foolish one. Fern understood danger. He understood the frustrations I had suffered in recent years, and I knew that Fern was a man who had taken his own frustrations into the firing range, or the gym, and exorcised them. He had worked for my father, and he understood me, and my family.

I had called him from my car, by instinct reaching out to the security of a familiar voice right after I called 911.

Now, when the police spoke to us, they consulted with Fern. Their attitude toward me was respectful, deferential, and they were happy to have Fern as a go-between. They nodded, muttering with him in the mist, while I tried to hide my shivering.

Fern stepped toward me across the sand, a few grains of it glittering on the black shine of his shoe. "No sign of her," he said.

Perhaps Fern was waiting for me to describe the woman's appearance. Perhaps he was waiting for me to say that I would never swim here again. There had always been an unspoken attitude: You hire me to protect you, and then you routinely nearly drown—for fun. I met his eyes and gave a shake to my head.

He sighed. "We have to go, Stratton. A body can wash up miles from here."

"I'll stay until they find her."

He let his voice fall to a world-weary pitch. "I know how you feel. I don't blame you. But it's pointless."

My voice was hoarse. "I should have done something different."

He waved aside my words. He had seen men die.

"I came so close to saving her," I said.

By now I was once again thinking that she had been a hallucination, a trick of the cold, the wind. What else could it have been? I was sure—and yet I was not sure.

"Maybe," I breathed, afraid to say what I was thinking. "Maybe she wasn't there at all. Maybe she wasn't real."

Fern put his hand on my shoulder. His grip was firm, well defined through my layers of cotton and goose down. "This is a dangerous place," he said, meaning, I knew, not merely this San Francisco shoreline, but the ocean, the world.

Only at the last did I see it, a luminous slip in the glistening sand. It glowed, as the figure had, and I knelt. I reached forth my hand, and closed my fingers around it.

I waited until I was sure that no one was watching, and that my silhouette would block what I was doing. I closed my hand around this source of light, and immediately my hand jumped back.

It was a feather.

What was the matter with me? It was just a feather—nothing more remarkable than that.

I thrust it at once into the deep pocket of my robe. I did not allow myself to look at it. I told myself that it was nothing, just another curiosity washed up by the waves.

But another part of my mind knew. I had found something wonderful.

Fern stood in the dark, his car parked at an angle behind mine. The police doors were thudding shut, engines starting.

"Did you find something?" Fern asked.

Show him the feather, I thought. Go ahead.

"It was nothing," I said.

And all the way home I wondered what had happened to me, why I had bothered to lie.

6

When I got back to the house I listened to Nona's voice on the answering machine.

It was painful pleasure. The machine duplicated the sound of the woman I loved, and yet she was far away from where I was. "How did your meeting with DeVere go? I was thinking about you all day." There was a long pause as Nona apparently considered the futility of talking, for the moment, to no one. "Everybody's interested. But I don't know if that translates into more funds for the children. Everybody says money is tight."

She sighed into the phone, a breathy whisper exaggerated by the telephone. There was a rustling sound, and I could imagine her looking at her watch. She made a mocking groan. "I have to run. I love you, Strater."

I did not like the silence of my house. I picked up the phone and calculated the time in New Orleans. I put the phone down again. Nona had sounded weary, distracted. She would be asleep by now, and I did not want to wake her.

When we love someone, we lose a part of our own lives, and even, in a sense, a part of our innocence. We can never be fully at peace away from the person we love, and it is no accident that tradition blames Adam's love for Eve for the fall of mankind. Without Nona, I felt that I had lost that simple self-centeredness I had enjoyed as a child.

I called Collie's name, hoping that she was here, by some

chance, in the pantry making one of her essay-long shopping lists. But, of course, she was gone. It was late at night. There was no one.

I nearly laughed at myself. I was afraid to be alone.

The house I lived in, the Fields family refuge, was a grand house among grand houses on Alta Street in Saint Francis Woods, although ours had been the first one built in that neighborhood. The house was a modified Georgian, beaux-arts-style edifice, with the pleasing handsomeness that is neither earthquake resistant nor easy to keep up. While the building had survived earthquakes, many of the rooms were rarely visited, and my favorite room, the study, had been in the midst of remodeling when I had been forced to delay further work.

Now some of my treasured books, and my favorite chairs and tables, were draped with plastic dust covers, shrouded, hidden by the work that had exposed the wooden bones of the walls. If I were absolutely free to live anywhere in the world I don't think I would chose to live in my family home, and yet I felt responsible for it, and respectful of the way the solid walls absorbed the sound of footsteps, the way each window looked out upon a prospect of flowers or ivy, lawn or copper beech hedges.

Some part of me said: Don't be alone. Call someone. Go somewhere.

The phone rang, and I clutched at it, but it was only Fern.

"I'm all right," I reassured him. "Cold, but fine."

He must have realized that I had hoped to hear Nona's voice. "Don't worry. I'll follow up on it in the morning."

What he meant was: Don't think. It was one of his enduring beliefs: Thinking got all of us into trouble.

He continued, "If there was a woman out there, she's dead by now."

That was another of his tendencies. Be brief, even if it means you have to be unpleasant. Fern was always honest, always reliable, and sometimes his words were a bit heavy. "That's one way of putting it," I said.

"You tried," he said. "There's nothing more you can do."

He was right, and I thanked him. I had to feel a certain steadiness in Fern. "I'm going to bed," I said, lying once again.

* * *

I did not feel sleepy. I bathed, and even after that hot, almost painful, soaking I was cold. What did I expect? I had always liked that lingering chill, the weight of the ocean staying with me long afterward.

But tonight I did not like it. And when I was dressed I did not put on nightclothes, but the sort of shirt and trousers I would wear to sit and draw. I did not think that I would be able to sleep even a little.

It was a source of light. Turning the plume in my hand it took on subtle hues, as the throat of a hummingbird will shift from sea green to ruby.

I was careful to put the feather in the pocket of my favorite jacket, the breast pocket, where it would lie across my heart. I wore the jacket now as I worked. I told myself that this plume was a charm, unimportant and yet compelling. I would keep the feather for luck.

Luck. It was an innocent concept. I tried to remind myself that *luck* was a word for children, for happy farewells, a word that bespoke friendship and a cheery outlook.

"Nice—too nice." I had lived with comments like this regarding my designs for years. I had sat here in this studio, this retreat in the family home, and adjusted the drafting table, the crook-neck lamp, hour after hour, scratching with my ever-shorter Berol H, designing roof gardens, pavilions, fountains.

"You make the world look the way it should," Nona had told me. Without knowing it, she had paid me the sort of compliment that hurt. Because this had been the problem: My landscapes and buildings were seen as impeccable art, but unworkable.

I turned on music that I expected to bring some sort of calm, something syrupy by Debussy, all wash and tone. I turned the music way down, and finally turned it off, leaving the only sound the thud of my heart and the high, fine dry hum of the lamp over the drafting table.

I sat in my studio now and reviewed my plans for the new Golden Gate Park. This time I had surpassed all my previous efforts. I was almost hoping to see my drawings as imperfect, but I could not. They were more than good enough to win.

The truth was, I needed to talk to someone. Well, I urged myself breezily, don't think about it. Keep yourself busy. I sat before a lightbox. I had, for a moment, thought of viewing some of the garden designs gardeners had actually brought into being. There were not many, a plot of plumeria and protea near Hilo, a knot garden for a retired film actor in Montecito, a tulip bed and a lawn with a ha-ha for the widow of a governor in Woodside.

The inner warning returned: don't stay alone tonight.

The translucent plastic radiated light through the miniature cells of color, gardens contracted to fine points of green and scarlet, each photograph a shrunken, jewellike universe. If a client had, in fact, met me here that night, this is what I would have showed them, my little contributions to the real world.

Crazy. I tested that word on myself. I was going mad.

And yet this self-diagnosis did not quite fit. I felt entirely lucid.

There had been no woman in the ocean. She had existed only in my mind.

But did insanity feel like this—alive, awake to every texture of wood and paper, aware of the solemn hush of the rooms?

I left the house and walked through the darkness toward the greenhouse. I paused and looked up at the grand, half-alive gingko tree, cutting a canyon out of the night sky. I wished there was some way it could recover and become healthy again.

The outbuildings were padlocked, their shutters tight. In these buildings I kept a bicycle or two, gardening equipment, and an assortment of teak lawn furniture.

In the hothouse, in the warm, tropical demi-world, I snapped on a light.

The stepping stones in the hothouse were outlined with green moss. The lobster claw heliconia and the ornamental ginger all blazed, technicolor and unreal in appearance, and even the vanilla orchid suspended from its perch overhead looked like a relic from a lost planet.

I had believed that we needed more sanctuary in our lives. We needed gardens, from rooftop to rooftop, interlinked, as a refuge for all of us. My drawings were found nearly universally "charming, tasteful," exactly the sort of grand illusion a gentleman designer would cherish.

I seized a pot and hurled it, and the sound of the exploding clay was loud.

I knelt and gathered the terra-cotta fragments. The pot had not been completely empty. A fan of soil spread across the moist concrete, and there were traces of delicate white roots.

Mustn't hurt anything like this, not here, not among all these living things.

The air was breath-warm, and as I knelt to gather the shards I felt something bend, like a wire, over my heart.

I wished that there was something I could tell Blake, some way of explaining to him what a mistake it was to align himself with DeVere.

Fight back, I told myself.

Powerless. I despised self-pity, but the word kept drifting back into my mind. Why was it, however, that as I stood there in the warmth of the hothouse I did not feel powerless at all?

7

The morning light slanted across the bedroom. The sunlight caught the tiny motes of dust. Every surface became dusty easily now, the restoration work downstairs standing unfinished.

The phone rang and I reached for it.

It was Anna Wick's voice. She was polite, friendly. Peterson was going to be on television, "AM San Francisco," the next day. Her voice did nothing to indicate the spite behind the message she was giving.

"They'll be showing his designs for the new Golden Gate Park," she said.

When I put down the telephone I realized the importance of this news.

Everyone would know.

DeVere was enjoying this.

Blake shook his head sadly. "I can't help you."

My first impression, sitting there in a leather chair, sunlight slipping through the plush curtains, was quite clear: This man has changed. He was not the avuncular, polite man I had known since childhood.

"As friends," I persisted, "don't you think we owe something to each other?"

"What would you have me do? Talk DeVere into liking you?"

His voice was sharp. I glanced around at the oak-and-crystal quiet of the club but there was no one who could overhear us. The lounge, a dimly lit room dominated by a fireplace, had been intended for a place of secluded conversation. We were alone with our balloons of cognac, although mine was largely unsampled; it was, after all, well before noon.

"I am in debt to DeVere," Blake continued. "In more ways than one." He looked at me and smiled joylessly. "Look at you—a vigorous man living in a house you should have sold a long time ago. Pursuing a dreamer's career. Give up."

"Look at me, Blake. You helped teach me chess."

"You liked the knights. You wanted to take them away and play with them." He let me enjoy this memory for a moment. "You've always meant a great deal to me, Stratton. You remind me so much of your father."

"I'd like to know how DeVere influenced you."

"You make it sound as though there might be some mystery about it. He bought me. Crudely. Without shame. He agreed to purchase my vineyards, and my stables, and my place in Newport Beach."

"Money."

"I can live without my own cabernet label. I can live without thoroughbreds. I cannot live without money." He made a gesture, a man throwing something away. That imaginary object being flung into the silence represented the things he loved.

He continued by changing the subject. "Don't you mind, living in your father's shadow? It might bother me."

"He was a good man. He cared for people."

"And so do you."

Nona had always said that she believed me to be "healthy in mind and soul." Does a man with a healthy soul want to risk his life? Even here in the club, snugly outfitted in cashmere and worsted, it seemed that I could still feel the chill in my bones.

"I look at you," Blake was saying, "and I see a man like myself —the way I used to be."

"I would never dream of comparing myself to you."

"I was a man of taste. But I wanted more of life. I wanted something grand," he said, working to keep his voice down, but failing. Someone stirred in a corner, a newspaper rustling.

"Tell me what's wrong," I said.

He gazed around the room for a moment, studying the shadows. This was a San Francisco copy of a London sanctuary for men, but unlike its British counterparts this place had always seemed pleasant to me. My father had brought me here often. I had first tasted scotch here. My father had not approved of the "pretentious old men of thirty," but he had taught me that a wealthy man had to be comfortable around all kinds of people, even the wealthy.

The last time I had seen Blake had been some months before, on the steps of Saint Paul's in London. It had been the memorial service for David King, the producer, and Blake had been there because everyone in film wanted to have a look at Blake, everyone wanted to be close to him. Movie people have ersatz respectability. Blake Howard was the real thing. He had paused on the steps as photographers' flashes in the gray day made his eyes spark, giving him a look both knowing and hungry. He had turned to lift a finger to Sarah Miles, a gesture courtly and familiar, and he had winked at me as he passed me. I was there because my father had known David King long ago, and because I was, for an American, old money, with just the extra zip of glamour for being a Californian whose father had seemed to endow every museum and hospital in the Northern Hemisphere.

Blake had returned to San Francisco to help judge the design competition and, the gossip columns said, "support the ballet company." We had not had a chance to meet since. Now I sat across from a virtual stranger. In these months Blake had altered. He had been robust that day in London, escorting a woman in a sable, a constellation of diamonds, grotesquely overdressed for a daytime ceremony of mourning but so freshly beautiful no one would dream of complaining. She was evidently one of those actresses who will never go anywhere in films but don't have to because they are already at the top, in London with a famous man.

Now he looked into the shadows around us, a fire just beginning its dance in the fireplace. I could think only one thing: He was no longer my friend.

I decided to be direct. "What happened to you?"

"You mean: to my money."

"What happened?"

"Bad judgment. Bad luck. Worse advice. This façade of ease, this role I play, is not cheap. You know all about that."

I knew.

Even in the muted lighting of the club, quiet drinkers and distant white-coated waiters all hushed, nearly silent, Blake was only a copy of himself, a reproduction with new lines around the eyes, and a hard glance.

"I don't expect you to forgive me," he said. "DeVere left me no choice."

Perhaps Blake had always been like this, and I was just now able to see him as he was. It was a painful thought. "You remember my fiancée? Nona Lyle?"

"How could I forget such a charming person. She's a psychiatrist," he said. "A delightful woman. You think I need her professional services?"

"Not at all. I want you to see the sort of work she does."

"I am in no position to make a donation."

"It might help you to see what real suffering is like—for children."

"Stratton, be realistic. You yourself have lived a very easy life."

"DeVere is stubborn, and so am I. I am going to persuade you, Blake."

Blake's low laugh surprised me. "Do you think we have souls, Stratton?"

I stalled, shifting my snifter to one side, leaning on the table. I could read people fairly well, but I couldn't read Blake just then.

"Immortal souls?" he added.

My father had hired the most brilliant tutors, essayists, psychologists. He had dismissed Stanford as too easy, although appropriate, so he had seasoned my education with long interludes in Italy and France. Still, it had been years since I had debated the possibility of miracles with a Jesuit surgeon or a nuclear physicist.

I hesitated to take the question seriously. Like most Americans, I find the big philosophical questions both embarrassing and pointless. There are times, though, I reminded myself—as when someone is dying—when the questions arise naturally.

"This isn't just a philosophical question," I suggested.

"Stratton, look at me—I'm a lost man."

"I suppose I really don't believe in the soul. But I don't know."

"Well, if I had a soul at one time, I no longer possess one. I've used it up, or traded it in. But even so, I'm reasonably happy."

I tried to joke. "Surely DeVere hasn't made a down payment on your eternal life."

"I'm not talking about DeVere. I'm talking about the choices I've made, step by step, day after day, all my life."

"Forgive me for finding this argument just a little bit irritating, Blake."

"You're angry." He laughed, and I could see a trace of the Blake I had known, the gentle, ironic man. "You know what the problem is, Stratton? You're likable. I can't help it. I like you. Everybody who knows you does. And it's hard to sit here and tell you the truth. There is idealism, Stratton. And then there is naïveté."

"I'm not helping my own cause very much, am I?"

"If people disappoint DeVere, they suffer. If they attack DeVere, one way or another, they pay. That CNN critic isn't on permanent holiday in Argentina."

"Are you telling me that there is danger in crossing DeVere?"

He smiled, with real affection. "You remind me of what I have given up." Blake took a pull at his brandy, then set the glass down as though the liquor tasted foul. Blake gazed at the table. There was a drop of brandy on the dark wood now, and the drop glowed and shifted with the firelight, a coin alive. "Do you know what one of your greatest flaws will turn out to be, Stratton?"

Blake had always had an avuncular familiarity with me, but even so I wasn't quite ready to hear about my defects.

He continued, "You are ambitious. You have looks and brains, but you want something more."

It seemed that as long as he talked about my character, and avoided trying to warn me, he was more like the man I used to know.

"What," I asked, "are you warning me against?"

"I canceled a meeting," said Blake. "I was supposed to meet

with Peter Renman tomorrow morning in Palm Springs. It was going to be a fantastic deal. I'm selling my art."

"You can do that? Live without your art?"

He did not respond, and I considered what he had just said. "You were going to meet with Peter Renman!"

"DeVere made the meeting possible."

Renman was a name to dwarf even DeVere's. The man was a Hollywood legend, a force in television, magazine publishing, professional sports, finance. The informed story was that he told presidents what to do, and when, and made sure their favorite liquor was waiting for them in the Renman villa in Palm Springs. If it could be said that DeVere had an empire, then Renman had the world.

"Renman!" I said, still stunned by the name. My father had known Renman, and Renman had some shadowy relationship with my mother's past. The great man had come to my father's funeral. He had been a short, quiet man behind a cordon of hired security.

"I canceled our meeting," said Blake. "I'm sick of all of it."

"These men can give you everything you want!"

Blake smiled wearily. "Can they? I think you want these men to be all-powerful because it makes your life simple. To fulfill your dreams, you defeat DeVere. I'm not so sure.

"Why don't you come over to my place tomorrow," he continued. "Breakfast. I want us to talk further about the power DeVere has, and Renman."

I saw another chance to win back his friendship, and I accepted. But as we shook hands, I sensed a sadness in Blake, or worse.

"I'm going to fight DeVere," I said. "You won't persuade me otherwise."

There was something in the look he gave me that startled me. I became fully aware of an undercurrent that had been present throughout our conversation.

"What is it, Blake? What's wrong?"

"Maybe I'm awake, after sleeping all these years. But just recently—very recently—everything is different for me."

Words occurred to me, but I did not utter them: Blake was disillusioned. He was depressed. Such emotional shifts were not unusual in thoughtful people. But at the same time I experienced a powerful anxiety. I could not leave Blake alone. Blake was more than a changed man. He was a broken man, a sick individual.

He seemed to read my thoughts. His smile was forced. "I'm fine," he said. "Too late wise—but perfectly all right."

The warning repeated itself in me. *Don't go.*
Don't leave Blake alone.

8

It is only afterward that we are aware of certain things. Only after the music has ended are we aware of how greatly it moved us, and only after a conversation has ended do we realize how strongly it has changed our sense of things.

My own family history has made me wary of the psyche's weather. People are not constant landscapes, paintings that age relatively unaltered from new to dusky to the point that they must be cleaned.

Blake was in trouble. He needed my help.

As I slipped into the cab that carried me from the club I was aware of a sensation that I did not quite understand. There was something in my jacket pocket, over my heart.

I had to smile. It bent with my movements, and as I stepped from the cab outside my home I felt it there, a wire, a fluted shaft of bone, but not dead, something else, something nearly alive.

When I was upstairs, in my office, the room with its clutter of pencils, T-squares and flat files, I hurried into my bedroom and pulled the big old Milton from the shelf. This large, calfskin-sheathed volume had been used by Rick and myself to press clover and coltsfoot blossoms. Certain passages of "Paradise Regained" were still stained with chlorophyll. I had learned to regret my youthful carelessness, but now the phrase "subtle thief of youth" was concave with the old imprint of a milkweed flower.

I sat on the bed with the book open on my lap. The treasure fluttered from my hand when I withdrew it from my inner pocket, and spun in the air. Silently, it fell to the bed. For some reason, I found it almost too beautiful to look at directly, like sunlight off crystal.

An azure plume. Or was it white? I couldn't tell. The eye prized the sight of this feather as it prized nothing else in the world. Surely it was white, perfect, steel and ice and quicksilver in a glance. I closed the book, pressing it around the light.

Nona's voice was on the answering machine, with bad news. She was coming, but she did not know when. "Tonight, I think. But, at the rate things are going, maybe a year from tonight."

That afternoon, I called Fern. He lived in a duplex in the Sunset District with a potted ficus and a VCR, and he answered the phone in the middle of the first ring. Fern was one of those men who use a laconic, vigorous manner to protect them from intimacy. I suggested that he drop by Blake's house, not for a visit, just a check.

"A check," said Fern.

"Make sure . . ." What? I had nothing but an uneasy hunch. "Make sure no one is after him."

He didn't respond. He was plainly waiting for the sort of anecdote he knew too well: homicidal fan, or someone bent on blackmail.

"What makes you think someone's after him?"

Intuition was something that Fern would trust. But when it came to bothering someone like Blake Howard, Fern would scoff at anything so nebulous as my feelings of anxiety. To think too much is to make mistakes. "I think someone wants to do Blake harm."

I was relieved when Fern said, "Okay." Meaning: I know all about harm.

"Just make sure he's home."

"And?"

"Don't disturb him."

Fern gave me a couple of ticks of silence, allowing me to see that I had stung his pride just a bit. "He won't know I'm there."

"The fact is," I said, trading a bit of confidence to soothe Fern's pride, "I think the trouble may be in his mind."

I had meant this to sound lighthearted, cheering. But as I hung up the phone I knew that the mind can be an assassin.

And I realized that I might be simply projecting my own anger with Blake onto the vague, shifting darkness of the City.

I was angry with Blake, that was true. But not so angry I wanted him to be hurt.

I reassured myself: I was not angry at all, really.

He was an old friend.

I adjusted the crook-neck lamp over my drafting table, and touched the pencil to the sketch of a roof garden, a drawing much like the one I had entered into the Golden Gate Park competition.

Collie tapped on the doorjamb with the back of her fingernails, a tap-tap-tap I would not have heard if I had not known it, and recognized it, as one of the subtle, dependable sounds of my life.

"Going to go," whispered Collie, cautious about disturbing me.

"Thanks, Collie. I know the house is a wreck. It looks like something blew up in the sun room. We live in a construction yard. I know how hard it is."

"No, sir, it's quite all right," said Collie.

The contractor was a good person, who hired brilliant people, students at the Arts School. There were more reliable, and more boring, contractors, but I knew that by supporting Packard I was supporting, indirectly, the arts. The trouble was that I was, for the moment, out of money, and I had asked Packard to delay for awhile. He had been mystified, but I told him that I wanted to sketch the walls in their stripped state.

"I did make some extra sandwiches," she said in a very low voice, virtually a whisper. It was the tone she nearly always used in my studio.

"I expect Nona tonight. She wasn't sure when. Apparently there was a strike in Chicago, and air traffic is a mess everywhere."

Collie was a tall woman with gray-blue hair. She was the last of my family's servants from the old days, the halcyon days before my mother tried to harm the staff. Collie had been in the London blitz. She had always fascinated me as a boy, saying words in a way I thought unique to her: gair-idge. "I had to take my car to the gair-idge."

A buzz bomb had landed in her back garden, a dud. Now she stayed with an elderly sister in Daly City, a woman who, ever since a fall down her front steps, was afraid to live alone. Collie's quiet courtesy did not make her seem meek. It made her, quite the contrary, seem stately and careful. "I know this place will look as lovely as all the others," she said, switching from a whisper to a beautiful alto. "All your work turns out so lovely."

When she was gone, I wished she had stayed on for a few minutes. I like to be around people like Collie, people with experience and deep feelings, and I sometimes find myself wearing solitude like borrowed, confining clothing. I adjusted the drafting table. The pencil made a satisfying whisper on the paper. The paper was the watermarked laid I bought by the kilo in Paris, and the hard-lead pencil soon lost its fine point as I roughed-in a sheaf of what I imagined would be asters, purple asters when I touched them up with watercolor.

Fern called just as I replaced the receiver. "There's a light in the house, upstairs, and another one on in what looks like the bathroom."

"So he's home."

"Someone is."

"That's fine," I said. "That's all I really need to know."

"He's burning something in the fireplace."

"That's what fireplaces are for."

"Paper."

I knew as well as Fern that newsprint and old letters smell different from applewood.

I called Blake, and there was no answer.

There was something wrong. I drew for awhile to give myself something to think about.

At last I threw down the pencil impatiently. I pushed redial again. No one answered. Now I was more worried than ever.

I nearly called my brother, Rick. My younger brother and I had a friendly but distant relationship, one that allowed him from time to time to call me to complain about alimony or his latest mechanic's bill, and it allowed me to hear someone lively, someone who reminded me of my father, if only in the timbre of his voice, his chuckle, and our shared memories.

I pushed redial again, persistent, faithful. Blake had always engaged a housekeeper. Surely he had a secretary. Nobody's phone simply rang and rang anymore. Something else always happened, a person or a machine took over to record your message.

I put down the phone and tilted my head, listening.

I wonder what it was that made me sense that the house was no longer empty. Collie must have slipped back, I told myself, remembering her sweater, or, as she would put it, her "jumper." Or Nona—surely it was Nona—dropping by on the way back from the airport.

There was someone in the house.

Someone downstairs.

I stood, and the chair I had designed behaved as it was intended to, scooting on its silent rollers, rebounding soundlessly off the wall. Nona called it my mosquito chair because it floated so lightly.

How transparent a voice sounds when it is trying to sound confident against the dark. I called for Collie, and then for Nona. My shadow fell before me. Floors were solid redwood from the Russian River, except for the study, which was floored in koa wood from Hawaii.

There was no question. I was not alone in this house.

I stood at the top of the stairs, in the bad light, then, slowly, sliding one hand along the almost imperceptible dust of the banister, began to make my way down. The stairs were one part of the house that did not creak. Some craftsman in the 1880s had determined that this would be the masterpiece of stairways, wooden pegs so tight-fitted they did not give, except for that very slight flex that all wood has, that property that keeps it from breaking.

It was not a person. It was a creature of some sort. There was the sound again. A fluttering, a big lift and fall, something flying. It was the sound of a bird, very big. Not like one of the African grays my cousin had kept in Santa Barbara. This was a very large winged creature, feathered and strong, fluttering with a noise like a sail loose in the breeze.

Christ, I thought. There's a bird caught somewhere downstairs.

And not just a bird. It's a condor, at least. My mind went blank, canceled by the single thought: the feather.

I took each step slowly, expectantly, descending into the dark vault of my home.

9

The light wouldn't go on in the first room I tried. The light switch in the next room worked, but only a carpenter's lamp flashed on, a shape like a helmet full of light. Furniture loomed under plastic, the plastic glazed with plaster dust.

I flinched. The rustling of the wings receded before me, a coy presence.

There is an instinctive sense of size, of girth, of the heft and presence of a large, living creature. That's what I felt now. There was a creature my size, or slightly smaller, in my house.

Not every room was being remodeled, not every room was stripped to its ribs. But now every room I entered, in the poor light, was one under repairs, dusty, shrouded. I did not want to speak out loud. It's terrible when that happens—when the sound of one's own voice fills a room, puny and unreal. "Show me where you are," I said, my voice sounding thin.

Was there a gap in my sense of time? There seemed to be. When I was aware of myself, and the walls around me, the sound of the wings was gone.

There was nothing.

I laughed, a sound that made the silence of the place all the worse. So, you see, I told myself. Everything is fine. No need to worry.

I experimented mentally with a phrase: auditory hallucinations. I reasoned with myself. I could be suffering a delusion of some sort. But why did I feel so wide-awake, so keen?

Jesus, I thought. What if it's happening to me?

But then—someone *was* there, in the distant hall, in the next room, plaster grit crisp underfoot.

This was not a winged creature. This was the step of someone human. I recognized this step. But surely, I thought, this is too wonderful to be true.

But maybe I was wrong. I shrank back against the solid expanse of a wall.

Real. She was real.

"That's exactly where I left you," she said.

The light, and the shadow, drifted over her. A small woman, dark, shapely. Anyone else would have been startled to find me in half light, but she smiled and put her arms out and held me.

"What happened?" she said. "Strater, you're trembling."

"Didn't you hear me?" I asked.

"No, I didn't. I just got here."

I kissed her. I held her close to me, and for a long time I did nothing but keep her in my arms.

Then I gazed into her eyes, hungry for the sight of her. She knew how I felt, and responded, kissing my lips, the lids of my eyes, as though curing me of every doubt I had ever endured.

She asked, after a long, intimate silence, "What happened with DeVere?"

"Nothing." I did not want to talk about DeVere, or about myself. Our time together was precious. "They haven't decided yet. About the award. The jury's still considering."

I could not shake the thought that Nona wasn't really here, that she was an illusion. I ran my fingertips over her face, her lips, the soft feathering of her eyebrows, like a blind man seeking to reassure himself. "They must be blind," she said. "There's nothing to think about. Your work is the best."

The sound of her voice was medicine. "The airports were a mess?"

"Unbelievable. A strike in one city, and people everywhere are sleeping on airport floors."

Her finger had healed. I kissed the place where I had put the Band-Aid.

"They loved my proposal," she said. "They loved it, Strater." She used my nickname with what sounded to me like special affection. "But I couldn't get any money out of any of them. Children aren't in fashion."

I cupped Nona's face so I could gaze down into it. "I'm so glad to see you," I began to say. But the words were not enough. I kissed her yet again.

We went upstairs.

Her hair was dark, not true black but black with a radiance, a reddish tint that caught even the weak moon from the clerestory windows, and held it. Her eyes were dark, too, and when she looked at me there was the strangest glow.

"I fell asleep on the airplane for a couple of minutes," she breathed. "And you know what I dreamed?"

She unbuttoned my shirt, each button taking far too long. I sensed some awareness in her, some discovery that made her look up at me, into me as though she could see something in my mind.

"You're trembling like someone who's gone swimming recently."

"I've given it up," I whispered.

"It's suicide," she said, but neither of us were drawn into conversation now.

She put her lips to my ear. "Do you know what I dreamed?"

I shook my head.

"I'll show you."

She was a glow in the darkness. Her lips tasted of cognac, although I was certain that she had not been drinking, and of something else, something unnamable.

Later, downstairs again, I made tea laced with the rum Collie kept in the cubboard with the Earl Grey and orange pekoe. Even in her absence, Collie's character was a part of the house, in the strong, naval rum, in the way the kitchen towels were folded, tidy and what Collie called "seamanlike."

Nona wore one of my silk dressing gowns. It flowed over her, and made her look like a sorcerer's apprentice.

My rooms were usually the picture of hurried efficiency, a marriage of software and oak furniture, ferns and phone proposals. Now each room looked like a quarry in the half light, and white dust, faint and visible only when smudged, covered every surface.

She took in our surroundings. "I thought they were coming to fix all this pretty soon."

Not even Nona knew the extent of my financial trouble. I nodded, shrugged: me too.

"Jesus, you can't live like this."

Nona is a woman who will not suffer delay, or fools. "They said they were running late."

"Running isn't exactly the word. What's the matter, Stratton?"

"It's you. You vanquish speech."

She smiled, acknowledging the flattery. But she was a physician. Human frailty attracted her eye. "I've never seen you so nervous."

"I'm worried," I said, trying to undercut the meaning of the words with a soothing voice. "You've never seen me worried before?"

"Not like this."

"There's something wrong with Blake Howard." I gave her the barest sketch of Blake's mood, my theories, and touched upon the subject of his unanswered phone. I didn't bother explaining that what upset me at the moment was that I was sure I had heard a winged creature, in this hall, in this room.

What I had really meant to say was: There is something wrong with me.

I was about to tell her about the wings. I parted my lips, dazzled by her, wanting to tell her everything. There were wings, I nearly said. Big wings, feeling the story melt and dissolve, because I knew it was foolish. The rooms were empty. There was nothing here, just as there was probably nothing wrong with Blake.

"They must have had some good things to say about your proposal," I said, sipping the fragrant tea.

"They loved it. Everyone wants to know more about what they are calling 'my children's dreams.' *My* children. As though they all belonged to me."

"They do, in a way."

"They're calling it a landmark study of children's dreams. Everyone says it would be great if we could spend more money on children. They say, 'We love your ideas, Dr. Lyle.' "

"But they won't come up with the money," I said.

"Money's a different matter altogether." She stopped herself. "I'm worried about you. Look at your house. Naked pipes. Struts. This is supposed to be your dining room. Stratton Fields's dining room. You're a famous man. My place should be a mess. I need malpractice insurance. I need a secretary. You don't need this. You have things on your mind."

She held me.

I was used to keeping problems to myself. It was a family tradition. My cousin, the one with the African grays, had been kidnapped outside a casino. He had, family rumor had it, crushing gambling debts. Something went wrong, and negotiations went awry, or perhaps the kidnappers quarreled among themselves. The cousin was found in a suitcase in Lucca, cut into pieces.

I told her the truth, as simply as I could. "I'm having a little financial trouble. A cash shortage."

She listened to my silence, as though she understood it more thoroughly than she understood my words. "You let things like that bother you?"

"My family has its secrets." This was understatement, but Nona could read the most brief comment, the gesture, the nervous cough, and see exactly what was being said. I had discussed my family only in the vaguest terms, and Nona was not the sort of person to linger over ancient sorrows.

"The house doesn't matter," she said. "Money doesn't matter. You matter. We matter."

The cup in my hand was empty, although still warmed by the just-finished tea. Nona took the cup from my hands, and she put it down beside her own empty cup on a dust-glazed side table.

Nona had a way of curing one of my headaches by applying her fingertips very gently to what she called "acupoints." These were points of her own discovery, I realized once while paging through a volume on acupressure. Her hands now found the pulse in my temple, the tension in my neck. Her fingers found the anxiety in me, and released it.

We were upstairs again, and as we made love I felt the city around us expand and dissolve, Nona beneath me whispering my name until it was no longer a whisper, but a cry of discovery.

I woke, remembering the sound of wings. This had happened to my mother, and now it was happening to me.

Her voice had been so beautiful. My mother's soprano was with me, as though, through the sound of Nona's steady sleep, I could hear my mother. Just like years before. When I had heard her talk. I had worked so hard to forget.

Surely everything would be fine. That was my strongest talent: faith.

I stared upward, into the dark.

10

She woke well before dawn, and she was into her clothes before I could fully stir.

It was that special, freshest part of the day, morning before it has begun to be light. It was night, but a time of night that promises. I could not help myself—I lay there for a long moment enjoying her loveliness, her tousled dark hair even now catching, or creating, auras out of the virtually nonexistent light in the room. She dressed with very little sound, and the dark light made it look as though I imagined her entirely. She was a figure in a dream.

"Do you have to leave so soon?" I asked.

"I hate to. But I have to get to the hospital early," she said. "I've been thinking about them every hour since I stepped onto the plane."

"I'm sure they missed you," I said, and I meant: So did I.

It was that simple: I wanted to be with her every day.

"I have time to do everything I want to do," she said, "if I stop eating and sleeping, and clone myself into about six different people."

"I can drop by the hospital for lunch."

She met my eyes. Her voice became serious, gentle. "The children would enjoy a visit. They like you."

"Would you like it?"

"You try eating lunch with a bunch of surgeons every day. All they talk about is golf and mutual funds. Today is really horrible.

I have to meet with the budgeting committee over chicken salad. I need to explain why hypnotherapy is as important as chemotherapy. Doctors forget that their patients have psyches. Sometimes I think half the surgeons on the staff would be just as happy if they treated horses and dogs instead of people."

"They forget," I said, "that people have souls."

Perhaps Nona hesitated with her hairbrush for an instant. "Exactly." Then she turned to look at me. "You are all right, aren't you?" she asked hopefully.

Leaping from bed, I hurried into my clothes. "I'll make some coffee—"

She saw me tucking in my shirttail and gestured that she had no time, a flutter of her hand much like a wave of farewell. "I have a coffee machine in my office that I never use. Morning is so important. The children need special reassurance in the morning, when they first wake up."

"Dinner tonight?"

"Someday we'll be able to do everything we want to do," she said.

"They teach you how to say no in medical school. Just go ahead and say it. It's a word of one syllable."

She kissed me, her lips lingering on mine, and on the special place in my forehead, that point where wisdom and peace were supposed to originate. "I know how you feel," she breathed. "There will be time for us, Strater. Someday."

"This is only the fifth time that we have even spent the night together. The fifth time in over a year."

She made a soft groan that I knew was a sincere expression of her feelings. She put her forehead against mine, and we stood as though in a small, confined space, a place of our own making. "I want to change the way we live. There's just so much to do—"

My feelings made it hard to speak. "I admire your work, Nona. It's part of why I love you."

The word *love* definitely made her pause. "Someday we'll have day after day together. Someday when I get real support, instead of the piecemeal dollar here and there. Someday, when my projects are funded—"

I kept the disappointment out of my voice. "Someday when there are no more sick children."

"They don't even take me seriously, some of them. Some of

the men, some of the dinosaurs with fat wallets. They can't even hear what I'm saying. They look at me and think: Just another hyperactive female. Just another pushy, plaintive woman. Just another lightweight. Besides," she laughed. "You'd get tired of me. Take my word for it—if you saw me every night you would become bored."

Day was coming. We could see without difficulty. We walked down the stairs together, Nona holding my hand, my arm trying to slow her down, hold her back.

I found myself wishing, whimsically, that I could visit a seer, a prophet who could tell me succinctly whether or not I would win Nona.

"You have to believe in the future," Nona was saying, as she reached the front door. She was bantering, refusing to take me seriously, and at the same time she realized how serious I was. "You're good at believing, aren't you?"

And I believe in you, I wanted to say. "Call me," I said, and then she was gone.

With her absence, the frustrations of my life all returned to me. There was simply the raw truth: My family had been wealthy, and now it was not. Nona knew a little, now, but no one beside my brother and I really understood the nature of our finances. Our cash reserves had suffered years of my father's benevolent mismanagement, money given away to promote everything from better acoustics in opera houses to computers in schools. What my father did not sow, Zeus-like, grand and loving, my mother finished off, but that was a story I did not like to even consider.

I kept up the illusion of brisk wealth, but it was only a pretense.

Collie had made a haven of the kitchen, and even in her absence it awaited her return, spruce and cheerful, like Monet's kitchen in Giverny, sun-yellow and spacious. Maui onions waited in a tumble on a side table, beside a rope of garlic.

I ground some Jamaica Blue Mountain and called Blake and let the phone ring. Bad thoughts pricked me.

Someone was keeping Blake away from the phone. Someone who was using Blake as bait. This was not a rational theory, and yet it simmered within me as I waited out the dark, the sun crawling across the old, warped glass of the leaded windows.

I turned on the portable Sony beside the teapot. I watched idly, and then cursed myself for turning on the television so thoughtlessly. There was "AM San Francisco," and our host, an amiable man I knew slightly, a man as mild and agreeably shallow as he looked, was introducing "one of Northern California's biggest talents, a man you're going to hear a lot more about, Frederick Peterson."

Frederick, I thought dully. Everyone I knew called him either "Peterson" or "Fred." It must be one of DeVere's suggestions. New clothes, new name, bright new future.

There was Peterson, lean and made up so that he looked more deeply tanned than ever. He wore one of DeVere's Scottsdale line of sports jackets, one of the so-called Western tweeds. It was not a bad-looking piece of clothing.

Behind the figures on the screen was the usual set, a beige wall, and a circle with a stylized seven—the station's logo. I had designed a few logos in my career—one or two had been accepted by local companies, a now defunct restaurant supply firm and a stationery store. I found myself wondering why beige was so popular, and if someone from the age of, say, Chaucer would have even recognized the color.

I busied myself with wiping invisible spots on the counter, unable to watch for a few moments. But there was something peculiar. The host's voice chattered idly, and I had the sense that the show was not moving smoothly. When I looked back Peterson was seated. "You've got some big plans for the way our city is going to look," said the host.

What had seemed self-consciousness now seemed a speech impediment. Peterson opened his mouth and could say nothing.

I felt myself sink into a very ugly realization. I said the words aloud. "Don't."

The television made a faint buzz, a tiny electronic reverberation behind the spoken words.

My voice again: "Don't do it."

It was a shock. Not long ago, Peterson had been thoughtful, articulate. Now he was a man numbed, lost. There was no doubt in my mind. I knew, but I was helpless, looking on, unable to reach forth my hand and shut off the sight of what was about to happen.

The cohost was a woman, a journalist of considerable intelligence who had retreated to the safety of morning talk shows recently after her helicopter crashed in the Middle East. Her voice accompanied the sight of Peterson's glazed eyes, his working lips.

"Frederick has some really impressive improvements in mind for the Polo Field at Golden Gate Park, and he has some good ideas for the Shakespeare Garden—"

Peterson spoke. His voice was hard to make out. "I wanted it all so badly."

The male host beamed and frowned simultaneously, so that he would be sure to have the correct expression in any event.

Peterson continued, his voice a gasp. "I wanted to *have* something."

"It certainly looks like you have some very fine plans for San Francisco, Frederick," said the brisk, female voice, "and in just a moment we'll be back to—"

"The competition was rigged. DeVere rigged it. Stratton Fields deserves to win." His words were spoken with the mechanical care of a man confessing after torture. Peterson stood straight in his chair. He fumbled at his sage-brown tweed jacket.

It looked almost comical as the camera panned back, the television crew in a hurry to move away from Peterson, to get him off and move on to someone else. Peterson seemed to take a large piece of chocolate cake from his jacket, put it to his mouth and work his mouth for an instant around the mass of dark color.

It was not cake.

The hand fumbled at the pistol. There was a crack that vibrated the speaker of the portable television, and what looked like cherry juice and chocolate was spattered all over the circle with its stylized seven.

An ad for something, a cavalcade of smiling people, flashed into view before I could stop myself. I seized the television, lunging at it instinctively, forgetting for the moment that what I had before me was an image. I wanted to grab Peterson, but in my embrace merely unplugged the Sony and sent it into blank silence.

11

It was a bright, perfect morning, as though there had never been a day before, never had been weariness, or doubt. It was sunny and cool, brisk yet warm, moss in the seams of the sidewalk.

Fern had been right. Thinking gets us into trouble. I tried to keep my mind empty.

There was no traffic. It was a quick drive. I stepped before Blake's house on Filbert Street, clapping my hands softly against the chill of the shadows.

I knew.

I knew as soon as I hesitated on the sidewalk, as soon as I wouldn't take the first step toward the front door. There was good reason Blake hadn't answered the phone.

I argued with myself—I'm good at that. Of course there was nothing wrong. But I couldn't shake the feeling: Call the police.

There was one of those large, twisting junipers beside the steps, and I found himself admiring the contorted plant. I sniffed the air for that metallic juniper spice in the air, and then I nearly had to laugh at myself. I was being childish.

You're stalling, I told myself, self-respect stirring.

The doorbell made a delayed toll, a bronze, rich tone far within the big house. The entire house was wrong. The curtains were drawn. Blake was a man who liked morning light, and he was an early riser. All the way back to the days at Tahoe, Blake and my father got up in virtual darkness for slowly illuminated, mountain-air tennis. All the curtains, all the way up into the third story, were drawn, and this was not right at all.

Maybe he's so sick he can't get out of bed. And here I am, I thought, standing here, totally useless. Blake is suffering from something pernicious and purely medical, and I am wasting time.

He flew to London last night. He decided to pop down to

Newport Beach. He's with a girlfriend. He drove down to see his horses, or north to gaze upon his vineyard.

Peterson was dead.

The doorbell rang unanswered once again, a solemn one-two far off in the depths of the house. The brass lion's-head knocker was bright and cold when I gripped it. I let the knocker clap. Many times. Too many times.

Stop thinking, Nona would say. Act.

There was always a housekeeper, at the very least. This was Russian Hill: staid, even pretentious. Surely one would answer now. But there was, if anything, even more silence from the interior of the house, a well of cold that sucked in all possible whispers.

I tested the door. It was a thumb-latch, the sort of graceful handle that the fingers wrap, leaving the thumb to depress the bright tongue and feel the satisfying slip of the bolt. Well-made, I thought, trying to ignore the cold that swept over me.

This door should have been locked. It was a quick thought, one I repressed at once. The door was opening, swinging inward.

Someone wants you to step inside. Someone wants you to be the first. Call the police. And an equally quick: You are definitely overreacting.

I paused in the foyer of Blake's elaborate Victorian. It was an ornate version of my own building, which was itself a proud three-story. This house had been done over by a designer featured in articles in several magazines, and walking into the sitting room was like entering the pages of an ad for Turkish carpets.

It was the sort of good taste that would make a casual person uncomfortable, except that it looked lived-in as well as handsome. Crystal decanters displayed scotch and vodka, and a gossipy Bloomsbury biography waited face-down on the settee.

You see, I told myself. All is well. Everything is fine. This is just a normal, civilized morning in Blake's house. There was a spill of index cards in one corner, beside a pencil with a carefully sharpened point, the sort of point a person puts on a pencil when he sharpens it for the first time. There was a spiral of pencil shaving in the otherwise empty ashtray.

I called Blake's name. There is something wistful in calling for someone when we have let ourselves in. "Hell—o" we say, making the greeting a tune, a song, an incantation: be home. Be well. I'm here.

These were the signs of haste. There had been hurry, and a desire to write something down, and an urge to find the right sort of paper. The index cards, all blank, were not the right sort of paper, and the hand had tossed the cream-pale stationery aside, spilling paper clips, each clip shiny, never used.

He had needed not fine paper, I inferred, but large sheets, paper roomy enough to contain hurried writing, desperate scrawling. I could not see any sign of Blake's handwriting, however. An organized man, a man who knew and treasured even the smallest detail in his life, had been in a hurry. I, as though to compensate, was in no hurry at all. I stood with one hand on the desk chair, drinking in the silence.

The fireplace was a black sierra of charred paper. I wandered the room, lecturing myself over what I saw: a man tying things up, I said. A man sorting things out. A man getting ready.

Of course I was wrong: there couldn't possibly be a smell. But there was a scent. It was a dark, meaty odor that made me grip a doorjamb and stay exactly where I was. There was the smell of flesh, and another smell that struck me as something out of alchemy, something that smacked of bad magic: sulfur.

I knew this smell, this combination of funk and chemistry. A thought, a single word, repeated like an endless drip: evil.

Don't think. Don't think, and don't move. But I did move, taking one careful step after another.

The hall was carpeted, except for a strip of wooden floor along each wall. My shoes kept slipping off the carpet and rasping along the floor itself. The steps were hushed, and then clunky and loud, and the contrast made me stop several times, as though the silence of my steps were essential. As though, I thought, someone were asleep.

The kitchen was an armory of frying pans and woks and utensils so nearly like weapons that it was clearly the place for carnage. The marble pastry slab was cold under my hand. The room looked never used. The roll of paper towels was unstarted, the first sheet stuck into place on the roll.

But the dining room had been used. The mahogany table was cluttered. Envelopes were arrayed, and then, as though a trembling hand had been unable to organize effectively, one or two envelopes scattered. I nearly expected them to scurry as I stood there, but they were still, reflected by the sheen of the table, each fat envelope casting a white shadow.

Legal-looking documents had been sorted, fanned, resorted. And a tablet of drawing paper, dog-eared, lay at the head of the table. The silence was like the water at the bottom of the swimming pool.

The library, I murmured to myself, moving my lips like someone reading a difficult passage. That was, after the kitchen, Blake's favorite room. No doubt Blake is up there now, listening to Wagner with earphones.

I called his name again, but this time my voice was a foreign sound, a noise I regretted making.

The library was upstairs, up the great, glistening sweep of banister. This handsome house was not as well constructed as my own. Each step creaked nearly inaudibly.

The upstairs hall was long and airless, stifling. The passage led me down what seemed an elongating tunnel of muffling carpet and dead-white ceiling.

I paused just outside the library. The smell was strongest there, and I held my breath, listening to the perfect silence of the room beyond. The quiet was punctuated by the clock somewhere deep in the library, and the ticking was slow, too slow in my ears to be telling the time.

Perhaps some instinct, or some subliminal shock, caused me to glance down.

There is nothing, I told myself. There is nothing at my feet. I have always been a man with faith that all will be well.

There was a substance like sheep's wool all over the floor. Upholstery stuffing, I decided. Except that some of it was dark. Some of it was hair.

Go ahead, an itchy mental voice told me. Don't waste time. Get it over with.

The door was open, but I was clutching the edge of the doorway. I slid one foot across the pile of the carpet, and then grew impatient with my own delay. I did not bother to gather myself. I stepped into the room.

Naturally. Of course. What had I expected?

Then: No, it can't be. Surely not.

I forced myself to look again, as though a steel hand gripped my head and turned it back to the sight.

The back of the chair was toward me. Stuffing had been blown out, and was stuck to the wall on either side of the door through which I entered, glued in place with the dark red mucilage.

I stepped to the side of the chair.

Surely Blake had not intended to look like this.

One black leather slipper had slipped off the pale, impossibly white foot. The port-black silk dressing gown was carefully, even artfully, sashed and knotted. Otherwise, what remained was not Blake at all.

A lightning crook of anger ignited me for a moment: I was going to help you. Why couldn't you wait?

My body moved on its own, stepping carefully to the side of what had been my friend, too late to take the weapon, with its sulfur scent of gunpowder, from the hands. The gun was hand-made, Holland & Holland. I knew the shop—13 Bruton Street, London. "The finest guns and rifles in the world."

Part Two

12

The lush grass at my feet was perfect. Such a small lawn, kept so flawless: grass as work of art.

From inside Blake's house came the muted sound of the official world, the authoritative sound of police dispatchers, and the quiet voices of men and women accustomed to aftermath.

I had told them that I would be in the back garden, and they had said that there was no need, that they could get further information from me at my home. But I could not trust myself to drive just now. I was mentally torturing myself with what amounted to a shopping list of guilt.

Life, at that moment, appeared a series of blunders. This sort of violent end was common, the way things really were. I huddled. Grief, shock, sorrow, always had their way with me. I was always the wet-eyed one at funerals. Rick, my brother, is always the dry-eyed one, reaching for a cigarette, tapping his foot through the Twenty-third Psalm.

A black shoe inserted itself into my view. The shoe was well-shined, and yet did not resemble the shoe one would wear to the opera. I glanced up, and stood, aware that I had been sitting there for a long time. I stood.

"Sometimes I think I was not cut out to do this kind of work," said Childress. "It's a little easier if you didn't know the guy. But everybody knew Blake Howard."

Childress was going to be an important man some day. Right now he was the best politician in Homicide. He had the cheerful courtesy of a man who had plans. He was just canny enough to know that you treated Matthew Fields's son with a little extra quiet when you saw he had trouble saying good morning.

He lifted a hand to say that he understood. "Simple. Simple and tragic. The investigation is over." Childress put his hand on my shoulder.

"All the documents on the table," I said.

"A child could figure it out." Childress let an appropriate silence pass. Then it was clear that the investigation was not *quite* over. "Did you know if he was depressed about something?"

"I talked with him yesterday."

Childress nodded, meaning: Keep talking.

I couldn't go on for a moment.

"Maybe he was sick," he suggested.

"There was something wrong."

"Maybe he couldn't go on living. It happens."

This was not the hard statement it sounded. Many were sick, troubled, lost in one way or another, and suicide was uncomfortably endemic in San Francisco. I turned away, but the white azalea, the map of leafless ivy on the garden wall, did nothing to eclipse the memory of the blood.

"It wasn't as though he seemed despondent." *Despondent.* That was a newspaper word, a television word. I continued, "Not too long ago Blake had been debonair. Christ, what an old-fashioned word. He had seemed gentlemanly and charming. But when I saw him yesterday he was different."

"In what way?"

I said, "He was a good friend."

"An old friend." It was not a question, and his voice was gentle, but he meant something he wasn't saying. He meant: Tell me everything you know. "How had he changed?"

I was aware that Childress was, as gently as Childress knew how, mentally beginning to fill out a form that had not yet been brought out into the back garden. Childress was solicitous. It was so routine that I was comforted, at first. This routine was the red tape of violent death, the way the law picked up the carcass and carried it away, and I was expected to be sophisticated, even in my state of shock.

My voice managed to find itself. "He was troubled."

"By what, exactly?" He said this a beat too quickly. As an investigator, he would be delighted to call this suicide and hurry on to life's greater challenges.

I couldn't answer.

There was, behind his diffident manner, a change of tone. "There are going to be questions like that," he said. "It's not my fault."

"I don't mind the questions."

"About the circumstances."

"Of course."

"There's the death on television this morning," he said.

I nodded, and my voice was ragged. "Awful."

"I took a call from DeVere a few minutes ago." He let the impact of the name sink in. "Here, in this house," he added, as though to emphasize some point I could not follow. "He says that we should take a close look at you."

I met Childress's gaze. I said one word. "Motive."

Childress made a sideways move of his head, a silent apology.

I continued, "He says that I had reason to want both men dead."

I knew when DeVere had arrived. Far off, doors thudded in the street, solid doors to the sort of limo DeVere favored. I could hear the murmur of detectives deflected from their duty to eye the famous man in their midst.

He looked good, one of his own overcoats, lightweight DeVere rainproof, tossed over his shoulders like a cape. The creases in his face were set in a mask of handsome malice.

I put forth my hand, and he shook it before he could stop himself, and I was the one who turned to Childress and said, "Please leave us alone for a few minutes."

One of DeVere's guards positioned himself beside the ivy wall, hands behind his back, but he was well beyond earshot. DeVere's security men were not window dressing. Credible rumor was that they had broken bones in the defense of their employer's good name.

DeVere's tone was almost friendly. "This is certainly a sad day for all of us. We're all speechless with grief. Absolutely speechless. Allow me to offer my condolences."

I gave a nod.

"I would like to know how you did it, Fields."

I did not respond.

"How did you arrange it?"

Our eyes met.

"You made a clean sweep," said DeVere. "I'm impressed."

I shook my head. I wanted to tell him how much he disgusted me, but I could only give him a bitter smile.

"I happened to like Blake Howard. A lot," he said.

"He was easy to like."

"I'm afraid of you," he said, in a voice that was firm, crisp, and anything but fearful. "And I will do everything I have to do to protect myself." He paused, no doubt to let the words sink in. "But I will not run away."

I had to laugh.

He continued, "You think I'm going to be worried? A couple of deaths and I'm supposed to be shaking? Maybe you wanted to humiliate me. You wanted me to see my protégé blow himself to shit on television, and you wanted me to see that you could destroy even an accomplished man like Blake."

His tone was nearly friendly, although surprised. He had discovered both an opponent, and a kindred spirit.

"Blake was a friend," I said.

"That's what impresses me," said DeVere.

I kept my voice low. "You think that I'm exactly like you," I said.

"Sure. It turns out you're a lot like me. But more foolish." Then there was a slight smile on his face. "I almost like this. Two complete bastards slugging it out."

I had to admit there was something admirable about this man. He would have looked good with a rope and horse. His eyebrows were tufted, and he had a sun-weathered look, although as I knew he had been seasoned by scotch and spread sheets, and not by endless horizons.

"You've done something brilliant," he went on. "I don't know how. Of course, you're going to pay a heavy price for this," he was saying, in a tone that was easy, almost cheerful.

I decided to gamble. "Agree to allow me to receive the award, and then, perhaps, you'll be spared."

I don't know what power induced me to say such a thing, but DeVere's eyes brightened. He did not speak for a moment, eyeing me with an expression that was hard to read. "I was so wrong about you. Jesus. How could I have misread you so totally? If I were dead there would be no one to engineer the award. You needed me alive to be certain that the award wouldn't go to Peterson posthumously, with some gaggle of young designers to put his plans into effect."

I shrugged.

"Or maybe you want me alive just so you can humiliate me. Make me eat the award, choke on it." He chuckled. "You surprise me. Don't take it as an insult. But I didn't expect this from someone like you."

I said nothing.

"I thought you were one of those weak people, one of those *good* people." He said "good" as though the word described something loathsome. "Maybe you have someone smart giving you advice."

I returned home, and changed clothes hurriedly, as though to disrobe from rags now grown unclean.

I sat and gazed at the white surface of my drafting table. I had always found solace in work, but now I could not concentrate. I needed to look at something otherworldly, something that would ease me.

I flipped the pages of my Milton.

A feather is an amazing act of nature. Like a leaf, it radiates out from a central stem, and like a leaf it is made to both withstand and to master air. This leaf was all colors at once, although white, the white of noon sun off a fjord, was the color that predominated.

Go outside, I told myself. Go out into the garden, where you can think.

I wanted to clip the privet bush, trowel the earth around the tulip bulbs, where any day now they would be erupting.

I hurried into my back garden. There was the lawn, the greenhouse, and the side buildings where, I knew, I could find everything from a chainsaw to a bicycle. I stopped.

Surely I was mistaken. This couldn't be happening.

The gingko tree was full-leafed. The leaves were tiny, still the greenery of early spring. But the tree was back again, as it had been years before.

13

The television stations played the tape of Peterson's suicide again and again.

At first the news readers warned viewers against "the shocking footage due up next." But after awhile they just played it, in slow motion. Someone on Pier 39 had a T-shirt printed up, the channel 7 logo splattered with gray and ruby. The shirts sold.

An editorial in the *Chronicle* decried "Golden Gate Design Prize Manipulation." DeVere appeared on the same television show that had seen Peterson's death. The backdrop was new, a more sunny shade of beige. The chairs were new, too. DeVere denied any "collusion to keep the well-known Stratton Fields from getting what he deserves."

The moderator, the amiable man, did not look changed at all from his up-close experience with death. "So you deny any involvement in trying to persuade the jury that Stratton Fields should not get the award?"

"I don't decide who gets the prize."

"Who does?"

DeVere gave his smile. "The jury."

"But it's well understood that you are the one who knows who should, and will, win."

DeVere did not bother to respond.

The host gave a smile of his own. "We'll have to wait and see?"

It was a contest of smiles, teeth, manly good looks. DeVere was winning.

The announcement of the award was moved up. There was no point, evidently, in making all of us wait a matter of weeks. DeVere was working quickly. There were hurried preparations. Calendar entries were scratched out, and plans were rearranged all over Northern California. No one wanted to miss the ceremony.

And no one complained about the short notice of the arrangements. After all, DeVere always got what he wanted.

Nona and I sat together in the pew at Grace Cathedral. DeVere sat nearby, and Fern was somewhere behind all of us, watching, and, I somehow knew, praying.

I was dazzled with that deep sense of dislocation an effective memorial service gives. Something grievous has happened, but the service offers hope, even promise, as though what has happened was an injury that can be healed. It is almost persuasive, the candles, the flowers, the prayers.

On this day, however, I found myself unable to concentrate on the prayers, which I had always found a source of sacred majesty, however unclear I felt about my own faith. My mind slid away from them, the words abstract and without flavor.

I kept repeating to myself the granite advice: Don't think.

Don't think about the suicides. Don't think about the prize.

I had nothing to do with either death. There was no reason to be uneasy.

We descended together, tugging on our raincoats, a few photographers flashing pictures in the drizzle. Nona was at my side, and she always gets the attention of a photographer or two by her looks, her carriage, the way her eye takes them in with amusement. You can hear them asking afterward, "Who was that lady with Stratton?"

Fern was there, too, behind his aviator glasses, tiny drops lashing the lenses, escorting us to the curb. The man had sat in on a presidential Commission on Violence in the Home, thanks to my father's influence. But something had always eluded Fern. He should have been a police chief, but now he was eying a crowd of tans and white teeth.

I was glad Fern was there, in the way I might be comforted by the presence of a familiar oak. DeVere and I stood close, protected by the crowd. Despite the drizzle, and the blossom of several umbrellas, no one was in a hurry to leave. With Blake's death an era had ended, a San Francisco name was gone, and few of the people there would ever be in the presence of so many actors and producers again. Besides, there was a crowd across the street, and the park was filled with a multicolored wash of onlookers. We were a subcontinent of famous faces surrounded by the more democratic sea.

DeVere looked outward, at the crowd of citizens beyond the haze of drizzle. "Look at them all," he said. "Like flies."

He stood beside me as though we were easy companions, and I could not blame him for thinking myself like him in some ways. In the face of an anonymous crowd, the two of us had something in common.

"The medical report is in. They leaked it to me," said DeVere. "Suicide. The same as Peterson. You've done something very smart," he added. "I'm going to figure out what it was."

Suddenly the crowd was a group of people who could eavesdrop, and I waited until the lion's pride of famous entertainers had moved away just a bit, leaving only Nona and Fern close enough to overhear.

DeVere sighed. "Sometimes I get sick of all of this," said DeVere. "All these people, all these faces."

He turned to me, as though sharing a secret. "Most of these people are lucky they can swallow their own spit. People are so stupid."

There was a sadness in his voice, though. There was something about DeVere's posture, the way he turned away into the rain, helped along by his own security people, that made me see him as a source of trouble. But as something else, too. He was a human being, and he had just attended a memorial service. Perhaps, in his own way, he was grieving.

The hospital cafeteria had that agreeable, fake feeling of so many institutional places. There was plenty of artificial, unnourishing light.

"He calls you the Man Who Makes Horses," said Nona. "The

way he says it makes it sound like your formal name. A ritual name. More serious than your legal name."

"I'm sure a judge would allow me to adopt the name. I like the way it sounds. Stratton-Who-Makes-Horses."

The Medical Center food was good. The lasagna Nona favored was made with fresh mushrooms, and what tasted like fresh rosemary. And I had that peculiar, wonderful feeling of experiencing moderate sexual arousal in a public place.

Nona seemed aware of this, meeting my eyes, giving me a knowing smile. "The children will be glad to see you," she said. "They always ask when you are going to come see them again."

Nona gossiped about the other people carrying trays to distant corners of the room, and I was warmed inside by how happy she seemed to have me with her.

Then, her voice dropped and she said, "I'm glad you're not too upset about Blake." She touched my hand, turned it over, and ran her finger along my lifeline.

"I'm all right." I found myself wanting to sound like Fern, laconic and sure of myself. I closed my hand around her finger, and kept it there for a moment.

She smiled. She understood. She added, "And maybe you think you can woo me by acting tough. Men are supposed to be that way."

I answered her smile. "Not in my family. My father would recite *The Tempest,* tears on his cheeks."

"He was an actor?"

Our words were calm, but behind each syllable there was a current of understanding: We knew each other, and we wanted each other. "He was everything. My father had old money. Old railroad money, and before that old shipping money, and before that old tobacco and iron-smelting money. I imagine them financing cannons and Yankee clippers. The Fieldses invested, and their dollars flowered, for generations." I spoke with a certain irony. "I was expected to do something aristocratic with my life."

"Children like you. That's important."

"Because children are a good judge of character?"

She laughed. "Children can be deceived. Just like us. But sometimes they can tell something about a person. I've always felt that to be loved by children is a very valuable sort of trust, and an honor."

"I like it when you look into my eyes." This was, it struck me, an unusually frank and even romantic confession for a hospital lunchroom. But having said as much, I added, "Although I wonder, sometimes, what you see there."

She opened my hand. I had never realized what a sensitive instrument fingers could be, or how erogenous the human palm actually was. She gazed at me with such warmth—and such gentle amusement—that I nearly blushed. "I see a man who should have more faith in himself."

We made the rounds, visiting her patients. We stayed close to each other, mutually enlivened by the touch and feel of our bodies.

They were all children that medicine had decreed incurable. She counseled them, listened to their dreams. She reassured them, but more than anything she understood them, and gave them a sense of companionship. She did it because, no matter what she might say, she loved the children more than anything in the world.

Before they had wanted me to draw pictures. Now everyone wanted a puppet, "like Stuart's."

Some of the rooms were like the private rooms of a home for the very old, for human beings aged beyond the expectations of nature. But in the bed, beneath the Porky Pig poster, there would be a child, withered as though with a century's hardship, meager head on a huge white pillow.

Stuart had the nearly bald head of a radiation victim. He had, Nona had told me, a disease very much like leukemia but hard to classify, a flaw in his bone marrow, a critical disease of the blood. He had been enduring for months, and at times seemed to be recovering and then on other days was faded to a figure that was almost translucent. His smile was corroded, his lips broken. He held out his hand for one of my better efforts of the day, a horse made out of cotton bond.

"Why is that you like horses so much?" I asked him, helping him fit the steed over his fingers.

He spoke, and I couldn't quite make out his words.

"Because they're so strong," said Nona, realizing that I had not understood Stuart.

"Lions are strong, too," I said, really just making conversation to keep the sympathy in me from making it impossible to say anything at all. "And so are bulls." But then I saw the look in Stuart's eye. "But I can't think of any animal that is stronger and faster than a horse."

His cheek wrinkled with a smile.

Later, over coffee, I leaned forward and asked, "Stuart has time left, don't you think?"

She stirred her coffee, looked up, and then looked down at the plastic stirring stick.

"I mean—a few months," I said. "Maybe even a little longer."

"Some very strange things can happen. What they call miracles," she said. "You never know."

"Children have all kinds of reserves of energy."

"Of course they do," she said.

That night, once again, I gazed upward into the dark, unable to sleep. I didn't want the prize. I did not want anything but Nona, and she was gone by then, in Seattle to do a radio show and tour the university there.

Innocent.

I was innocent, and that's all there was to say or think. How could I have had anything at all to do with the death of two people, miles from me. Two people I liked.

There was no question about it in my mind.

14

*G*Q had once listed me as one of the "Ten Men Who Look Best in a Tux." It was not the sort of honor I sought. It was my opinion that Tutankhamen's mummy would look pretty good in a tuxedo.

Even when the audience that filled Davies Hall was hushed there was that wash of sounds that makes the presence of a thousand people known. But then, as the envelope turned in the fingers of the master of ceremonies, and the thick, soft paper began to tear, the audience took in its breath.

The auditorium was silent. It was that quiet I love, tension about to be broken. The spotlight reflected hard off the microphone clipped to the master of ceremonies' black lapel. The envelope tore, and the off-white card was half lifted from its paper housing, and then caught. The envelope fought back somehow, clinging to the card within it, one corner snagging, as though the name of the recipient shrank from human touch.

The master of ceremonies blinked to adjust his contact lenses, perhaps, and with the timing of so many such stagestruck speakers he took one second too long to acknowledge that he knew something the entire assembly did not.

The master of ceremonies was the president of a major corporation, an impeccably attired patron of the arts, and he was a man accustomed to working in private, in the boardroom, in the oak-and-leather box of an office. He enjoyed this attention, and he wanted to keep it, feeling in the beam of the stagelight a power that he, for all his accomplishments, relished.

The emcee spoke, and to me the syllables were for an instant entirely unfamiliar.

Not me, I thought, in a confused attempt to protect myself from disappointment. Surely it's somebody else.

Nona was squeezing my hand, gripping it hard, with a clench like terror, except that she was smiling, her beauty smiling into my eyes. People were turning to clap their hands at me.

What an incantation a name is, meaningless sounds that are, at the same time, as intimate as a gland, or a first memory. I was dazed. I made myself repeat the syllables he had spoken, to make sure that I had heard correctly.

My name.

Christ, they'll think I'm milking the applause. More faces were turning to look, still smiling but touched, now, with curiosity. Eyes were on mine.

I pulled myself to my feet, the applause swept me onto the stage. Fortunately the stage had that reassuring artificial look, the look of a place that was hyperreal, lurid and awash with light and at the same time fake. The floorboards gleamed. The podium was far in the distance, a monolith I could never reach.

The audience was comprised of professional designers and architects, and the critics who approved and derided them. Then, naturally, there were the hundreds of people who employed these professionals.

I reached the podium and accepted the award, a simple, purist-pleasing rectangle of engraved paper. I turned, and for a moment it happened.

Peterson would be standing here, I told myself. Blake Howard would be sitting there, at the end of an aisle, his usual sort of seat, smiling toward the stage.

How strange the theater looked from where I stood. I surveyed the blur of faces, and what I saw resolved itself into individual countenances. These were the well-fed, wrinkles surgically erased, hair transplanted, jawlines lifted, women long past childbearing kept eerily teenage-thin.

These were the men and women I knew well, some of them friends since my childhood. Isn't it wonderful of Stratton to take up architecture, family friends had smiled, but at the same time it had been obvious that they generally thought it just a bit odd that I shouldn't content myself with horses and a tasteful and slightly dull collection of eighteenth-century oils.

There was DeVere, his eyes hard.

I began to speak, and the years of training, practicing careful diction under the attention of a gifted man who was at once teacher and servant, and the years of watching my parents at ease in public, all stood with me.

I praised Peterson's work. I offered the solemn memory of the promising architect, and of "San Francisco's best friend," Blake Howard. By instinct, I was able to choose exactly the words people wanted to hear. Looking upward, up the slope of the seats, through the haze of faces and the glints off jewels here and there in the audience, I sought Nona's face, and found it, continuing to offer my thanks, my appreciation to my fellow designers and architects, sustained by the sight of her encouraging smile.

It was then that I saw a new person, a stranger, slip into the room.

She stepped through the doors at the end of the aisle, declined with the easy wave of a hand the assistance of an usher, and slipped into a seat at the end of the very top row. It was a glimpse, only, of a figure with white hair, a latecomer, wearing something moon-bright and resplendent, a gown.

My voice was steady. But as I spoke there were thoughts edging in on me, pressing upon my pleasure. Now, I thought, they'll start to actually build one of my projects. Now they'll take me seriously and let my gardens take their place in the real world, and not only in a few out-of-the-way corners. I would get commissions from around the world.

I should have felt joy. I should have felt the bliss of honor. What I felt was anger. They had withheld this sort of public acceptance from me for a long time. Too long. I had redesigned a cardiologist's mock-Tudor, managing to make the residence into an office building without making it look cheapened. I had doctored a multistory parking complex so that it now looked more like a set of hanging gardens, gracing San Francisco instead of punishing it. But most of my dream gardens, dream landscapes, dream glimpses of what structures could be if we gave ourselves over to trees and ivy, natural wood and native stone, remained in the realm of the unlikely, sets for plays no one would ever produce.

I had designed birdbaths, wading pools. Now, I thought, I can actually accomplish something real, and not be rewarded as a visionary, a man of dreams that are too beautiful to be made concrete. "You think too much," my brother had once said. "Beauty's a luxury. All that prettiness is so much perfume—nice, but not worth the earthquake insurance."

Now all that futility was behind me.

The reception was what the society columnists would call a "sparkling affair." I shook hands and accepted warm congratulations. It was obvious that Peterson's lurid death was eagerly put out of mind for the moment, and Blake's loss was not enough to dim the event. The celebration was all that I could have wished.

Barry Montague, my doctor, clapped me on the back and said that this was the best thing that had happened for a long time. We promised each other again that soon we would play tennis, "like the old days," said Barry. "Although I think you'll clobber me." He patted his stomach. "Too many doughnuts."

Fern fingered the stem of an empty glass, beside the rush of palms into which he had just emptied his bubbly. He looked much better in a tux than most big men, and I had to remind myself that Fern was experienced with protecting the lives of ambassadors, a man who was accustomed to wearing a gun under any sort of clothing.

To my surprise, my brother was there. He made his usual pistol-shot with his fingers, the way he usually said hello, what he called "the silent hi." I nearly always had the same, simultaneous linked thoughts when I saw Rick.

I thought how good it was to see him, and at the same time: I wonder what sort of trouble he's in now. There is something electric between the two of us, something that springs from our shared memories. The woman with him was a dream-vision of high couture and something vaguely dissolute, a fashion model turned courtesan.

I made my way through the crowd, unable to attract the attention of Nona. She was chatting with women in brightly colored dresses while dressed herself in something subdued, dark blue, clothes that made her look like a woman who had taste and, at the same time, someone who could save your life.

"Of course you won," said Rick with a smile. "You're a winner —like me."

Rick was a little thinner than usual, still looking like a man who could get a job as a model himself, Suits for the Man on the Go. He introduced me to "Honey—that's her name—right out of a storybook," the sort of meaninglessly pleasing statement Rick had made a specialty. I studied his face, his eyes, for signs of drinking, drugs, even recent accidents. He had crashed a string of sportscars, including that near-fatal crash at Devil's Slide not so long before. Physically, we looked very much like brothers.

Rick put his arm around me, my younger brother acting like the protective sibling. "I'm proud of you, Strater."

His compliment warmed me inside. I thanked him.

"I knew you were a winner, all the way, even when we were kids."

It was the kind of boyish nonsense Rick manufactured nonstop, but this once it worked with me, and I was pleased.

"That news about Blake was really bad. Really hit me hard," he said. He was being truthful, I knew, but he had probably been skiing in the Alps when the news had reached him, and he was too lively and unsentimental to bother with memorial services. "You ought to drive up and see Mother," he said. "Tell her about the award. She'd like that."

I wasn't in the mood to talk about Mother. "She was never enthusiastic about me drawing pictures."

"I'm not exactly something for her to show off to the nurses. I saw her a few months ago."

"How was she?"

I rarely saw Rick looking so thoughtful, or troubled. All he said about her was, after a long moment, "Quiet. Not peaceful, exactly. Just quiet."

The doctors had asked us to stop visiting her. After our visits, the word had been, she was "uncontrollable for days, except under chemical maintenance." I knew what that meant—the sort of sedative that sent a patient into a virtual coma.

"But go on and have your party, for Christ's sake," Rick laughed. "We'll talk about Mom some other time."

I left my brother to Honey and made my way through well-wishers, feeling buoyant despite the talk of my mother and the strain in my brother's voice.

DeVere caught my eye. I stepped up to him, wishing he would vanish from my sight.

"Enjoy the prize," he said.

15

In Pieter Brueghel's painting of the Tower of Babel there is an open mountain like a volcano, except that it is not a true mountain at all. It is composed of the arches and spans of a magnificent unfinished edifice. This mount is, at its summit, streaked with cloud.

There is little sign of confusion—of babble—at all. The divine aphasia that has rendered language both nearly useless and multifoliate had either not taken place yet, or has had the effect of making the human beings present cautious rather than confused. The structure stands seemingly vacant, apart from both human aspiration and scorn. A few figures gather, others scatter, and it is plain that above all else in this landscape the building is most lasting, even unfinished as it is. Humans flee, or wander, or stand where they are. With that Flemish talent for diminishing human stature, the painter shows us that human beings are not terribly important, although human endeavors may be. It is the tower that endures.

It was this picture, Brueghel's oil and wood reproduced in an art book, that fascinated me as a child, more than any of the Annunciations, more than any of Gustave Doré's biblical nudes. This building was a marvel, even though its construction had begun so much human confusion. I believed, in my boyish way, that the polyglot citizens of the land must have found some use for such a great tower in the years yet to come, if not as a citadel then as a quarry for future cities. It is this painting, I think, which lay the first stone in my desire to be an architect, my aspiration to span the sky with sanctuary.

The reception was a crush of light and voices. Standing there, champagne flute in hand, surrounded by the murmur of so many lives, I remembered this painting. We need safe havens, strong buildings to act as theaters for our dreams because our dreams are fictions, as we are.

DeVere's security men stood along a wall, beside a stairway, watching. DeVere found a place for himself where he could both greet well-wishers and watch the crowd. I had a bad thought: Fern is outnumbered.

Why did I think such a thing just then? Nona and I smiled at each other from time to time. She was speaking to a real-estate developer and a coffee heiress, no doubt explaining her work at the hospital, and describing the need for money.

Someone touched me. I turned. I took a step back, unable to speak.

She was pale, her hair a remarkable color, like moonlight. She was dressed in a silvery gown that trailed upon the floor.

She had touched my hand. The touch had been cool, and yet I lifted my hand and cradled it, as though I was in pain. She smiled, as though knowing exactly what I was thinking.

This was the woman who had entered the hall as I accepted the prize. I must have said something, some stammered pleasantry, because she shook her head, just slightly, to keep me from saying anything more.

She stepped close, and despite her beauty I involuntarily took a further step back. She swept lightly upon me, and touched my lips with hers.

Her lips were cool, and there was a fragrance in the air that warmed, as oil of cloves or essence of spearmint will both warm and numb the lips. I wanted to thank her for her congratulations. But I made no sound.

I have met many remarkable women, and a gentle kiss on an evening like this can communicate exactly the right sort of charm. This woman did look vaguely foreign, so perhaps her command of English was not equal to her poise.

But I looked into her eyes. It was not the usual moment in which one fumbles for words, embarrassed, distracted. This was something quite different. I knew this woman. But I could not guess how.

The woman left me. There was a swirl of gown upon the floor. There was a wash of light that followed her through the crowd.

I stood, my fingers to my lips, and people were talking to me. Familiar faces were beaming at me, and I had to say something. But I was aware that all the sounds, all the voices and gentle laughter, had been silent for a moment in my ears.

I found Nona and took her elbow, leading her to one side. After we had talked about the people she had met, the actor with the conservatory theater, the executive with Clorox, I stepped as close as I could to her, as though confiding a secret, and said, "Did you see that woman?"

"Which one?"

Nona was teasing me, I knew. She was being coy. Everyone here had to be aware of the pale woman in the silver gown. I described her, and Nona smiled and put her nose to mine, both playful and mildly mocking.

"I didn't see this queen of the evening," she said.

I persisted, and Nona put her hand in mine, the same hand the woman had touched. "No, Stratton. Honestly. I didn't see any-one like that."

16

After the reception, Nona and I found a favorite restaurant for a continuing celebration.

The owner welcomed us with a cry. I felt slightly embarrassed at his apparent delight in seeing us. We made our way to a secluded corner.

"You're a champ, Strater," said Nona, lifting the flute of yet more champagne. Her eyes dazzled me, the candlelight reflected in them.

We touched glasses, the crystal making the appropriate music, and I made a heartfelt but flowery comment about being inspired by her presence.

The award, the champagne, the North Beach restaurant to which we had retreated, were all like the facets of a new kingdom. Even the sight of Fern at a corner of the bar, sipping what looked like a diet cola with an impressive amount of ice, made the evening all the more perfect. Shouldn't someone as splendid to the eye as Nona have a courtier or two, a palace guard this late in the evening?

She ran her forefinger over the lip of her crystal, and it made the slightest ringing chime. This should be the beginning of a new point in our affair. I knew that she wanted it to be, as badly as I did.

But she had a report to write, a proposal to fax to Brussels, an article to finish on neuropathology, and we both knew that this was going to be little more than an interlude between obligations. Even now, she should be in her apartment, revising her proposal.

"They're cutting back the number of beds in my ward," she said. "There's talk of eliminating my ward totally."

I was incredulous. "How can they justify that?"

"My kids generate publicity during the Shriners' game, and

from time to time a basketball player drops by to have his picture taken with someone like Stuart. But my patients aren't going to get better. They aren't suffering dramatic illnesses. They're just kids facing death."

Her offhand way of discussing it made her message all the more impressive. I said, truthfully, "The kids are lucky to have you."

"There's a problem, though. I don't spend enough time with you," she said.

I knew enough to keep silent.

"I'm always flying to Detroit, or Brussels, or Guadalajara to give a paper on dream imagery among critically injured children. Or childhood reformation of earliest memories. Or any of a dozen other subjects. They are all important. More important than people think. I think no one really understands children. I think I have a chance to open the subject to the eyes of the world. To make them realize how wise, and alive, children are."

I took her hand.

"I know I keep promising this," she said. "But someday we're going to have a life together."

Someday, I thought. That vague day, that smudge on the horizon that never arrives.

Fern drove the armored Mercedes, the big car rolling up and down the San Francisco hills. There was a blush of city lights in the clouds overhead, and the night was cool.

Nona and I kissed, and I let her slip into her apartment.

I would happily put the evening on rewind all the way back to the restaurant owner crying, "The beautiful couple! Over here— I have your special place," in a voice so loud everyone in the restaurant turned to look. I could replay our time together over and over, tirelessly.

When Fern and I were on Nineteenth Street, he said, "There's someone following us."

I craned, looking back. Perhaps I was out of practice. There were headlights. Municipal railway tracks gleamed in the dark.

I settled back into my seat. "It's like the old days. Kidnappers. Terrorists."

Fern did not speak, and he did not glance into the rearview mirror.

"Maybe my ex-wife hired a private detective," I said. "Satisfying her curiosity. Keeping track of my love life." I could not keep a certain grit from my voice with the last two words.

Margaret would never have hired someone to follow me. On the other hand, Rick was *always* being followed. Some woman's husband had him trailed—it happened fairly often. Or else he owed people money, strong-arm Vegas types.

"Remember that time you dropped that photographer's camera at the film festival?" I said.

"These aren't reporters."

"How do you know? You're always making these pronouncements. And of course neither of us will ever know whether they were reporters or insurance salesmen, so you end up sounding like you know everything."

"It was a nice reception," said Fern. "Congratulations."

Fern drove to Lake Merced. I did not ask him to. Perhaps he knew my moods, after all these years. This was like the old days, too. I used to come here at night. The lake was a surprise to the eye, even when one expected it, and at night as at day it was a chance to look upon something not made by human beings. In the months after Margaret and I split up, Fern and I would drive here, and I would stroll to the edge of the lake and skip stones, sipping cognac from a flask, Fern waiting patiently.

But Fern did not stop the car. He drove into the neighborhood adjoining the lake. I waited for his professional opinion.

He said, "Maybe it's the police."

"Looking after me. How thoughtful."

He drove, his broad shoulders at ease, his head tilted sideways. "Making sure you aren't heading for the airport."

"The idea has a certain appeal. But why should they care?"

He did not answer directly. Silence was one of Fern's devices. He was a quick man who worked slowly. "How are you going to handle DeVere?"

"The police will protect me," I said. I meant this ironically, and Fern laughed silently.

He turned a corner. Shadows of trees rippled over us. "Maybe it's DeVere people," he said. "Showing off."

"What's he got to show?"

Fern said nothing.

"Are you trying to make me nervous?"

"If he hurts Nona, what are you going to do?"

I was ready to laugh. Fern was being ridiculous. Then I couldn't laugh. "That kind of thing isn't going to happen."

When Fern did not respond to this, I continued, "Don't worry about DeVere. I can handle him. The world isn't the kind of place you think it is."

Fern parked the car in the garage. He locked the garage and muttered something about doing a "visual" on the interior of the house.

"It's all right, Fern. You're going to make me nervous squinting around at things like that. I think you guys get most of your training watching television, I really do."

He did not laugh.

"The kind of thing you're worried about," I began. "That kind of violence. We don't live like that."

"If you say so," said Fern, and he left me.

I entered the house. I switched off the burglar alarm, locked the door, loosened my black tie.

Upstairs, I hurried through my studio, into the bedroom. I splashed a little postaward cognac into a glass, and as I slipped out of my jacket I felt something in the pocket. I was puzzled, because I could see the Milton there on its shelf.

But it was an envelope, not a feather. Inside was the award. That's all it was: paper.

This was the prize. Once I really looked at it, it did resemble one of the more elaborate stock certificates, or the sort of diploma one could buy from the University of Beverly Hills, except smaller, small enough to fit into a pocket.

All of that fuss, I told myself, all of that ambition over a little piece of paper, a wedding invitation, the announcement of a new partner.

I had been aware of something as I moved about my room. The light was not the same as it should be. My house lights are on timers, and timers can fail. But this was not too little light. Nor was it too much. I gazed about me.

And it became clear. I could not tell how I knew, but I did.

Was it a trace of perfume in the air, or the weight of a presence, a special, pregnant variety of silence?

I was not alone.

17

The light in the room had changed. It was brighter, each object glowing. There was a sweet flavor in my mouth.

I let myself linger at the door to my bedroom, and to my amazement the jamb gave at my touch. It was impossible. Surely it was only in my mind. But the doorway was alive, composed of sensate flesh, taking pleasure as I brushed through it and hurried to the top of the stairs.

It was a rare moment: I wished I owned a gun.

I told myself to go back this moment and call Fern. Tell him—Tell him what?

There was a fluttering, and a waft of air touched me as I stood, gazing down the almost perfect darkness of the stairwell.

I told myself to stay right where I was and think for a moment. Think about what was happening. Too much champagne? Or something else. Something chemical slipped into the victory bubbly, a little hallucinatory juice to speed the revel?

But there was no question about it. There really *was* someone downstairs. Were they stealing something? I listened, but there was only the whisper, as of a blanket shaken, a flag rippling. Perhaps it was not a person at all, but some creature.

I began my descent.

There was a source of light preceding me, slipping down each gleaming stair. I stopped. I clung to the banister. I told myself to stay where I was.

Call someone, I thought. Get Fern on his car phone and tell him he was right. Call the police.

I glided to the doorway of the study. The light was in there.

Why wait, I asked myself. Why stand here in your own house, afraid to make a move? Go on in.

Someone is looking for the family treasure. Everyone assumes that's what you have here, I told myself. Platinum and the kind of old gold that reminds the eye of sunset. Everyone knows that's what you have, in a wall safe, or just sitting on shelves, so much bric-a-brac.

If there were thieves I wanted to confront them myself.

I stepped into the room.

The light was only a fire in the fireplace. Nothing more. Flames snapped. The shivering light made the shadows of the shrouded furniture tremble. Perhaps Collie had lit a fire, and left it. The floor seemed to tremble.

My feet crunched the glaze of plaster dust on the koa-wood boards. A plastic dust cover crackled as I leaned against a bookshelf. The woodsmoke was fragrant, the scent of mature cedar.

Just as a feeling of domestic calm was beginning to allow me to enjoy the fire, there was a gentle movement against a wall.

I turned, ready to seize the poker.

There in the shadows was the figure of a woman. Her gown rustled across the dust floor. She was easier to see as she approached the firelight and stood before me, looking into my eyes. I recognized her. She was the remarkable woman who had attended the reception. I was happy enough to see her, and at the same time felt that she should not be where she was.

Her eyes were dark. They reflected the fire.

My voice startled me. "How did you get in?"

She offered only silence. She was stunning, and as awestruck as I was at the sight of her I was also aware of a mild sense of outrage. She was trespassing. The thought had the weight of moral authority—she should not be here.

I took a step back to get a better view of her, and to sense whether she had any companions. I had the further sensation that we knew each other well, as though this woman were an old and treasured friend whom I had forgotten until this night.

I heard only the snap of the fire. "Are you alone?"

She still kept her silence, but her gaze was searching, and there was another impression I had as she looked upon me, studying me.

"Forgive me for being blunt," I said, my voice calm now. "But now and then I meet someone who means harm. There are people who for one reason or another are dangerous."

I did not have to ask the question explicitly: What sort of person are you?

Her hand was on my arm. "You must believe in me now," she said.

I hesitated for an instant. She had answered my question, perhaps without knowing it. I knew how to handle this: I would humor her. She must be an eccentric, or deranged. She was unsettling, but there was no need to be unkind. "I never doubted," I said.

"You must begin to understand what I can do for you."

I realized that I had not entirely understood her first remark. Or perhaps I had. It is wise to be polite until it's clear that courtesy is useless. "I can't tell you how happy I am tonight," I said, attempting to keep the conversation on solid footing.

"This does change everything for you, doesn't it?"

I tried to turn away and stir the fire, but she kept her hand on my arm. "It does indeed."

"It gives you—a future."

She used the word *future* as though she did not quite believe in it herself. I agreed that I supposed it did accomplish just that, but she lifted a finger to silence me and smiled.

I continued my course of using hospitality as a form of self-defense, at least until I figured out what else to do. "May I offer you something?" I said. When she did not make a sound, I added, "A drink?"

"I see that you don't quite understand me."

My eyes must have communicated a question, for she answered what I had not asked. "I am an old friend," she said.

For an instant I believed her. Then I wished that I had Nona with me to overhear such an outrageous and yet strangely plausible remark. "I'm sorry this room is such a mess," I said.

"You got my gift."

I watched the firelight in her eyes.

"The feather," she said.

Some power in me kept me steady. I laughed, self-consciously, but I was not at all comfortable. I made it sound easy. "Who are you, really?"

"But surely you have guessed by now," said the charming woman, both elegant and oddly out-of-date in her gown.

"I'm afraid," I said, "that you are the most puzzling creature I have ever met."

She laughed. I had once known a soprano, one of my first loves, with such a laugh, only perhaps not as musical. "You are happy, aren't you?"

I glanced around, hoping to be rescued by some idle activity, sweeping ash from the hearth or arranging a book on a shelf.

She said, "Of course you're unsure of yourself."

There was something else going on here, something I could not guess. Perhaps she intended us to be lovers. I found it hard to breathe. "I wish that I could say I understand what you are talking about."

"It's not difficult to comprehend."

Deepest puzzlement kept me from speaking for an instant. "I really must have had too much champagne."

"You have to decide what you are going to do next."

I tried to caution myself against talking to her. "Regarding what?"

"You can't leave things as they are."

Ask her to leave. Now. "I'll begin getting real commissions," I said. "I'll have a career, not just a string of minor contracts. Things will be fine."

"You'll need help."

Who *was* she?

But I responded to her statement with a gesture. Maybe I would need help, and maybe not.

"Tell me what you want," she said.

The thing to do, I warned myself, is to stop talking to her. Now. I stepped away, and glanced around. "I have what I want. Really."

"I trust you, Stratton."

For some reason this remark took my breath away, perhaps because she had used my name.

Of course she knows your name, I told myself. But you certainly do not know hers.

She continued, "Let all the harm that has fallen you cease, from this point on."

"Yes, that would be a pleasant thought, wouldn't it?" I did not want to hear any more.

And yet I could not break away from her eyes, the sound of her voice. I did, indeed, want to drink in more of her words. She touched me once again lightly on the arm. I shrank back, and she withdrew her hand, saying, "You've always wanted our help."

"I'm afraid you're confusing me."

"I think not."

"I don't understand you."

"But you do."

My lips were stiff.

"You are right," she said, "to be afraid."

I was past thinking that my alluring visitor was mad. I could not make any sense of her at all. I tried to clear my throat, to speak, to behave as though reality made sense to me.

"You knew," she said, "exactly what you wanted, and now you have it. You asked for our help, and we helped you."

My mouth was dry. "What are you doing here?" This was the tone I used with nuisance-suit lawyers, with photographers outside nightclubs at two in the morning.

"We know you so well."

Don't waste your time talking to this creature, I told myself. Make a telephone call and get her out of here. I bowed, as I would to any aristocratic madwoman at a time like this, preparing to take my leave.

"It's too late for that, Stratton."

"Too late to ask for help?" I couldn't laugh. I felt queasy. "Thank you for coming tonight," I said. "It was wonderful to see you."

That was truthful enough. I knew her from somewhere, some hidden part of my life. She was familiar, a sibling I had never had. She smiled. "Your enemies are ours."

"I don't," I said, as smoothly as I could, "have any enemies."

She laughed softly, and slipped toward me. She lifted her lips to my ear. Her breath was warm. "Tell us what to do."

I could not keep myself from moving away from her.

"You know how," she smiled.

I brushed against a side table. A vase fell and burst on the floor. The sound made me bite my lips. When I turned back to look at her, I blinked and took a few steps forward.

She was gone.

It was impossible. No one could leave so quickly.

I hurried into the hall and tried the front door, which was latched and solidly locked. I searched from room to room, until I began to be convinced that I had never received a visit at all that night.

Surely that was the explanation. I had been experiencing a vivid fantasy, a waking dream.

But this was a disturbing thought. I stayed by the fire, letting the warmth knead me into a more settled frame of mind. I gradually convinced myself that I had endured a brief interview with a very unusual visitor, and that my shock at the shattering of the vase had rendered me unable to hear her leave.

But I did not want to go upstairs, into the even deeper solitude of the dark.

18

I was afraid to sleep that night.

I was afraid of what I might dream. When I did sleep, a little after dawn, I was awakened by the ringing of the telephone. There were many telephone calls, one after another. The answering machine kicked in each time, but I was aware of voices on the speaker, some of the voices familiar, some unknown to me, offering congratulations, offering commissions, urging me to call. The distant-sounding voices were a reminder of the city, the real lives, around me.

As a result of these calls, the following day was a pleasant one. I was on the phone all day, when I was not meeting with someone from the mayor's office at one of the sunny, flowery restaurants off Civic Center. They wanted to begin work on rebuilding the park immediately, and I had a delightful meeting with a firm of landscape architects in the Bank of America building on California Street.

I forced myself not to think about my visitor of the night before. I warned myself several times: Put her out of your mind.

Often throughout the day a delicious word formed itself on my lips: *success.*

This was it. This was what I had wanted. Some of the calls I did not respond to, from film producers and the representatives of real-estate developers. Some of these deals would have excited me a few days before. Now I was not interested in drawing up my ideas for a carp garden in Honolulu, or a saguaro fantasy for a retired movie director near Tucson. One or two of the film projects looked exciting, including the sets for a movie about the building of the Eiffel Tower, with a "version of the Tuileries as that area must have appeared back then."

I tried to reach Nona by phone all day, but she was in a meeting or out to lunch, according to an assortment of receptionists. All morning, and all afternoon, I persisted.

Nona eluded me.

Only in the evening, after supping briefly on a veal with mustard sauce, one of Collie's best dishes, did I have time to sit for a moment in the studio near my bedroom, and try to gather together my sense of what was happening.

My thoughts were interrupted. I was aware of a familiar laugh downstairs, and aware that Collie was happy to see someone. I was pleased to recognize my brother's voice, but only when I hurried down the stairs did I fully realize what Collie was saying.

"It's terrible, the things we have to put up with today," said Collie. "To see such good people suffering. It's a terrible thing."

"Your house looks like a storehouse for phantom furniture," said Rick.

The sight of Rick silenced me for a moment. Then I managed to sound cheerful. "Things are going to get better. Commissions are starting to come in again. This will all get fixed."

There was something wrong. Both of us pretended that all was well, and our conversation remained superficially cheerful. "Patient—you're a patient guy," Rick was saying. "But look at that armoire, shrouded like that. And look over here. You expect to see a mummy sitting under a chair like this." He lifted a plastic drape and it settled, stiffly, over the structure it protected, an Empire vintage sedan chair. The slightest spill of plaster dust sifted to the floor.

Rick thanked Collie and said he did not want coffee. He motioned me up the stairs, and when we both sat in my studio I could see clearly what was wrong, and why Collie had been upset. I had been trying to deny it to myself, saying that surely he didn't look as bad as I thought.

One of his eyes was swollen, the flesh around it blue. His lip had been cut. He withdrew a handkerchief from his pocket. The white cloth was starred with blood. He dabbed at his nose.

"You know what I think, Strater? I think you have about as much money as I have."

"There's something you wanted to tell me," I prompted him. I poured brandy from the decanter in the corner.

He did not respond at once. "Trouble," he said. He took an inelegantly large swallow of cognac and had to blink his eyes.

"It stings your lip," I suggested.

He nodded, and yet he took another swallow.

I had endured my concern over my brother by ignoring it, suppressing it, pretending to look the other way. The truth was that I had been, at times, worried about him, finding in Rick the capacity for recklessness that I recognized in myself.

"I might as well hear it now," I said.

"I had a little difficulty this evening. Nothing overwhelming. Just a little unpleasantness."

I waited, saying, with my eyes: Tell me.

"First of all, I owe people money," he said.

"Gambling," I said.

He made his finger-pistol gesture. "But the problem is: I've always owed people money. People let it slide. They know they'll eventually get their cash."

"Something has changed."

Rick studied me for a moment. "Suddenly they want it all back now."

"How inconvenient," I said dryly. Then, at once, "I'll help you if I can, Rick. How much do you need?"

"I can come up with a few dollars. I'll sell that Miró. I won't like parting with it. But I'll buy something to replace it some day. And that odd Cornell, that box that looks like the view out a hotel. That's worth a lot, and that's one piece I never really liked. So it's not the money."

I spoke for him. "It's the sudden pressure."

"The suddenly very vigorous pressure. That's what has my attention." He dabbed at his nose. "Do you think about money as much as I do, Strater?"

"Probably."

A cruel and unfeeling observer would have said that my father was profligate. It was after my father's death eight years before that my mother began to make grievous mistakes. She had been a woman with a steady gaze and long silences, cool where my father had been jovial, calm where my father had been energetic. Awed by her fine profile, and her way of offering a cheek for me to kiss on arriving and departing, I had loved her without, I was to ultimately understand, really knowing her.

My father's death destroyed her. Beneath her peaceful smile, which we assumed was a calm sustained by religious or at least philosophical strength, was a deep passion for self-destruction. Within less than a year she had donated extravagantly not only to my father's favorite charities, but to charities no one had ever heard of before, foundations that sprang up, it seemed, with little purpose but to batten off Fields funds.

It took an effort, even with dwindling resources, to immolate the estate, but by the time I responded, in the midst of my own travels, to a call from the family attorney to the effect that "Mrs. Fields has been secretly and cunningly committing financial suicide," it was too late. By the time I took a moment from my own career to survey my mother's circumstances, the family estate was abysmal, and only the fact that Rick and I had inherited some money directly from my father had protected us from losing everything. My brother had, characteristically, spent his money quickly, and his wives had relieved him of what reserves he seemed too busy to consume himself. Stories regarding my brother involved baccarat and thoroughbreds. There were hints of bribes in order to avoid jail after sportscar races or New Year's celebrations gone awry.

The two of us enjoyed the silence, and then Rick asked the question he had been withholding. "Is there any reason that someone would want to punish you, Strater? Get back at you somehow, I mean?"

"You know who it is."

His tone was kind, philosophical. "What are we going to do about it?"

"I won't let them hurt you, Rick."

He shook his head with a thoughtful smile. Rick was always an active man, all color and energy, a man women liked and men mistrusted. He had confidence, but now something had snapped in his spirit. "We can't fight these people. Well, we can literally fight them, if and when it comes to that. I did fairly well tonight. But tonight was just a friendly tap on the shoulder. We can't really fight back. Not in any way that matters."

"I'll talk to DeVere."

"Good idea. What will you say?"

I felt punished, for a moment, by his sarcasm. "I'll think of something."

"You shouldn't have made him mad, Strater. He'll stay mad. He doesn't have our forgiving nature." This was said with more than a dash of irony. Rick had a way of thinking as I thought, physically resembling me but at the same time unlike me, the same coloring but a slightly different mold.

"He won't hurt you again."

"I know things about the world that you don't." My brother stood and began to pace. "The world is a contest. A long war. You link up with powers, the law, government, organized crime, you name it. But we all need some sort of power behind us. By ourselves, alone—we're nothing."

I listened, thoughts and feelings churning.

"So the point I'm trying to make, Strater, is—there's not a thing you can do."

I did not answer.

"What weapons do we have? You know how long it takes for lawyers to do anything, and we can't afford much in the way of representation anyway. The police? They do what the DeVere people want. Sure, they'll be sympathetic. But months will go by, years will go by. And the people he knows. They have long memories."

"It's going to be all right," I said.

I was a different man now. No more harm would be done to us. I would not let my brother suffer. I would not let myself suffer further indignity. It was all changed now, transformed. I could not fully comprehend how I had achieved this new confidence, but it was real. It would not fade.

I laughed.

Rick was startled, although, even in his anguish, a little pleased to see me so spirited. "This is funny?"

"There is nothing to worry about," I said. "Everything is different now."

"There are people who don't care about human beings, Strater. They aren't like us."

"Don't worry about them."

"We were raised innocent, like it or not. The world is ruled by violence, and we've always tried to finesse it, be polite, get by on charm."

"They won't bother us."

Now Rick laughed, incredulous, hopeful. He could see that I meant it, and he was almost willing to believe that I could do something. "You always take this view of things. You always believe things will be all right."

"It's all over. All the gray, dead times are done." I stood and took him in my arms, and I felt him stir with surprise, because we had never been an affectionate family. And then, slowly, but with feeling, he returned my embrace.

Rick had been my father's favorite. This had never been talked about, but if my father wanted to read Plato to someone, or if he wanted someone to massage his shoulders, he called Rick in from play to be near him. "The allure of the youngest son," my mother had called it, and I had wondered if she shared my father's affection for their younger, more lively offspring.

How could I be sure, I wondered, that my new confidence was not misplaced? My mood might be the afterglow of the award, combined with the memory of a woman who might have been only a reverie, a hallucination.

My brother gambles, I thought.

So do I.

But as soon as he left me I tried to call Nona. She did not have her answering machine connected.

In my disordered mood I watched television briefly, pacing the channels through canned laughter and ads before letting the screen go blank. I paced, tried to reach Nona again, looked through magazines. A recent *Wall Street Journal* had an article that caught my eye. The article ran beneath a pen-and-ink sketch of DeVere, one of those finely detailed portraits about the size of a thumbprint.

The article described DeVere's empire as "losing its marketing stamina." The newspaper detailed a series of disappointing products, sluggish sales, and a failure to "regroup before economic realities." I hurled the pages away, the large sheafs of newsprint wafting to the floor.

This article was absurd. Everyone knew the extent of DeVere's power. Men like DeVere and Renman could do anything they wanted.

I stepped outside and across the lawn in the darkness. The conversation with my brother had troubled me deeply. I needed time to think, because on this day everything had been happening so quickly that I could not focus, I could not begin to sort my emotions.

They would not hurt Rick. I would not let them. And yet, as I surveyed the things that I could do I felt a growing feeling of impotence replacing my earlier confidence.

I unlocked the hothouse. I fumbled for the light. I found the switch, and stooped to unravel the hose, its bright brass nozzle draped across a steppingstone.

I straightened.

Disbelief kept me from moving. This was impossible. It couldn't be true. I had to put my hand out to the potting bench. I could not take a breath. I closed my eyes. I opened them again.

The smell of the place had changed, too, from something fertile to a sour, dead place. The hothouse had been lush and green, the flowers richly colored, the leaves gleaming.

Now each leaf was bleached and limp. The heliconia dangled, pale and withered. My fingers went out to yellow, wrinkled leaves. Stems were slack. Blossoms were brown.

The entire hothouse, every plant, was dead.

I covered my eyes with my hands. I had seen this before, in my botanical studies in Hawaii. The highway department kept certain roads clear by using chemicals strong enough to do this. Someone expert had used a powerful herbicide.

I had to admire his thoroughness.

*   *   *

The feather drifted to the floor, spun, lifted, and wafted upward, in a new direction, toward my outstretched hand. The plume was all colors at once, like the splendor of a hummingbird, white, yes, but then vermilion, then Lincoln green. Radiant alternate colors raced across its filaments as it swung, fluttered, and fell at last upon my fingertips.

Rick, and then my plants. What would be next? When would they get around to Nona? When would someone decide to pay a visit to my mother?

DeVere, I thought.

Stop DeVere.

19

I t did not take long.

Perhaps it should have surprised me, but it didn't. A call came just before midnight.

It was Childress. He wanted to see me, at the scene of a crime. That was the word he used: *crime.* And the word reverberated in my mind, a painful syllable, a word like *cry.*

Whatever you do, I told myself, don't think. Don't think about your feelings, don't think about anything.

I did not trust myself to drive.

The evening was cold, but it was a cold that was beginning to fade. The streets were glazed with a drizzle that did not fall from the sky so much as drift out of nowhere, sideways, idle and weightless. The tires of the cab hissed, and the Financial District was both ablaze with the lights of offices and deserted.

I sat in the backseat not sure what to think, afraid to think.

It looked like a movie being filmed, bright lights and a tangle of people. In a giddy, uneasy way, I convinced himself that perhaps it wasn't true. It was all a mistake. Surely nothing bad had happened here. They *were* making a movie, nothing more.

I slammed the cab door, thrust some currency into the cab-driver's hand, and then hunched in a gust of wind. I made my way toward the activity, the bright illumination, the flash of emergency lights.

A fire truck was rumbling slowly into position. The streets were quiet otherwise. The cloudy sky was blocked here by the buildings that made it even colder, and the street vents exhaled vapor that streamed into the air and vanished.

I could still feel the struggle to deny wrenching at me. *Not true —it can't be.*

Just keep repeating that charm, I told myself. Just keep saying that. Maybe reality will change. Maybe you'll be able to lie to yourself so well you'll begin to believe it. Didn't you always believe in magic?

The window glass glittered on the sidewalks, and crunched under the feet of men in long, yellow plastic raincoats.

I shouldered my way into the light and then stopped. My breath caught. The plastic sheets did not begin to be sufficient. My shoes made sucking sounds on the pavement. Red was sticky underfoot.

One or two cops greeted me, solemn, courteous, "Hello, Mr. Fields." "You don't want to see this, Mr. Fields."

I could not move.

"We're sure who it is, in case you're wondering," said Childress. Not: Good evening. Not: Why don't you step away from here and spare yourself.

The best politician on the police force, Childress, a man destined to do well in interviews, was panting like a man out of breath.

"I'm sure you're right," I said, sounding, I hoped, both ignorant and innocent.

My tone must have irritated Childress. To shock me, to make me eat the truth, Childress whisked the plastic sheet aside.

The falling body had struck a parking meter. The steel fist had punched through the skull, and yet the impact was so great that the violation tag stuck out of the mass on the sidewalk.

Childress made a remark to some of the policemen nearby and

gave a command. He was letting me take a good, scalding look. Then he turned to me.

Surely I was mistaken. Surely—it was an ugly hope—this was a stranger.

"It's DeVere," said Childress. The deferential detective, kind and yet burdened with the task of filling out forms, was gone. This was the real Childress, a man who did not like his work. He wanted television, press conferences, headlines. He did not want this.

I asked, "What happened?" It was a way of trying to deflect, unsuccessfully, what I was seeing. Ask questions. Talk. Don't just stand here looking. Such a sight should blind, but it didn't.

"What happened," echoed Childress.

"Was he pushed?" I said, my voice thin but steady. There is, in a man like Childress, despite his polish and earnestness, a dislike for the rich. It is the dislike some men have for very beautiful women, a resentment: Some people have everything.

"Don't even suggest murder," he said. "We won't even consider such a thing."

I would not please Childress by shuddering, looking away. There was a long pause while the death-heavy lights did their job, illuminating everything. And then I must have passed the test. The plastic sheet was settled back over the mess.

"He jumped," said Childress after a long time, during which he looked at me with something like apology.

I could think only of the fall, the arms and legs swimming, the street swelling to fill his eyes.

I rasped, "How can you be certain?"

"We're sure." Childress cleared his throat. "People don't push each other out of men's-room windows. He had to climb on top of a toilet."

"Someone was chasing him, perhaps."

"Who?"

I was afraid to guess. "This is the suicide capital of North America," I said, as though that ugly label would make either one of us feel better. "You want to ask me some questions."

"Again. More questions."

"Why did you call me? Why did you ask me to come?"

"I wanted to see if you'd show up."

"You don't think this was a suicide, do you?"

He led me up the sidewalk several steps, out of the hearing of the other men. He gazed at the sidewalk. "The security in this building isn't very good. They're putting on a new roof. There are scaffolds, doors left unconnected to the alarm."

I said nothing.

He eyed me, as though to verify that I was not an illusion. "Why would DeVere want to take his own life?"

"I have no idea." I was stunned at what I had seen. And yet the world continued: buildings, cold darkness.

"Why was DeVere investigating Blake's death?"

"Was he?"

Childress waited. He was unwilling to irritate me, but seemed dogged, even proud of having someone like me to question. At the same time he knew it was a simple case. A man had jumped. "He did not believe Blake simply shot himself."

"They were associates." There was a catch in my voice, and I recalled that DeVere, for all of his shortcomings, had felt real respect for Blake.

Childress's eyes glittered in the emergency lights. He turned so his face was half-hidden, and he stood so he could see my face clearly. "He was putting pressure on me to investigate you. He hired private detectives to follow you around. Rumor was that he was obsessed with you."

There was the sound of a car door at the end of the street, a thud, and a distant patter of voices.

"The media," said Childress, as though uttering an obscene phrase.

I understood the core of Childress's anger. He did not like corpses, and he did not like being saddled with another possible homicide. It was natural to take out his disgust on me, a knowledgeable man who knew so little about mortality. I needed to lean against a wall to strengthen myself. He put his best expression on, a manly, set-jawed look that hid all feeling.

I said exactly the right thing. "You're a good cop, Childress."

He looked at me and lifted an eyebrow. Maybe, he meant to say, and maybe not. He had a broad, pale face, the sort poor at disguising feeling. "It doesn't have to make sense. It doesn't have to be logical."

"What are you trying to tell me?"

"The DeVere people are going to figure you did this."

"What do you think?"

"What I think doesn't matter."

He turned back to his work, rich in experience I would never understand, a man only a little older than myself.

It was easy to hate the casual efficiency of the men and women there. As I watched them work I tried to reassure myself. This might have nothing to do with me. DeVere might have lost his grasp on hope, on life.

I tried to lie to myself.

When the ambulance was gone the fire department hosed down the street, and the gutter ran with black. I followed the stream along toward the drain, where the flow reflected the building lights. The current ran red and then faintly pink and at last clear and empty, finished.

I couldn't lie to myself any longer.

I was dirty inside. I had that feeling that is out of fashion, that feeling that is so rarely discussed in polite conversation. I felt sinful.

I trod sand until I was far out of sight of the Great Highway, out of the flick and lick of headlights. The surf would be too cold tonight. I was making a mistake this time. This was, though, what I had to do. I loosened my tie, worked at the knot, let it drop.

Subliminally, or perhaps by an act of memory tinged with imagination, I registered the warning on the weathered, dark signs: Dangerous.

My clothes left me. The sand was not subtle, fine stuff. It was marred with gravel, and the crisp, toastlike remains I recognized, in the dark, as chunks of charcoal.

There was a storm coming. The air smelled not only of sea, but of land, of a land far away, an ocean away. Experienced as I was, I crouched, naked, panting. The wind was rising, and the waves were huge. Don't go in, I told myself. Not tonight.

I was polluted. I had done something wrong.

A sin.

I stood naked, clear of the fling of the foam. Mountains lifted, sloughed half their bulk, and then ascended again. Cliffs marched forward and collapsed. A range of breakers combed in from the side, and the clap the mountains made colliding was a steel smack, a freight-car coupling, a canyon wall going down.

I stepped carefully, as if upon ice. The water was not warm. It stunned. It was nearly ice, and muscular. I let myself cringe, dance backward, and then I strode forward, and plunged.

I dived under a wave, and surfaced, shaking water from my hair. My body contracted, scrotum, lips, the very soles of my feet tightening. I was swimming, hard, and had been swimming for quite some time, I realized, chill-dazzled, unable to sense the passage of time.

The air I breathed tasted of iodine. I climbed a cliff-face of water. The surf-sheer grew as I worked upward, growing taller. Then it leaned backward, hesitated, and straightened again. It was an unfeeling thing, a happenstance of bulk and power, mass given force. It fell forward, taking me with it.

I rolled, kicked, found the roiling afterwave. The cold hurt. It stopped aching. It was pain. How much of this could I withstand? It was the cold. It would take my life.

Perhaps this was what I wanted. Perhaps this was what I deserved.

I turned back and began to seek the shore. I had hoped that the surf would awaken me, sweep the sight of DeVere's blood from my mind.

But it hadn't worked. Instead, sparring with the waves, fighting to keep breathing, I knew something. I knew something that did not make sense, any more than the slamming of the breakers around me represented logic: I had caused DeVere's death.

It was not too late. I could return to the simple shore of everyday life and escape whatever the woman represented. But as I swam, with strong, steady strokes toward the pinpoints of light, safety, home, I could feel the power leave my limbs. The cold was doing its work.

That's all right, I told myself, that boyish confidence returning to me as it often did here in the surf. Don't worry. The waves will wash you back onshore. It was the irony of such waves—they weighed like boulders but could not crush.

There was something wrong. I was swimming hard, but I was going nowhere. I had always been curious what it would be like, and now I would find out.

This was a riptide.

20

A riptide slices outward, away from the beach.
   It cuts through the line of waves, a horizontal tornado of water that drags a swimmer far out, far away from land. Fighting against it is generally useless. The only chance is to swim across the riptide, parallel to the shore, because it is like a violent stream—deadly, but not wide.

A riptide is ugly, even at night, the boom and roll of surf flattened, choppy and thick. A riptide even smells different, less like an ocean and more like salt waste. And they are quieter than the ocean, more silent, and thick with sand clawed from the bottom.

Nona had said I was flirting with suicide. What would I choose to do, now that dying would be so easy, if not without a certain anguish toward the end?

I forced life into my arms. I knew the waves. This sport was one I understood and I made way across the riptide, only to realize that this current was wider and stronger than I had expected. I was much more weary, and stiff from the cold, than I had anticipated.

What are you? I asked myself. Aren't you a man who wishes other people dead? Aren't you a man who can make things happen with a thought?

That doesn't happen, I reminded myself. Wishes have no power. The body has power, and the ocean does. But thoughts are next to nothing. I swam hard, exhausted. The opposite bank of the riptide shrank away from me, as though my outstretched hand was surrounded with a force field.

With a last burst of strength I struggled out of the riptide. I reached the relatively powerless tossing of the surf, and treaded water there, my head back, panting, joyful.

I was elated. So that was a riptide, I thought. Not much of a challenge, really. You might even consider them overrated.

A nasty little thought flickered: far from shore. Too far.

Could I be this far from land? Was that vague streak to the east the beach? There wasn't any shore. There was no sense of direction. A wave broke over me.

Too tired. When I spluttered to the surface to see a massive comber, I was eager to take advantage of it. I pumped my limbs to reach the same speed as the wave, and when it broke I let the flow crash around me, over me, thundering over my head, pressing my eardrums, momentarily deafening me.

The water tossed, churned, seethed. I did not have long before hypothermia would steal me away, make me leaden, light-headed. But I was still confident. After all, the ocean is only so much water.

The sea around me changed, thickened.

The surf was quiet. I was being tugged even farther from shore. I understood what was happening but registered it as a bad joke.

This was a riptide.

The sea made a humming, moaning sound as the water changed from a fluid that was all confusion to a cylinder, a gleaming black wall. I gulped air that tasted like powdered steel so I would have enough oxygen in my lungs.

I was treading water with legs that were nearly impossible to shift. My calf muscles knotted, twin cramps that would have been agonizing if my limbs were not numb.

The tide dragged me. The wind spun my hair, whipped my eyes now with spray. There was a cry, a long, human wail that I recognized only after several seconds was my own voice. The cry depleted my lungs, emptied them, spent all my air on a futile song. It was not a cry of fear so much as a cry of awe, a cry to accompany the thunder around me, as the bellow of a crowd might cause one's own voice to rise.

I recalled a voice: *What do you want?*

Maybe you did want to die, all along.

It pulled me under. I was crumpled, flattened, pressed to the sand. This was not the wave-licked sand of the shore, either, but a hard, gnarled sand, stretched thinly over stone. This is what I felt. I could see nothing through my salt-stung eyes. The water was heavy. It was all darkness. All solid, like a man poured into the core of something, to harden, as though my body were gold and I had been allowed to flow deep within a crack in earth.

Breathe soon.

I will have to breathe soon.

My thoughts were distorted. I was warm. Yes, this is how it happens, said a voice in me, a travel narrator. First the swimmer is overconfident. Then he forgets. He can't swim. He can't breathe.

Then all thoughts slipped away, like the long, satin trains of a wedding, the half-thought: It's over.

Save me.

If I had spoken the words, if I had been able to articulate my lips, the sound would have been quiet, but intense, unmistakable. It was a prayer.

Make me strong.

Aren't prayers futile? Aren't human wishes mere garlands, things turning into air? But this nothingness was no longer the flat slab of weight that had existed just an instant before. Something had lifted, the density of the water, or of my own body, was transformed.

Something had my arm. My arm was lifted upward, and my body began to rise upward, too, trailing after my arm in a way that struck me as barely comprehensible, as though my arm had become an eel, a vibrant, living creature of its own. And my other arm. And my legs, too, thrashing, driving me.

Part Three

21

Easy, I told myself wryly: a night's swim.

A wave smashed over me, around me, carrying me to a place where my feet scrabbled along a sandy bottom. The surf erupted around me, but it was a beach, now, with the breakers dying on the sand.

Nothing to be afraid of.

I spat brine. So soon back, I marveled. So soon saved.

So this was earth. I had that profound sense of gratitude and dislocation that arises after danger. The waves hissed, bubbling, simmering to where I stood, so I strode higher, leaving suction scars on the wet sand, until I reached the flour-dry sand of the beach the waves rarely touched, sand graveled and littered with stones, and trash that rustled in the light wind.

Sometimes we take refuge in the certainty that life continues, the stars rolling gradually along their slope. But at times it seems inexorable, inhuman, the dull squat of objects upon the earth. There it was, the pile of clothing, where it would have been, loyal to nothing, if I had drowned.

The wind was strong. I hated the insensate nature of my

clothes as I approached them. How dull and common everything was. I despised the warning signs, the sight of the tiny sparks of headlights on the road. Surely I would be unable to dress.

That is, however, exactly what I did. I planned my way into my clothes, and the plan worked. My skin was salt-sticky, but the sleeves accepted my stiff arms, the pants my clumsy legs, and I felt like a man purloining clothing that the very act of theft caused to become not only his own, but his own fit. My tailor, a patient man with a by-appointment-only shop off Union Square, would have been pleased.

It was difficult to thrust my sandy feet into the socks, but I welcomed the sensation. I usually left the surf glad to be alive, but now I felt life-stunned, dazed.

What had happened? I had found the strength to swim back to the shore. That was all. There was nothing remarkable about that.

I drove carefully. The passing streetlights, the CLOSED signs in the liquor-store windows, all were of the ordinary, the steady, reliable world.

Nona's apartment was dark, her bedroom window a rectangle, and a gray, vague curtain. This was not unusual. She was working late, or gone: Dallas, Vancouver, Mexico City.

I locked the garage door. I tugged at the heavy padlock, testing it. Cold, and gritty with sand, I found my way into the garden in the darkness, and gazed up into the giant gingko tree. I could not understand the full green it now displayed, the vast full life that lifted and swayed in the wind.

Why was I reluctant to slip the key of my own house into its lock? It was raining now, and warm. My hand was shivering. The key missed, scratched, and finally found its slot.

I have to talk to someone about this, I thought. I have to talk to someone very badly. I'll talk to Nona—or have her suggest one of her colleagues.

But where would I begin? Surely one of my old teachers would help me, one of the defrocked priests, the sort of men who declined evil into its categories as one might study Latin verbs.

I wandered the house, making an inventory of the familiar half-finished rooms with plastic draping the furniture. I ascended the stairs and poured myself cognac. I was pleased to get out of my limp, sandy clothes. I was sticky, and I felt the beginning of a soreness in my calves. Collie would see the sand all over the bathroom tomorrow and would, as always, not comment on what she considered yet another Fields eccentricity.

I took a hot bath, the water so hot it hurt. But I stayed in the steaming tub, adding some of the bubble bath I always bought when I was in Paris, at the shop in Rue Mouffetard. I let the water absorb the arctic from my muscles.

Don't think, I told myself. Don't think about DeVere, or what was left of him. Don't think about the feather.

When I was out of the tub, monk-robed in terrycloth, my feet in slippers, I began to feel the first stirrings of appetite. A swim does that to me, and cold does it, too, and I had certainly, I thought dryly, been experiencing a little cold and wet lately. I would pad down through the shrouded furniture and find something Collie had left in the kitchen, perhaps one of her country terrines, or some of her hand-crafted sourdough.

I tried calling Nona, but she did not answer. Rick's voice told me that I had reached his telephone number. I left a message: "I just wanted to make sure you were okay." And as I spoke I became aware of the change in the house, the subtle alteration in the silence.

I listened. There could be no question. I put down the receiver carefully. I stood, my breath hushed.

I crept down the stairs. I leaned against the wall, just outside the study.

There was a fire in the fireplace.

So what? It's just a fire. Some smoldering kindling had ignited. This was not, however, a small, minor fire among forgotten splinters. This was a blazing fire, a classic sort of crackle-and-glow.

I stepped into the room.

I hated myself for being disappointed. There was no waiting figure in white. Was I actually looking forward to seeing her? What a fool I was! It was like looking forward to an episode of psychosis.

Many people would trade places with you, I chided myself. This was an opportunity to see for myself what was only the subject of superstition, of legend. But as soon as this weak enthusiasm erected itself, I turned away from it. It might be madness— it might be the worst evil. Either way, I would leave it and return to my normal life. I did not comprehend, for the moment, how facile my thinking was. Like many optimists, I am primarily capable of keeping myself from grief, and from horror.

On my way through the shrouded sitting room I stopped. The half-plastered walls, the peaks of the plastic canopies over the furniture looked both eerie and homey. I made my way to the wall, but the light would not switch on, and I had not expected it to.

But my eyes were accustomed to the firelight by now, making it quite easy to see. All was well, I reassured myself. There was nothing amiss. But why did I stand there, unmoving? My hand was on the useless, obsolete light switch, the pushbutton type, the type attached to cloth wiring. I could not move from where I stood.

I could not take a single step, because there was something wrong. It was impossible to see what it was. But it was real. There was something that was not right.

Then I heard it.

The slightest rustling, the briefest whisper of a plastic drop cloth. Not a cloth being lifted, and not a cloth riffling in a wind. There was only a briefest noise, as of someone sitting quietly, turning his head, his head and body covered by a dust cloth.

And that is exactly what it was.

There was someone sitting in the radiance from the fire, light both poor and brilliant enough to make me wish I could mistake what I saw, the profile, the posture. There was a man sitting under that translucent canopy, and I knew who it was.

I knew, and I couldn't breathe, shrinking to the wall, groping for something to keep me upright. I could not bear to stand just as I was, unable to turn my head.

And I didn't want to look away. I didn't want to do anything but stand as I was, with time finished, the world stopped completely.

I knew now why Mary falls to her knees in so many of the paintings of the Annunciation. If a messenger from Heaven arrives, even with good news, we cannot be human beings and fail to experience the sensation: May this not be true.

Even when the beloved voice spoke I sensed that this was not a voice from Heaven. As charged as I was with love I wished I could have fallen utterly deaf before I heard those words.

"It's too late, Stratton."

I stretched forth a hand, but could not take a step, wanting to speak, my tongue powerless.

"It's too late," he said again. "You can't go back."

It was my father's voice.

22

The plastic canopy over the shadow figure shifted, began to slip away, and then fell clear with a slithering whisper as the figure lifted its arms.

My father, dead for eight years, sat stretching, as he always had when forced to wait, a way of releasing his cheerful impatience. He flexed, his fingers interlocked, his arms extended: handsome, graying. He wore one of his hunting shirts, a wool check that looked manly and outdoorsy, hand-tailored, and, I knew, as soft and easy to the touch as old linen. He stood and looked at me, as though wondering at my reason for holding back.

I had backed all the way into a corner. I wedged myself among wall studs and strips of lath, the vise of the corner gripping my skull as though it would have me look hard at this human figure, this wraith that looked as solid and breathing as any man I had ever seen.

He gave that half-smile, that eye-crinkling grin that I had known for so many years. He looked a little embarrassed at his sudden appearance; he had always preferred the low key to the dramatic. "I'm proud of you, Stratton."

His words, so exactly what I needed, and wanted, to hear, suffocated me.

"You have," he said, "done well."

I commanded myself: Don't listen.

"I knew you would. All those years of drawing. I remember

watching you draw the Ferry Building one afternoon, do you remember?"

Madness. Can't be happening.

"I'd had lunch at Tadich's, I think it was, and was taking a stroll. And I came upon you, sitting there on the sidewalk, drawing the hands on the Ferry Building clock. I think that's the first time I really knew what sort of person you were."

I commanded myself: Whatever you do—don't talk.

My father watched the fire, shadows shifting on his face. "What are you going to do now?"

I would not speak.

"You can't turn back, now, Stratton, because They've already done too much for you." The voice was reasonable, earnest.

Just stand here against the wall and don't make a sound.

"Besides, now you're in real trouble. The DeVere people are busy right now, this minute. They'll never forgive you."

He regarded me, waiting for me to respond.

"You have a responsibility to your mother. To Nona, and her children. To your brother. To yourself. You have a great deal to protect."

My own voice was a hiss. "What are you?"

He did not answer my question. "You have to accept what has happened to you, and take it seriously." It was my father's old tone, a lecture both formal and kind, like a vicar on a Sunday afternoon, still warmed by his own morning sermon. He stepped toward me, and when he stood just before me he stretched out his arms. "We're allowed to have a bear hug."

It's the way he always put it: a bear hug. The phrase allowed us to pretend we engaged in a brief tussle rather than a show of love.

I did not move.

He chuckled. He put forth his hand, and a palsy overtook me. And yet I could not flinch, wedged in as I was. My breath stopped. His fingers approached my face, and my eyes froze in my head.

He touched me. His fingers brushed the tears on my cheek. See, his eyes said. You can't pretend any longer. I am here.

"I missed you," I coughed, the words painful. "I missed you so much."

He held me, firm, warm, solidly corporeal: my father.

I withdrew from his arms, but kept him by the hand. I took a step so he would turn and the light could play across his features. Every detail was correct, including the tiny scar on the bridge of his nose, a childhood injury, the family nurse bumping him against the rail of a balcony. He was not a vague copy. He was himself. He looked as he did that day, relaxed, ready to spend a day on the bay, or hiking the East Bay hills, a man arrived at both health and wisdom.

"Mother," I said, steering toward profound understatement, "isn't doing so well."

"I know."

I had trouble speaking.

"You should go visit her more often, Stratton," he said. "I know it's difficult. I know the doctors don't think it's a good idea. But you don't know how confused she is most of the time."

My eyes were downcast. "I'll go see her." But then I rallied, aware again after a few moments what an enormity was taking place. My voice was a whisper. "But this can't be."

"They are so powerful, Stratton. So powerful that the ways of fire and skies are like toys to Them."

It was my father's diction, a man who would have loved to be a priest or a professor, a teacher or an actor, someone in command of the attentions and the affections of thousands. Instead, he had been a solitary public figure, and the only vocabulary his position offered was that of money. He had endowed scholarships and research, and he had saved his lectures for his family—for me. My mother had always been courteously detached from my father, despite her great love for him. She was more worshipful than attentive, and Rick had always played the role of the restless kid, the itchy youngster, even in early manhood.

"You left things in a mess," I said, steadying my voice. "Financially we were in bad shape. And you shouldn't have trusted Mother. Leaving so much in her hands didn't turn out to be the best alternative."

My voice lost strength. Here I was chiding a shade, an apparition I both longed to hold again, and did not believe was anything but an illusion.

"I know it, Stratton," he said with what sounded like his old, gruff-voiced regret. "I know I made mistakes. I didn't know I was going to vanish like that, walking down the stairs. I walked and walked, and then I realized I was not walking at all, anymore. My face went numb. *Bang*—like being hit with the Sunday paper. And then—" He looked at me steadily. "It makes a noise, dying like that. A noise in your skull, in your brain." He kept my gaze, telling me: I know, and you, my son, do not.

Then a smile crinkled his eyes. "Don't stand here like this. Come and sit down. And what on earth is happening here? I thought you were a designer. Plaster dust everywhere."

I stayed where I was.

"I'm not here for long. I'm here to prepare you. You should go upstairs and get dressed. Someone is coming for you."

I shook my head.

"You have no choice anymore, Stratton. The powers you have enjoined are at your beck, but not at your command."

This odd phrasing *could* have been my father's, but it sounded strangely unlike any statement I had ever heard him use. His diction had always been bookish, both straightforward and polished. "Rick is doing fine," I said, offering him news, buying time while I tried to believe that this creature was, in truth, my father.

"I remember how upset you were," he said. "When you thought you had hit him so hard sparring. You were under the impression that you had permanently damaged him." He sighed, half laugh, half sorrow. "You were the son I was fondest of, Stratton. You must have known that."

Emotion swept me, seared me. When I could speak, I said, "I was worried about Rick. I always worry about him." Again I was aware of water on my cheeks, and used the sleeve of my terrycloth robe to wipe my eyes.

"You've spent too much of your life worrying," he said. "You've been concerned with the good opinion of people who should not have mattered to you. It's time to give something to yourself, or, as Buddha would suggest, to accept that which is given to you."

"It's not easy being your son," I said. "You were so admired by everyone. Including me."

"I deserved the admiration. It's true—I did. But I neglected you. I overlooked the people around me, wanting more. More than a man should want."

I prepared my question guardedly, choosing the words. "What

are these powers being offered to me?" I lowered my voice. I did not want to ask the next question. "And who offers them?"

He put his hands in his pockets, in a way that meant: At least we are talking business. It was another gesture I recognized from former times. "Someone is coming to see you."

"I don't want to see anyone."

"It doesn't matter." His voice was light, manly, but his words were so at odds with his tone that I was not certain that I had heard them correctly.

I turned away, feeling a stubborn twist inside me.

He continued, "Accommodate Them—you have no choice."

"The soul," I said, my voice ragged. "So we have souls, after all."

"Who mentioned the soul? You're confused, Stratton. The soul has nothing to do with this." He thought for a moment. "But maybe that's the best way for you to understand this. You remember the story. The Faust myth. A man interested in magic—in the darker kind of magic—makes a pact with Satan. He does it for power, and for knowledge."

"I'm familiar with the tale," I responded, my voice hoarse.

"He has years of power, and even makes love to Helen of Troy." He smiled, as though seeing it before his eyes, the copulation between Faust and the immortal. "In Marlow's *Dr. Faustus,* when Faustus knows that he is lost, he stands looking upward on the last night of his life and he utters an apostrophe, to the sky, to the rolling of the planet that gave him life. It's a line fashioned from Ovid. *'O lente, lente, currite noctis equi.'*" He paused, as though uttering Latin took his breath away. " 'Run slowly, slowly, horses of the night.' But the night is never slow enough. It always ends. Once you have enjoyed congress with these powers, you will not escape."

"Faustus could have escaped."

He tilted his head. We had loved our philosophical jousts. "How?"

The argument was one I did not believe, but we were so far into the cellar of theology that my own opinions barely mattered. "By asking God's forgiveness." Perhaps I had expected the air around me to throb when I spoke of God, but there was no sound, no movement.

"It was too late."

The argument belonged in an all-night drinking session, matching whiskeys with one of my ex-Jesuit tutors. I felt my innards contract, as at the sight of my own name on a death warrant. "I don't like this."

"They come for you tonight. Don't make the mistake of hubris, on the one hand, believing you can outwit Them, or cowardice on the other, attempting to flee. You have lost all your freedoms. It's time to accept your prize."

"I have entered into no contract."

"You have, just as Rick has so many times in dealing with loan sharks, just as I did in agreeing to a price for a work of art at an auction by waggling my fingers."

"I've done nothing."

He lifted his hand. "You're about to say that you're innocent." It was my father's tone exactly, the way he didn't look at my eyes when he spoke but looked to one side, as though playing to an invisible audience.

This is all incredible—and yet, why not play along for awhile? Choose your questions carefully. "Why," I asked, "do they want me?"

"Who can say?"

He looked younger than I would have expected. My next words were a shock to me. They were heavy, ugly. "You're dead." I did not mean this to sound as wooden as it did. When my father laughed, I recognized beyond doubt that whether this was an illusion or not, this phantom captured exactly my father's gentle imperiousness, his humor, his impatience.

I saw, too, how much I had changed in the last eight years. Eight years ago I had been twenty-seven, and an immature man, in some ways, eager to win my father's approval, eager to establish my name in a profession. Now I was not so hungry for praise, from my father, or from anyone else.

I did not move. I did not believe it. It looked and sounded right, but it was not.

"You have to get dressed."

"Does it matter what I'm wearing?"

"You are about to engage in an important transaction. Your allies understand the importance of costume. You don't," he said, quietly exasperated, as so often, "have that much time, Stratton."

"I would have thought that the powers we enjoined were time-less."

He made a cheerful gesture, waving off my remark. "We aren't."

"Not even the dead?"

"One of us is still alive."

It was his sort of argument. I saw how equal we were in intelligence, in temperament. I suspended judgment. This was my father, and yet it could not be. I loved this man, this fleshly, apparently real human being, and yet I was not certain what this creature might really be. In radical, stoic confusion I ascended the steps to change my clothes, and reserved all critical judgment. I was experiencing something no man ever really experienced. And yet here I was. I could not understand it; I stopped trying.

I turned back, and there was his figure in the hallway, looking upward. He even cast a shadow, a long, distorted shape flowing behind him across the koa-wood floor.

"Wear a business suit," he prompted. "Nothing too formal."

"We're going to be doing business, are we?" I asked, intending irony.

"*You* are," he said.

"Will you," I asked, fighting to keep the tremor from my voice, "stay with me?"

"Not for much longer." He saw my pain. "I can't."

"I won't leave you."

"I promise you that I'll wait."

I was going to lose him, all over again. I could not take another step. I wanted to throw myself back down the stairway and cling to him. The fact of his physical presence, the fact of his fatherhood, struck me as thoroughly as the force of gravity, or the heat of a fire.

"I will wait right here. I promise. Please hurry, Stratton." It was the way he had urged me as a boy, as I dallied, toying with my socks, fighting with my brother over a favorite toy. The taste of my own childhood was in my mouth. This was not nostalgia. It was all back again, all here. My father had returned, and joy was beginning to flower in my heart. I saw that anything good was possible.

I hurried into the sort of suit that I would wear to a board meeting to stand before myopic capitalists with a pointer and blueprints. I was, without thinking, dressing as a young man would, to please his father.

As I dressed, hiking a lightly starched shirt over my shoulders, I stepped back, aware that I had nearly stepped on the plume. I had not left it there, on the carpet, and yet I did not doubt that the plume could shift and twitch, and ride currents of air like a living thing. I knelt, quickly, and when I settled the jacket over my back, and shot my cuffs, I slipped the plume into my breast pocket.

When I was dressed, still adjusting my tie, I was down the stairs quickly and into my father's presence full of questions. Questions about what to do with Mother, questions about Rick's character, questions about memories I knew he would share with me.

He was beaming, delighted, staying where I had left him. He made that slightly pouty, upside-down smile that meant: I'm giving you my most critical appraisal and you look great. I wanted to dance, to run around him in a circle like a pup.

There was a knock at the door.

Our eyes met.

"You will find that in this new life you have assumed," said my father, "time is always bleeding away."

"What will happen if we do nothing?" I said.

"Stratton," he said gently, "you have already joined with Them, long ago."

I must have looked incredulous.

"It's true—with your love for power, with your ambition, your fascination with your own future."

The knocking had stopped. But now it continued, each blow echoed by a shudder of my body. Each blow slammed the solid oak of the door, wrenching it in its frame.

We do not lose our minds as we might lose a credit card, or a car, or even an empire. We lose it, and gain something else.

This knocking would awaken every sleeper in the neighborhood. This thought was a link with a knowledge I had suppressed: All of this could not be happening. It was impossible. I was mad, inescapably ill.

And yet, I told myself, the pounding at the door shaking the

very air in my lungs—did it matter? Did it matter—if my madness made real things happen? Or if every good and bad thing
was a coincidence—did that mean that I had to flinch from the
pleasure, the joy?

I was like a man who had swallowed an elixir, a liquor that
destroys the perception and loses the memory. The toxin was a
part of me. I could not turn back.

"Hurry," said my father. "Open the door."

23

The knock resounded, an echoing imperative. Each blow
made me wince. It seemed unending, the knock persisting,
so heavy the floorboards quaked.

This was not an ordinary reverberation in the air. This was
another event that was both real and not real, within time and
beyond it.

When I opened the door I would be taking a further step in
agreeing to something I did not understand. I looked back at my
father and his expression was strained, his smile forced. A good
man, he had often said, stands up to what he fears. I saw now,
though, that much of my father's sure-handedness, and much of
his insouciance, had been an act. My love for a dangerous sport,
risking riptides, may have been the desire to prove myself equal
to a man who was by no means equal to himself.

He must have read my thoughts, or sensed them like high-amp
voltage through his own considerations. "You've always been
slow to make up your mind," he said.

I tried lying to myself. It was only a knock, and certainly, I
reasoned, it may be someone innocent, a neighbor in need of
help. The knock came again, and my instincts made me want to
cringe, hide. "I won't. If I don't answer it, nothing bad can hap-

pen." I felt reduced to childishness, and reduced to a boy's diction, and a boy's stubbornness.

He did not speak for a moment. "There's no sense putting it off forever."

I nearly asked him what he himself had done, what he had bartered and what he had gained, in dealing with such an army. "I won't talk to them."

He could not keep the slightly patronizing tone from his voice. "You're being foolish."

I began to argue, but he put his fingers to his lips. I turned back to the door, certain that my father's love for me was strong enough to keep me from harm. The pounding continued, the barrier shivering with each blow.

"I will never open the door," I said, in a whisper.

There was a breath behind me, at my nape, and I turned to see my father sweating, his hand taking my shoulder in a grip that was not strong so much as urgent, a bony pinch, the clench of a desperate man.

I saw that if I did not release the latch and let the barrier swing wide, he would suffer. He was suffering now, with a look in his eye like the pain I had seen in Blake's. He could not say it. He could not beg. He was proud. If much of his courage during life had been an act, it had been a good one, a noble act, even, a reliance on manners and good humor.

"We have to accommodate our visitors," he said, "since they are so insistent, and since we have no real choice."

"A contract coerced," I said, quoting one of my old teachers, "is no contract."

"Remember this," he said. "I love you."

The words took all the light, all the dark, all sensation from my body.

I turned. I strode across the hardwood floor to the door, and the walk stretched, each step falling shorter than the one before it. I would never reach the door. I would never stop my father's pain and cut short this pounding, each blow staggering the house, now, shuddering the walls. Nails squealed in the joists and the foundations groaned.

In the midst of my eagerness to spare my father, in the midst of my hatred for the fist hammering the door, I had begun to change. The doubt was beginning to return. I was aware that it was all for my benefit, this theater. I felt myself imprisoned in an opera, a stage so exaggerated none of it could be believed for a moment. Only my love for my father was real, and it was with that love that I approached the door.

The door handle was cold, beads of condensation greasing it, water drooling to the floor as my grip closed around the brass. The metal grew even colder. My thumb found the latch tongue, and depressed it. Too cold, I thought, feeling my flesh stick to the handle, the handle growing colder with each heartbeat, until my skin was joined to the metal. The cold sang into the bones of my arms, into the muscles of my shoulder.

I wrestled with the door and began to drag it open, and yet the door had taken on the weight of something massive, swiveling on corroded hinges. Except that I knew the door was not more massive, and I knew the brass of the handle was not cold. It was my own weakness that made them so, and I was frail because I was afraid.

The door was open, and I stepped back.

I turned, beckoning to my father, and he was gone.

The knowledge made me stumble, and I caught myself against the wall. I called out, and yet my cry was a whisper. I called again, knowing the futility of it.

There was no need to search for my father, no need to cry after him. He had vanished into a void inside me, in my own psyche, the same wound that had produced him in the first place.

Doubt now replaced the joy, diluting even the fear. I had been deceived. This had not been my father. My tears, my love, had been wasted on a hallucination. All of this was a sham. But would a specter, a demon garbed in my father's appearance, have expressed his love so fervently?

The silence was perfect.

The door was open, and there was nothing there. The staging had gone awry, and a character had missed his cue. I made a sound, half yelp, half growl. You see, I wanted to declaim to an audience, to a colisseum of assembled souls. You see—none of this is real. This is pageantry, this is the dazzle and the thunder of illusion.

As I stood before the black rectangle of the open doorway I felt something like disappointment. Because I had anticipated the sight of a divine being, a god, if only an evil, fallen god. And here was silence. I laughed. I mocked myself, shaking my head.

And I had been convinced, I told myself ruefully, that they would be able to hurt me, to torture that trick of light and reason that I had believed was my father. The legions I faced were frightening but swordless, empowering only the imagination. This was a little more than a new caliber of nightmare. I had survived such dreams.

The house was silent. The floor was solid under my steps as I reached the door, and swung it silently shut.

But it would not shut entirely.

Someone was out there.

Coming in.

24

S he had changed.

She was there before me, a figure of white, her hair and her gown floating in a wind that was silent, that stirred nothing else.

But she was different, taller, perhaps, or younger. She touched me as she stepped across the threshold. Her fingers were icy as they brushed my lips.

The door closed silently, as though moving with its own will. For a moment I was relieved to see her, grateful, nearly, that it was only her, this charming creature who both disturbed and delighted.

Then I understood. This was not just another visit. This was different. I sensed the hush of a crowd around us, through the walls, like the silent and yet audible weight in an opera house, a thousand lives weighing on the air.

But these were not lives. We were being watched by others, other creatures, other beings, invisible beyond the walls.

Trapped. Of course, I *could* run. There was the door. But why should I flee my own house?

Her eyes met mine. "It's time," she said.

It was hard to breathe. She turned at the entrance to the studio. She was, indeed, taller than I had recalled, and at once more slender and youthful and beyond age.

Tell her to get out. Flames snapped and spat in the fireplace. The color of the fire deepened, and the fire leaped higher, blue, and scarlet.

Despite the silence I felt rising within me, and the growing need I felt to take flight, I kept my voice firm. "I think it's foolish," I said, "to put me through this theater."

She did not respond.

I could only whisper. "It was brutal. That—that thing—was not my father."

The plastic canopies had been stripped from my furniture, and the chairs themselves were huddled together, like living things, mastiffs, drawn in closer together for protection. The furniture was unfamiliar to me, transformed.

The touch of this furniture, this brass-tacked leather, was enough to make me queasy. The leather had glazed itself with something like hair, the fine, sharp coat of a horse. The room around me was peeled of all familiarity. I was aware in a vague way of the unplastered walls, the gleam of nailheads, but what I saw were the glints and shiver of an armored host. Eyes, I thought, or spear points. I did not let myself look after a glance or two.

It was a fever, I told myself, a sick dream.

She gestured, inviting me to sit. The chair absorbed my weight, welcomed it, seemed to pleasure in it with a quiet groan. The leather breathed under me, around me. Some being held me lightly, taking its pleasure.

I stared into the fire. Don't look to the left, I told myself, or to the right. I should have been furious. An assault had been made against my emotions. And yet, there was something about her, that sense that I knew her from long ago, that stilled me from being completely angry. I was mystified, but I could feel no hatred toward her.

She spoke. "You're ready."

I took a deep breath. I experimented with an incredulous

laugh, something to buy time. Use your wits, I reminded myself. Stay steady. She had chosen a conversational tone, like a woman who had stopped by for a cup or two of Earl Grey. I kept my tone equally light. "Perhaps I should be grateful."

She did not answer. I knew how a grandmaster must feel, considering openings in an international tournament, the eyes of a crowd upon his hand.

"But I'm not." I turned to gaze at her. "What are you?"

She looked me up and down, mocking, seductive. "Surely you know."

The words thrilled me.

I had always known the truth was like this. I had always, in the back of my mind, understood that behind all good fortune was some ultimate power. I felt used, battered, and yet all I wanted for the moment was to stop having to experience the wash of such strong emotions. But that is how they—whatever They were—would want me to feel.

"Names are essential in such matters," I said. Names, I did not add, were the key element in conjuring. The ancient scribes of Judah would stop copying and undergo ritual cleansing every time the name of the Lord appeared in the sacred text.

She spoke after awhile, as though my speech had to be translated for her. "Names are important to human beings. We are not so interested in them."

I leaned toward her. "Where do you come from?"

"I am not here for conversation," she said.

"Where?" I repeated.

There was another silence. I began to understand. Speech was crude, a debased communication. "What do I seem to you?" she said.

On the surface this was mere conversation. This was a late-night visit, two people sharing thoughts. I felt, however, the formal quality of the transaction as an undercurrent. This was not chat—this was a deposition, a gentle but inexorable form of interrogation. Something like a system of law had been engaged. I did not know what judges with what sensibilities might weigh my words.

I would have to choose my words with care. "My father—my real father—would not want me to trade my soul for power."

She laughed, gently.

I continued, uttering words I could not have anticipated. "I won't do it."

She laughed again. She soothed the cloth over her breast, a voluptuous gesture that aroused me.

"Did you kill DeVere?"

She waited before answering, as though remembering her response from long ago. "We watched you from birth, and marked you as a friend."

"I don't believe it." But I sounded stolid, sullen, even petulant, staring ahead into the fire, able only to overshadow my thoughts with a fistlike skepticism. "And I don't want to enter into any contract."

She was silent.

"You will find me stubborn. Not so easy to deceive."

She watched me.

"I want to end it," I said. "Whatever we've begun. Tonight. Now."

Her eyes glittered, as though in me she saw a great prize, a pearl of price.

Then I spoke from a deep sense of what was happening, one of those bursts of truthfulness that are more than Freudian slips, a whole paragraph of honesty, like the blank frankness of a drunk or the chattering of a patient anesthetized with sodium pentothal.

I was not trying to thwart her, and I was not playing for time. "There aren't any angels. They're mythical, things we wish could exist but can't. There's no Heaven, and no Hell."

The only answer was the snapping of the fire.

I thought for a moment, and then turned aside in my chair. The leather eased around me, ecstatic with the movement of my body. I was sickened at this sensation, and I tried to tear myself away from the chair. The leather crooned after me as I escaped, and yet when I leaned against the mantelpiece I felt the solid, glossy timber shiver at my touch.

She was waiting for me to speak. I loathed the touch of the mantelpiece, the way the floor itself stretched beneath my feet, trembling nearly imperceptibly, wanting the impress of my footsteps.

A thought snagged me. I turned away. I forced out the words. "Are you," I said, "Lucifer Himself?"

Her laughter was lovely. "Stratton," she laughed, "you are the most delightful human being."

I waited. "I'm relieved," I said, with at least a little truthfulness.

The room changed. The fire did not flicker. Each flame went up straight. She gazed at me without a smile.

"You will decide tonight," she said, her voice throaty and low, still lovely but no longer touched with laughter.

"Please leave me."

She did not move.

"I've made myself clear," I continued. "I was told to be ready to transact some business with you. I must tell you that I am not interested."

The house had been silent. Now it became more than silent. The stillness touched me, shrank my heart. I continued, "If this is the way the powers you represent extort the human soul, then you have lost mine. You have played for me, and failed. My father is asleep with the dead, or with God, wherever humans go when they die."

Before I could shrink back, she had reached me and was touching me.

I could not deny my own delight. My own sense that at last I was ascending to life. Show me, I thought to her. Show me what you can do.

She touched me as my father had, on my cheek. "So lovely," she breathed, her breath the scent of gardenias.

"So lovely," she repeated.

Show me.

I could not think. I was experiencing a lust beyond sensation, something like agony.

"Ours," she said, her breath in the gentle mechanism of my hearing, entering the organs of my fancy, my faith in life, my dreams.

Don't do it, I warned myself. Keep your mind a blank.

She was a woman, and beautiful. And yet I knew that she was not female, not human. It was the fluid nature of her body that captured me, and drew me in, the sight of her nakedness arousing me, the sweep of her gown at our feet poured about, beneath us, like milk, like quicksilver.

She wasn't real, I knew. She was a hallucination. Surely that was it. I was simply losing my mind.

The sexual arousal I experienced was painful. My mind, my consciousness was gone, pricked like a bubble.

I was falling.

There was the nonsensation of oblivion, that empty bliss. But my lust was hard, and what swept me was a wet passion, an orgasm like something an innocent would experience, a child unable to emit seed but able to discover for the first time the hook nature had given him, the pleasure that commands.

25

I could hear something. Something steady, and indistinct. There it was again, that sound of continuous rise and fall.

Breathing.

That much was certain. There was the sound of breath, and the sensation of it, too. It was the lift and swell of an easy surf, comforting, but resonant, too, promising something more than simple calm.

This was the sound of my own respiration. This was the sensation of my life continuing.

Continuance. This was what nourished, not triumph, not vengeance, or knowledge. I lifted a finger. I lifted my entire hand, and bunched it slowly into a fist. I would not open my eyes—not yet. But soon, very soon, I would make that effort.

I said Nona's name, or thought it so strongly that my tongue shaped the syllables. One eye opened. It beheld a flutter of russet and auburn colors, golds and autumn browns playing across what looked like a blank screen above me where there should have been sky: the ceiling of my house. The screen was marred, or defined, by the stiff swirls of a trowel, a plasterer's application some time in the past, perhaps long ago.

I was on my back. I was naked. When I tried to lift my head it was too heavy. But I knew enough. I was in my own house, alive, unhurt, and the sense of an impending crowd, of a spectacle in progress, was finished.

I rolled over. I climbed to my feet, moving cautiously, expecting with every movement to feel the pang of injury.

I was wobbly, but I was unhurt.

Alone.

Was that a trace of dried sperm on the carpet? I found a sponge in one of the bathrooms, one of the large, natural yellow sponges, and used it to wipe away what might have been semen.

I dressed in the clothing that was scattered on the floor. The dustcovers had returned to the furniture. I examined the plastic coverings carefully. There was a sift of dust in the folds of the plastic. These coverings had not been removed recently.

I touched the chair where my father had appeared.

I closed my eyes. "Father—you wouldn't do that," I said.

Would you?

I felt comforted by the sight of dawn seeping into the house. The fire in the hearth had vanished, leaving a white residue, like the haze breath leaves on a cold window.

The sight of morning made me hope that the entire night had been a train of illusions, a hallucination that had stretched from horizon to horizon. Maybe, I thought, none of it had happened.

Maybe DeVere wasn't really dead.

And then I felt it, supple and stiff at the same time, a presence near my heart. I slipped it from my breast pocket, and looked at it as it rocked in my hand, responding to the unfelt currents of the air.

It was easy to forget how beautiful it was. Visual memory could not store such an array of colors.

This was not a feather anymore. It was a quill—a writing instrument. I examined the point, and saw how it had been sharpened, pared, readied for the ink. Had it always looked like this?

I could picture it vividly—signing my name. That's what this was for.

But there was no ink in the bone-gray shaft. This plume had never been used for writing.

The fact of this feather in my hand meant that they still had, however feebly, a claim on me. The feather, insensate, rich with color, shifted in my hand as though it knew.

The thought was a sour flavor in my mouth, but I knew what I had to do.

I found a match, one of the thick, lavender-and-white-tipped matches that fit the silver Hoffman-designed box. I returned to the fireplace.

I struck the match on the brick of the hearth. I let the flame touch the softest down at the spike of the quill, perhaps hoping that this star of filament would not ignite.

The walls seemed to step back. The room became a huger place, and darker, despite the dawn. The feather twitched, writhed in the palm of my hand. And then as instinct forced me to whisk my hand out from under it, the feather was made of flame.

Each filament was gilded. The feather spun, dancing, lofted upward by its own heat and its growing weightlessness, following the spire of its own smoke up the vault of the chimney.

And then it was gone.

26

"You look different," said my brother, gazing straight ahead at the road.

"Better than usual, or worse?" I said, trying to make easy conversation.

"For a second there I almost didn't recognize you."

"I must look really great."

"You look good, actually." He shrugged. "Just a little strange. I'm sorry I mentioned it."

It was later that morning, and Rick was driving me north at my request. He looked bruised, slightly puffy.

I was still shaken. Burning the feather had been the right thing to do, a final, capping farewell. But I sensed that it might have been a galling insult.

If the Powers existed. Here I was, thinking such thoughts. I needed help.

"Terrible about DeVere," said Rick.

I went cold.

Rick sighed. "He always looked so sure of himself."

I heard myself utter the words, "The news stunned me. I'm a little tired—wasn't really able to sleep."

"You don't look tired so much," said Rick.

"Haunted? Fugitive? Demented?"

He took his eyes off the road and took me in, studying me with a glance, a brother's glance, both knowing and affectionate. "You look like you could sleep for a week. But on you that's a good way to look. The rumpled *bon vivant.*"

I thanked him, a bit of mild sarcasm that made him smile.

I was trembling. I gripped my hands together so he wouldn't notice.

Rick drove fast, working the little Alfa through its gears. We were heading through wine country, but skirting the more celebrated vineyards. The countryside that whipped past us was nearly Tuscan, the gnarls and stumps of grapevines, intermingled with an appearance that was quite western, men in white straw cowboy hats leaning against pickups, horses nosing grass behind barbed wire.

Rick changed lanes to leave a slow delivery truck, painted to advertise a popular brand of corn chips, far behind us. He took a curve with either careless skill or recklessness, and his tires complained. I wasn't certain whether Rick drove this car out of special fondness for it, or if it was the last car he owned, all the others sold off—or wrecked. "I'm glad you decided to see Mom," he said. "Not just because I think it's a good thing to do."

It was odd, in my ears, the way he called her "Mom." It was so casual, affectionate, ordinary. I thought of her as "Mother." On this day, more than any other, I needed to see my surviving parent. "You want to compare notes on her."

"I think it's a good thing you're going to see her." He had said this so often that I was beginning to wonder if it were true.

"You think she's . . ." I hunted for a kind word, and couldn't think of one. "Hopeless?"

He gave a tilt of his head. "What made you want to come and see her so suddenly?"

I considered my answer.

"I know I encouraged you to come," he continued. "But I'm just wondering what made you change your mind."

There was something about his tone I did not understand. "I worry about her all the time," I said. "That's why I can't stand to see her. To see her makes it impossible to deny the truth."

"When you're away from her," Rick suggested, "you can pretend that she isn't really so ill."

Sometimes I find it impossible to use words. They stick to the truth like labels the post office applies to packages, as though a red-and-blue sticker means safe passage. " 'Ill' is a good way to put it," I said, and gave no hint of the inner debate I was experiencing, questioning my sanity, the sanity of the world. "Tell me, Rick—do I look like someone who could kill another human being?"

"Sure."

"I do?"

He laughed at the concern in my voice. "Anybody could be a killer, Strater. What sort of person would you be if I thought you absolutely could not hurt anyone?"

"What's good about hurting people?"

"It's horrible to hurt people. A terrible habit to get into. You're very peculiar today, Strater. Even your voice is different."

"You think that I'm the sort of person who could kill someone to further his career?"

"I don't know about that. But you could definitely protect yourself, if you had to."

"It's a matter of masculinity, isn't it? A man is supposed to seem capable of homicide."

"Doesn't it say something like that in the U.S. Constitution?" He drove for a while, and then said, adjusting and readjusting his hands on the wheel as he spoke, "You know what people are going to think? Not everyone, but the DeVere people. They'll think we hired someone to dump DeVere out the window."

Maybe I did it, I thought. Maybe I am so sick that I could do something like that and not know it. The thought was nauseating. I cranked down the window to let air stream over me.

"Those people who are after me," said Rick. "The people who

are after me for money. My creditors." He said the last word with what he had intended as an ironic edge. "That's what *they'll* think."

"It doesn't matter."

"These are serious men, Strater."

"It'll be all right."

"It definitely will not be all right. You're just like Dad—so optimistic I think life ought to slap you around a little. I love you dearly, Strater, but sometimes I think you have no idea what the world is all about. You expect life to be good. It isn't."

I let the rolling scenery answer for me, corrals, tractors, the occasional barn. From time to time there was a circling pair of wings high above a rocky creek.

My father had known an ambassador from a Middle Eastern country who enjoyed after-hours blackjack and, at the same time, grew overfond of the wrong set of women. This gentleman, who had visited our family at Christmas over the years, had been found in a canyon in Big Sur punched full of small, twenty-two-caliber holes. My teenage years had been shadowed by only partly apocryphal tales of rich kids who got tangled in drug stakeouts, blackmail capers, wee-hours contretemps with private detectives.

"I'm going to make lots of money," I reassured him. "Big commissions. We'll pay your debts."

"It's not a matter of money. The DeVere people will want us dead."

"I'll arrange things," I said.

"How?"

I didn't know how, but my silence seemed to express confidence.

"I don't want to think about it," he said. It was his way of expressing gratitude for what he interpreted as my easy attitude. "Look at this scenery. This kind of place makes me happy. It makes me believe in things. I can't b*elieve* the kind of people I've ended up dealing with."

It was characteristic of my brother that when he did deal with philosophical matters he used bold, unmixed colors—mortality, faith. He had the stout, simple diction of many people I knew, the sort of man who has such conversations only while driving fast, or while drinking.

When we approached the Place he began to slow, downshifting, delaying.

It made both of us quiet, the sight of the iron gate swinging inward after a videocam had observed us for awhile. The road was well tended, hills and oaks, and new blue-gray gravel spread on the verge of the road.

My brother and I called it "the Place," but it was a private hospital for a few patients, the most distinguished being Mother, widow of the man who had served for years on the board of directors. Los Cerritos Sanitarium never displayed its name, nor did it have any of the outward trappings of either a hospital or a prison, except that after a long drive there was a chain-link fence surmounted by a long spiral of barbed wire and then, at the distance of a stone's throw, another, parallel fence.

It had been part of the deal: we had paid to have the Place made maximum security, or at least as secure as the state hospital for the criminally insane at Atascadero, where the prosecution had been eager to deposit her.

There was a no-man's land of bare dirt, raked weedless. The fences were tall, perhaps thirty feet high. A security guard waved his clipboard at us. We parked, and sat for too long in the Alfa.

"Dad would like the wisteria," said Rick, indicating a late winter vine on an arbor, and redwood benches. The cement walks were still new-looking, and the grass had that recently mowed look that left the lawn in a pattern of parallel stripes.

"Do you think Dad would be proud of the two of us?" I asked. "Do you think he would make the point of saying so, if he met us?"

"He'd be proud of you, no question."

"He wouldn't try to talk us into something . . ." The word did not come easily. "Evil, do you think?"

Rick did not answer at once. When he spoke there was a hint of tension in his voice. "Dad made mistakes. But ask anyone and they'll tell you that he tried to do the right thing."

"If you saw him—his ghost, an illusion, perhaps, what would you ask him to test him? To see if he was real?"

Rick was thoughtful. "I would never believe that he was real. I just wouldn't believe it. It can't happen."

We both sat silent for what seemed like a long time. Then Rick said, "By the time I reach the parking lot and turn off the engine, I'm always nervous."

We shook hands with a row of nurses and orderlies. The doctors were at a meeting in Napa, although this was not bad news. For once I wanted to see my mother unencumbered with professional commentary regarding maintenance doses and bedsores.

The new head nurse was Mrs. Lamb. She welcomed us, told us about the new Jacuzzi. She showed us into the library, the patio, the view overlooking the lawn. There were other patients here, in addition to my mother, but I was aware that they had been whisked out of the way. We had phoned ahead, and we were like royalty, people who go through life convinced that the world smells of fresh paint.

"You both look exactly like your pictures," she said. "I'm so happy to be able to say I saw you at last."

"How is she doing?" I asked.

"She's doing just fine." Mrs. Lamb beamed at Rick, and then at me. She was a plump, pleasant-looking woman, with white teeth. "I think it wouldn't cause any trouble at all if we let you peek in at her."

"We want to see her."

"That's what I mean—"

"We want to talk to her."

Her smile brightened. Her teeth, I realized, were false. "That's going to be a problem."

I gave her my best tea-party smile. "We insist."

Mrs. Lamb looked at Rick, as though for support. Rick gave her a smile of his own, and winked.

"It's a very bad idea," she said, solemn, subdued. "It might cause complications."

"Has she been making progress?" I asked.

"Of course she has," said Mrs. Lamb. "Of course she has been making excellent progress."

"Then perhaps she will be able to withstand the strain."

"It was a staff decision. One person can't alter policy."

I used my most gentle voice. "We certainly wouldn't think of asking you to alter policy. That's out of the question. Perhaps, in this one instance, you could happen to be looking the other way . . ."

Mrs. Lamb's face was set, with a lingering smile that now looked spiteful. "It's families," said Mrs. Lamb.

I must have looked mystified, because Mrs. Lamb added, "Please forgive me, Mr. Fields. But I've seen it so many times. Some people think government is bad. Some people think the police have to be watched all the time. People ought to take a look at the family—the harm *it* does."

I softened. "Maybe it's not such a good idea."

Mrs. Lamb's manner was brisk. "No, I think you're right after all. I'm sorry to have seemed so rude. Let's all go have a nice long talk with Mrs. Fields."

"We don't really have to—"

"Besides, you always get what you want, don't you?" She was walking away from us, and reached a door. She held it open.

"What does *that* mean?" I asked.

"That's what someone said on one of the talk shows. The Fieldses get what they want. A lot of people even admire you for it. Nobody stands in your way."

27

In Irving Penn's portrait of my mother she has a hand to her head to press down the crown of a broad-brimmed hat. The photograph is in black and white, but it is plain that her glove is black, her hat some dark color, red or blue, and that her lipstick is probably deepest scarlet. She is smiling, and is both charmed by the camera and shy in its presence.

My mother was not shy, particularly, but she did dislike unnecessary spectacle. I have often wondered what remark, what passing mood, might have inspired her smile. The photograph was taken during my early childhood. My mother looks like a stranger, someone connected to reality, someone enjoying life.

The woman sitting in the hospital had white hair, and a fine profile. She looked out through the glass door, at the lawn, and at the trees in the distance. Her hair had been brushed, and her lipstick was a muted rose-pink.

She did not glance our way. She said, "The horse pavilion is getting wet. Isn't it?"

Rick and I exchanged looks. Her choice of words was often vaguely outdated. She spoke for people long-vanished, men who lived for their horses, for golf, for sleek yachts.

She looked my way.

"I don't think it's raining," I said.

We kissed, formally, like diplomats. She was shivering, the result of the drug she took to keep from hallucinating.

"Stratton," she said. "However did you find your way here?"

I told her how well she looked. It was true, and yet, as so often when seeing someone after a year or more, there is the strangest sensation that someone has fussed with the sketch. It was simply not that there were new wrinkles, or a more age-bleakened look to her eyes. Her hair had grown fuller and her face had a too-pale look that I associated with a drawing imperfectly erased. There was something missing in her, a glow, that had been present as recently as a year ago.

"Rick drove me," I said, clumsily literal.

"That was kind." She made a gesture with something like her old graciousness. "It's very pleasant here," said my mother. "I can sit and watch deer feed off the aspens, or whatever they are. Those trees out there which have, alas, no leaves on them now."

I enjoyed the way she expressed herself, phrasing out of another time, a time well before her own birth. "Birches," I said. "And they're getting some leaves. Quite a few of them."

"Birches poison deer," she answered.

I did not want to discuss poison. "It's a very pleasant view," I said.

"Ah, 'pleasant.' Yes," she said, "that is precisely the word I would use. It is constantly on the tip of my tongue. I am always saying to myself, 'Look out at all that and enjoy it. It's so pleasant.'" She had a slight tremor in her voice, too.

I picked my words with care. "Sometimes we think we shouldn't come see you. That it upsets you too much."

She regarded me. "You could help me get out of this shithole."

The word hurt. She had been so reserved that a society columnist actually retreated to his thesaurus, he confessed to me once, to conjure "ethereal."

"I'm sorry you're unhappy," I said.

I felt myself growing edgy already. Edgy, and sad. She had always had that effect on me. Her tone was imperious, her mind jumping back, always, to the prime question: why we kept her caged.

"I'm sorry," she said. "Forgive my tongue."

"There isn't," I said, "much we can do." I did not want to mention that she had been sentenced here by Judge Bieglitter, the very man she had admired when he ran for lieutenant governor.

"It's all right, Stratton," she said. "Really."

I could not look at Rick.

She wrenched her wheelchair to renew her appraisal of me. I backed away, quite without thinking.

Her shoulders rose and fell. She would begin to weep, now, or collapse into a stoic rage. She fought the straps that held her, and Rick put a hand on her shoulder.

He looked hard at me for a moment. "We hope," he said, brave enough to persist, "that you can get out of here someday."

It had been a bewildering and agonizing series of episodes when it had all transpired, but looking back it seemed simple. My father's death had unstrung her so completely that she had suffered the delusion that he was still alive, residing in Montreux, beside Lake Geneva, with a mistress. The servants, she had been convinced, *looked* like the familiar servants, but they were jailers, paid to spy on her and keep her trapped.

She had used less ingenuity than I might have expected in poisoning the staff, employing oleander tea, boiled to a concentrate, in the Christmas fruitcake. She had never been original, or imaginative, only caring and proud. Two people had died, although Collie, who herself had spent time in the medical center as a result, had reassured me that "old help like ourselves don't mind dying in the line of duty, as it were." I had discerned in this attitude perhaps a bit too much wartime ethic.

It was true that both of the staff who had succumbed to the poison had suffered from weak hearts, and both had already been taking digitalis. The addition of the toxin in *nerium oleander* was just enough, as the coroner put it, attempting to ascend from his usual medical prose, "to dramatically and irrevocably eclipse cardiac function." The law could not overlook Mother's behavior as eccentric, and the family attorney, to his credit, had salvaged this simple future for her.

My mother ran her hands along the wheels, approaching me. There was something like honest doubt in her voice. "I used to count on you, Stratton. You." She uttered the pronoun with heavy emphasis. "I used to feel so close to you. You, who only cared about your pencil drawings."

"You always call them that. 'Pencil drawings.' I draw in all kinds of media . . ." I faltered.

"Stratton won a prize," said Rick. "He's going to redesign everything."

"Help your mother, Stratton. Help me!" She was weeping.

I had, in the backwaters of my intentions, planned to ask her about my father. What had he been wearing that day? One of his old hunting shirts? I had almost wanted to say: I have seen him. He is alive in the Other World. It had been a ridiculous plan, one of those hopes that dissolve under full awareness. One thing was certain: seeing the phantom of my father had made me aware that one of my parents was still alive, still with us. "We are your sons," I said, the words bringing me to a point of great sadness. "We love you."

I could see it in her eyes. She did not believe me.

I took her head in my hands and I kissed her. She was rigid, a woman enduring a passing agony.

"What can I tell you that would make you trust us?"

Her voice was sad when she said, "Nothing. I can no longer tell what to believe, Stratton. I don't know what's real. And you—you men. You think you know."

"We don't mean any harm," I said.

" 'Harm!' " she echoed, scornful but affectionate for a moment. She regarded me. "I lost my daughter. My little girl."

We never mentioned this. I could not meet Rick's eyes. Before my birth there had been another pregnancy. It had ended in a miscarriage, and unspoken family tradition understood that the baby would have been a girl.

"In the days before your father, I used to go riding," she continued. "In the canyon, to see the palm trees. Some young man or other would offer to ride with me in their creaking new riding clothes, but I wanted to see the palms and I wanted to be alone."

As so often before, I realized how little we knew about her life as a young woman. We had a smattering of images, photographs, impressions. Her father, a man I barely remembered, had been a "Virginia planter," an archaic description I had always taken to be a shorthand for "wealthy enough to do nothing." Tobacco, I had always assumed, and racehorses. Her widowed father had lived for awhile in Palm Springs, the old money side-by-side with people like Jimmy Cagney and the young Peter Renman, already a major producer. Why Palm Springs, I had sometimes wondered? Why not Beverly Hills itself, or, for that matter, London, Paris, or one of those Mediterranean enclaves created to keep the well-tailored quietly out of sight? Still, Palm Springs must have been charming. The old and new money had enjoyed each other.

I had been forced to fill in details with my imagination, a kind of fiction. It was not difficult. If a constellation can look like a bull or an archer, a few glossy photographs and a house of heirlooms can look like a coherent family history. The mind builds connections, the secret to both government and motion pictures. We want to be deceived. There were secrets, though, canyons of family history that ended abruptly.

"I am afraid," she said. "I have not been a good person. I have not loved you the way I should have."

I held her. I could not stand to see such anguish. She wept, and gradually subsided.

Mrs. Lamb stepped forward to steer Mother away from us. "She is not doing so bad," she said. "Only sometimes."

"On a day like today," I said.

"Oh, no, today is a pretty good day for her. Isn't it, Mrs. Fields?"

We stopped in Mrs. Lamb's office before we left.

"Dr. Ahn?" she echoed, in response to my question. "No, Dr. Ahn never sees Mrs. Fields anymore. Dr. Ahn retired."

"I'm sorry to hear that," I said, and indeed I was.

"We still have all of Dr. Ahn's books. Whenever Dr. Ahn would visit it was like—having a movie star come to visit. We were all so proud."

The nurse showed me one of Ahn's books, *The Woman at the Well: Hallucinatory Experience and the New Jerusalem*. The book was signed in a strong hand, "To all my friends at Los Cerritos, Elizabeth Ahn."

"Dr. Skeat will be so sorry he missed you," said Mrs. Lamb. Dr. Skeat had suggested that we curtail our visits to Mother.

We walked in silence to the parking lot. The air was cool but the sun soaked through our clothing and felt warm. I drew a breath of the scent of the hills. High above a hawk circled, or a vulture, a dark chip in the blue.

"Dr. Ahn understood her better than anyone," said Rick.

I agreed. I wanted to talk to Dr. Ahn about quite a bit that was on my mind. And, at the same time, the very thought of Dr. Ahn was an irritant. Something in me froze at the thought of talking to her. Psychiatrists could be so annoying, with their abstract labels for human passions. Ahn probably retired because she found her efforts entirely futile.

"Mother's not getting any better, is she?" asked Rick.

His voice woke me from my thoughts. "Someday I'm going to get her cured," I said. "Someday. When I have money again, and can find someone who knows how to wake people out of that kind of sleep. Someday I'm going to wake her up, Rick."

Then there were tears, and I could not say any more.

Later, as he drove south, Rick said, "Do you have any idea how heavily she has to be drugged, just so she can sit there like that?"

His tone kept me from answering at once.

"Some people never get well," he said.

As we entered the flow of Bay Area traffic, slipping from lane to lane, I felt the shadows of the trucks fall over us as we passed them.

"People will still have a high opinion of us," said Rick. "They'll like us. They figure rich old families like us have all kinds of power. DeVere screwed up. He shouldn't have stood in our way."

I remembered growing up this way. Every child is taught a general fear of strangers. We were trained to avoid solitude, cars that slowed down, admirers, especially when they stood at a curb. Each car could become a weapon. Every road was a trail that could close.

And your mind, I told myself. You will devolve to the point that you will be like your mother. The disintegration has already begun.

How long do you think *you* have?

28

I found Nona sitting beside Stuart. I could not suppress the thought: He was too thin to live much longer.

"Stuart was just asking for you," she said. "He just told me his horses need more friends."

She slipped me a sheet of lined foolscap from her notebook and I crafted the paper into a horse. I tore the corners into ears, and used a pen to describe a flowing mane. The horse had flared nostrils, and the eyes of one of the steeds of the Parthenon. Examined with a certain open-mindedness and imagination it was a fine horse, and it fit over Stuart's fingers.

Stuart brought forth another horse from beneath his pillow, and the two horse puppets were an act of theater, a story, two figures of power introduced to each other. What happened next could be battle, or partnership. Stuart's hands worked the puppets, one much more worn than the other, and I could see him debating the course of their relationship.

"The new one is stronger," said Stuart. He had the pinched, deep-creased look of a middle-aged man who has lived hard.

"But the old one is crafty," I said.

He didn't understand the word.

"Crafty means 'smart.'"

He gave me a mildly skeptical look: Smarts aren't worth much.

"Strength isn't everything." There is an artificial heartiness some adults use around children, especially sick children. I tried to keep this fake tone out of my voice. The idea of strength troubled me under this circumstance, but I knew it was false to pretend that power, of one sort or another, did not constitute the major character of the world.

Stuart thought. Perhaps such considerations wearied him, but he kept the two horses before his eyes. "They are," he said from his pillow, "both smart."

"What do they think about?"

"They worry," he said.

"What about?" I asked, although I could tell what he was about to say.

He closed his eyes, although the horses were still on his fingers. He opened his eyes again, and the horses seemed to gaze at each other.

Nona closed her door, locked it, and then kissed me. She slipped off her shoes, sitting behind her desk, skimming a brace of pink memos to one side. She kept my hand in hers, not wanting to let me go. She looked into my eyes, though, and her smile faded.

Her hand squeezed mine. "What is it?"

"Nothing you should worry about. You have enough on your mind."

"Are we being a little coy today, Strater?"

She rarely used her office, on the ground floor of the medical center, and yet it bore marks of her character. There was a yellow sheet marked THINGS TO DO on the wall, but it was blank. Nona could always remember what she had to do, and get it done.

"I saw my mother this morning," I said.

She gazed down at my hand, and then back up into my eyes. "How is she?"

I told her about my mother's condition, and she listened with an air of compassion. When I had concluded my brief description of the visit she did not say anything for awhile.

Perhaps I seemed to be waiting for a prognosis, because she added, "Maybe there will never be a return, Strater. Maybe she will always be as she is now."

"You want to prepare me for disappointment," I said.

Nona's face was rarely sad. She was too lively, too direct. But there was a touch of melancholy as she said, "There is so much that we can't change."

There was feeling in my voice as I said, "And the children here. Stuart, for example."

She didn't answer.

"They don't have much hope either, right?"

"I think we have to have hope. As human beings—we have to have faith to keep on living. But there is such a thing as a false hope."

She meant: Stuart did not have long to live.

She seemed to read my thoughts. "They don't even know what's wrong with Stuart."

"Whatever it is, he's dying," I said, my voice husky.

"I help them in my way. There's only so much I can do. Stuart was found in a dumpster as a newborn, abandoned. He's lived with a string of foster families."

"I used to believe the world was going to get better and better. We'd abolish things like sick children."

Nona gave me a wide-eyed, knowing look and said, "You've been through something recently, Strater."

I slipped easily into mock-cheerful denial. "Like what?"

"You've changed."

I tried to laugh. "I'm in love."

She smiled in response to that, but then she added, "You are keeping a secret. Don't try to deny it."

I had always intended to tell her. But I was not prepared to begin the story now.

She continued, "Are you in trouble, Stratton?"

The formal form of my first name made me look away. I could not lie to Nona, but what sort of truth could I tell her?

"Do you need my help?" she asked.

"Soon," I said. "I will be able to tell you everything. But not now."

A long silence. She whispered, making a joke of it to protect her feelings, "I know what it is—another woman."

"I believe," I began, "that there are Powers in the world that can pluck us as we might pluck an apple." Having started, I wondered at my choice of words, at how I could possibly make her believe what I myself could barely accept.

"Do you mean," she asked, "supernatural powers?"

"Not exactly," I said.

She slipped behind me, and her fingers found the places in my neck and in my skull where the tension seemed to reside. "You had better tell me now. Whatever is bothering you, I want to know now. I won't wait."

Her fingers were wise. Calm pooled inside me. It had been a long time since I had felt anything like this.

But I couldn't tell her. I had to keep my secret.

I stood and strode to the bulletin board, feeling caged in this office. Her eyes were aglow with the question: What is it?

And then I realized that Nona was the only person I knew, and perhaps would ever know, with whom I could share such a tale. I took a long breath. "It might not be safe to be with me right now."

She waited.

My voice caught. "I'm a dangerous man."

"I'm not that interested in playing it safe. I see children die."

It was a decision as deep as the moment in which a person picks up a weapon to defend his life, or decides to leap from a burning building.

Telling her, letting the events slip through my fingers like a line, I did not begin to imagine what impression the story would make on her.

It took a long time. I told her all over again of Blake's suicide, of DeVere's apparent suicide. With a trembling voice, I told her of my father.

"You've been through all of that," she said at last, "and didn't think to tell me even a hint of it?"

There was no glib response to that. "Do you believe any of it?"

"What you say disturbs me, Stratton."

"What do you think?" I added, with a rasp in my voice, "Give me your diagnosis, Dr. Lyle."

"I believe that something wants your soul."

"Something real?"

"Does it matter?"

"You know it does."

She watched me, actually saw me, the way few people look at another human being. "It's real for you, isn't it?"

"I don't know." I let the admission, the confession of ignorance, linger in the room.

"I think you want me to tell you that it's all impossible."

"If that's what you think, please do."

"I don't think there are such places as Heaven and Hell, Strater. I don't believe in things like that."

"Psychosis."

She was thoughtful as she rose from her desk and plucked a thumbtack from its place on the bulletin board.

"That's the word you're trying to avoid using, isn't it?" I said, pain in my voice.

"I don't know what to think," she said. "But we might have to consider the possibility."

"You're being too nice about this," I said, with a flash of impatience. "Go ahead and say it—I'm ready to move into the hospital with my mother."

"I would say so, if that's what I thought. Your father taught you to be noble and generous. Mine taught me to be honest."

"If it's not psychosis, then I'm in even worse trouble."

She lifted an eyebrow.

"Because that means that what has happened to me is actual. Real."

She gave the tack a toss, and it nestled in the wrinkle of her palm. She seemed to be weighing it.

"Besides," I continued, "a man who dares riptides as a form of recreation can hardly be called normal."

"I never said you were 'normal,' Strater. Every potential hero has to be a little bit in love with death. Only a little—but it makes the big risks possible."

"I never quite saw myself as heroic."

"I always saw you that way." She replaced the tack, down by the frame of the bulletin board, and pushed it in carefully.

"But you see why it might be dangerous to be around me. I don't know what I'm going to see next. Besides, DeVere's people will be after me. You might not even be safe in your apartment. I'll ask Fern to arrange some security for you."

"You rely on me, don't you, Strater? As a source of common sense. You think that I'm going to be able to answer your questions. You almost hope I have some sort of medication that will put these images to sleep."

I answered truthfully. "I wouldn't mind."

For the first time that afternoon, and perhaps for the first time since I had known her, she seemed defeated by something. Listening to me had spent something in her, and I sensed that I was about to discover something about Nona I had never known before.

"My father was a physician," she said. "Not one of these doctors who spend their afternoons playing tennis with their investment counselors. One of the real kind, the kind with a black bag and a practice of people who can't pay their bills. He had a general practice in Oakland, years before it was stylish to want to save the inner cities, and then after it was no longer stylish."

She gave me a glance, and I told her with my eyes: Please go on. She rarely spoke of her family.

"He died of overwork. That's hardly a medical description. But on a death certificate there is a step-by-step breakdown. There is the primary cause, and the secondary cause, and the contributing cause to that. A cerebral hemorrhage killed him, and that's all that they bothered typing in. But they could have accurately given fatigue, and the weight of too many sick people, as the contributing causes.

"He died when I was in college. It broke my mother's spirit. It forced her back into her past. In a way, she reacted like your mother, only much less violently. She moved back into her old neighborhood, and lived quietly and peacefully in a world of soap operas and bridge games where she was born and raised, in Minneapolis. I think seeing me reminded her of what she couldn't bear to remember. My father was that special. When she died it was as though she made up her mind not to breathe anymore.

"I would be proud to accomplish one-third of the good he was able to work in his lifetime. And one thing he bequeathed to me, one precept, that I swear to live out each day: Be true. Be honest. Don't lie, especially not to yourself. If you don't know, admit it. Be ignorant and brave."

I had never heard her describe her parents in quite this way. There had been, naturally, the occasional anecdote. I had thought that I was getting to know Nona. But now I saw that she was a person I was only beginning to know, and that I could spend years with her, as in a new, unfamiliar country, and still find her amazing.

"I never mentioned why I decided to study psychiatry," she said. Without waiting for me to respond, she continued, "I had problems of my own. They are all far behind me, thank God. I got the help of someone very capable."

"I think your father would be proud of you," I said.

My words touched her. She ran her hand through my hair. She kissed me, her lips the flavor of cinnamon, sunlight. Then she kept her hand there, on my head, as though in an effort to bless me, to give me peace. "Something is after you, Stratton. After your soul. I don't know what it is. But I'm going to fight with you against it."

"It might be a mistake."

"Whatever it is, Stratton—it makes me afraid. And it has convinced me: I'm moving in with you. Today."

29

Anna Wick, DeVere's long-time "right hand and confidante," as one TV reporter put it, spoke at DeVere's memorial service, an invitation-only affair at the Palace of Fine Arts. The service resembled a pageant more than a ceremony of mourning, and police video cameras swept the crowd. "Looking for crooks," said the matron behind me in a stage whisper.

"One thing is clear to all of us today: we will never forget Ty DeVere," said Anna. Black suited her well, as did an expression of thoughtful sadness. She had evidently taken diction training at an early stage in her career. She had the clear tone of a woman reading poetry on educational radio, or a stewardess accustomed to working first class. "His name will be forever a part of our times. When they think of us, they will not remember our individual names, or our faces. They will remember Ty DeVere."

At his request, his ashes had been scattered in the Pacific. This was a surprising decision, dictated by DeVere's attorneys, although it is possible that DeVere had seen this as less a final annihilation than a way of blessing that largest of oceans with his remains.

Dr. Skeat called late one afternoon. "Please don't visit her again without my permission," he said.

I prepared myself for bad news. "Is she worse?"

"We adjusted her medication."

"I'm sorry," I said.

"An apology won't do a whole lot of good," said Dr. Skeat. "She needs to be protected."

"But it's a pretty terrible situation when a woman has to be protected from her sons."

He agreed that it was. "Apparently you don't realize the corrosive nature of your family."

"We're loving people—"

"Family love isn't always motivated by wisdom, Mr. Fields. It can be possessive, manipulative, and it can kill people. In your mother's case, we have a reactive trauma if we so much as mention your father."

My voice was ragged with feeling. "We love her."

"We have to be careful. Especially in a family like yours."

He must have sensed my anger over the phone.

"Please, Mr. Fields. Stay away."

It wasn't fair, I thought, hanging up the phone, stepping to the window. But this was a feeble complaint. Since when was the world just? Besides, Dr. Skeat had been chosen by my brother and myself out of a long list of "sensitive professionals."

I gazed out the window at the street. My family was—I groped for pale, dried-up phrases: honorable, civic-minded. We were decent people.

I could not keep myself from wondering if the occasional figures strolling in the dark, walking a dog, smoking, were decent, innocent people, or individuals sent to watch us, to remind us that they were out there, waiting.

A few days went by, cue cards splashed with bold letters: good news. More money. Commissions, interviews.

Strengthened by Nona, I entered each new day, very much a man who expects to be attacked, taken at any intersection, any restaurant or gallery. I kept myself at ease, inwardly alert. I was anxious. I was happy.

Fern arranged his hours around my schedule. He drove us to the symphony, to my appointments with potential clients, and I was familiar enough with the way of such guardians that I came to enjoy him without giving him much thought, as one enjoys the shade of a landmark elm.

Packard, the contractor, finished the walls, plastered, painted. The house looked now as I had dreamed it would.

Collie arrived each morning to whisk her ostrich-feather duster about the new furniture arrangement, offered the usual assortment of splendid salads for lunch, and yet I could tell that she understood the household to be under some manner of siege. She appeared pleased at the thought, involved in an important ordeal, inspired, perhaps, by my calm.

My career was unfolding. International calls imprinted themselves on my answering machine, and the planning chiefs of what the financial pages called "energy consortiums" and "communications empires" were planning visits to San Francisco. Notice of my career was printed not on the society pages, and not in a paragraph in a review of local art shows, but on the business pages. It was clear to me that not only was success coming my way, it was coming quite literally to my doorstep.

Time magazine flew its chief photographer in for a sitting. *Vanity Fair* magazine shot me playing frisbee with Nona at the Marina. The events of these days seemed sacred, devoid as they were of any taint of the uncanny. Rick, and his creditors, played no further part in my life for the time being. This was not unusual. It was typical of Rick to spin through my life with a vivid problem and then vanish.

In all ways my life was becoming a chain of ordered, connected events. It is that characteristic of dailiness that makes us enjoy films, stories, even travel. We intuit that the flow of things, the episodic spill of occurrence, is the natural state of our lives. It is only when a death, or something flavored with death, takes place that we awaken.

People accepted DeVere's death as a suicide. Collie suggested that people at the checkout at Lucky's felt it was "bad conscience he couldn't live with because he tried to hurt the Fieldses." People doubted his death was murder, apparently, but would not have been terribly outraged if I had, in truth, taken DeVere's life. When an article in the Sunday supplement referred to our family as "the modern day Borgias" it was intended as a compliment.

Fern was tight lipped. When I asked him what was wrong he would say, "Let me take care of it." He would shake his head, keep driving, keep standing behind me at the art gallery, keep his place at the curb while Nona and I window shopped.

I glanced up from time to time to wonder if the van at the stoplight next to me was really a carpet cleaner's. But with each lulling hour I was becoming tarnished, sleepy, returning to my faith in life.

I believed, as days followed one another, that the troubled times were behind us.

30

One evening Nona and I were dining in Christophe's, off Geary, enjoying the post-posttheater quiet. We enjoyed brook trout, Montrachet, and candlelight in a corner of the restaurant the maître d' always managed to have reserved for me.

It was that time of night that is actually very early morning, a time so far removed from business and appointment books that one can actually believe that no further harm will ever take place in the world.

Nona's dark hair was more radiant than ever, the deep, hidden burgundy hue of her brunette catching the candlelight. She was peaceful, in a way that was distinctively her own. She was sure of herself, and of her life.

Landscaping was a matter of illusion, I was saying. "If you want a blue garden to look blue, it should be twenty percent yellow," I said. "If you want your garden to look old, plant poplars. No tree grows faster in Northern California."

I had managed to spend an hour or two that afternoon begin-

ning to restore my hothouse. I had been busy composting, opening new bags of potting soil, writing orders for new plants.

"It's all magic, then," said Nona.

"It's a matter of glamour. In the sense of 'artifice.' The flower
has to attract the bee. The blossom is a natural form of cosmetic.
A botanical fashion statement."

Coffee arrived. We chatted about recent staffing changes at
the Medical Center, the progress of a local theater, my own good
prospects for a contract with a Japanese financial firm, and then
she reached out her hand, and closed it over mine, a gesture that
I recognized.

She had something important to say. I encouraged her with a
look, but she was oddly reluctant to continue.

At last she said, "There's someone I want you to talk to."

When she did not immediately continue, I urged her. "Please
tell me."

"You'll be angry."

I laughed. "Impossible."

"You will, Strater. You'll think I've been working behind your
back."

"Have you been?"

She paused. Nona rarely needed to be encouraged to share her
thoughts. I opened my hands to say: please go on.

"I shared your story with someone I know—someone who understands such things."

For some reason I decided to be just a little bit difficult. "Such
things as what?"

She waved her hand: you know.

I did not want to remember the hallucinations, or whatever
they had been. I sipped my coffee. "Who is this remarkable individual?"

"His name is Victor Valfort."

"I've seen his books. He was one of your teachers."

"Something of a magician, too."

"In the sense of 'artifice'?"

"He uses hypnotherapy. He is an adept, if I can use that word,
in dealing with the trance state. He's been very successful at
curing what used to be called hysterical symptoms."

"But it's been two or three weeks since I had any sort of vision." I tried to give the word *vision* a certain spin as I said it, as

though having a hallucination was like having a cramp, or a spell of dizziness. I did not convince myself. I know I did not convince Nona.

Her voice was low. She toyed with her spoon. "I study dying. How it happens, and what it means to the psyche as people—especially children—approach it. I can help children. I don't know how to help you."

"And this man does." It was not a question.

"He's in Paris."

"When will he be here?"

"I'm suggesting that you go see him."

"You must be joking. You've seen all my appointments. I'm too busy." I lowered my voice. "I'm all right now. Look at me—everything's fine."

"Your symptoms are probably situational," she began. "They will return when the conditions that caused them return. Right now you're satisfied. Things are going well. In a crisis, your body chemistry will change. And your visions will come back."

"You have it all figured out."

"I knew you'd be angry."

"I'm not angry. It's just that I think there's no emergency."

"I don't want to say anything that might hurt your feelings," she said.

"Such as?"

"I think there's something inside you. Buried. Some secret, or series of secrets."

I did not quite understand why her comments made me feel so tense. I glanced over at Fern. His radio was plugged into his ear, a black coiled wire out of his jacket collar that he kept adjusting. His eyes met mine. I tried to read his expression. Was there something wrong?

I watched the candle flame, its untrembling blade tapering to a long, golden needle. The candlelight on Nona's skin made her look like a woman shaped from oldest Egyptian gold. Her face was the mask of a Sybil. "I want you to promise to go see him," she said.

"I love Paris. When I get the chance—"

Her hand was on mine now, squeezing. "Soon. Please."

My laugh was easy, relaxed. "I think I'm beginning to feel jealous of this magus."

"There's no reason to."

"He certainly made a strong impression on you. Nona, look at me. I'm reliable. Steady. Sane."

"It's called denial, Strater. Sooner or later, the hallucinations will come back."

31

The night was calm. There were low clouds overhead, and a light drizzle. Some of the taller buildings seemed to vanish in the mist.

Fern slid into the front seat, started the car, and the Mercedes floated into the traffic. The armored vehicle moved at a stately pace.

"I have a good deal of faith in Dr. Valfort," said Nona. "But I think you should be forewarned."

I had not agreed to see him. She was pursuing the subject. I chuckled, hoping to feel as good-humored as I sounded. "Don't tell me. Let me guess. He's not one of those physicians who study the psyche because he's completely mad."

"He has very strong opinions."

"That's the warning?" I could not stand the friction between us, so leaned to her ear and kissed the soft, invisible down of her earlobe.

"Maybe we can take the trip together," I said.

"Promise?"

Denial. Maybe Nona was right. "Put on some music for us, Fern," I said, and he seemed quite happy to steer what must have sounded like a troubled conversation into steadier water under the temperate strains of Telemann.

We were another couple enjoying a San Francisco evening, sedated by music, and I forgot all but the moment, the gliding movement of the car, the jewels of the headlights. Sometimes there was drizzle on the windshield. Fog crept lower, closing over the tops of telephone poles and trees.

" 'The darkness which is not art,' " said Nona.

The lights of the traffic flowed over her, the shifting shadows of buildings, the rippling spill of headlights followed by the falling shaft of yet another shadow.

I recognized the quote, vaguely. I asked her to repeat what she had said.

"It's one of your own phrases, Strater. From that article you wrote for *Design Quarterly*. You said that we are the ones who discover light, and music, all the ingenuity we use to make life an experience that we can endure. But beyond us always is the darkness that isn't art, the Void."

"That's a nice, cheerful line of thought to take at a time like this." But I was a little disturbed. I was forgetting my work, my thoughts. Even now I had trouble recognizing the quote as my own.

I patted the back of Fern's seat. It was a more solid than usual piece of equipment, and I sensed that it, too, was armored, plated like the seat of a fighter pilot. "Let's slip on down to the Marina," I said.

"You got it," said Fern, his jaw working a wad of gum.

We surmounted a hill, at an intersection I did not recognize, and fog was suddenly dense, ragged, swirling. It would break only to show a dash of distant lights, a glimpse of parked cars, and then it closed again.

Slow. Beyond our control. Deliberate. The evening a video of itself that we reviewed from a point far in the future. The fog lifted. A car swept into the lane ahead of us. It was a dark shape, its chrome bright. The car squealed sideways. It blocked the street.

Fern stepped on the accelerator, then slammed on the brakes as the car jockeyed to a new position, wedging us in. Fern worked the Mercedes into reverse, and backed up, driving fast.

I turned to look and could see nothing. Beyond the car windows was an absence, a blank. There was nothing out there, only fog.

And then there was a dark shape, a car rolling toward us down the hill, its headlights dead. Fern stood on the brake.

"Keep going," I said.

That was the rule we had all learned. Keep moving. Don't stop, ever.

No hurry. Plenty of time. Fern looked at me for an instant that began to unfold into several seconds. He said, "Hang on."

He stared down the hill, his jaw working at the gum. He jerked the Mercedes into drive, and the big car accelerated. There was a feeling like joy at the sensation of speed. And there was another feeling: nausea and ice.

We crunched into the dark shape before us, our own car lurching to one side as the tires howled. Fern gunned the engine, and both cars churned down the hill with a smell of sulfur from the rubber. Then Fern yanked the transmission into reverse, and shook off the crumpled hulk before us.

Our car was slammed from behind, rocked from back to front, all of us thrown.

Fern fumbled at the glove compartment. It would not open. Fog shrouded us. A wind stirred the blank wall of drizzle, and the fog broke into tatters, into streamers and spinning wheels of vapor. We could see again.

But the street had changed. There was movement, people in the dark. Cars were rolling into place on the sidewalks. Car doors opened. Figures were hurrying toward us, black-garbed men with dark stockings or ski masks pulled over their faces.

Hurry, but with a certain lethargy. There were heavy thuds, chassis-shaking blows. I threw myself over Nona, taking her in my arms. Gunshots, I registered, my intellect gathering in the data while my body was rigid, nearly unable to move.

Shotguns. Fern pounded the dash, fumbled at the glove compartment. The door would not open.

Nona and I sat up, bracing ourselves. I wanted to say something to encourage Fern, but when I opened my mouth I could not make a sound.

Fern pumped the accelerator, and we slammed back and forth, our vision blurred, Fern wrestling the car into one position after another, trying to run down men who escaped only by leaping walls or their own crumpled cars. But the Mercedes listed. It was faltering, the stink of scorched rubber burning our nostrils.

We were slammed from behind again, and this time something had us. Fern floored the accelerator, and we dragged the wreck of a vehicle behind us, only to crumple into a car that blocked the hill.

A car struck us from the side. The Mercedes rocked far to the right, then fell back. Our bodies were flung, wrenched, half-tumbled, seatbelts cinching hard around our waists.

The music had continued until that last collision, a harpsichord's spindly sound dashed into silence.

The glove compartment had fallen open with the last crash. Fern reached into it. He had a pistol in one hand, and was wrenching at the steering wheel with the other, powering the engine. The car skidded, shrieked, shimmying in place, going nowhere.

"Stay in the car," he barked.

There were sounds from the car roof, dull thuds. They were on top of the car now, these dark figures. The butt of a shotgun or a rifle struck the window beside me, and the glass did not shatter.

Fern's handgun was big, a .45 automatic he had praised for its "swamp-grade stopping power." Fern levered the door open, and was outside.

The big pistol made a *wham* that rendered one half of my head numb, and deafened me. Fern braced himself against the car and fired again. Fern kept firing, hanging onto the gun with both hands.

And then he was gone.

Down. Fern was down, and the car door was open.

But surely that was a false impression of what had happened. Surely Fern was not hurt.

There was a subtle vibration. The engine block creaked. The car began to moan. The windshield shivered, and spidered, fragments like chalk, like bone fragments, bursting inward. The car was buckling, forced back upon itself. The doors were jammed within their frames, and the windows exploded.

One of the cars pressed the car door shut. We were in a fortress, and the fortress was beginning to cave in. The cars around us were pressing in, crushing the big, armored vehicle. The car trembled, durable enough to take the punishment only for awhile. The cars around us were big, too, and when the Mercedes would not crumple the cars methodically rammed its bulk.

The seatbelts would not unbuckle. The straps cinched us tighter, restraining us, squeezing the air from our bodies.

Nona was tight-lipped but calm as I contorted my way out of the grip of my seatbelt, without being able to work the catch. I helped her out of her harness.

Free.

We were out of the car.

Chemically tainted steam exhaled from under the curling hood. Gasoline rained from the tank onto the asphalt. The structure of the car was strong, but very gradually the car squeezed back upon itself, steel whining, crying out, metal popping loose and whistling past us.

32

We both saw it at once: beside the battered, steaming Mercedes there was a figure on the ground, in the green water that trickled from the radiator. It was a man in a suit, and as Nona and I hurried toward it, it was clear that the man we knelt beside was Fern.

His head was crushed, black and glistening remains streaming onto the street. Nona lingered with a physician's urge to attend, to make right.

Arms grappled for me. Figures had Nona. I struggled, freed one arm, and lashed out with my fist.

It was the leisure of it all, the ease with which it all took place, that amazed and sickened me. It was a game, surely. No one was really going to be hurt. Fern's injury was sham, and the police would be here soon.

They held Louisville Sluggers. The labels on the bats were clearly visible in the unreal light, black tattoos on the flesh of the wood. Men stood ahead of us, beside the steaming hulk of the Mercedes.

They had Nona. She was crying out.

I registered this as I wrestled with the arms that held me,

grappled me in place, a grip on the back of my head, in a knot of my hair, forcing me to watch.

I fought, kicking, twisting. I wrenched my shoulders, and I was free. One of them crouched before me, his bat in his fists. The man took two quick, sideways steps and lifted the bat to strike my skull.

My right fist caught his mouth, a sharp slither of tooth and lip behind the black nylon mask. He exhaled hot breath upon my fist. He gathered himself to strike. I charged him, knocking him down. Someone else's bat whistled through the air, and caught my arm.

There was a wet *crack*. I staggered, wallowing in a world that was suddenly sideways, lopsided, aswim and quaking. The pain was so great it wasn't even pain, a neurological white noise.

They're hurting Nona.

This time when they grappled with me, they held me harder, and there was no way I could work free. The hand at the back of my head, the hand digging into my scalp, searing my skull, forced me to look on.

Nona was on the ground. She was hurt.

The men worked hard, kicking, beating with bats aimed carefully, stabbing blows, work so quick that I could not associate it with Nona, except for the thought, wending through my semiconscious.

They are killing her.

I prayed, as I had prayed in the surf. *Make me strong.*

I had no thought for myself. I called out for Nona, again and again. They worked her expertly, twisting her one way and then another with their blows, shifting the angle of my body so I could watch as they took their time, like figures engaged in ritual slaughter.

Part Four

33

Whenever I opened my eyes, Rick was there, his hands clasped, his face taking on a smile when he knew that I was looking. But I always saw the look that had preceded the smile.

Above me was a white, dead expanse—acoustical tile, with the holes in rows. I did not have to ask where I was. The familiar walls surrounded me, with that thick, glossy paint, paint so shiny passing people cast not only shadows but dim reflections. I recognized this place. I was in the Medical Center, a few floors from Nona's children, and from her office.

"You're looking good," Rick would say, and my eyes would roll back to him.

There was one thought that returned again and again, amidst my morphine-coddled sleep: not dead.

Nona can't be dead.

I felt the insistence, the denial, working against what my rational mind knew had to be true. Remember, I told myself: the sloppy crunch of the blows.

The sickening, ugly sound of the bats.

It's better not to know. It's always better. That way you can pretend that everything is the way you want it to be.

Whatever you do: Don't ask the question.

I couldn't wait any longer.

I braced myself, and stared up at the ceiling. "How is Nona?" I asked.

But my words had been soundless, airy nothings. I tried again as Rick knelt close. This time my words were audible.

"They won't tell me," he said.

I tried to sit up.

"They won't say anything about her," he said. "When I ask they just give me that look—that doctor look."

The opiate was too strong, the pleasant lucidity lifting me, and yet pulling me from what I had to know, needed to know.

"But I'm sure everything will be okay," said Rick.

Meaning: He wasn't sure at all.

I was alone.

I grasped for the call button and missed. I took a moment to catch my breath, and this time I closed my hand around it and depressed the button.

The male nurse who fussed over me said, "Don't worry about her. You're looking fine." He was a big man, overweight, panting as he tucked in the sheets.

Fine, I repeated to myself. The word was a steel blade, the sound of meat sliced. *Fine.* It was the sour echo of the word *lie.* I had suffered a serious concussion, and such patients need peace. You might even lie to a person like myself to keep that patient calm.

"How is Nona Lyle?" I asked.

The television was on to a news program, a handsome, silent woman giving voice to some information about Europe, I gathered, as the map of that continent spread into focus behind her.

The nurse gave me a smile. "You're supposed to be resting."

"I need to see Nona."

He pinned me to the bed as I struggled.

My own family had been furtive when it came to injury and sickness. If one of us had ever been shot we would have stumbled home, and in answer to an inquiry about our health would have respond, "I'm fine, thanks." There had always been that formality about our home, a calm that was both benign and maddening.

I made an interesting discovery as I let myself relax, pretending to surrender the effort: I was not critically hurt. My arm was weak, badly bruised. I was stiff and ached all over. But I was not a wreck.

As soon as the nurse reached the door, I worked my way to the edge of the bed. I sat up, posed dizzily, and stood.

I was attached to various apparatus, tangled in transparent cords that reached into every limb, into one nostril and down my throat. When I lifted an arm a bag of saline solution swayed and a pole threatened to fall.

As a tennis player, Barry Montague was gifted with a brilliant serve. His weakness had always been the quick strategy of the game. I had usually found him easy to work out of position, a victim of the well-timed counterstroke.

Just as I began tearing adhesive tape off my arms so I could free myself, Barry was there. It was good to see him. I needed to hear the truth, and I knew that Barry could not lie to me if I had him by the hand and looked him in the eye.

Barry helped me lie down again. The room swayed slowly one way and then another. He adjusted the blanket over me, and then our eyes locked. He was hoarse. "Her condition is very serious."

"Is she still alive?"

Why did he hesitate before answering? "I would tell you if she wasn't, Stratton."

I choked on the words. I tried to sit up. "I don't believe you. She's gone."

"She's not gone," said Barry gently. "She's still with us."

Tears flooded my vision. I turned my head so they could spill from my eyes.

He gave a tired smile. "But she still has a long way to come."

"What does that mean?"

"It means that her recovery is slow. You've been here three days. You're doing well." He hesitated. "Nona is struggling."

"Struggling," I echoed.

"She's strong. She's a fighter."

I searched his words, echoing them in my mind. It was like

translating Caesar in my student days, easy sentences, interesting stories, but at the same time oblique and hard to tease into sense.

To swallow my saliva took an effort. The plastic tube felt like the shaft of a pencil caught, maddeningly, in my throat. I said, at last, "You're hiding something from me."

"I'm trying to," he said with a rueful smile.

"What's wrong?"

There was a long pause. "She's not responding."

"What does that mean? 'Responding.' Talk to me like a human being, Barry." I flung off my blanket. "I want to see her."

"It might not be good for her. She's too badly injured, Stratton." He adjusted my pillow, giving it a little punch from the side. "Everyone is very optimistic about you."

My lips formed the words: about me?

"Well, for both of you. The telephone has been driving the receptionists mad. There's a mailbag of cards in the mailroom. You've been beat up. Not one-tenth as bad as Nona, but you took some tough hits."

I weighed his sports-announcer diction against the way I felt about him, and decided not to be too critical. "I want to see her now. Help me out of this bed. Christ, it's not a bed—it's a web. Jesus, I have a—my penis is hooked up to something, for God's sake."

He said my name with that sharp, clear tone I remembered from the classroom, and from visiting people with disobedient dogs.

I was still, but I gave him a very hard look and he dropped his eyes for a moment. "As soon as possible," he said.

I waited.

"First thing tomorrow," he said.

I clenched my teeth, and found my tongue to be raw. I was aware of myself as I might be aware of another person. I was furious, and even in my damaged state I was stronger than my old tennis partner.

I was connected to poles, sacks of fluid. I was out of bed, and wires and cables clung to me. Urine spilled from a sack beside the bed, and flowed across the floor. I disconnected the catheter, with a yank that made me gasp as the long, hot wire pulled all the way down the shaft of my penis and fell to the floor.

I whipped the IV out of my arm. Barry called to someone just outside, in the corridor, and looked on as two large male nurses shouldered into the room. I gave them a move, a stutter step, a feint, but I was still too weak to dodge them. They stabbed a needle into my hip.

The two men wrestled me into the bed. I could feel the drug dissolving my strength. "If she dies, Barry, I'll never forgive you."

The drug had me. Pain, anguish, even love, was nothing. I tried to fight the sedative, but I couldn't.

Barry looked back from the doorway. His eyes were friendly, and I knew that he was a man I could trust. I took in the array of plants at the far end of the room, under the television. This greenery was a violation, I supposed, of hospital rule, but was the evidence of the handiwork of some of the City's more expensive florists and also the respect that the hospital owed my family.

"The first thing tomorrow," he repeated, and I lifted a finger in agreement, and in command.

I woke. Childress stood over me. I tried to sit up. The drug held me, sapped me. "You let this happen! You knew what they would try to do."

He sat down, said nothing.

"Don't even pretend," I said.

He looked tired. "We're looking for suspects."

I no longer had a tube in my throat, but even so my voice was rough. "You don't expect to find any." I recalled Fern's body lying in the street, and grief made it impossible to continue.

Childress picked at a callus on his palm. "Tell me what you remember."

"They wore masks."

"License-plate numbers. The makes of the cars."

I did not respond.

Childress blinked and rubbed a hand over his mouth, either uncomfortable or all-too sympathetic. "If you could give us any kind of description at all—"

But I wasn't really listening. It took a moment for me to realize that Childress had spoken. I was caught up in a violent reverie, a fantasy of revenge that surprised me, and I had to stir myself, shifting my head on the thin hospital pillow.

"These are violent times," he said, as though he couldn't bear the silence.

"Do you know anything about Nona's condition?"

"The doctors don't talk to me," he said. "Any kind of description. Size, age. Any impression of what race—"

I closed my eyes.

Childress's voice was easy, intelligent. He wanted so much to be liked by me, but his dislike for police work was too plain. "This is common when there's a violent crime. There's a selective amnesia."

"The light was peculiar," I offered, feeling the need to apologize, and to be kind to this man who wanted to be everything at once: cop, fellow citizen, sympathetic visitor. "Not bad, so much as shifting, all glare and shadow."

"That's very unfortunate."

We gave each other a long look.

"Can I tell you a secret?" said the policeman.

He wandered to the window of the room, an opening in the wall that disclosed virtually no view except for the sight of an angle of wall, concrete painted adobe yellow. I found myself once again liking this difficult cop.

I encouraged him to share his secret.

"If DeVere or Renman paid money for this, there's a limit to what we can do."

Once again, I missed Fern. He had thought of danger as so much rubbish to be removed by expert hands. A threat had brought a test pilot's glint into his eye.

"I'm going to post a guard in the corridor," said Childress. "Just to be safe."

"They didn't want to kill me, did they?"

"I guess not," he said.

"You know what I want to do."

"Understandable," he began.

"If I find one of them. Just one."

All that night I kept waking and thinking: Nona.

What are they hiding from me?

34

"**I** have to tell you something," he said. Barry blocked the doorway with his body. "I want to warn you," he said. He did not add anything further. He expected me to understand what he was trying to say.

"Get out of the way," I said.

"You'll see why I thought it was a bad idea."

My first impression was that Barry had taken me to the wrong room. There was a stranger in the bed, someone I did not recognize.

I took an uncertain step and stood mystified. My hand hesitated, then reached forth, and I touched her.

The white wristband read: Nona Patricia Lyle.

Nona was a mummy, blue, tube-festooned. She lay contorted, her hands bunched into fists.

I leaned over her. "Nona?" I said, speaking into the greenish cloth that swathed her skull.

I said her name again, and then Barry said, "It's best to let her be still."

I met his eyes.

"You've seen her," he said. "She's alive."

Her eyelids were blue bruises. Her lips glistened with glycerin or petroleum jelly.

"She can hear us now," I said.

"There's not a whole lot of reason to expect much in the way of cognitive function."

"She can hear us," I said. "That's one of the things Nona discovered. That people critically hurt, even dying, can hear us." This was a rebuke, and a reminder to Barry to remain upbeat. But it was also a message to myself, in wonder: She was still with us.

I kissed her.

"You will be well," I promised her. "Whatever it takes."

I leaned against the wall in the corridor. Barry leaned beside me. Neither of us wanted to talk.

"The prognosis," he said, "is anyone's guess."

"What's wrong with her?"

"We expected subdural trauma. After all, she was hit on the head pretty hard."

It impressed me once again that Barry was not articulate. "And?"

"She should be in better shape than she is."

"Her condition baffles you."

"That's right."

"She'll be all right."

Barry folded his arms. "I think you should be prepared," he said.

"She's not going to die, Barry. Somehow or other, you'll find some way to bring her back."

"We don't even know what's wrong with her."

"That can mean good news. If you don't know what's wrong with her—"

"Don't you see what I'm trying to tell you? Please don't make me spell it out."

35

"It's your mood," said Barry.

It was an effort to tie my shoe, but I managed.

"What's wrong with my mood?" I asked.

"It's inappropriate."

"I can't help it," I said. "I've made up my mind about something." I knotted my tie. Rick was in the corridor, talking to the policeman on duty, waiting for me. I stuffed my shaving kit into the overnight bag.

Barry adopted his most brisk tone. "I want you to stay here for another day or two. We can have you work with one of the staff psychiatrists."

"You always said that, except for Nona, they were a bunch of bores."

"Well," he said, regretfully, "they are. But they might be better than nothing."

"Barry, look at me."

"You suffered a deep concussion. They can be unpredictable."

"What are you afraid of?"

"I'm afraid of what you might do."

"Revenge?"

Barry did not answer.

"I have something else in mind," I said.

I knew how to win Nona from the place which had claimed her. I was beginning to understand that life was a series of bargains. Effort is expended for reward, money is exchanged for pleasure. I knew what Nona's life would cost me, and I would pay.

Rick had ordered the flowers, and the type of floral arrangement that dominated was a lush confusion of heather. They did not look like the usual flower for this sort of event, and I think that is what Rick intended, hoping to remind all of us of the more lively sort of garden, the one that is not the well-kept haven for the permanently asleep, but the sort for children and painters, and lovers.

Many people had known Fern, and liked him. It rained. It didn't matter. Black umbrellas were everywhere, sweating dark domes under the fine rain. The people who don't go out in the rain, my mother said, are "people made of sugar." By this she meant that these people were soft and without drive, and she was, I think, trying to prevent me from becoming a decorative male, like so many of the tall, well-tailored men who lounged in and out of my parent's parties, all good looks and money and, one sensed, without any strength unless it was the ability to drink until five in the morning.

It was not a downpour. The sun broke through, only to dazzle us like a trophy, far above anything we could attain, and then it resolved itself again into a tablet of calcium, a trace, and then nothing but the flowing, sun-bleached clouds.

There were many police. Childress was between two marble monuments in the distance, talking to a uniformed cop.

In the background, along a ridge, was a picket line of photographers aiming their cameras, some of which were on tripods. The cameras made a faraway squeal and whine whenever the figures of the mourners parted, giving the photographers a clear view of myself gazing at the cherrywood casket under the canopy, or looking down into the grave.

They were drawn to me. My story was still on the front page, after four days. There were diagrams of the street, estimates of the number of "club-wielding assailants." My fight with them was described as "heroic."

I was the center of the target, even now.

I had come straight from the hospital, dressed in a suit Rick had picked out from my closet. My left arm was in a sling, but I had stamina, and a sense of purpose.

People kept their distance as I made my way through the crowd. Snipers have been known to miss their targets.

Anna Wick wore bright red lipstick. She was now the sole captain of the DeVere empire. I was surprised to see her there, and then I realized that she must have come to catch my eye.

The earth from the grave was a small hill disguised by bright green artificial turf. I did not listen to the prayers, to the eulogy, finding the drone of the clerical voice irritating, forcing me to the back of the crowd.

I greeted Collie and her sister, a square-jawed woman with strong-looking arms who spoke in a whisper.

Only Rick stayed near me during the service, and afterward he kept close, as Fern might have. I told him that the flowers were beautiful.

"This isn't what I had in mind. I thought just a quiet service, graveside, intimate, was the best idea," said Rick. "It's hard to feel intimate with the media around, though."

"It's a beautiful afternoon," I said, awakened to the scent of grass by my stay in the hospital.

"It's terrible about Nona."

"I don't think there's any reason to be worried, Rick. She'll be all right."

"You're so sure of that."

"It's just one of those strange things that happen," I said, perhaps too airily.

"That's the difference between us," said Rick. He looked drawn, tired.

"Why do you suppose Anna Wick bothered to come?" I mused.

"She needs your help," he said, putting his hands into his pockets.

"Her people killed Fern."

"That's not what happened. She runs the DeVere empire, but most of the Renman people see her as expendable. She wants your help to consolidate."

"You're smart," I said, remembering in that instant the conversation I had enjoyed with Stuart. One could use craft, or strength, rarely both. "I wonder if I'm as cynical as you are."

"I would keep away from Anna," he said.

The photographers had packed their gear. They trailed away toward an assembly of subcompacts and vans, looking like hunters mildly satisfied with the day's kill.

Rick waited for me to enter the car, but I held back. I told Rick that I wanted a private moment beside the grave, and Rick sounded almost relieved to say that he understood. This was the Stratton he could understand, serious, thoughtful, loving.

Anna Wick had beckoned to me.

We walked together under a row of cedars, my leather soles squeaking on the wet grass. "I know the people who did this," she said.

"Why tell me?"

"They'll try again," she said. "And this time they'll kill you."

"I think I'll survive," I said.

"The cops won't help, Stratton. They don't even want to."

Rick was watching from a distance. Even from here I could sense his disapproval.

"She's just trying to set you up," said Rick. "You better have a talk with Childress."

We were in the back of a limousine, the day screened by the
tinted glass. "I'm not that worried about it."

Rick made an incredulous laugh. Then he grew somber. "If the
doctors can't do anything to help Nona. If they can't help her."
He was thinking something he could not bring himself to say.

"Are you saying that Nona might as well be dead?"

Rick opened his hands and let them fall. "It's a thought that
occurs, isn't it?"

"No, it doesn't," I said sharply. "Not to me."

He gave me a satisfied look, as though I had passed a test.
"Let's have dinner together. I'm putting together a security team,
and we can sit right there in Trader Vic's like presidential candi-
dates and nobody will lay a finger on us."

I told him that I couldn't.

I had plans.

36

The night was clear and it was warm.

The warmth came out of the ground, radiating upward. I
walked the streets to the Great Highway, and, swept by the
beams of the occasional pair of headlights, I hurried along the
shoulder of the road for awhile. Then I ran across the lanes of
the highway to the beach.

The beach there was broad and flat. There were a few
iceplants, straggling succulents, like barbed wire gone green and
slack. The plants were planted to keep the sand from blowing
into dunes across the highway.

There were stars. The sand was white, littered in places with
aluminum cans and scraps of charred driftwood. I made my way
to the edge of the water, to the spindrift, the lowly fleece, all that
is left of the surf when it has died on the shore.

There was no sign of any gift from the surf. Nothing glowed on the glistening wet sand. No voice called to me. There was only that buffeting near-deafness of the surf.

When I saw one at last I did not stoop to seize it. I waited, wondering if it was the one I sought.

It was the feather of a gull, upright in the sand right at the line where the wet sand and the dry meet. It did not glow, it did not possess a flush of color. But it was the only one, the only plume along the beach.

So at last I plucked it from the sand. It was the right size, and the point of its quill would do. I slipped it into my jacket pocket.

I hurried home, not looking at the houses I passed, not looking up at the passing men and women on the sidewalk. I could not be distracted. I could not be persuaded to take any other course.

I knew how to save Nona.

I lit a fire in my study. The room was finished now, and the new ash paneling reflected the light of the eucalyptus wood fire. From the pantry, I brought one of the cups my mother had prized, thin bone-china that was translucent and fragile. I went up to my study and returned with a large, uncut sheet of super-opaque paper and a fountain pen. I also brought down an Exacto knife, one of the razor-tipped wands I used for precise cutting.

I spread the paper on the cocktail table. I uncapped the pen. And then I could not write a single word.

This was the way to save Nona. I knew that. But I could not keep from wondering at what I was about to do. What had I come to, this night?

On the page I wrote, carefully: *My soul in exchange for power.*

I could not move.

Does it really say that? Had I written that, with this hand?

I stood. I backed away from the page, all the way to the mantle.

My hands were trembling. I could barely cap the pen. I knew that this was the end of my life as a human being. From this night on I would be something else, something like a man, but not.

At the same time, I felt absurd. This made swimming in rip-tides look like a dull effort indeed. I was crazy. I made a sound, an ugly, dry laugh.

My soul. What was it, after all? A thing of legend, an artifact of myth. There were no souls. There was no life beyond death, no essence within a living creature that could be described truthfully by such an ancient concept. So what I tendered was a thing that did not exist. There was no reason to be concerned for even an instant. I was cheating the Powers, whatever They might be, offering Them a currency that was worthless to me.

I was a fool. Nothing would come of this. Still—there was something sick about what I was doing, something unclean. Why? What could possibly be wrong with me?

People did worse things every night. People destroyed lives, depraved, cruel people, and never suffered a moment's conscience. Who was I to quail over this trifling deed?

And yet all the fears I had ever had about dying arose within me for a moment. Men and women dedicated whole careers to saving the soul, keeping it from endless suffering. Could I argue that not believing in the soul made this step any less serious? Perhaps. But I had the sense that I was about to do something ultimately sinful.

For Nona, I breathed. Or was it? Wasn't I interested in the other rewards that would spring from this?

I had already enjoyed a taste of the prizes They could bring me. I was shivering. Wouldn't I take my own life to win Nona back to the world of daylight? Of course I would. Then, what a cheap price my soul would prove to be.

The doctors were useless. The police powerless, or even in collusion with my enemies. I could not turn back. What was I waiting for? Didn't I want to hear the sound of Nona's voice?

I nicked the end of the quill, cutting a notch into it.

Then I lifted the sharp blade, a wedge no larger than a fingernail, before my eyes. I steadied my hand.

I cut my tongue. I let the blood from my tongue flow into the bone-china cup. The cut was deeper than I had anticipated. The blood made a chiming sound as it ran into the container, the sound growing deeper and more muted as the cup filled to one third of its capacity.

It was not too late. I could still turn back.

At first the cut had not hurt. Now it throbbed, and I found myself swallowing blood. I dipped the quill into the fluid. I squinted, making sure that the shaft of the feather was filling with the red ink.

Then I knelt over the sheet of paper, and signed my name.

I had to dip the feather into the cup twice, but when my signature was finished the final letters gleamed in the firelight, before they, too, faded to a brunette cursive.

Blood on a page, in the light of a fire, looks like tar, something originating with a living thing but far removed from it, a by-product rather than the stuff of life.

There. Done.

And everything was fine. The firelight was bright. The cut on my tongue didn't hurt anymore. Everything was going to be as I had wanted it. All I had to do was unwrap the night like someone receiving a gift.

And take what was mine.

37

I had never felt so alive.

I ran without tiring, with the steady stride of a marathon runner. There were almost no people out this late, and little traffic, but the streets were alive, the glistening reflections of bedrooms and stoplights pulsing in my sight.

For long periods I was aware of nothing but a sweet flavor in my mouth, and then I would wake to full consciousness and find myself, unexpectedly, in a garden, observing the slumbering carp, or in an alcove, aware of the drowse and murmur of sleepers above, around me.

I could taste the lives around me, as thoroughly as I could have tasted the smoke of a fine cigar, rolled it on my tongue, inhaled, and breathed it out again, enriched and poisoned.

It is in the closed places, the rooms, the hidden courtyards that we will never visit, that life takes place. The act of passion, the bribe, all begin the changes that will construct the life the streets can only deliver to be unpacked.

Listen, we say, pausing under a window. Someone is making love, or urging an infant to sleep again. Life possesses itself, complete, private, the wellhead sealed with the potted geranium, the stone saint staring into the crypt. It is a marvel.

And it is mortal. The people around me were distinct and comprehended, books I had read. I hurried, unaware of my footfalls, slipping from door to street to shadow. My clothing, my damp human garb, clung to me, the remnants of a life I was already forgetting.

Streets passed beneath me as I ran. "I see how beautiful it is," I breathed.

I had spent my soul, and a new life had been given to me.

The Medical Center was a blaze of fluorescent lights. There was activity there, in contrast to the sleep of the rest of the buildings I had seen. One ambulance backed up, and the rear doors were flung open. Another approached, red light lashing the dark.

Once I associated this sort of emergency with myself, feeling that I, too, could have an accident, suffer, lose my life. When I was inside the hospital I glided past the desk, and the two women holding conversation there did not even stir to look in my direction because I willed them deaf to my presence.

An elevator would be too slow. I pounded up the stairs. I reached the room where Nona had slept, and hurried into it, aware that the chamber was too dark, devoid any sign of her. The room was empty.

She was gone.

An adjoining room held a man wide awake, staring into the half-dark. Another room was occupied by a gray-haired woman whose hands fidgeted on the coverlet. I plunged past room after room.

"What have they done with Dr. Lyle?" My voice was as calm as I could make it, but it still ripped the silence of the nurses' station, a small domain of clipboards and scratch pads provided by the manufacturers of painkillers.

The nurse there considered me, and then, after she had finished thinking, continued to look at me blankly while her hand reached for the telephone. "Dr. Lyle?" she responded, stalling. "When was she admitted?"

I leaned over the counter. "Where have they taken her?"

The sound of my voice made her snatch at the telephone, and

miss. The other hand clung to a ballpoint pen, one of those cheap, black, institutional implements. "I'll have to check her file."

"Do," I purred, all courtesy and implied—but barely implied— impatience. For some reason she was not charmed by me. My tone did not strike her as well-mannered. I smiled, and she picked up the telephone.

I reached over the counter and took the receiver very gently from her hand. "It won't be too much trouble, will it, if you look through those files there beside you?"

"I'm not sure that I can help you—"

"I believe you can," I said, with a smile that made her drop her pen.

She searched, hurriedly. "I don't see it here, sir. If you would just let me make a call or two—"

Crush her, I thought. How dare she stand in my way?

Something about my eyes made her give me a fake, painful smile. "Please," she began. "Maybe someone from security can help you."

I had a struggle, within myself, for a rational thought. *Make her tell me. Make her find out, without alerting anyone.*

The nurse took a sharp breath, like someone pricked. There was a long moment. Then she picked up the phone and punched numbers.

At last she hung up and turned to me, her eyes bright with good cheer. "She's been taken to the Omega wing," she said.

The corridors had never seemed so narrow. The hospital had never seemed so jammed with trolleys of soiled laundry, with empty gurneys, with wheelchairs lined up against walls.

Omega wing was locked. I entered a side door, through a passageway of crisp, fresh white uniforms on shelves, dodged past a stack of boxes, and entered a hallway of muted light.

There was none of that sense of abandoned bustle here. There was nothing that reminded one of the fretful promise of most hospital wings. This place was badly lit, and the nurses' station was unattended.

I had never realized how artificial the air of a hospital is, how empty of living fragrance.

Nona was curled in her sleep. There was a glaze of perspiration on her forehead. She was breathing, very slowly. As before, her hands were curled into fists as I looked down upon her, this concourse of fluids, this woman dead to life.

The only light came from the red numerals in the medical equipment, and a gray glow from the hallway.

"Nona," I whispered. "Wake up and speak to me."

The power was in my touch, and I felt my fingers hum as I touched her face. "Wake up, Nona, and be with me."

Nona slept, and I could feel the dumb weight of her, the slung-down bulk of her flesh and bones, her stricken-animal stupor.

"Nona," I cried in a loud voice. "Nona, I want you to live!"

Make her live, I cried in my thoughts.

I knelt to the floor, trembling. It was happening. Surely it was happening. There—her breath was quickening. Look—the red digits of the machines that measured her metabolism were flickering, the registers ascending, her pulse responding.

Surely she was stretching, about to whisper, about to roll upon her back and open her eyes.

I was on my feet again, and turning her over, a plastic bag swaying above me on a steel pole. I rolled her gently, tenderly, afraid that I might wound her somehow, aggravate a needle thrust into a vein. I kissed her.

I kissed her, willing all that I wanted, all that I needed to share with her, into my lips, into her. I held her, weeping, calling her name, over and over, the incantation, the one word I knew.

I wished, with all the power I had purchased with my soul, for Nona to return to me.

And nothing happened.

38

There was a sound I barely recognized as my own voice, calling her name. I swept her into my arms. One arm dangled. The metal pole that suspended the plastic bag of saline solution swayed and nearly fell.

She was slack in a way that disturbed me. She was thin, her bones apparent in the feel of her body in my arms. But she had no spark of even twilight awareness, no roll to settle inward against me, no sigh to show her relief to be in my arms.

Careful, I cautioned myself. *Don't hurt her.*

She was beyond feeling. Her gauze-wrapped head lolled. One arm was bandaged, and her legs were swathed. She did not breathe so much as tug in air just a few slack inches and then, almost soundlessly, work it out again, like a person breathing the same exhausted breath over and over again.

I ceased abruptly. Someone was coming. I did not move, listening hard to footsteps in a far-off corridor. The steps pattered, receded, and at last left us alone together.

Lowering her to the floor, I slipped the IV from her arm, withdrew the catheter, carefully as the most skilled nurse, working to detach her from the courses and alternates of her bodily fluids. I cradled her recumbent weight, and I made hushing sounds, as though to encourage her to sleep. "Don't worry," I whispered. "Don't worry, Nona."

I would not surrender her. I would take her away. I would flee with her—I stopped myself, holding her there in my arms. Where would I take her?

Nowhere. I was outside the room, but I did not carry her any farther. Where would we hide?

I did not move again for a long time. Then I hurried toward a green EXIT sign.

I was determined: No one would take her from my arms. My

feet echoed in the stairwell. There was a scent of old concrete dust. Light reflected dimly off the handrails. I was climbing upward, carrying Nona.

I leaned into the pushbar of a door. The door did not budge. I leaned into it again, hard, and the heavy barrier made a scraping rumble, and slowly gave way.

The smell of night surrounded me, the sea air, the tannic flavor of trees, the purr and mutter of faraway traffic I had never been alive to before this night.

I stretched her on the gravel of the roof, massaging her hands. She did not stir.

She was waking up, I told myself. Keep talking to her. Keep massaging her arms. She's coming back. Look.

Her lips were parted, unmoving. Her eyes were closed, her breath so slow I could barely hear it, even when I held my own breath.

I swung a fist into the dark around me. "You lied!"

There was no response, but the silence was like that of a retreating wave, a falling back full of capability—and promise—to return.

A step pressed the surface beside me, a sound that was inaudible but which I felt in the lacquer of my own thoughts, like a sensation within my own flesh, a brain surgeon's probe calling forth this memory and that desire.

At first I felt joy. So, I thought, I was not alone. This was not insanity.

My joy did not last. "Lies," I whispered.

This presence was a source of light. I could not look at her. Her gown made a sigh as it brushed the skin of air, the last remaining heat of sunlight radiating from the roof.

"That's all you offer, isn't it?" I heard myself say.

The light did not answer.

"Perhaps I lied to myself," I said.

There was a long silence. Then a voice, like a whisper at the very edge of hearing. "There is a way for you to stir her," the voice said. "But in your selfishness you will not discover how."

Gravel scattered. "Tell me!"

There were no further words.

"Tell me how to wake her!"

The thought came: Soon you will forget all about her.

I said, carefully, deliberately, "We have no contract."

A force wrenched me to my feet, and slammed me against an air-conditioning duct. A weight pressed my ribs. The breath was crushed from my lungs. All the air was flattened out of me, and I went numb. I struggled, my arms twitching. I could not make a sound, or think any thought except: air.

I was suffocating.

The invisible grip let me drop, sprawling to the sharp stones. I tasted my own blood, and wiped the water that flowed from my nose on my sleeve.

The whisper again, a sound I could barely make out. "You think of us as evil," she said. "So that is how we appear to you."

"How can I win her back?" I asked.

There was no response. Her presence was like the flickering fragment that precedes a migraine, like the shard of light associated with a blow to the face.

They won't give you Nona, I said to myself.

What can they give you?

Sometimes the cheers of a crowd are so complete that they deafen, a solid wall of noise. Sometimes a leader steps before his adoring subjects and, when he speaks, is silenced by the love his supporters feel for him.

I was this prize, this man who stood before the senate of the dark and found myself buffeted by their acclaim. I was no longer a man who had lost his humanity. I was one of their creatures, and while I had no hope, what hope did any man possess?

For a moment I thought I could escape, forgetting that what I breathed was the same air that sustained Nona, except that she was still alive, however vanquished, while I already felt the socket in me, the stump that had been my soul.

I gathered Nona into my arms. The gravel was unclean. So was I.

Perhaps I had struck a bargain with nothing more than my own insanity. I lectured myself in a wry, peevish inner voice: Your own mental illness, your own circus of hallucinations, would make nothing happen in the world of plasma and blood gases.

Whatever I had bargained with, I could not turn back.

"Let them attack me again," I said. "The people who did this."

Again—silence.

"That's what I want. Let them try again."

There was a silence, and the light around me was dimming.

"I can have that, can't I? If I can't have Nona, then I can have revenge."

There was no answer.

39

It was a bad question to have to ask myself: How did I get here?

I did not recognize this room. There was firelight, and I was not alone. That peculiar fear had me, that sensation of not knowing the walls, the floor, the furniture.

There were two people with me. I was very near to guessing who they were.

I was on a sofa. There was a soft footfall. Rick adjusted the blanket that covered me, a heavy afghan. It was the sort of action our mother must have made when we were children, a lift of the blanket, and a careful folding over and adjusting of the counterpane. A bed, even a temporary one such as this sofa, is a magical place, a place of refuge, of dream, of procreation and healing.

"Everything will be all right," said Rick. It was that ancient optimism, perhaps the first lie one family member ever told another.

But it was a comforting sound, the low murmur of Rick's reassurance. We were in a comfortably messy study, large volumes on bookshelves beside computer software and stacks of journals.

"He looks okay," said Rick. He sounded eager to convince himself.

A familiar voice said, "He's physically quite sound. When I got to the hospital I saw him as he is now. Physically quite well, his blood pressure normal, his pulse rate a steady fifty-six per minute."

Rick accepted a bourbon, and both men settled into chairs, but it was with a false ease.

Barry could have been fishing for an explanation. Rick said, with a trace of pride, "Stratton's always kept himself in good shape."

"That's one way of putting it."

"We heal fast, too." "We" meant: our family, and, in light of my mother's condition, Rick might not have been quite truthful, but I was touched by his words.

"I suppose I understand," Barry said. "He visited Nona, and was overcome. I don't blame him."

"I didn't feel right about leaving him tonight. I kept calling, and after awhile I was so nervous I dropped by his house."

"Did he seem to have left in a hurry?"

"Stratton's always been the organized member of the family. I've always admired that."

There was a long, silent reverie on the part of both men, Barry's silence more complete, Rick's quiet of the restless sort, legs crossed and uncrossed, liquor sipped, and then gulped. "That's great bourbon."

"Twenty years old," said Barry.

Rick accepted more. Barry commented with enthusiasm on the oaky flavor of the bourbon, and I knew that Rick was being polite, as well as simply solicitous of more liquor when he had finished this second drink. Rick had never cared for overelaborate discussion of food or wine, but Barry prided himself on his knowledge of liquor and tennis-racquet technology.

"I suppose he can hear us," said Rick.

"He might, but I doubt it. He's in a sort of torpor."

"His eyes were open when I came in."

"Maybe he's awake, then. Ask him."

"Strater. Can you hear me? Wiggle something."

I listened to the snapping of the fire in the fireplace, intent on the silence between their words.

They both waited for me to make some movement of arm or leg, but I did not care to stir.

Barry thought for awhile. Then he continued, "I took a risk bringing him here. Medically, maybe it wasn't the smartest thing to do. But I thought of how much Stratton would hate this kind of publicity, and I also reflected that he needed something more than what our hospital can offer in the area of psychiatry. Now that Nona is—" He worked towards a better word, and failed. "Now that she's gone."

They were both silent. Then Barry continued, "I came close to letting the neurologists do a serious workup on him. But I looked into his eyes and made one of those snap decisions . . ."

Perhaps Barry wanted to be congratulated, or at least reassured, that he had made the right move. Rick understood this a moment too late, but he was warm in his expression of gratitude, his praise for Barry's good judgment, and went on to admire the library, and the stonework of the fireplace.

"The look in his eyes bothers me, too," said Rick. "It has for some time."

I could sense the shake of Barry's head. "Medically he is a remarkable specimen. He doesn't even look the way he used to. Have you noticed? He looks stronger and even younger somehow."

"He was always a good-looking man," Rick said, with a touch of fraternal protectiveness. For a moment Rick did not speak, or could not. He cleared his throat, and said, "I'm so glad he's in your good hands, Barry. You've done a very good thing."

"Listen, when my brother died a few years back I was so broken up I couldn't eat or sleep. The thing is, though, that after awhile we forget. We simply forget, and go on living."

"He's taking it hard."

"Nona Lyle was a tremendous human being."

After pouring himself some more bourbon, the scent of the liquor reaching me, Barry said, "Sometimes I wonder what I'm doing. What it is to be a physician. The money is satisfying, and the sense of being somebody. But you realize how little even a skilled doctor can do."

Rick made his question sound motivated by civilized concern, but I could tell how deeply troubled he was. "It's a crime to keep her alive like that."

"She's self-sustaining. Breathes for herself. She's very much alive. But . . ."

"I don't call that life."

Barry did not speak.

Rick was done with his drink, too, and I could hear the glass slip across the surface of a table. Rick was no longer making conversation.

"I have to ask," said Barry. "As a doctor, and a friend—what is Stratton up to?"

"What do you mean?"

"Did he want to take Nona's life?" He had stepped to the fireplace. His shadow bulked across the ceiling.

"By dropping her off the roof?" Rick said, sounding dazed.

Neither of them had to mention DeVere's name.

Rick spoke softly. "We can't do anything without Stratton's consent."

"How is your mother doing?" asked Barry, no doubt about to embark on the possibility that mental instability had a genetic root.

I sat up.

There was a silence. Then the two men greeted me, encouraged me, said that I had been found unconscious at the hospital, and brought here to the warm fire, both men adopting a simplified form of speech, the way one addresses a sickly child. Or perhaps it only sounded that way to me. I knew, now, how undernourished our psyches are, how little we know of the truth.

I was vibrant, clear-headed. Even my vision was sharper. I was aware that Rick's eyes were on me, glittering with firelight. Barry was easy to counter-lob, a player I could outmaneuver. But Rick would anticipate me.

"You had an accident," said Barry. He stated this hypothesis as a certainty, something he had ascertained beyond a doubt.

"Really?" I said, my voice the tone of mild and courteous interest, a man learning of the minor misfortune of someone he did not know. "An accident?"

"You lost consciousness, at the hospital." Barry's voice was kind, but wary.

"I appreciate the care you have shown," I said. "I have never felt better."

Rick was silent, studying me, his head cocked to catch my tone.

It was true. I had never felt quite this way before. I felt affection for Rick, and friendship toward Barry, and loyalty toward both men. But I felt a strong contempt for their human ignorance, their puniness, their feeble grip on the major passions of life.

"I'll take you home," said Rick.

"How is Nona?" I asked.

"She was in your arms," said Barry. "On the roof."

Both men waited for me to offer an explanation. I straightened my tie, wishing for a mirror.

"I was about to suggest something," said Barry.

"I think Stratton just wants to go home and take it easy," said Rick.

"I was about to suggest," Barry continued, "that you tell me— and your brother—what you are doing."

I made a flippant remark, responding that, for the moment, I was enjoying the fire.

"There's something wrong with you." Barry's clumsy earnestness made me laugh.

They did not join me in my laughter.

"I'm about to suggest a period of rest," said Barry.

"You mean 'confinement,' don't you, Barry?" I kept my tone quiet, but the question had an edge.

"Unless you have an explanation—"

"Is that your recommendation as friend, or as physician?" I said.

Rick had stood, and he did not speak for awhile. He leaned against the mantle, studying the fire. He stirred the embers with a poker, and then he set the iron aside. "Stratton couldn't stand to see Nona like that."

I did not respond.

"Maybe he was thinking that she wouldn't want to go on the way she is," said Rick. "I know the feeling."

"You wouldn't let them put me away," I asked abruptly, "the way we put Mother away?"

Rick made an involuntary jerk of his head. He would rather not have this conversation in the presence of anyone else, even someone as kind as Barry. "You're not like Mother."

"But I make you nervous," I said. I could not keep myself from pity for my brother, who could not know the world we inhabited as I now knew it.

Rick turned away and would not look into my eyes, and that made his words sound all the more truthful. "There is something wrong with you. You're different than you used to be. It was happening before we lost Nona."

It was Barry who caught my eye, stepping to his telephone, holding his personal telephone book open with a finger.

"I'm suggesting quite an advanced place. It's a private sanitarium," he said when I turned so my shadow fell over him. "Discreet and professional. You don't know how many famous people have been secreted there while they worked through one sort of crisis or another."

There had always been something a little prosaic about Barry. He was a good doctor, and an alert human being, but he allowed himself to choose the most shallow expressions. I was not about to "work through" a crisis, and I did not consider myself to be simply a "famous person," whatever definition of "fame" I might have considered.

"Hang up the phone, Barry," I said, very quietly.

"I'm going to ask them to expect us in—" he glanced at his wristwatch—"half an hour."

"You amuse me." I said this with a bored tone.

Barry's face twitched. "Let's face it, Stratton, I can't in all conscience let you go on like this."

"Put down the telephone," I said.

Barry made a fake laugh. "Good heavens. Listen to you. You sound close to strangling me. Doesn't he, Rick? Sound close to wringing my neck?" A forefinger was busy as he spoke, punching numbers.

"I'm not going anywhere," I said, but Barry was talking, announcing his name, and asking "with whom am I speaking?"

Then he moved his mouth, shaping words, and made no sound. He made a dry squeak, gaping, wide-eyed. I had my hand around Barry's wrist, and his hand was white.

His fingers quivered. He gave a cough. I squeezed harder. He went limp, and sat down, still holding the telephone, still making silent words.

Rick called out, telling me to stop.

I squeezed harder. He replaced the receiver with his other hand, missing and finding the telephone. He looked at me, and he looked at Rick, and shook his head, bright with sweat.

I released his wrist.

I wanted my voice to be gentle, the sound of someone telling pleasing but fairly unimportant tidings. "There's nothing really wrong with me. It's just that, for the moment, I want to be alone."

"Jesus, Stratton," said Barry. "You hurt me!"

I washed my face in Barry's bathroom. The water felt wonderful. I did not look any different to myself. My usual, guarded self-examining gaze, my hair tousled. I had never liked looking at myself, always feeling that for all my decent looks Rick was the one with the face cameras loved.

Was I wrong? Was there a certain light to my eyes now?

I thanked Barry, and then turned to my brother, his face care-worn in the firelight. "Take me home," I said. "I have so much to do."

"Really?" said Rick, hopeful and skeptical at once.

I was puzzled with myself. For the briefest moment I had trouble remembering my brother's name.

40

Rick drove me through the dark streets. We didn't speak until we parked outside the house.

I told Rick that I didn't need his further attention. "There's nothing wrong with me," I said to his unspoken objection. I had to put on an act. I had to pretend to be a human being.

He let the engine idle at the curb. When he spoke he said, "I couldn't stand it if it happened to you," he said. "I couldn't bear to see you like Mom."

There was a car parked up the street, two men sitting. I could not see their features in the dark. Rick followed my gaze. "I hired some security."

I felt a great rush of fondness for Rick. "We grew up being afraid, didn't we?"

"Of everything," he said.

* * *

There on the cocktail table was the document. My signature
had darkened even more. The clotted letters could have been
written in feces instead of blood. The paper made the slightest
whisper as I carried it up to my bedroom and placed it in the
pages of the Milton.

The quill was clotted with blood aired nearly black. I slipped
that into the volume, too.

There was so much around me that was false. Newspapers,
magazines—distortions. There was even a copy of *The Economist*
featuring an article on Renman's "fading empire." I knew that
Renman's empire remained all-powerful.

I burned that magazine, and others filled, I was certain, with
similar lies. Then, without hesitating, I spent what remained of
the night burning my drawings, my plans, my photographs—all of
my work. It took a long time. The photographs were nearly all in
the form of slides, and they were easy to burn. They burned with
a bright blue flame, gem-size gardens vanishing in an instant. The
bigger pieces, the works on paper, the drawings rolled up in
tubes, years of it, took time, and yet my life's work did not even
heat the room.

Paper burns brightly. At one point the fireplace and the chimney rumbled, the conflagration loud. It was true that I could not
burn the work no longer in my possession. I could not burn the
work on exhibit in various places, and I could scarcely destroy the
actual fountains and gardens I had created. But I burned all that
I could, every drawing tablet, every sheet of acid-free bond. They
left winking citadels of ash, which I broke up easily to gray dust.

The shelves, the closets, the drawers, were empty when I was
done. The work I was going to produce in the future would be
finer than anything I had managed to produce in the past. I knew
now how the compact worked: I could not have the woman I
loved, but I could have everything else.

I stepped from the elevator in DeVere headquarters. The secretary there recognized me at once, and she fumbled for a button
on her desk.

A security guard stopped me, a man in a camel hair sports
jacket and the sort of bearing that is intended to communicate
the single impression: I have a gun.

There was a sense of frantic movement beyond my vision. Telephones were snatched up. Computers were switched off. People scrambled.

The guard saw the look in my eye and took a step back. I expected him to say that he was going to have to ask me to leave. But when he jockeyed into position behind me it was as though he wanted to prevent my departure.

Two other guards joined us, and we walked down the corridor together. The entire building seemed to grow silent.

"You came alone?" asked Anna Wick.

I was keenly aware of the nuance of speech, the quality of light. I heard a guard's stomach grumble, and I could smell the correction fluid on a distant secretary's desk.

Make me so alive they cannot kill me.

I held forth my hands: alone.

"I'm very surprised to see you here." Anna was in the doorway to the office, a red plastic folder in her hand. "Surprised," she said, "but happy."

She was more than surprised. She was frightened. "We have business to discuss," I said, amazed at my own calm.

She managed to speak in her usual tone. "Security in this place is the shits. Until they get done tarring the roof."

She dismissed a small group of assistants, and the young men and women fastened their portfolios and scurried from the room, none of them, pointedly, glancing at me.

She shut the double doors behind us. I absorbed the virtual silence, the whisk of her shoes across the carpet.

Alive. I felt so alive.

She gazed upon me with a look of pleasure in her eye. There was another feeling there, too.

"You look like a man in a hurry," she said.

"I decided that we should have a talk."

"I like that." She seemed to roll my words on her tongue. "I admire a bold approach. But tell me, Stratton. What is it you're going to do?"

She waited for my response, and when I didn't make one she laughed. "You can't do anything here without Renman's permission."

I allowed myself an expression of surprise. "I'm not worried about Renman."

She smiled. "You're so sure of yourself." She slipped the red folder into a drawer in a file cabinet, a sunset-russet bit of office furnishing so well made that the drawer was virtually silent. "I find that very attractive in a man. You're so ready to take."

I stepped behind the desk. The great wooden plateau was scented, vaguely, with beeswax. There was a vase of black Oaxaca clay and three long-stemmed roses, the hybrid Silent Lady, the name for which had been inspired by my mother. The petals were a port-black, a color I doubted my mother ever wore.

"But it's Renman you need to see, not me," she said.

"You'll help me."

"Why should I?"

I recognized the look in her eye. "Because you're afraid of me."

"Did you kill him, Stratton?"

I did not answer her.

She was a woman used to disguising her emotions, but her smile was too bright. "As long as Renman thinks you did, you're a dead man."

"You think I shouldn't have come here," I said.

She hesitated, making a small motion with her head: We were being overheard, recorded. I saw something in her eye. She had resented DeVere, and the thought of his death pleased her. "You might even consider it justice. He wasn't a nice man. But what I said in the memorial service was true. People will remember him. God, I hated that service. All that cheap perfume, all those overweight people in black. But I was sincere, in a way. He was the real thing. He had talent."

I sat in the desk chair. I studied her for a moment. Her blond hair was loose, her blouse a lavender silk chiffon. This was not the usual DeVere look. DeVere had disliked what he called "flower hues," preferring colors of earth, colors of hillsides, of mesas and red rivers.

I took in the décor, the paintings, the carpet, the way the office was not a rectangle but a trapezoid, a shape that gave a sensation of space and freedom. The room was a study in DeVere style, a look that one magazine had called "half Siena and half Santa Fe." This was where DeVere had humiliated me.

This was where he had sat, running his world from behind this massive, naked desk. It was all so huge, now, without his presence. The Bay Bridge commanded the view out the window, the bolted steel orange in the morning light.

"Maybe he was in my way, too," she said. "Maybe I don't miss him all that much."

I said this more to myself than to her: "The future is going to be nothing like the past."

"It's your future now," she said, as though she did not quite believe it.

"If I survive."

She sat across from me. "It was a mistake to come here."

"I know what's going to happen."

"The next time someone attacks you, it won't be amateurs."

"They were amateurs?"

"One of those gangs." She shrugged. "Chinatown, the Fillmore. All it takes is cash."

I could not bring myself to describe what they had done to Nona.

"The next time," she said, "it will be someone professional."

I rested my head against the high-backed leather chair. "My brother has people watching me. And the house has a fairly decent alarm system. It's not unbeatable, but it's good."

"The next time someone attacks you, it won't be so simple." She poured herself water from a crystal decanter, and I saw the way her fingers struggled with the grip. I saw the way she met my eyes. Her mouth was dry. The water tasted good to her.

"It wasn't simple last time."

"You should go now." Her eyes said *hurry.*

"Men and women never used to talk like this," I said. "Conversation between the sexes became fashionable only when tea was introduced, something for gentlewomen to serve with their own hands to their male guests in the withdrawing room. Before then, the women had no interest in conversing with men, the drunken, genteel hound breeders."

Her eyes were wide. She was smiling, moving the glass from one place to another across the surface of the desk. "I tried to warn you, Stratton," she said. "Didn't I?"

"That's why I came here. I'm not afraid."

Her voice was husky. "But you should be."

Alive, make me alive.

"My mother used to love roses," I said.

When a door opened, the stealth of the step, and the location of the door, surprised me. I did not expect an entrance from the side, and I did not expect such a swift response to my presence. I had been willing to wait.

I did not turn to look. I had never had such good hearing. I could smell the new presence in the room, a mid-grade after-shave, and a sense of human bulk. The silence in the room changed. Whoever he was, he was big.

Anna did not want to witness this. I read her eyes. She was one of those people who like to be insulated from violence. If harm was done, she did not want to see it. Her eyes told me that I had a few seconds to get out of the chair. I felt compassion for Anna. She did not, when it came down to it, want to see me killed.

He can't hurt me.

It was almost amusing to see her features stiffen, her smile go hard, her eyes telling me that it was too late.

41

Why does the rose, that slender stem, have thorns? For protection, of course, but why don't the honeysuckle vine or the climbing wisteria have thorns? Some careful absence of good fortune pruned the rose into its meanness. Evolution is accident. It consists of what does not happen as well as what does. It consists of absence, a lack of water, of light, or the purest absence, the lack of creatures who can digest the thorns and must select instead the new shoots of timothy.

I watched Anna Wick's eyes, and they told me all I needed to know.

I spun out of the chair and lifted one hand. I was slammed back into the chair, writhing, my arm paralyzed. I kicked hard against the desk, and forced the chair backwards.

My chair fell to one side, and someone fell with me. I struggled on the floor, unable to do anything but wrestle in one place with a wire held, garrot-fashion, around my neck, my arm, and part of the headrest of the chair.

I was pinned. But there was a moment of stillness inside me. The loop of wire was in no position to do me much harm. There was a lucid interval in which I realized that I was trapped, but not in immediate danger of dying. And there was another, starker understanding. In a moment my attacker would release me just long enough to get a new grip on his piano wire, and then he would try again.

And next time the wire would not miss.

I jammed the chair backward, pushing with my feet, and we scuttled back, a monster made of two men and an executive chair. The force of my kick slackened the wire just enough.

I wrenched my shoulders and was on my feet.

He was a large man, with gray hair on his head and tufts of it in his nostrils. He did not hesitate. My escape was of little interest to him. His expression was determined, but not malicious. It was the intensity of a plumber, the frown of a carpenter fumbling for his hammer.

The loop was around my neck again. His fists met, but before he cut into my neck I kneed him in the crotch, hard.

He did not go down, but I confused the effort, the wire losing its bite. I forced his head back, kicking, kneeing, all the while forcing him against the wall where I began, methodically, pounding his head against the plasterboard.

A large chunk of the wall caved in. We were showered with white dust. Big slabs of wallboard attached themselves to our elbows and shoulders. We worked ourselves out of the fragments of wall, and he was stronger than ever, gouging at my eyes with his thumbs.

My vision squirmed, lightning and galaxy-scarlet in my sight as he stabbed at my eyesockets. I seized a thumb between my teeth, and bit as hard as I could, down into the bone. I shoved his head back against one of the steel wall studs.

I began pounding again, and this time the wall did not give way. The beam was blue-black, still decorated with the yellow crayon of the construction foreman years ago. Blood flowed from his thumb into my mouth, the thumbnail on my tongue like a thorn. His free arm tried to loop the wire around the back of my skull, fighting for a place around me, but I slammed the gray-haired head into the steel beam until the arm began to weaken.

For years I had stepped into the streetlight to avoid the passing car, eyed my mail for a letter bomb, a ransom demand, a scissor-and-paste missive of hatred.

Those days were done. When the head became sloppy, I spat out the thumb, releasing the arm streaming with blood. I kicked the body as it hunched, trying to cover itself up. One hand still fished toward me with the wire. There were grips of black electrician's tape, wound around and around to make handholds. A knob of black tape struggled toward me, the wire having a vitality of its own, like a plumber's snake, a fight quite independent from the fist that held it.

I snatched the wire, and pulled hard.

The length of wire in my hand, I stepped before the white-powdered, bloody mess before me. I whipped the wire around the neck, and cut into it, using all my strength.

Anna had shrunk against a far wall. Her hand, with plum-dark fingernails, was to her face.

What was I doing?

What am I doing with this wire?

I dropped it. I fought free of the body and stumbled away from it.

The man made a retching sound, rising to his knees. His hands were at his head. He tried to get up and could not, falling back against the wall, his weight caving in another section of plasterboard.

I was not a human being.

42

I put my hand on the telephone, and Anna said, "Don't!"
I looked at her, mystified.

"I'll take care of everything," she said.

I thought for a moment that she must mean that she could call an in-house physician, or bring some sort of miracle to pass.

I called 911.

It wasn't that easy. I was trembling, and the numbers on the buttons did not look like numbers to me, but something unrecognizable.

I told them that I was Stratton Fields. I said that I thought I had killed a man at the DeVere offices on Montgomery Street.

I could not bring myself to look at the body.

Anna handed me a drink. I tasted it and then left it on the desk.

"You know what you're doing," she said in a tone of quiet amazement.

The roses were still there, upright in the vase. There was the softest velvet sheen on the petals.

I could not speak to her.

"We're going to make a good team," she said.

She showed me to a washroom, a large room with a bathtub and a sheaf of dried rushes in the corner. The soap was unscented coconut oil with DeVere's signature imprinted in it.

My eyes in the mirror showed no feeling. I had enjoyed the fight. That is what disturbed me. I had planned it, anticipated it with pleasure, and when I saw my attacker's blood I had relished the sight.

When I stepped from the washroom there were police, there was the damaged wall, and blood, but there was no sign of my gray-haired opponent. Anna was deep into an explanation. Strong words. Lost tempers. No real harm.

The police officers greeted me respectfully. "Do you subscribe to this description of the events?" one of them asked, a young one, fresh from textbooks and the firing range.

I told them what had happened.

"Self-defense," said the older one.

"Do you know the name of the assailant?" asked the other. I had the impression that they were interested in arresting him, and were on the verge of congratulating me.

I was trying to make a confession. Their attitude told me that they would not mind if I beat one of DeVere's myrmidons to a boneless pulp. I knew how things stood: public opinion did not favor the DeVere empire. DeVere had tried to manipulate the award. The distinguished Fields family deserved satisfaction. The police were concerned for my health, wanted to know if I thought I would need medical attention. Someone from the department would contact me when it was convenient to take a statement.

Then they left with Anna to look for what they had begun calling "the suspect," leaving me feeling that I would be able to do anything I wanted—anything at all—and get away with it.

"If there was a body, Anna Wick took care of it," said Childress.

I had wanted this conversation far from any of Renman's people, far from any possible listening devices, and far away from my own house, with its Milton on the shelf to remind me of what I had done.

I had been a little surprised that Childress had been so eager to meet me away from tape recorders and underlings. I understood, however, when he said, "It doesn't matter if you killed him, or who he was. No one would blame you."

My tone was one of disbelief. "It doesn't matter!"

"Do you want it to matter?"

We walked through the shadows of Golden Gate Park. A photographer walked backward ahead of us, squeezing off shots of the two of us. I had become a walking photo-op, and Childress was rumored to be close to announcing his candidacy for supervisor. We were trailed by a couple of plainclothes police, men chewing gum and watching everything that happened around them in a way that reminded me of Fern.

"I thought it was a sin to kill someone," I said.

We kept our voices low, our expressions the sort of public unconcern that appears so often in newspapers and news videos of politicians and celebrities.

"I don't know about sin," he said. "You realize what people are saying about you."

"Enlighten me."

"They say some people should be excused if they decide to cut their way through life. Used to be they said it about DeVere. Now they say it about you. DeVere was hungry. He made deals wherever he could. If he wanted a better price on Egyptian cotton, he dealt with importers who weren't, maybe, totally legit. He helped a friend, he got helped."

Childress considered for a moment, and then continued, "And with Dr. Lyle in what the papers are calling a 'vegetative state,' nobody would blame you if you decided to strangle someone. You have public opinion in the palm of your hand."

I thought for a moment. "I've expected DeVere's old associates to see me as an irritation."

He laughed, a sound like a grunt. "They hate guys like you."

"What do *you* think?"

He took his time answering. "One or two people in the police department have the same idea. Maybe you killed Blake. Maybe you killed DeVere."

"You're keeping something back."

He smiled without mirth and shook his head. "I hate being a cop."

I said nothing.

"Some people," Childress continued, "say they saw someone vaguely answering your description in DeVere headquarters the evening he died. The witnesses are not definite, but the question has come up hard. Maybe you did it."

The sugar-frosting conservatory, the Hall of Flowers, gleamed before us. The splendid construction was modeled after the glass-and-metal flower sanctuary built by Prince Albert for the London Exhibition.

I motioned Childress into the conservatory. It worked—the camera did not follow, and the two dark-suited cops stayed outside. The hothouse was too overgrown, and did not offer the opportunities for pleasing camera angles, and many policemen are suspicious of closed spaces.

"If you did something. If a man did something. And came to regret it." Childress thought for awhile. "He could use some help."

The air was a paste, heavy on the tongue. Childress was a little less happy than I was to be in this elaborate hothouse. He surveyed his surroundings without love. "No one," he said, "wants to see Stratton Fields go to prison."

The windows were washed with white, and sunlight radiated through the white transformed from the light of a star to something subsumed and traduced by plantlife. It was nearly hot in the conservatory. The smell was rich: mulch, wet concrete, and the nonodor that was the exuded carbon dioxide of so many broad-leaved plants.

"It's all so easy," I said.

"Detectives have been asking questions," he said. "Legitimate private investigators, the kind that handle Beverly Hills divorces. The feeling is that we won't prosecute because you're an old San Francisco name. The fact is, we don't have a case. Yet."

I spoke again, knowing that I had heard enough. "What can you do about it?"

"Not much. Tell you to take care of yourself."

"Do I look worried?"

"That beating that killed Fern, and . . ." Childress had the good sense not to mention Nona. "We don't know who they were, but there are more like them. People admire you. Maybe that bothers people like Renman."

"I'm an innocent man."

"Are you," he said. He said it flatly, without any intonation except one that meant he did not believe me. "Innocent, guilty." He sighed, as though to say: What difference does it make?

The atmosphere in the conservatory always made me feel enlivened and stifled at the same time, the humidity and the wealth of life combining to make a place that is a part of no other world. Perhaps it was this building alone that inspired my career. Make a new world, I had told myself as a much younger man, a new world more like the world than the earth itself.

"What's going to happen next?" I asked.

He answered easily. "Another attempt on your life."

I turned to look at him.

Some plants remind me of people. They live in soil so leached of hope that they have to steal nourishment. We stood before a pitcher plant, a jungle survivor that drowns insects and absorbs their proteins.

"What would be the fun," he said, "if we knew when?"

I laughed, and for a few moments Childress and I understood each other, liked each other again, and did not want this conversation to end.

"You want to quit being a cop," I said at last. "You want to be somebody."

Childress touched a leaf with his forefinger. He was sweating. His lips formed an answer, but he did not speak.

"You don't like it in here, do you?" I asked.

"I hate it," he said.

Our passage stirred the leaves around us, and water pattered from the spouted leaves. We made a wrong turn, lost for an instant along a sidewalk so long-damp the green stain of the moss had begun to dissolve the concrete like acid.

When I spoke again, I said, "You'd make a good mayor."

"A month ago you were just a respected name. Now—" Childress shrugged. "Now you can help people."

"I'm going to talk to Renman. I'm going to get what I want from him," I said.

He considered this. "Remember your friends."

The air outside was cool, nearly cold, drenching us with light.

I might have killed Blake, and DeVere. I was almost certain I had killed a man today. And it didn't matter.

43

I cried her name.
  Nona.

I sat up, panting. I clutched the sheet to my throat, staring into the dark. I sat sweating. I worked to convince myself that this feeling was nothing at all, not even remotely, like fear.

But I was terrified at what was happening to me.

When I was a boy a plane had crashed at the very edge of Lake Merced. I had been playing tennis with the robust pro my father had insisted was the right trainer for us, a man impatiently strong, his serves white blurs that *thwacked* against the chain link before we could twitch. Only I had gradually learned to chop the serves back with some efficiency and, from time to time, I lobbed a ball back cleverly enough to make the instructor serve all the faster.

After these matches I welcomed a walk by myself, and it was on such a walk that I saw the plane falter in the sky.

It was a yellow plane, with a single engine, the sort of aircraft the eye loves to follow. The airplane glistened in the afternoon sun. The wings banked, and then the aircraft found a wrinkle in the sky, a crease invisible to the eye.

Every child, I believe, wants to fly. I wanted to fly more than most children do. Airplane flight was not what I sought, and fantasized, and dreamed of so fervently. I wanted a hawk's power to soar. I wanted wings.

And yet airplanes attracted me, as well as birds. And I watched with pleasure as this plane lifted its nose slightly, the same careless lift I had watched airplanes perform before, human will being exercised high up and far away. And then, abruptly, the plane tilted downward, a buzz-saw burr from high up, the sound of the engine following the airplane, trailing it in that familiar delay that never fails to puzzle: sound, the means by which we learn and receive warning, is so slow.

The airplane was no longer descending. It was not diving. It fell, the wings wagging, the drop without coordination, graceless. The aircraft was transformed from a weight-defying trace of craftsmanship to so much structure dropping, fast.

With people in it. Even as it was still falling I ran. With people in it, my mind shrilled. People are falling. And yet why I ran toward the place where the plane was falling, my boy's legs pumping, I have no idea. It would have been better to have run away, for help, or to escape the truth. Perhaps even in my extreme youth I had that overly muscular sense that all would be well.

The plane was down, and without a sound. Then: a clap, a smack that was too distant to be anything associated with the plane. And I knew from movies that there would be a plume of smoke, and there was no smoke, only the bright afternoon. So, I told myself, all would be well. There would be no sad discovery at the end of my run. The thoughts all occurred within me with a hopeful lilt. See: no one's hurt.

The lake brooded to the left, too blue, as always, in contrast to the late summer gone-to-seed foxtails. The housefronts beyond were bright as those chalky mints the hand loves to sort through for the right shade of pastel.

The plane had come down and disintegrated, although it took me several moments to acknowledge what I saw. Sheets of white and yellow lay in the fields, and there was a smell of hot metal and scorched rubber. In a recess of the wreckage a valve or tube exhaled, or a part still spun invisibly. A Plexiglas pane of windscreen gleamed in the branches of a cypress at an impossible distance from the crash.

It seemed that there must have been only one person in the aircraft, and the sight of him was almost pleasing to me, as I panted up, slowing down, my long run completed. So there he is, I thought. He must be all right, in his short-sleeved shirt, sitting in the cockpit. And then my mind sorted through what it beheld, and made sense of it.

A fence rail was stuck into the man, lancing him, passing all the way through him, and through the seat, upward all the way through the now skeletal fuselage. This was not a man, but a new sort of creature, like a centaur, a man with a bright shock-bright-ened span of redwood through him, a man with a fixed, angry expression.

I could not talk about it. My father, in my view, was a man who needed to hear good news so he could keep on being a good man, and my mother needed it to keep herself from having head-aches. Furthermore, I felt guilty, as though the crash, the impale-ment, had been my fault, a shameful discovery, a monstrosity that I had perpetrated.

That crash had been my first real encounter with a truth: peo-ple can be hurt—badly.

Before she had been hospitalized, my mother had been in therapy with Dr. Ahn. Ahn had warned me that the "dissociative mental life" is seductive. This was Ahn's way of warning me that my mother might never recover, or, at best, would recover slowly.

Perhaps I should try to contact Dr. Ahn. I saw this therapist's books in airport bookstores and on the bookshelves of men and women I respected. Like many well-known individuals, Dr. Ahn had become both ubiquitous and remote, more of a name and less of a person one could actually meet.

Besides, why did I have to think of myself as mentally ill? Perhaps my life had given me a rare opportunity. I felt nausea, and cold, and a feeling like a fall that would not end.

People have been hurt. You know that's wrong. You *know* it.

And what are you doing to help Nona? What are you doing to help Stuart, and all the other children? What are you now?

Doesn't a human have *something*? Some essence, an interior shadow. A soul. I had sold it.

44

My handwriting had never looked quite this elegant, each letter an example of penmanship. It scarcely looked like my handwriting at all. I was dressed, feeling crisp. A pair of my great-grandfather's gold cufflinks made a rodent-tiny rustle against the paper.

There was another, similar sound in the room—the gold nib of my pen against the paper. I was writing a letter to Fern's sister, retired and living in Toms River, New Jersey. It expressed, in phrases millions of people had used before me, my honest condolences. I sealed the letter and pressed it carefully, as though my state of mind might cause it to become unglued, to become unwritten, to make the entire communication vanish.

I was anything but mournful. Fern had lived, and he had died. The writing of the letter struck me as quite remarkably absurd for a moment. But I knew that it was important to continue to behave like a normal man.

I had another bit of paper that required a personal check and a postage stamp: a bill from a towing company. The armored Mercedes was in a foreign auto salvage yard in South San Francisco. I understood debts.

My neck was sore. I was stiff. My tongue, too, was still healing from its cut. But I did not feel badly injured. Any sense of regret was fading in me. What was given to me in the place of conscience was the keenest sensation of being alive.

They must not know. They must not be able to see by looking at you what has happened.

"You look so well," said Collie. "Despite everything."

She said this with a tone of approval. Grief had always been well hidden by my father, tucked in and knotted, dressed in well-cut worsted. And yet what I felt could not be called grief.

Your body is a disguise. Your feelings are relics.

"Despite everything indeed," I said. But it was not simple happiness that made me feel clear-headed.

"Black doesn't look good on some people," she said, pouring my coffee.

"I've always admired black," I said. "Not over other colors. The other colors are more lovely. But black gives the figure a certain definition. It gives everything definition, don't you think? Light contrasting with dark."

"I really can't say, but I've always liked colors, myself, a little foolishly, I suppose. I always liked the greens and the oranges."

"You're a cheerful person, Collie," I observed.

"I do appreciate you saying so."

"How do you stay so happy?"

"My sister wonders the same thing. Sisters aren't always alike, you know. She's the one who worries. Watches the news and can't sleep. It's a habit, really. Or a gift, if you like. But you certainly look pleased with things this morning, if I may say so."

This morning my hands had, quite without conscious guidance on my part, selected black trousers, a midnight-blue tie, and a black jacket. I watched myself butter toast with a detached interest. I wasn't hungry, but I ate because that's what a normal man does. He chews, he sips coffee.

What is our old friend Stratton Fields going to do today?

I should be taking notes. Something for a PBS special: what it's like to have no soul.

Forget the latest fad in recreational chemicals, the latest sex manual, the latest computerized reality. Let's check in with a man who has traded his soul for—for what?

Tell us, Mr. Fields—what did you get in exchange for your soul?

Well, for one thing, it turns out I can get away with murder.

Quite literally. And the odd thing is that I like it.

That's fascinating. And what else have you noticed about yourself?

The Children's Hospice had never been so small, and the light there had never been so dim before. The door swung shut behind me.

I thought: He simply has to be here, still, in his usual bed.

But the place had changed. Nona's ward had never resembled a hospice when she was in it. With her presence it had transformed from a hospital wing of children not expected to recover to a place of life, the kind of classroom that is a joy.

The pictures she had pinned to the bulletin board were still there. They were the artwork done by the children themselves, red, scraggly suns, big-eyed, lively humans with stick arms and legs, the style of drawing that children take to with pleasure.

The bright colors and the spritely figures announced to the viewer that the world was a place to stir the hand to take up the crayon and the chalk and try to get it all on paper—for fun, as an act of purest happiness.

I hurried down the corridor, my shoes squeaking on the freshly waxed surface.

To my relief, Stuart was there, turning his head to see who was at the door. His eyes brightened. His face wrinkled into a smile, and he held out his hand to me, and I took it. His hand was thinner than before.

Picking the right words might prove difficult, I thought. To speak would be to talk about Nona, and about her absence.

He touched a bead of water on my raincoat. He said, "Dr. Lyle is sick."

"Very sick," I agreed.

"Everything will be fine when she gets back," he said.

Stuart looked away, up at the television. The silent set was a cartoon, multicolored androids of some kind locked in conversation, the animation jerky, nothing moving but the robot mouths.

Stuart stirred in his bed, as he often did during a visit, impatient, perhaps, with lying down, or with the feel of the sheets over his body. "I ate all my JELL-O," he said.

I told him that this was good news.

I had picked out some special paper on leaving the studio in my house, a French drawing paper from a shop on rue du Bac, and I folded it carefully, slowly, into one of my puppets. It began, of course, as a stallion, but ended looking, after I tore one of its ears clumsily, and then botched the other, like a horse wanting to transform into a creature that could fly, a beast with talons and a beak.

Its ears looked like feathers standing forth along its neck, so I made a few more such feathers. I told Stuart that it looked more like a bird than a horse, and he said, "A flying horse."

"Possibly."

"I liked your other horses better."

"This one looks strange doesn't it?"

"A little bit," said Stuart, dismissive but kind.

His bed was nearly covered with comic books; muscular, Vikingesque men battling metallic monsters, steel-clad creatures with pincers and hooks for limbs battling deathray-blasting titans. The epic battles looked both exciting and unimaginable, a boy's universe.

Do this child a favor. Smother him.

I made another puppet, a well-turned horse, and Stuart laughed. He took it from me, and we made a little game of mock combat, the two horses outbiting each other.

But he was tired. There was no doubt that he had lost more weight, and the whites of his eyes were slightly yellow. I stood, ready to leave. In a sleep-heavy voice he said, "I had a dream about you."

Do it. Kill him now. You believe in mercy, don't you?

"I'll have to hear about it sometime," I said.

"You were in trouble."

"What kind of trouble?"

"You were hanging off a mountain."

"Off of a cliff?"

"Off a cliff," he agreed.

This story, idle as it had seemed, did not please me when I stopped to think about it. "What happened?"

"I had wings," he said.

"That's sounds like fun."

"I saved you," he said, sleepily.

I offered to turn off the television, but he did not seem to hear me, only holding on to my hand as he turned away and drifted off, his lips moving, like the lips of the creatures still offering what looked like taunts or threats to each other on the screen.

One of the nurses was at the doorway as I turned to leave, and I wondered if perhaps she had been warned to keep me away from the children.

"It's so good to see you, Mr. Fields," she said. "The children ask after you when you don't come. Especially now."

It would be an act of mercy to kill them all.

"I really had to stop by and see them. I think about them all

the time," I heard myself say, with the smooth tone of a diplo-
mat, an accomplished actor, a liar.

"Do stop by again. Stuart asks for you."

I found myself lingering in a corridor. I urged myself to go and
see Nona. To say good-bye.

To take her life.

Go back and show her mercy, too.

I stood there, breaking into sweat. Just a few quick steps to the
stairway, just a quick walk across these polished tiles. Why did I
hesitate?

Kill Nona.

Part Five

45

The wind was brisk, but I found myself not needing to button my overcoat. The cabdriver at Charles de Gaulle airport was doubtful. He looked at me with his mouth turned down and his eyebrows up, but I repeated the address. He looked at his map book and put the car into gear.

I was not sleepy, after my hours of sitting in first class, declining the champagne and the claret.

A great, long barge made its way past Notre Dame, and the sky was gray. The river reflected the sky, and the wavering image of the city around it. A bus had changed lanes unexpectedly, and a Citröen had been slightly damaged. Traffic went nowhere. Police in white helmets whisked up to the scene on tiny motorcycles, blue lights flashing. The cabdriver wrestled the steering wheel one way and another, and we managed our way onto the Quai Voltaire, past some of the shops where some of my paintings, and a good deal of my furniture, had been purchased.

I had called from San Francisco, before leaving for the airport, and while I had not spoken to Valfort himself, a woman's voice had spoken clear English. I could hear her pause to make a note, and then she said that they would be expecting me.

Hadn't there been, I wondered, a certain hesitation in her voice?

It had been more than a year since I had visited Paris. I had lectured, the last time I had visited, at an institute of design and architecture on rue Dupin. My lecture had been a comparison of Frank Lloyd Wright's work in San Francisco, which consisted of the building he had designed on Maiden Lane, and the buildings he had drawn for possible construction on adjacent streets, but which had never been built. "Perhaps," I had explained, in slow English, "in a city both charming and earthquake prone, he did not trust the landscape enough to commit his favorite work to it."

The students had listened alertly, but my name had not been one to call forth a tremendous crowd, and I had been happy to be able to stroll toward the Luxembourg Gardens with a handful of polite students, as interested in smoking cigarettes and examining the clothes in shop windows as they were in anything I had to say.

The cabdriver was expert. As we turned from rue du Cherche Midi onto a crowded street I realized that I knew this neighborhood. And I saw that any progress was going to be impeded by the trucks double parked before us. I thrust currency into the hand of the driver, thanked him, and made it clear that I had decided to walk.

I found the street without much trouble. Rue San Mames was a tiny street, a demi-lane between fashionable apartment buildings. It was a short walk from Bon Marché, the big department store, but it was, as so often happens in Paris, in a neighborhood out of another time. There was a market in progress, aubergines and cheeses in stalls, and I could not keep from pausing, even in my great hurry, to take in the sight.

Things love what they are, the courgette, the sheaf of leeks. How little they desire, the iron-dark beets beneath the hide of root callus, the black cylinders of wine. Only humans hurry from place to place, declining this potato, that sheaf of white onions.

I walked quickly, and when I reached 19, San Mames I was not surprised to find that the heavy glass door was locked. I was, though, surprised that there was no speaker box, no way to signal one's arrival. I was on a street of considerable bustle, and could see no way to make my entrance.

The door buzzed, and I became aware of a camera high above me. The door opened easily at a push, and then closed firmly behind me, a solid and transparent door that reminded me of the windshield of my demolished Mercedes.

A voice spoke to me, a female voice in rapid French I could just catch. I marched forth my own fairly rusty French and told the intercom that I was here to see Dr. Valfort. I announced my name.

There was a long hesitation. The sounds of the Paris street were muted through the glass. I could easily guess the way my name sounded to the French ear, and could hear it, in my mind, being uttered with some distaste at the Anglo uprightness of the syllables.

But the wait went on too long. I sensed indecision, or even irritation. Or perhaps it was something worse. Perhaps Dr. Valfort knew my sort of case all too well, and received my visit, however expected, with regret.

Another buzzer released me into a courtyard, and I gazed upward at the shuttered windows, the walls stitched with ivy. Somewhere a baby was crying.

"It's so kind of you to visit us," said a voice.

A tall, very thin man stepped toward me across the courtyard. He was gray haired, and wiry, with steel-rimmed spectacles. He looked like a kind raptor, a benevolent hawk. He had a gray mustache, closely trimmed, and wore a jacket over his shoulders. His handshake was strong.

"I'm delighted that you could spare the time to see me," I said.

"Dr. Lyle is a woman I admire tremendously."

This sounded like simple courtesy, but his eyes looked sharply into mine for a long moment.

Upstairs, he introduced me to a young woman in a dark blue dress. Her name was Marie, and the dress was both delightful and unfashionable, a full, pleated costume that recalled to my mind Paris of the Second World War, fashion created out of sparse wardrobes. She took my coat but did not seem to want to meet my eyes. He suggested that we work in the sitting room of the apartment, a room that adjoined this foyer and was equipped with heavy, brass-fitted doors.

"You will want to eat, and perhaps a glass of wine." His English was markedly accented, but apparently quite fluent.

"Some coffee," I suggested, "would be nice."

"You aren't hungry?"

"No."

"Or tired at all?"

I admitted that I was not particularly tired.

"You do not mind, I hope, if I serve you coffee which has been decaffeinated." He stepped out briefly to arrange for the coffee, and I had a moment to my own thoughts.

I did not want to be alone. My solitude frightened me.

"Why did you feel the need to see me, Mr. Fields?" His accent made the question sound both polite and sinuous, a question I should answer with care.

"Surely Nona described me—"

"In your own words," he said, with a kind smile.

Don't tell him, I told myself. He won't understand. I took a deep breath. "I'm afraid."

"Of what?"

He won't understand a word of this. I cleared my throat. "I believe that I have sold my soul."

He leaned back in his chair across from me, gazing at the ceiling for a moment.

"You'll think me absurd for saying this," I continued. "Or foolish."

His gray eyes met mine. "Before you tell me what has happened to you," he said, "perhaps you would like to know more about me. About my work."

"I've decided already that I trust you."

"This is kind of you. But some people find my work a matter of controversy."

"Nona mentioned this."

He smiled thoughtfully. "I use hypnotherapy, and I have a great deal of respect for traditional beliefs." His voice was gentle.

But something about his words disturbed me. "Traditional beliefs of what sort?" I found myself asking.

"What others call obsolete religious concepts. What could be called 'superstition.' "

His words made me very anxious. I stood and gazed about me.

I experienced a great need to change the subject. The sitting room was large, with earth-red tiles and a huge fireplace. Age-blackened oak beams supported the ceiling, and a display of flowers held court on a side table. The flowers were unseasonable, and remarkable for another reason.

They were common, ordinary flowers, not the sort of orchids one would feature in a hothouse. There were pink and delicate asters, the sort of wide-awake looking flower Collie liked to put on the breakfast table. There were grasses, and what looked like —and upon close examination were—stalks of wheat, all introduced into the same vase, a magnificent profusion.

I paced the room. "Your taste in flowers," I said. "I admire it."

"The grasses come from a favorite shop of mine," he said.

I knew the shop, with its sign announcing: VEGETAUX SECHES DE TOUS LES PAYS. It had inspired me, during one visit to this city, to draw a series of sketches of dried grasses, oats, and rye. The drawings had been described as "charming" in more than one art magazine. I had burned the drawings in my fireplace with everything else.

Coffee arrived, the dark-clothed young woman hurrying from the room.

I tried to make the comment sound offhand. "She acts like she's afraid of me."

"Marie is a very wise woman," he said.

We chatted easily about shops, and fashions in clothing, and for awhile he let me direct the conversation toward safe, pleasant subjects. I sat across from him again.

Then Dr. Valfort said, "I have had a very interesting experience, one that redirected my studies from ordinary psychiatry to the sort of work that I do now. Three years ago, while I was being operated on for a gall bladder." He waited, perhaps to see if the words *gall bladder* communicated anything to me. "And, in the surgical theater where I lay, my heart failed. And I died."

"How awful," I said, my words sounding inadequate.

"Indeed." He continued, "I recovered my life. The surgeon was very skilled. But what I saw at that moment I died, the impossible-to-express vision which I had, altered my life."

The coffee was black, sharp, delicious. I did not want to hear what Valfort was about to tell me.

"Regardless of what you have understood in the past, Mr.

Fields, regardless of what the people you know may believe, I have discovered something unavoidable. Something more real than our own lives."

I did not like these words, but Valfort's voice had captured me.

"I discovered our ignorance. We know nothing of Heaven. We know nothing of God, or Hell. Our ignorance is deep, almost what one would have to call magnificent."

"I'm certainly willing to concede the possibility of that," I said with a dry laugh.

"In traditional terms, it is not possible to sell one's soul," he said. "What you have done may seem to amount to the same thing: you have mortgaged your soul. You have put it up as surety. In exchange for your soul you have received something."

"I have received quite a bit," I said, my voice low.

"What have they given you?"

His use of the pronoun *they* chilled me. I had entertained some doubts regarding Valfort. I was here not because I knew or understood his work, but because I needed help badly. But now I began to wonder if Valfort knew what sort of powers I had engaged.

I had trouble speaking, but forced myself. "I have received what you would have to call career advancement. I have a new feeling of tremendous . . ." I could think of no better word. "Power."

He waited, his eyes bright.

"I feel so alive." My voice broke. "I think I am losing my mind. I can't tell what I'm going to do. I think I might hurt the people I love."

"And you are afraid," he said.

I nodded, silenced by emotion.

"You have every reason to feel this way," he said. "You are a very dangerous man."

46

His words angered me. "I don't even believe the soul exists."

"But you do, Mr. Fields, or you would not have mortgaged it."

"I don't believe in Hell." The word stopped me, capitalized in my mind, and standing for something out of Dante, out of the mouths of late-night preachers on television.

"Then tell me what you think is happening to you."

It was difficult to say it. "I'm afraid I've killed people."

He closed his eyes, and the slowly opened them. "Do you want me to help you?"

"Can you?"

"You don't believe I can?"

"What will you do? Teach me to pray?"

"What would you pray for, Mr. Fields?"

The question hit me hard. "I would pray for my soul's return. I would pray for Nona—to have her back again."

"You think you can have your soul back so easily—by asking for it?"

"This is all academic. There is no soul."

"Ah." It was a simple sound, a mild exclamation which the French use to accept and dismiss at once. "Have people actually died?" There was something sly about his tone.

"You know they have. Ty DeVere was practically a cultural hero in France."

"Of course. What you say is true. I did, though, want to hear you admit it. So something real *has* happened."

His voice was soothing. "I don't know if I can help you, Mr. Fields," he continued. "Do you want me to try?"

I said that I wanted him to help me.

"I could not quite hear you, Mr. Fields."

"Please try," I said.

"Pay attention to what I am about to tell you. I am going to listen to your personal history. Then I will put you into a trance. We will discover what has really happened to you."

"I'm not sure I want to be hypnotized. Can't we just talk? As we are talking now."

"You think you killed them, don't you?"

"I want to know the truth."

"You don't really, Mr. Fields."

I did not like the way the wall shivered in my vision. I did not like the way the room was too quiet.

The story was a longer one than I had thought, reaching into my childhood, my career, my love for Nona, my love of the dangerous surf. Valfort listened with a look in his eyes of genuine caring, and I found it easy to tell him all that I could.

When I was finished, Valfort took the glasses from his eyes and ran a hand over his brow, like a man who has studied too late into the night. He replaced his glasses. His eyes, when they found me again, were kind, but he said something that stung me. "Mr. Fields, you have been in tremendous danger, every moment since your first encounter in the Pacific."

"I am afraid—even here."

"Who—or what—do you suppose it was calling to you in the surf that night? Who took your hand?"

I did not like the sound of his voice. "What do you want me to say?"

"You're angry."

I could not deny it. But I was confused more than angry. It was Valfort who seemed to have all the answers. I had memories, delusions.

"You have made," he said, "one mistake—blunder is how I might describe it—after another."

I could not respond.

"And you come into my home expecting me to help you!" he said, in a virtual whisper.

"You must help me," I said, bending forward. "What's happening to me?"

His manner changed, once again, to that of compassion. But I could see anguish in his eyes. He reached into a notebook and withdrew a slip of paper. "Tell me what you see here," he said with a smile.

I expected something like a Rorschach inkblot. What I saw was a photograph of a statue. The statue was an unnaturalistic depiction of a huge man—judging from the human figures around it. This giant was in a trance of some kind. "It's a Buddha."

"Very good. Tell me, Mr. Fields, what this is." He gave me a second photograph.

"I don't want to do this," I said. I could not recognize my own voice.

This new picture was a crude, medieval work, utterly unrealistic, but with the charm of that sort of art. It was an icon. A mother held a grotesquely misproportioned infant to her cheek, looking out at the viewer with sad eyes. This was one of those little sheets you can pick up at St. Germain-des-Prés, or a hundred other French churches. *Prions chaque jour pour la paix du monde* read the inscription.

"What is it?" asked Valfort.

There was a vague flickering in my vision. A migraine was beginning.

Was I hesitating too long? "I don't recognize the artist. The subject is the Virgin and the infant Christ."

He had more, pictures he withdrew from a large brown envelope. Photographs. Sacred images. He had Tibetan mandalas, crucified Christs, Romanesque saints, a handful of such samples he was prepared to hand to me, one by one, for my examination. As he handed them to me I felt an accumulation of nausea. My hands were cold.

When we were finished he said, "How do you feel about these images?"

I tried to adopt the tone with which I would decline a certain variety of mustard, or an opportunity to watch television. "I don't like them."

"If you were going to make a work of art depicting Satan, how would he look?"

"I don't know," I said. But I stopped myself. "Like one of those. One of those sacred images." Like a woman in white, I nearly said.

"Are these images sacred?" he asked.

"To some people," I said.

"You want it both ways," he said kindly. "You want to be rational, an unbeliever. And yet you believe you can form a pact with the unseen, harness it to your desires."

"Tell me what's been happening to me," I said. I was impatient, perspiring, chilled. We seemed to be involved in a form of intellectual fencing.

"If Satan came to you he would disguise himself as something beautiful, wouldn't he?" said Valfort.

"Perhaps. But I don't believe in Satan."

"That must make it all the easier," said Valfort. "For Satan."

"Your views are antique," I said.

He allowed himself a smile. "You judge me too harshly. These divinities may not exist apart from us, or they may. I have discovered that it makes little difference. The angel speaks. Mary is startled. The messenger foretells a birth. It matters to the scientist whether or not the divine messenger is real. But to the Virgin —it makes no difference. The message is true."

"There is a soul," I said, "even if there is no soul."

"I remember Nona Lyle very well. I loved her."

His words startled me.

"She was a gifted student. She had the ability to understand. To listen and to hear what someone was saying. She loved children. You don't like to talk about her condition, how near to death she is." He observed my discomfort, and added, "You are partly responsible, if only in your own mind."

"The doctors don't understand what's wrong with her."

"I think that there are many secrets you have hidden from yourself, Mr. Fields. And that is one of them."

I stretched out on the settee in Valfort's sitting room. He had been solicitous, gentle, giving me a glass of sparkling water.

"Are you ready to begin?" he said, from off in a distant part of the room. He closed shutters, drew curtains over the windows, and there was the sputter of a match, and the rattle of wooden matches in a box.

He lit a candle. The candlelight threw a hush into my mind. The single candle shivered as he walked, carrying it toward me.

"I need to know if I killed DeVere. And Blake. I need to know what really happened."

He did not argue with me, or say a word to reassure me.

"It's already too late," I said.

"It's true," he said, "that it can become too late. The last, magical night draws toward dawn. The question is: How far away is dawn for you, Mr. Fields?"

I wanted to know the truth.

"Let nothing disturb you," he said. His accent made the simple words elegant: "nothing" became "nussing," a childish, charming word.

"Lie quietly," he said in a low voice. "Look into the candle flame. Count backward with me."

I shaped the numbers, forming them, picturing, at his suggestion, steps leading downward. We started with the number ten. And then downward, each number a step into darkness, as he had suggested. Or, at least it seemed that he suggested it.

It wasn't working. The hypnosis was a failure. I wanted to sit up.

And I did sit up. But then relaxed, letting my body fall back again. Because there were steps, and they did lead downward. And there was a flame with a sleeve of perfect blue that coated the wick, and protected what it consumed.

All the way to the truth.

47

I sat up, and blew out the candle.

No. It wasn't possible.

Something about the garden. About my mother. Something about—

I could remember it all. And just as quickly the memory eluded me. I found myself huddled against the wall. I would not think that way. I would never think that way.

The memories were gone. I wrapped a blanket around myself, and huddled there in the dark of Valfort's sitting room. His hand must have fumbled, groped, and found a light, because there was a rattle, a lamp went on, and I blinked.

Valfort was at a distant wall, his eyes on me, his arms crossed, his entire posture communicated one powerful emotion. He was outwardly steady. He was professional. But he was afraid.

"That's enough!" I said. My words erupted, my voice ragged.

The remains of the candle smoke drifted. There was a long silence. Valfort did not make a movement, waiting, I sensed, to see what I would do.

"Did you learn anything interesting?" I asked. Why did I ask this with something like a sneer?

"It's so difficult for a man like yourself, to see the truth after such a long time," he said.

"What did I tell you?"

He did not answer.

"Tell me!"

"You would not believe me."

I bunched the blanket into a wad and threw it on the floor, where it swooped and drifted, skimming the surface before it fell. "I want to know the truth."

"You might say that Satan does not exist, and that none of the powers you have contacted are supernatural. That may be only a way of describing it, a manner of thinking. But it is clear to me, Mr. Fields: a career of marvels awaits you. You will be more famous, more important, more influential than DeVere ever dreamed of being. You wanted good fortune. Now you have it."

What sadness, I realized, embellished each one of Valfort's words.

I asked, "What do you know about me now?"

"It would be wrong for me to tell you. You will have to discover the truth you have hidden from yourself."

He must have read my eyes. "As soon as you surrendered possession of your soul, you ceased to love. Soon Nona Lyle will mean nothing to you. You will forget."

"Impossible," I said, my voice hoarse.

But I may do something to hurt her.

"Perhaps Nona was injured simply so the Powers could trap you."

"Using her as bait. So I would agree to sell my soul. But it didn't work. She wouldn't come back to life."

"Do you know why Nona Lyle turned to the study of the mind?"

"She was influenced by her father. He was a physician in Oakland."

"She had a history of psychological troubles as a young girl. She had a tendency toward a hysterical reaction which made her slip into a form of trance so deep it resembles a coma. My primary work with her was to cure her. I had reasonable success. I see the look of hope in your eyes. I must caution you. Don't be reassured. What has happened to her may be worse than anything purely physical. She may have collapsed beyond hope of any recovery, forced into a preconscious state by the shock of the beating."

"I don't want any of this—I want to go back to my old life, the way things used to be."

"That's impossible."

"Even Faustus in the legend could have asked for forgiveness—"

"Faustus believed. Besides, what Faustus wanted was knowledge, and experience. He wanted to know the workings of the planets, and to make love with Helen of Troy. What you want is yourself."

He was astounding, this wiry, keen-eyed man. "What should I do?"

"There is a secret in your family. Several secrets. That you will not allow yourself to acknowledge."

"Did I kill DeVere?"

"You believe you did."

I could not control myself. My feelings snapped. I picked up a chair and hurled it. It stuck the solid wall and bounced off. The chair spun on one leg, and then fell to one side and was still.

"You'll never beg to be forgiven for anything, Mr. Fields," he said. "Look at you."

I struck the mantelpiece so hard the timbers above us vibrated. "You will help me!"

Valfort was calm. "That's what you wanted. More life. So much life you can kill. Your ambition killed DeVere and Peterson, and your old friend Blake Howard. You are responsible for what happened to Nona Lyle."

I turned to him, and my shadow fell over him, or perhaps it

was the shadow inside me, rising up and covering him as a dust storm falls upon a sole figure on a plain. I would make him stop speaking such falsehoods. What did he know, this man who had tricked me into a trance, this stranger?

There was a whisper behind me, a step, the light sound of a presence. I spun, and the young woman was there, her eyes wide with terror.

I glanced at Valfort, feeling suddenly numb, speechless. "Why are you both so upset?" I said, in something like my old manner. I shook myself. I tried to laugh. "You must forgive me."

French money crackled in my hand, new notes, fresh from the change window at the airport. I left a bunch of the colorful currency on the table, their leaves shifting slightly after I had tossed them down. "You must think me a terrible creature," I said with an approximation of good humor. "The way I acted just now."

As Valfort looked on, the young woman shrank back against the doorpost. "There's no need for this display of fear," I said. I touched her cheek, and I knew.

I knew as surely as I could see the five fingers of my hand. I would trade my soul again in an instant for another taste of the power I had experienced just now, the sensation of strength, the knowledge that my name was, in truth, going to master the world.

The world. The scope of the future occurred to me, like the taste of salt air recalling the vast empty expanse of horizon. Valfort was a little man, a weak, small man, but he had insight, a mouse's glimpse at the truth. I would lift myself out of the characterless accomplishments of my life.

"What did you do, to make me feel so wonderful?" I asked Valfort, my voice husky with lust. A lust not for woman, but for air, light—for everything.

"I spoke to your lover," he said.

I blinked.

"The woman in white, that demon resident in you."

"Ancient superstitions," I said. "Ancient and glorious."

"And true."

I laughed. "You do have a certain courage, Valfort. And for that I will spare you."

Valfort stood on the doorway of the sitting room. "They chose you because you were noble, Mr. Fields. Because you were loving. Because you tried to live by an old standard of conduct—to do good. But They have won you."

"This is the way you help me?" I laughed, feeling almost merry.

"I admire you, Mr. Fields. You had a quality that is so rare."

"I thank you for your advice."

"Nona's hospitalization is doubly tragic because she was on the verge of a major triumph. She got wealthy and powerful people to agree to come to a meeting here in Paris. It was to have been a major achievement for her, a chance to establish an international committee to help children. It was not going to be easy to get these people of ease and power to part with their money, but Nona would be able to do it. Now, her plans are nothing."

The sunlight was bright, spilling across the stairway. I looked back and asked, leaning against the railing, "What was it you saw, when you were dying, Valfort? How little you had done with your life?"

The streets outside were sunny. The wind was cold. The gutters were filled with running water, the flow directed into drains by rolls of toweling.

I wandered, fretful, even feverish.

The traffic was the usual hectic Paris rush, but at the same time it was without the malice of the traffic in other cities. I watched my reflection glide across the shop windows.

To not know, I told myself. To not know. That is to be free.

I stood outside the Cluny Museum, the ruins of the Roman bath before me. Wind shivered my trouser legs, but I did not mind. Valfort did not know me. I had strengths against more than one sort of riptide.

I turned into the wind and stepped into the street, alert for a cab. I have always weighed the consequence of what I did, and sometimes I have mourned. But, in the end, I have always returned to life.

How little Valfort knew, that man who had seen himself die.

A cab squealed to a stop. I seized the door handle.

But then I realized what I was doing. I understood that I was about to return home more lost than before.

* * *

I hurried through the streets, and at last found myself on rue San Mames once again. I pushed the door, and it would not open. I pounded on the heavy glass, shook it, but it made only a metallic rattle.

"Please!" I called. "Not for me! For Nona!"

A man in a uniform was at my side, asking me what I was doing there, banging on a door. Where was my key? Who did I want to visit?

Rapid French words wrapped around me briefly, and escaped, losing me.

48

A woman's voice called my name as I paid the cabdriver at de Gaulle Airport. Despite the decorative spin her accent gave my shouted first name—*Stray-tone*—I recognized it at once.

It was Marie, dressed in an overcoat of the same dark blue as her dress, looking both out-of-time and contemporary. She handed me an envelope, and when I began to speak she put a finger to her lips.

She left me without speaking. I did not open the envelope until I was on the plane. That was because I knew from the feel of the pleasant, auburn-gold paper what was inside.

When I had buckled the seatbelt, and declined yet another glass of champagne, I could not delay any further. I slipped a thumb under the flap of the envelope, which was still slightly moist from the tongue of either Valfort or Marie, and it opened without tearing.

The money I had left was there, folded up within a sheet of paper. But there was a surprise, too. On the paper was a strong, almost illegible bit of handwriting: *I will do what I can, but it's nearly too late.*

There was a signature, too, a *V* like the sketch of a flying thing, a hawk rendered too quickly to allow for a head, feathers, the outstretched talons. I wanted to feel hope. But I recognized the truth.

I got off the plane in San Francisco while the other passengers were still stretching and fumbling for their coats. I threw my black leather overnight bag over my shoulder, and walked fast.

Even so, the lounge was crowded. I was eager to escape the tangle of people, but as I walked the long corridor away from Gate 67 someone fell into stride with me, and on the other side was someone else, another man in a suit, another man in dark glasses.

I stopped, and they all stopped with me. "Mr. Fields?" said one of them, a man with a white scar on his lip.

I was surrounded by a wedge of men. One or two carried small black transmitters. My first thought was that Childress had changed his mind or had been demoted. The men were blank-faced and wore gray suits. They did not, however, recite my rights, nor did any of them touch me.

Instead they walked as quickly as I was walking, and the airport security men nodded to us as we passed.

Beautiful, I thought. A top-of-the-line kidnapping.

That was perfect. It was what I deserved, and it was exactly appropriate: I step off the plane and fall into the sort of trap I had spent years avoiding.

"How was your flight?" asked Lip Scar.

"Fine," I said, reaching into my pocket for my passport. So, I thought, we're all going to pretend to be normal. That should be fun. "The flight was wonderful. I didn't watch the movie. There was, at one point, a little bit of turbulence."

We were waved through customs, and as we stepped out onto the sidewalk, I took a breath of cool night and diesel fumes and wondered when they would shove me into the trunk of an Eldorado and head toward the landfill near Foster City. I would kick the one nearest me, the one with the radio with the wiggling black antenna. I would kick him hard in the knee, and skip around the Skycap struggling with a mountain of suitcases.

Then Lip Scar said, "Miss Wick wants to see you."

There was a brisk walk through the chilly dark. There was a smell of jet fuel and that ordered sense of power that an airport often gives. A chain-link gate was unfastened, and I was hustled up the steps into an executive jet.

Anna Wick handed me a martini glass and waited for me to settle myself in the seat.

"It can be so pretty there this time of year," she said. "How was the weather?"

"I didn't get what I wanted," I said.

"How unusual."

I did not touch my martini. The stuff looked viscous, poisonous, the olive distorted by refraction. She observed my reluctance to drink, and made no move to taste her own.

"I used to think you were one of those people who were too good to get anything done," Anna was saying, running a finger around the edge of her glass. "Too nice. Too well manicured to fight."

"You aren't disappointed," I said.

"Renman wants to meet with you," she said.

My pulse tripped. "I want to meet him."

"He insists that we fly down tonight. He says it can't wait. He has news for you."

She picked up her drink but still did not taste it. "Renman probably wants you dead. He and DeVere understood each other. If I share all of the DeVere empire with you—he won't like it."

"I want everything. Where it says 'DeVere' I want it to say 'Fields.' I want everything that DeVere had. And then I'm going to make everyone forget all about DeVere."

"You expect me to help you accomplish all that."

"Yes."

Her eyes were smiling, but her voice was serious. "Why should I?"

"You don't have any choice."

"I can't tell if you're threatening me, or offering me something amazing."

"Medford, Oregon," I said.

"I beg your pardon," she coughed, but she knew exactly what I was talking about.

"Lumber town," I said. "Mountains of sawdust, and everywhere you look you see truck ruts and dusty houses. It should be a pretty place, but it isn't. In the middle of forests and all you can see is barren lots and piles of sawed-off trees. And you can smell the lumber fermenting. Starting to rot. That's how it all begins, the houses and the towns, even the books. Piles of sawdust. Your hometown."

"Just when I was starting to think you were so much fun."

"You're gambling, too."

"Am I?"

"You think I'm the future."

She took a sip of her drink and some of it splashed. She said, "Renman's going to be very surprised."

We were taxiing. The small jet jounced with the unevenness of the runway. In the distance, beyond the curtained window, was the Bayshore freeway, billboards, glittering traffic. "He thinks he can scare you. Don't laugh. He should be able to frighten any normal man."

I did not have to speak.

Far away, beside the freeway, I could see the billboard displaying DeVere's rugged, handsome face. Its expression seemed to have brightened since DeVere's death, as though the image of the man knew what had happened and needed to hide the truth from itself.

"You want that taken down," said Anna in a matter-of-fact tone.

"Replaced," I said.

But I knew that I was playing out the last act, milking the applause, staying on for just the last, lingering sensation of triumph. I was getting what I wanted.

But it was too late.

49

The executive jet had been outfitted with Mojave-yellow leather seats and sage-gray seatbelts. The impression the color scheme gave was that this aircraft had grown out of an outcropping in New Mexico, from the side of sandstone mesa, a miracle of geology equipped with landing gear.

Anna kept looking over at me, looking up from the contents of yet another red plastic folder. When our eyes met she always gave me a DeVere-quality smile. She returned to her work, whisking various words and figures with yellow highlighter.

She looked over at me so often I began to wonder if she thought I would vanish, or turn into some other sort of creature altogether. And what was that hint in her eyes? Something about me pleased her.

At night the desert is pure abyss. A human settlement is a sharp concentration of pinpricks. Freeways cast a mange of light, and cars pushed light ahead, bulldozing the dark.

The jet glided onto the runway at Palm Springs. There was the flavor of desert night in the air, and a flavor of lawns, too, of sprinklers raining over bermuda hybrid.

A limousine met us, yet another armored vehicle intended for both comfort, easy ostentation, and the sort of shaded glass window that could, with any luck, stop a bullet. A white-and-blue Palm Springs squad car slipped into the traffic behind us.

"The police take care of Renman," said Anna.

"Good friends of his," I said.

"He makes them nervous."

The truth of this made me smile. Renman's name was linked with assassinations and vanished labor union leaders. The story was that what DeVere had known Renman had taught him, if only by example. Renman bought television stations, closed movie studios, and dictated what VCR technology would sit on shelves in homes around the world.

My family viewed Palm Springs as a place for the newly moneyed, the refuge of entertainers and their politician cronies. I had flown down occasionally for tennis, and once or twice a wedding or party had called me here. But it had been a few years since I had visited these streets of tall palms and walled gardens.

When we stepped from the car, I looked up and caught the faint pallor of starlit snow high up in the San Jacinto peaks. There was a glimpse, in the artfully lit garden, of pink raked sand and the spikes of an ocotillo cactus. Then we were within the walls, and in a separate world.

The villa was a masterpiece of security. Cameras tracked us. Polite, tailored men greeted both of us, opening doors for us, and then, noiselessly closing them, and, I sensed, locking them behind us.

The dry air was chilly. Fish, large, scarlet creatures, slowly worked their way through an immense pond, a design I recognized: one of my Japanese friends, a man well known for his ponds of philosophical fish and tastefully arranged, nearly unnaturally pristine, reeds and rushes. The pond was lit from within, and there was a musical trickle of water.

"I keep forgetting how cold it can be here," said Anna.

She was nervous. I was surprised, before I reminded myself that she had no idea what Renman had in mind.

"This is all going to be free entertainment for you, isn't it?" I said.

"I have feelings," she responded. "Don't you?"

Perhaps they would try to drown me among the fish. Perhaps they would slit my intestines, in the style of Japanese assassins, and let me bleed to death among the dwarf apple trees. I had the feeling that if there would be an attempt on my life it would be something classical, a beheading with a ceremonial sword.

He was making us wait.

And watching us? I did not think so. Renman would have his Swiss Guard tracking us from distant television screens. The man himself was bathing, or reading, not giving us a thought.

"He's coming," said Anna.

There was at that moment a sound—a click, a door opening.

In the dark, far across the Japanese garden, there was a whisper. There was a movement. There was a silhouette in a doorway.

I had seen him last at my father's funeral. He had put on weight. He was stocky, short, and wore some sort of flowing gown. His figure was composed not of color but darkness, his head and shoulders blocking the light.

Even now the man was not watching us, I sensed. He was simply taking the air, ignoring us, perhaps barely aware that we were here. But he must have had enough sense of theater to know that his entrance was perfect.

My father had always spoken of Renman as a "field marshall of the real world." The man was a legend, and like many legends he did not have to appear in public to be a public figure. Even more than DeVere, Renman was a man who had created the age we inhabited. If Petrarch had embodied *his* age, then Renman embodied ours, and the legends of his influence over both the underworld and politics were the stuff of what journalists called the "subtext of our culture."

When he stepped from the doorway he was invisible. Then, not so invisible. He drifted toward us, stopping to finger the ornamental oranges, pausing to watch the pool and the scarlet and orange-splashed behemoths drowsing there.

He looked older than I had expected. White haired, with white eyebrows, he looked smaller than I had recalled, too, and more weary. We shook hands.

He turned his back to us and watched the pool for awhile. There was a quality about him that was unmistakable: he existed, and the two of us did not.

He shook his head, as though disputing some argument only he could hear. He waved us into chairs, but I preferred to remain standing, as he seemed to. He stepped into one of the beams of light from a hidden lamp. He let me study him, but did not bother looking at me, examining the stunted pine beside the pool.

"You do look like her," he said.

I made no sound.

"Like your mother," he said.

Anna sat, arranging herself like someone getting comfortable for a play. I could not keep myself from experiencing an unpleasant thought: That is where she will be sitting when my bowels spill onto the gravel.

"When you were younger the resemblance wasn't so strong," he said. "But sometimes that is what maturing is all about: becoming what you already are."

I don't know why I sounded so carefree. "Anna thinks I won't leave here alive."

He did not look her way. "And what do you think?"

"I sold my soul to get here."

I could not read his reaction to this words. Perhaps he was assuming that I was speaking metaphorically. He did, however, consider my statement for awhile. "Was that a wise thing to do?" he said.

We both knew he was not joking.

"First of all," he said at last, "I owe you an apology. I did a bad thing, and I'll make it up to you."

I prepared a quick response to this, about to say that I certainly saw no need for an apology, but he flicked my unspoken words aside with a finger.

He did not continue for awhile, regarding me briefly with dark eyes. "I thought you had killed Ty. Now they tell me otherwise."

"Who?"

"My people."

The water made its gentle music.

He sighed, as though I had made a remark, but he was responding to thoughts of his own. "The man who attacked you in Anna's office was named Palmer. Mark Palmer. A well-known man in certain circles. He's still alive."

I closed my eyes with relief.

"I am the person who's done harm. I killed someone recently," he said.

I didn't understand.

He went on, "I was rash when I heard about Ty's death." He used DeVere's first name with affection, like the name of a brother. "And Blake. He was like family. He'd fallen on hard times in recent months. But he was on his way back. Ty was going to help him. Ty was like that. Good friend, hard enemy. I'm a man with a certain feeling for people. I had been drinking a little. I said someone ought to teach you a lesson. Some hotheads got the wrong idea. Some baseball bats were used, and harm was done."

He patted the pockets of his dressing gown, like a smoker who has forgotten his lighter. "I'm responsible. Nona Lyle was a good woman. Fern was an admired man, a good man the way some cops can be. I financed a special on Nona Lyle once. The Japanese loved it. It played there on television with a title like 'Warrior Children,' or 'Little Sunset Heroes.' Something like that. I used a pound of Kleenex when I saw it. You ever see it? She did good work with those sick kids. I know how you must feel."

What a fool this man was. I nearly said this aloud. And I nearly said these words: *A power greater than yours was responsible for that attack.*

I said nothing, however, surprised at something that was only obliquely related to his words. He had spoken Nona's name, and for an instant I did not know who he was talking about.

I had forgotten her. I had forgotten the woman I loved. And then I reminded myself of that empty gully in me, that still-fresh void.

I told myself this, and yet I was cold, far colder than the chilly evening warranted. I was queasy. The man's words made no sense.

Renman was quiet, as though speaking used up some power in him. "I'm disgusted with myself," he said. "You do a bad thing and you can't undo it. It stays."

"Why did you ask me here?"

He lifted a shoulder, looking at me with surprise or curiosity. "I'm going to let you in."

He saw that I did not quite follow him, and added, "As a way of making it up to you. It's very simple. I feel sorry for you. I do. I feel a very real kind of pity for you."

"Pity," I echoed.

"That's right."

"You fool," I said softly, but quite distinctly.

The words were like a slap. Nothing was said in response. Renman did not flinch, or turn away, but I sensed his reaction.

"You have no choice," I heard myself say. "You are forced to give me what I want."

Renman surprised me with his calm as he said, "What will happen if I don't?"

"They'll destroy you."

He nodded as though in complete agreement with me. Then his eyes flicked to Anna.

"I told you he was crazy," she said.

"Did you?" said Renman thoughtfully, sadly.

"He's great fun to be around," said Anna with a laugh. Her voice was bright, unkind.

"Go inside," snapped Renman.

The sky was empty, except for the pinpoint lights of the stars. The stars, and the empty black. My chest was heaving.

He waited for her to leave, enter a sliding door, and vanish into the house.

A fish splashed.

"She knows a lot," he said. "And she works hard. I've never thought knowledge was that important. And work . . ." He made a silent, thoughtful chuckle. "Anyone can work hard. Work's not that important."

I was distracted by the wriggling lights of the fish pond. "What is important?" I asked, my voice rough.

"I know what you want," said Renman. "I know what kind of emptiness eats at a person who feels that his life doesn't add up to anything." He knelt, perhaps to get a better look at the fish.

"I may be more disturbed than you realize."

"You mean I might be too late?"

I could not tell him how right he was.

He straightened. "You can't live to punish people. You can't breathe hate, or eat it. You can despise me because I want to help, and all I can say, Stratton, is that I am not a good man. I've done some bad things. But maybe I'll do something right where you're concerned. I'm going to try to help you. Call it a gamble."

My words flowed without any awareness on my part. My tone was one of wonder. "You don't have any choice. I see how it's working. Perhaps you sold your soul, too, a long time ago. I've won. I have what I want."

He took my arm, kind, gentle. "I think maybe you came here thinking you would kill me."

"Why would I want to do that?"

"I know your family."

50

When the shore is reached, the life-pocked surface, what do we call out, what claim do we make, possessing the new-found land? Without king, without emperor, carrying a flag of no country, the discovered continent is land, so much earth, nothing more than another home.

I no longer knew what I wanted.

I could kill him. I could kill him and get away with it. He had admitted responsibility for harming Fern and Nona, and justice would forgive my wrath. And weren't there, after all, powers belonging to me, whether satanic or the more subtle reins of fortune? With the help of my own good luck, I could make this villa, and Renman's empire with it, my own.

Was there danger here for me? This would be a perfect moment for that knife in my throat, I thought. Talk me into a pensive mood and then strangle me on my guts. My bruises hurt for a moment. My throat was raw, my arm aching where the bat had struck it. The pretty splashing of the pool would hide a footfall perfectly.

Destroy Renman. Take his life.

You don't want his "help." What will you do? Design clothes? Produce movies? Control a president, manipulate a government? What you wanted, all along, was more life.

And how can Renman give you that? On the other hand, how can killing Renman give you what you want? Is that what it comes to—if you can't do anything else, do harm?

Renman tied the sash about his waist a little tighter. "Did you know your maternal grandfather?" he asked.

This question was a surprise. "He died before I was born."

"Heart trouble?"

"Both sides of my family have had weak hearts. Imperfect valves. Murmurs, squeaks." I was trying to make a mild joke.

"But not you. And not your mother."

This subject made me feel just slightly uncomfortable. "Maybe this is why I've always been so interested in being in top condition. My heart's healthy, and I want to keep it that way."

"Your father had a bad heart?"

"This was a family secret. I think he had trouble with a defective mitral valve."

"That killed him?"

"His heart did."

"That sort of death is such a shock," he said sympathetically. "There was no autopsy?"

"No."

"I attended his funeral. I admired your family, from a distance. You were in many ways what one of those jeweled mavens, those society witches, called 'one of the first families of America.' My own background was simpler."

"Simpler and more fortunate, you mean. You were the one I admired. I thought of you as Olympian."

"Godlike?" He tilted his head, considering the possibility with apparent amusement. He put his hands into the pockets of his dressing gown. "Maybe this is how gods really are—distracted, worried about people, always saying or doing something stupid. And then regretting it. I always thought of the Greek gods as eternally working on their tans."

Even now, when I tried, I could recall little of my father's funeral. For some reason—perhaps the weight of my shock and grief—I had a streak of amnesia regarding the aftermath of my father's demise.

Was that a figure in the shadows? Was that a step on the gravel? I kept my voice steady. "I've enjoyed this visit tremendously."

"Good manners," he said. "You have manners, I'll admit, despite your troubles. Do you know that I used to be very fond of your mother?"

I stiffened. I did not like this man mentioning my mother again. Besides, many people loved my mother from afar. She had graced society columns for years. "You have a good deal to say about my family."

"And it bothers you, doesn't it? It must bother you that everybody knows the truth—everybody who matters—but you."

"You were saying that you loved my mother."

"A bit of the old Fields anger. Yes, it suits you well. That sharp glance, the barely controlled desire to throttle me. Go ahead. Give it a try, Stratton. You won't be able to accomplish much, and I won't blame you."

He chuckled, observing me. "Love? Well, that's hardly the way to put it. Maybe it would be more true to say that I worshipped her. Her father was a rancher here. He owned nearly all the Coachella Valley at one time, a sweet-tempered man, from Virginia. I don't think he liked desert. I think he was one of those men who look out at all this aridity and see one of nature's mistakes. He tried to irrigate it, and turn it into another sort of land entirely. He made a small fortune, and I bought land from him and made a very big fortune."

I was skeptical regarding what he was telling me, but I knew that it was probably true. My mother had always skipped over certain details of her parents' life. I had been handed the "gentleman from Virginia" lore. There had been no details such as lettuce growing, if that is the crop he raised, or irrigating.

He turned to me. His expression was serene. "What did your father do, to make her so miserable?"

I tried to say it with a laugh. "You despise us."

"If you killed DeVere it wouldn't be like me paying someone to finish off a crook in some alley. It would be—how would you put it? A lord's right, a ducal visitation, complete with a sword."

He caught my expression and laughed. "You're surprised that I know how you think."

I tried to change the subject. "Everyone confuses me with my father."

"I never would. He was the most selfish man in North America."

"He was a good man. He endowed hospitals."

"Oh, sure. So he would be loved by everybody. He was a glutton for love. He ignored your mother, I believe. Treated her like a piece of pretty furniture. Am I right?"

"Absolutely wrong. He was a loving man, affectionate, good-humored."

"Is that what you really think? That explains a great deal. I think the bad things you've been pretending never really happened have come back. To haunt you."

*   *   *

He left me in the hands of "a few helpful people" while he slipped away to make some calls.

I was held in a benign sort of arrest, imprisoned and pampered at the same time. Renman's villa was not a place that knew night or day. Windows were lit up, security gates were clicking shut, even under starlight. I was ushered into a room DeVere must have decorated himself, a hideway of timber-browns and cinnamon red, Argentine leather and redwood everywhere I looked.

As though to underscore the western motif, there was an etching of a cowboy on one wall, a Borein in a handsome wooden frame. There was a video camera above the dresser. I wanted out. I could feel the invisible eyes of security guards watching me.

I sat in a sauna, and then in a spa scented with a fragrance I could not place, peppermint, I thought, or some other mildly astringent herb. I was joined by two men with muscular shoulders and arms, both men looking like slightly over-the-hill lifeguards. They wore identical blue shorts, and while these two men were plainly unarmed I did not mistake their purpose.

Their eyes crinkled pleasantly when I greeted them. They both watched me when I departed the steaming water, rubbing myself with a fresh white towel, a deliciously crisp towel, nearly big enough to be worn as a robe. Another man watched me from the shadows.

I returned to the room I was beginning to think of as Cowboy Country. I dressed in a clean chambray shirt from my black carry-on, and felt that never again would I need to sleep, not even for a minute.

I stepped outside, into the cool, sterile air, feeling a kind of sadness foreign to me. I no longer wanted anything that Renman could offer me. My face smiling down from the billboard in South San Francisco—was this the triumph I had wanted? My gardens in cities I would never visit, my signature on bars of soap —was this the long-sought prize?

Anna was there, her shoes in her hand. She had been dangling her feet in the carp pond, and now she drew herself close to me. "You're a lucky man," she said. "Renman likes you. I've been listening to him on the phone. No one will ever say no to you again."

Her arm was around me, and she was wearing a scent I could
not identify as one of DeVere's.

"What I want to know is," she was saying, "how will I be able
to help?"

From time to time one of the fish would splash, or perhaps it
was the sound of something falling into the water. Once I had the
definite impression an animal was lapping the water, splashing
with its tongue. That was entirely impossible, I told myself, because we were in a courtyard, the buildings of the villa forming
an enclave around us.

Renman reappeared with his hands in the pockets of his robe.

It was still night—dawn was hours away. The water made its
music. "You know the story of the goldfish," said Renman. "You
put a goldfish in a pool this big, and it's supposed to be able to
grow and grow. And get big. As big as these."

The fish floated unwavering, splashed with color, like creatures
which had been wounded.

"But I don't know." He was silent. "I don't know if it's true,"
he said. He stirred himself. "I've told Anna what to do. You'll
need all the help I can give you. You are not a well man, Stratton."

I wanted to laugh. He was the one who looked shrunken,
drained, reserving for himself a residue of peacefulness.

"As a young woman your mother came here once or twice a
year. She had a great deal of contempt for all of us parvenus.
She'd drive out from San Marcos and stay a weekend during the
season, in February. We deserved her contempt. This was just
after the war, and all kinds of useless people had a lot of money.
But I remember riding with friends to look at the palms in one of
the canyons here. It was quite a ride. Rocky. Dead scorpions, or
maybe just their exoskeletons. Dry. Unbelievable how dry it can
be."

He laughed wistfully. "I was a would-be cowboy, with silver-
chased chaps. What a young dandy I was. A silly kid. Born in
New Jersey, taught the alphabet in a public school, and there I
was in the saddle next to Gary Cooper. Of course, I paid his
salary, but still—he had that look. And we came upon your
mother in a dry creek of that rough canyon, all boulders and

dead things—lizard skin, dried-up rattle-snake rattles. And she was speaking sweetly to the canyon air."

I blinked.

"I mean she was talking," he said. "To nobody. To herself? Maybe. Talking like someone holding conversation with an invisible being."

I chose my words. "I find that hard to believe."

He considered this. "My father made his money selling shipping pallets. And then cardboard containers. And then he owned railway cars, and refrigerated trucks, and he seemed to own people. People who could get things done. He did harm to get where he was. He was a feared man."

"Why are you telling me this?"

"Go home, Stratton. Give your mother my regards, if and when you see her. I'm going to help you."

"Who killed DeVere?" I asked.

"An old evil," he said.

He turned to Anna, who was several steps away drinking from a glass filled with ice and what looked like chartreuse.

"Anna, you look like an angel," he said. "Take Stratton away before he asks too many questions."

51

People tell the same stories, over and over again, and it is both a pleasure and a minor source of impatience to realize that one is about to hear once again an anecdote, a dream, a scene from an old movie, which one had heard many times before. One of my father's favorite stories was dusted off over port at least three times during my childhood. It was a bit of musical history, a story from the life of Johann Sebastian Bach, that had caught my father's imagination as a boy, and encouraged him to study the piano.

The carriage ride was long, and the old rutted road dusty. The feeling of travel seeped into the bones, the rocking, the clop of the iron shoes. At last Bach reached the court of Frederick the Great, and climbed down from the carriage. Attendants hurried him at once, dusty and hungry as he was, into the imperial presence. Frederick the Great proposed a difficult musical problem, a theme almost impossible to play, something that would make a musician's hands, in my father's phrase, "spider up and down the keyboard." He asked Bach to improvise a sketch based on this challenge, and then sat back with his eyes half closed.

Bach played. What was travel, and its weariness and disorientation, compared with a chance to make music? Bach performed, in the candlelight, before the hushed court of the emperor.

The story changed at that point into a sketch of my father's studies, a sunlit summer in Salzburg, hours of conversation with cellists, conductors, and the eventual tale of my father's dislike for playing scales. "I realized I couldn't sit still that long and play the same thing over and over. I was an audience member, a delighted consumer, not an artist at all." The point of the story dwindled into a simple thesis: My father was not Bach.

But while most people are somewhat aware that they are repeating an old story, my father's telling grew smoother, and at the same time more detailed, and he never seemed to recognize in his audience—usually simply my brother and myself—the very slight reluctance to hear this fragment of musical history again.

We left Palm Springs, flying northwest into a headwind that buffeted the small jet. In the pocket beside my seat was a blue folder. In the folder were several Sony micro floppy disks. On the foldout desk before me was a Toshiba laptop.

I looked over at Anna and she seemed to sense my gaze. "We'll be developing you tomorrow."

When I did not respond, she continued, "A video, still photos. Stratton Fields: the legend."

"You'll put my signature on bars of soap."

She took a moment, and added, "It's what you dreamed of, isn't it?"

As the jet bobbed and ducked in its flight, I reviewed files that at first made little sense to me. The files were labeled enigmatically, in the way of such computerized data, but it took me only a few minutes to begin to scroll through columns of numbers, paragraphs of explanation, drafts of letters and memos. These were Renman's own records, copied, apparently, for my edification.

The files included movie projects DeVere and Renman had discussed. They described loans to foreign governments in exchange for suppressing labor unrest that might have an effect on the cotton harvest. Memos involved highways through rain forests to "access raw material." U.N. guidelines on worker exposure to insecticides were being indefinitely delayed. A Renman-controlled company owned coffee plantations in Brazil and needed to keep the costs within limits.

Not all the projects smacked of what some journalists would have called exploitative strategies. Schools were being rebuilt in Armenia, to replace those lost in a major earthquake. Tuberculosis was being studied in China, the funds coming entirely from Renman's sports profits. A vitamin supplement was being provided to infants in Africa, and mothers were to be encouraged to nurse their children. But there were opposition leaders to be persuaded, unions to be infiltrated, governments to be rewarded for their willingness to be "partners in progress." The theme of Renman's files dwindled to: We give, we take away.

There was a file labeled FIELDS. I had unlimited access to ready money. It would all come out of medical research funds.

But the files contained lies, too. Some of Renman's interests had been losing money, according to one report. One consultant recommended "thoughtful cutbacks." Renman had deliberately given me access to information that showed his empire faltering, failing around the edges. I was angry. I knew that he was trying to disguise his power.

It was dawn.

From DeVere headquarters there was a view of the East Bay hills. Headlights still glittered on the Bay Bridge. The big building was silent around us, DeVere's desk a slab that reflected the light of the rising sun.

"I don't know how you managed it," said Anna Wick, handing me a cup of coffee. When I didn't respond, she continued, "Renman's getting old. He's losing it."

"That's ridiculous."

"You don't know him."

"The man can do everything he wants to do."

She gazed with me out at the view of the bay. "Not everything," she said.

She surprised me by leading me to an elevator secreted behind a panel in the wall. We rose one floor, and stepped out into a suite with a broad bed, oak furnishings, and another view of the predawn Bay Bridge.

"We'll get it redecorated. All these earth colors make me feel dirty." She waited, as though for my reaction.

The furniture was all mission-style, some of it authentic early Californian. The worm holes and minor blemishes gave a feeling of gnarled authenticity. DeVere had not felt entirely happy in this tall, air-conditioned building, I realized. He had wanted something more real, more enduring.

"Renman's giving me what I wanted," I said. "He had to."

She considered my words. "He makes mistakes. He's making one with you."

I did not enjoy her tone. I asked, "What kind of person was DeVere?"

She sat on the edge of the bed. "DeVere lived here for awhile. Here in this room. You might say he didn't really 'live' anywhere, though. This was his address, but you couldn't say it was his home. He was always meeting with someone, or on the phone. Even when he was here his mind was somewhere else. He was looking at videos, or spreadsheets."

"He sounds a lot like you."

"Men have often found me brittle. Too interested in work. Too amused at the wrong things, too interested in what I can get out of life."

"Too interested in money."

"Power. You deceived an old man. That's what Renman is— soft and tired. He decided to be generous to you. You tricked him. I don't know how—but you did. Congratulations."

I switched on the sound system, dialed through a jazz station and various spurts of static. When I found some Elizabethan music, nearly comical in its jaunty rhythms and bleating instruments, I drew close to her.

"We're not like Renman," she said. "And Ty was never happy with any of this. He wanted to escape his past, and ended up wishing he was a farmer. I've decided that Ty didn't have an empire so much as a sort of minor cattle drive."

I let her talk.

"You're crazy," she went on. "But it may work. And if you're going all the way, I want to go with you."

The room resounded to the sound of recorder and tambour. I smiled.

She unbuttoned her blouse, and eased off her shoes. At my touch she closed her eyes. At the touch of her lips I felt something inside me go cold.

Not right.

This wasn't right.

"We'll have time," I said huskily.

She kissed me, and did not seem to sense the reserve in me, the feeling I had that there was something wrong. Or if she did, she thought she understood. What was lust compared with power?

"Yes," she said with a smile. "I believe we will."

The rest of the day was a series of conference calls, faxed messages, employees hurrying in. Photographers clicked away at me as I studied designs. The big desk was covered with blueprints, contact prints, folders.

Anna fumbled now and then for a vial of pills, and she smiled apologetically when she knew that I saw her swallowing three at once. "I'm not like you," she said.

DeVere had been in the midst of a deal to have his trademark signature on a pack of cigarettes. DeVere had insisted on top-quality Virginia tobacco, the cigarette company had wanted air-blown Maryland and "other well-regarded tobaccos" along with flavorings and "enhancers." DeVere was moving heavily into the field of handwashed silks. There were sketches of women in flowing blouses, and samples of imported silk, swatches of the stuff, some of it raw, with that wonderful creamy scent.

Renman was building two new stadiums. He was building a hospital in Denver "exclusively for the study of cancers of the internal organs." He was buying a da Vinci cartoon. He was buying a chemical company that was momentarily weakened because of a lawsuit. He was denying any knowledge in the disappearance

of a Teamsters Union official who had vanished years ago but
kept showing up in tabloids as a subject of controversy.

I flipped through folders, printouts, fired off questions to Anna
and a string of assistants. I took pleasure in every minute. There
would be a Stratton Fields edition luxury car out of Detroit, and
there would be a Stratton Fields sportscar out of Italy. I decided
that it was perfectly all right to raid the medical research funds
for some of my projects. We could always repay the money in the
future.

I did not let myself be deceived at the hints that Renman was
losing control over his empire, that the rust that eats at all empires was slowly weakening his.

My brother must have found out where I was. He called three
times, but I didn't have time to talk to him.

The sketches I made were some of the best work I had ever
done. The reading I did was stored in my memory. The presence
of power refreshed me. I was more intelligent now. I was more
energetic. I found myself thinking—knowing—that I could make
no mistake.

But in the midst of conversation with Anna Wick regarding the
new DeVere scent I stopped. The cologne was being test-mar-
keted in Tucson and Omaha, and Anna had been explaining to
me that these cities were ideal for such experimentation.

She passed me, running a finger over one of my eyebrows
possessively.

Her touch awakened a memory.

What was I doing?

Anna leaned forward with a frown, blinking to clear what I had
begun to realize were contact lenses. "Are you all right?"

I said that I was fine. "But maybe this isn't a very interesting
subject. Perfume for men is a little dull."

I let the file remain open on my lap.

Too late.

I looked around myself with new eyes. It was late afternoon,
the bay taking on the neutral gray that would soon fill with darkness and begin to reflect light.

Anna's touch had reminded me of the woman I loved.

*   *   *

"You look so tired, Mr. Fields," said Collie.

She was just leaving, buttoning her coat. "I feel great," I said, barely recognizing the sound of my own voice.

"You look just a little bit weary, if I may say so. I made something for you, just a beef burgundy, because I didn't know really where you were . . ."

"That will be fine," I said. I was not hungry. I had not felt any appetite for what seemed like a long time.

"Please let me stay and see you comfortable, just a little bit longer. It troubles me to see you so—"

"I have never felt better in my life."

"Things are shipshape here," she said. At some point in her personal history Collie must have known and admired someone whose life took him down to the sea. It might have been this naval tradition that allowed her to accept my polite but firm insistence that it was time for her to leave.

I knelt and shaved kindling, and lit it. Gradually I nursed the fire into a blaze. Here, I reminded myself, was where I once burned a feather.

This was where I burned my work.

Now what I needed more than anything was to have that audience again, that court of Presences.

"I've needed you so badly," I breathed.

I was trembling, sweating, unable to hold a thought in my mind, except for a sensation of self-loathing.

I continued, speaking as though to the fire, "I need to ask you some questions."

There it was at last, that faint flicker of light. A woman's figure, a distant galaxy, a wrinkle in my own aura—a thing I could barely see.

I whispered, "There are things I need to know."

She did not make a sound.

"The people I love," I said. "I can barely remember them."

She did not have to respond. I could sense the answer: What did you expect?

Is that what happens when there is no soul? With its loss, does memory go, too? Because love is in large part memory, bringing the absent voice, the absent face, into being.

This is what I had exchanged for my fortune. Exchange: That was the essence of life, giving one thing for another.

I turned to speak to the source of light, but she was gone.

I supported myself against the mantel. I knew what I would have to do.

Hurry, I told myself.

There is a way to bring Nona back.

52

"**D**r. Montague asked us to call him if you dropped by," said the receptionist. "And your brother wants you to give him a call, Mr. Fields, and—" But I had given a wave and a smile and was in the elevator.

I glimpsed the receptionist as the doors slid shut. She was reaching for the phone.

"Good evening, Mr. Fields," said an orderly.

"It's a quiet night," I said.

"Yes, sir," he agreed, pushing the rolling bin of laundry, "very quiet."

Then he called back to me, "Did you report in, sir?"

"Of course."

But I could sense him watching me as I hurried away from him.

The tile floors gleamed. A buffing machine hummed far off, a man directing it methodically from one side of the corridor to another. The hospital at night was subdued, but still very much a place of power, a place where lives were lost.

The floors gleamed *too* brightly. The murmur of the machine was an orchestra.

"They told us to get permission before we let anyone see her," said the rent-a-cop at the door.

"I don't think you have to worry about me," I said.

His eyes were full of apology. "Dr. Montague mentioned you especially," said the tall, dark-skinned man.

"You know just a look won't do any harm," I said.

The man was pained, leaning to one side, unable to give permission.

"Everyone has procedures," I said. "You have to have them. Otherwise, you really wouldn't know what to do when something unexpected happens."

"This is true," he said.

"I won't really go into the room. I'll just stand in the doorway."

There was a hesitation of just a second or two. "Right," he said with a smile, letting me into the room.

She was no longer curled up, but her head was still swathed. Her eyelids were sunken. She had resolved into a creature at once less tortured in appearance, and even further removed from life.

There was a long whisper in the half-dark, and then, after a long time, another long airy syllable. She was breathing. But her breath was so slow it nearly stopped during the turn-around, the waiting period between inhale and exhale.

The word came to me out of old tales, legends: deathbed. A commonplace-sounding word, but the actual bed, the actual death, has the feel of an abyss as one stands at the edge.

There was another sound, too. It was insistent, approaching, a squeak and patter, soles against waxed surface. I could hear the footsteps of people hurrying closer behind me.

Now I knew what it was I had to do.

"Nona," I said. "Everything will be all right."

The words had always been sincere, when I had murmured them after lovemaking, uttered them with delight or affection in my voice. Now they were a promise, a truth, a change in my life brought on by the advance of my own knowledge.

I knew the secret.

Life was an exchange, a cluttered trading pit. I knew what I could trade for Nona.

As I left the room Barry ran down the corridor, slowed when he saw me, and fell against a wall, panting heavily. Security guards ran along behind him. The tall, dark-skinned man tucked a transmitter into his belt, and looked at me with something like apology.

When he had recovered his breath, Barry gave my arm a squeeze as he passed me. He switched on a light and bent over Nona's recumbent body.

"You seem to think you can do anything you want," said Barry. He switched off the light and tucked in his shirt, still winded, trying to pull himself into something like professional appearance. His eyes looked puffy, and he had that new-born look of someone who has been asleep. I knew what he was about to say. He was about to say how concerned he was about me, how worried he was about what I might do.

Whatever he said, I didn't hear it.

I was gone.

53

The door to the stairwell was locked, despite the fact that the door was labeled EXIT, in glowing green letters.

I knew this hospital. I had stood with my father while we contemplated the blueprints of the new wing, the new laundry facility, the new emergency room, my father's fingers slipping across the vacant rectangles that indicated the chambers of refuge and healing.

I found another door, to another stairwell, and this one opened.

My steps echoed in the shaft. I bounded up the stairs, from time to time gripping the handrail as I leaped three or four steps at once. Below, far below, was the slam and echo of pursuers.

The lower stairs were well worn, the rail's paint flaking to bare steel. As I climbed higher, however, the steps were newer in appearance. Each doorway was surmounted by a green exit sign, and I kept climbing, beginning to breathe hard, all the way to the top.

The stairs ended. I struck the barrier with my fist and the

resulting sound was loud. This was a trap, a cul-de-sac. I had run so far to end up nowhere. The top door was padlocked and chained, and the links rattled as I tugged at the latchbar of the door.

I plunged downstairs, and a door I had raced past was labeled, clearly and in bright red letters: OPENING THIS DOOR WILL SOUND FIRE ALARM.

Footsteps slapped the stairs below me. The sound of the steps had a continuous, reverberating quality, like the splash of water in a cave.

As I tugged at the door I heard a faraway trill, a very faint shrill of fire alarm, which I knew was connected to my activities here in the musty air of the stairwell. A further notice on the door read: DOOR TO REMAIN UNLOCKED AT ALL TIMES.

The pursuers were closer. There were voices, gasps. Far-off doors were flung open, a metallic thunder.

I pushed. The barrier gave way, barely. It was unlocked, but it stuck. I slammed into it with all my weight. It burst open with a steel chuckle, scraping the crushed rock that had somehow worked its way under the door.

My feet crunched gravel.

Everything was quiet, open. There was freedom—air, sky. I was on the roof.

So you understand at last.

Her steps did not stir the crushed rock of the roof. She hovered there, as though a wrinkle of skin, a shrink-wrap sheath over the earth, kept her from touching the fragments of stone.

She was indistinct, then, and just as quickly distinct, a source of pain now as well as light, as though the early symptoms of petit mal seizure had blossomed into hallucination.

I was panting hard, unafraid. "It's all a matter of cost, isn't it? It's all a matter of what a person is worth."

Her voice was the sizzle of surf on sand, the flutter of wing. "Nothing more. But, Stratton—you still don't understand what I am."

"What you are? What difference does it make what you are? I know what you can do."

I took no pleasure, anticipating what I had to do. And yet I was sure of myself. I had that clarity of vision that comes from having no choice. I ran.

Did I hear that voice in me, that source of light, calling me, telling me to go no farther?

This was the sort of roof that should have been a garden, a landscape away from the tumult in the building below it. Instead, it was another waste. The roof in the dark was a disorienting desert. Vents brayed and vibrated, big metal hoods and domes. The smell in the air was like the clean, starchy smell vented from a laundromat.

I stumbled, and recovered my stride. There was a walkway across the gravel, flat slabs of cinderblock set as steppingstones across the rough gray mesa. I followed this path, running easily.

It was all a business, all a carnival, a noisy flea market, a brawling auction. I had guessed the secret. I climbed the dull, rough-surfaced edge of the roof, a low wall.

For her. To bring her back. I was paying a life for a life, and in the blathering stock exchange of souls I had guessed right.

54

As I fell forward, something hooked my throat.

A force tugged me back, and upward. The pressure increased. Something had my arm, a warm, bruising grip. Then something had my other arm, grasping, squeezing.

"I have him!" I recognized Barry's gasp.

I was dragged back. Gravel scraped the heels of my shoes. Arms held me.

There were voices, commands. These were people—nothing supernatural. People! I wanted to laugh. Human strength was nothing. The grasp of three men was not enough to keep me there. I climbed to my feet encumbered by their weight, but barely slowed by it.

They could not stop me.

Barry fell away, the exertion having spent him, sending him

sprawling over the stones at my feet. Two more orderlies joined the men who held me, and they tried to wrest me off my feet, back to the roof's surface where they could pin me. I could escape them easily, I was certain, but Barry's eyes made me hesitate.

His eyes beseeched me, and his hands clenched my pantlegs. "For God's sake, Stratton, please!"

His voice switched off a current in me.

I relaxed, and with something like instinctive understanding, the men released me. I backed away. I fell to my knees.

More figures joined us, and they played the nervous beams of flashlights into my face, around the metal vents on the lunar wilderness of the roof.

I saw what Barry was, at that moment. Not simply the harried, work-wasted man. Not simply the man who could play a capable game of tennis. He believed in saving lives. Medicine was not a moneymaking career for him. He was a friend.

I gazed through the twitching pools of light cast by the flashlights. There was Rick, beside a vent that resembled the great head of a robot. Rick was watching, and I did not recognize the expression in his eyes.

All I could think was: Nona.

Had to help Nona.

The two men were talking. I sat in a chair, gazing at the floor. I was trapped. Outside the door was a very large orderly who kept looking in as though to make sure all was well. Barry had given me a shot, a syringe of what I imagined was Thorazine, in the muscle of my thigh. I could feel no effect from it, but perhaps that in itself was a result of the chemical. If the patient wonders if the drug is taking effect he is already calmer than he was.

Trapped. Can't help Nona.

Gradually the drug made me feel thick-tongued, mildly concussed. I stood, and both men froze.

The best scheme was to try to seem completely peaceful. I would express regret at having caused such a fuss. I spoke as calmly as I could. I took a deep breath and managed to clear my head. "Don't you see how ridiculous this is?"

"Sit down," said Barry, "or I'll have you put into restraints."

This formal way of putting it made "restraints" sound old-

fashioned and grim, something out of Bedlam and the most remote *gulag.*

There was a flash of anger inside me. I did my best to disguise
it. "You'd be overreacting," I said.

"Hardly."

"There's no reason for me to be here."

Even now there was a measure of caution in the way Barry
treated me. I was, after all, Stratton Fields. "Please sit down,"
said Barry. "You make me very nervous."

"I'm not even trembling. Look at my hands. Steady." I looked
over at Rick. "Have you ever seen steadier hands?"

"Maybe you should sit down, Strater," said Rick, with iron in
his voice. "You're giving Barry a nervous breakdown."

I sat once again, and knitted my fingers together. "Penning me
up here will do no good. It's not necessary. I suffered a fit of
anguish." I deliberately used a phrase I thought Barry would
respond to.

It almost worked. I could see Barry revolving "anguish" in his
mind. "A fit of suicidal anguish," he corrected me. "And now
you're entirely recovered—is that what you want me to think?"

I lifted my eyebrows: Why not?

Barry made a tight little smile: We both knew "why not."

We sat in an examination room. A long table was against one
wall, and rumpled white paper covered it. There was a small
desk, with a writing tablet taped into place, a spray of paper-
wrapped thermometers and a tablet of prescription forms.

For a moment I could think only: I've lost Nona.

Barry looked very tired. It was an hour after our struggle on
the roof. It occurred to me that Barry had been virtually living at
the hospital. "I'm not just a physician in this case. We're friends.
Maybe that blurred my judgment."

"This wasn't hard to understand," said Rick. "Stratton thought
Nona was . . ." He fumbled for a word and couldn't find one.
"He couldn't go on."

"I can understand it." Barry's voice was breathy, torn. "But I
can't let it pass."

"Release him to me. I'll take care of him," said Rick.

Barry shook his head. Someone happening upon us would
have thought that Barry was the distraught mental patient, and
that Rick and I were soothing counselors. "I've sent for someone

who knows your family. I wouldn't do it unless I thought Stratton was an emergency case. I admire your family. I admire you, Stratton. I'm scared, Rick. I think he's really got problems."

"He's upset," said Rick.

"There's family history we have to consider."

Rick made a snort. "What do you know about our family?"

"You have to face facts. The time has come."

Rick laughed, a jeer. "Christ, Barry. Listen to yourself. Do you realize how stupid you sound? 'Face facts.' You sound like a small mind, a little greeting-card intellect. We've suffered year after year in the public eye. I have too much champagne or scrape a fender on Taylor Street it's in the paper. In the gossip column, Barry." His voice had hardened, and Rick was on his feet. "People like us are expected to live like public monuments. Elegant, civilized. We can't have careers, like your kind of person. We have to say the right thing, stand in the right places, like famous, boring public buildings."

His voice was gaining power. " 'Face facts.' Your sort of person can go around uttering trite phrases like that while my brother— my brother, a man I love—is suffering from years of having to be a gentleman in a world of people made of plastic and stapled together with wise little phrases like 'the time has come.' "

I had never heard my brother speak with such feeling, not since boyhood. "And you think that this hospital, which my family helped build with its own money, is going to be a prison for Stratton Fields? Do you think I'm going to stand around while you put my brother in 'restraints'?" He said the last word with something of Barry's nervous manner.

"How will you stop me?" said Barry.

"You ordinary people," said Rick quietly.

"Are you going to get your family attorney on the phone? What's he going to say? Do you think he's going to talk me into letting Stratton go? I'm right, Rick. You're wrong. Stratton's my patient."

"I won't let it happen." Rick's voice was quiet and fierce. "I won't let your kind of ordinary person abuse one of us. We've never allowed that. We never will."

Barry was blanched, and Rick glanced at me and laughed unsteadily. "I've let my feelings show at last. That's not our usual habit. I've given a little speech, haven't I? Barry will think the two of us ought to stay here together. I wonder, do they actually have rubber mats on the walls, like in a gym. We can wrestle. You were always pretty good at wrestling."

The frankness with which Rick had spoken could not be withdrawn, and I saw that Barry was struck by Rick's manner. I recognized Rick's anger. It was an anger we shared, but I had never realized how furious Rick was.

"It won't work," said Barry quietly. "I have a legal responsibility." There was a weakness in his voice, however. He was not certain he could wage a battle against the forces of law and public opinion Rick and I could muster.

I could see Rick readying a response.

"I'll stay," I said.

Both men looked at me.

"I'll stay—if that's what Barry advises. He's my doctor. Not that I agree with you, Barry. I agree with Rick, my eloquent brother. However—under protest—I will submit myself to whatever you have in mind. For a day or two."

This bit of diplomacy quieted the two men, and I could sense Barry's gratitude. Rick, however, met my eye with something like a merry glance of his own. And winked.

We would pretend to cooperate. We would placate Barry. After all, why damage an old friendship beyond repair? But in our own way, in a convenient moment, we would do exactly what we wanted to do.

It was hardly a surprise to see a nurse in the doorway. Rick's voice must have carried through the door. "There's someone here to see you, Dr. Montague."

Barry opened his hand as if to say: We're in the middle of a crisis here. He looked at me with a touch of weary humor, as if to say: I can't get a moment's peace.

But the nurse stepped inside and whispered into Barry's ear.

"Good heavens!" said Barry. "Here?"

The nurse whispered something else, and Barry stood.

55

How impossible it is to understand this surface that springs from nowhere, this moment-to-moment. What falls is neither the sparrow nor the night, because those things only appear to descend, called by weight or the roll of earth toward the planet's core. What falls is what we dreamed of, prayed for, and were always certain would happen in just this way.

Dr. Valfort entered the room briskly. He adjusted his necktie and gave me a knowing smile. I was not as surprised as I should have been. I thought: of course.

Valfort looked for a moment at Rick. I knew that during my hypnotherapy I must have said some interesting things about my family.

Barry was beginning introductions, but Valfort lifted a hand. "I should have flown out on the same plane with Stratton. I was jealous. I sulked."

"I am very happy to see you," I said.

"I am a man of moods, and I apologize. Marie scolded me. I realized my responsibilities. Here I am."

Barry continued to struggle through introductions, and Valfort shook hands all around, but there was an undertone of impatience to his voice. He looked rumpled, but jet lag agreed with him, softening the hawklike glance. "Stratton will understand what I have done. He and I are aware of Nona's needs."

"We'll be able to make some real progress," said Barry. "And the staff will be delighted to meet with you—"

Valfort spoke sharply. "The staff here is not interesting to me. I did not come here to 'make progress.' Nona Lyle has a history of hysterical trances, something that you will not find in her records, but which first encouraged her to study the mind. Please don't interrupt me, Dr. Montague. I have examined Nona Lyle already. I do beg your pardon. I took a liberty."

Barry looked pleased, but reserved. "I'm delighted. I look forward to your conclusions."

Valfort silenced Barry with a wave of his hand. Valfort stepped before me, and although he spoke to Barry and Rick his eyes were on mine. "Stratton made an important decision tonight, I am told."

"Decision?" said Barry.

"They tell me that you tried to take your life tonight, Stratton."

I acknowledged, with a nod more than a word, that this was true.

"Did you think that you could exchange your life for hers?"

My voice was husky. "Yes."

He closed his eyes, then slowly opened them. "It doesn't work that way. The Powers we enjoin cannot do good. They give us good fortune only through harm. Surely you know that by now."

"And yet—here you are."

There was real warmth, and real sadness, in Valfort's eyes. "You will misunderstand what I have been able to do," he said.

"It will be an honor to work with you, Doctor," said Barry.

Valfort studied Barry without a further word for a moment. "Dr. Lyle is very weak. In addition to her emotional trauma there was the physical drain of the probably unnecessary surgery."

Barry worked to control his temper. "You are late arriving to help us. We're glad to see you. Of course. Distinguished and colorful. International. Perhaps when you have taken time to review every step we considered—"

"Time is not important, although you are wasting mine. Dr. Lyle is conscious. She is asking to speak with Stratton."

As I strode with Valfort through the corridors of the hospital I was elated. The institutional colors of the walls and the floors were bright and the air was sweet.

He squeezed himself before me, blocking my way. "I have not given permission," he said.

I ignored him, squeezing by. He walked fast to keep up with me. "I'm not at all certain what you will do."

"What sort of person do you think I am?"

"I know one or two things about you, Mr. Fields. That's why I am worried." But he seemed to make a decision, relaxing his expression slightly. "Don't say anything that would trouble her," Valfort was saying.

I reassured him. The thought was outrageous. I would do nothing to hurt Nona in any way. Besides, I didn't want to stand there talking.

Valfort took my arm and turned me to face him. I was irritated, tugging myself away, not wanting to waste time with argument.

But there was something urgent in his manner. He held me with one hand, a firm grip on my shoulder. His dignified, weathered face was right before me, his eyes earnest.

"I know you," he said.

Two white-clothed attendants had appeared, one on either side of me.

"I know what you think must have happened, Mr. Fields," he was saying. "You think that you have saved Nona by using your powers. This is your belief. But what has happened is not an evil miracle. It is a matter of medicine. Of flesh and blood. If you see her return to life as a pact with your Powers then this is a very bad thing. It would be better for Nona to have stayed as she was."

I stiffened. "How can you say that?" I tore myself away from him.

He took my arm again. "I know what you think you are capable of doing. I know what you think you are."

My voice was a hard whisper. "I want to see Nona."

He gave a quiet laugh with little humor. "A man without a soul has nothing to bargain with."

His words angered me, but they also stirred my doubt. Of course, I was forced to remind myself, the Powers would not have been at all interested in returning Nona to me. And what madness had possessed me all along? A man does not win his lover's life through suicide.

He perceived the sort of inner questions I was experiencing. "I want to save her life," he said.

"So do I."

"Please think of me as a friend. A difficult friend, but a real one. You do not live in the same world the rest of us inhabit."

The very slight effort it took him to choose the right words in

English gave his communication greater weight. "You must hate me," I said.

"Do not hurt her, Mr. Fields."

I could hardly speak. "I can't possibly hurt her."

"I hope what you are saying is true."

I wanted to joke, to turn aside his words with a laugh. But I could not. Perhaps I did not know my own nature after all.

She was asleep.

It was so simple—sleep had her now, not unconsciousness. Her skin had a hint of rose, of the old liveliness I recalled.

I can't wake her, I told myself. I will stand here and watch. I will stay here, in this vigil, without tiring.

She stirred. Her lips parted. Her eyes searched behind their lids. How did this body before me hold within its flesh the spirit of the woman I loved? All the maps wither. The stars vanish. At a time like this there is no north, no south.

She spoke.

It was a breath, only, an exhalation. But that span of air had been a shape I recognized, that airy sound had been a word. I leaned close to her, my ear at her lips.

A vigil.

A long wait, guarding a border, beyond the empty place that is not human, from which humans come when they approach from illness, from sleep.

Valfort had me watched, more carefully than Nona was watched. These attendants were not the usual orderlies. These were alert, and had a more practiced bearing, young and wary of me. They were, however, polite when I commented on the warmth of the room, or on the slow passage of the time.

The time did not matter. It was Nona who had come so far only to linger just beyond us. From time to time a nurse touched Nona's lips with a moist cloth. Sometimes Valfort came into the room, and when he did it was always to observe me as much as the sleep of his patient. He was not an adversary so much as a man who knew the things about me I had forgotten, or chose to forget.

Sometimes a glass of water, or orange juice, tasting strangely sour, was pressed into my hands. The hours that passed were the great, rolling passage of glaciers, or eras of geological time, but I was steady, there, waiting for her, a man watching the north, peering into the wind for a rider he knew would come.

Someone said: "You must be tired."

Someone said: "You must be hungry."

Each breath she took was another step for me, another moment on a climb across the cliff face.

Remember, I told myself, the quick acts of love she committed, the force behind her life. "I can't stay," she used to say. "I'm in a hurry." "I'm due at the hospital in ten minutes." "There's a new child. He needs so much." In that winter that follows loss we feel that we cannot consider the absent person. When we think they are returning, then we allow ourselves the pleasure of remembering.

It is not enough to love. We must enact the love, turn and walk back up the path, swim across the lake, and climb up upon the new outcropping that no one owns and which is never old, another day.

How did we find ourselves so dependent on accomplishment? How was it that we learned the way to believe in the future and ignore the flat, sun-warm soil at our feet? I had that awareness, that sensation that a hospital gives, that what surrounds us, the glossy, thick-painted walls, is the empty vision. What is real is what is gone.

She spoke.

My lips touched her ear. "I'm here."

She stirred, just barely, a movement too slight to be noticed except for the fact that I was so close to her. Her head rolled, a slow, barely perceptible movement. Her lips, her eyelids, seemed to vibrate from some inner tension, some inner pleasure, like the shimmer of feeling on the features of a skater about to spin across the ice.

56

"I dreamed," she said.

Her voice was a thread.

Her eyes closed again.

No, I wanted to cry out to her—please stay with me. And then I remembered that it was this selfish love that had been so shallow, so false.

Nona slept.

I began to feel an appetite for food again. Rick brought me snacks, a ham-and-cheese croissant, a chocolate bar. Valfort looked in frequently over the next several hours, and sometimes Barry stepped to my side, patted my shoulder manfully, and gazed at Nona with both joy and disbelief.

There have been times in my life when I thought that war might destroy our world, and when I considered this I wondered: how would we rebuild? It was not simply a childish fear. I had been raised knowing that hydrogen bombs would seek out the ports of San Francisco and Oakland, and the naval bases of the bay. The places I loved, like the people, could be blown out like a host of flames. The solidity of the buildings I loved was an illusion. The world was composed of space interlaced with happenstance.

If the world were erased, and yet enough people survived, as we rebuilt what would we neglect to include in our new recreations of life, what precious shadings of reality would we forget to replace? We might forget the charm of clutter, the pleasure of a footpath worn across a public lawn, the serenity of waiting while someone slept, and reconstitute a new civilization without the minor graces.

* * *

She opened her eyes.

I could not speak.

She let her strength gather. Then she said, "You talked to Dr. Valfort."

"Yes. He helped me. Just like you said he would."

"He's very wise." Her voice was weakening. She was about to drift off to sleep once again.

"I don't think he likes me," I said softly, believing that I was talking only to myself.

She moved her lips, and her eyelids parted once again. "The dream I had. It was a bad dream," she said.

"We can talk about it later," I said. "We'll have time."

A frown creased her brow, a small furrow. She tried to lift her head. "Something bad," she said. Then, lifting a hand, stirring herself, "Something is after you."

"No, nothing's after me," I said, not aware of telling a lie, wanting only to reassure her. "We don't have to talk about it now."

She fought to speak. "Something—"

I tried to hush her.

Her voice was a whisper. "Something real."

She rested, still conscious, letting her strength return.

I repeated my reassurance. We would talk later. We would have years, and I felt the presence of this future inside me. I knew that I was telling her the truth. Seeing her alive to the world was all I would ever want.

"Someone tried to kill me," she said.

"I know." How could either of us forget the darkness, the broken glass, the baseball bats? "But you're going to be—"

"Someone here. Here in the hospital."

57

The room was gray.

The floor, the ceiling, the walls. There were no sounds. There was no show of pictures in frames, the kind of décor sported by the other rooms of the hospital, the Klee prints, the anonymous reproductions of seascapes and forest streams. There was no television with its flicker of smiling faces. Even the matter-of-fact dignity of the hospital room was missing here.

There was the flow of my breath, and the tread of my heartbeat. There was nothing more.

I had insisted. Barry had said it wasn't necessary. He said there were better plans: private hospitals, brilliant psychiatrists, long walks under rows of ornamental plum trees, Mozart and saunas.

"You need help," he had said, "but we don't have the kind of facilities for someone like you."

I was afraid.

I was afraid that I had, myself, with these hands, tried to hurt Nona.

Forgetting: That was the key. I had forgotten so much. There was a life, a world, I had repressed. I could not guess what sky I had fallen from.

The room acknowledged the harm a person could do. Just as a visit to a nursing home dashes away all complacency about the nature of illness and age, so a place like this room told everything about what the human will might descend to.

This was the rubber room of joke and legend, the mythical chamber of the madman. The rubber mats were gray, puckered all around from the plastic sealed rivets that spiked them to the walls. The smell was that of a clean locker room—metal, concrete, rubber.

*   *   *

Voluntary commitment, Barry had explained, would mean that I could leave whenever I wanted. Barry himself could have kept me in the hospital for forty-eight hours' observation, "typical for someone who is suicidal."

I had stated it as plainly as possible. "I want to stay locked up until I'm sure I haven't killed anyone, or tried to kill anyone."

"But this is hardly necessary," Barry had said. "This kind of room is for someone who's really . . ." Then he selected his words carefully, continuing, "This is the sort of room for someone in the most disruptive stage of behavior. Rooms like this aren't even necessary anymore. We still need a sort of pressure-release place like this for someone in the rocky stages of detox. Or a terminal alcoholic, someone who throws turds at people. We can have you so quiet with injections of chlorpromazine that you might as well be a zombie."

"That hardly sounds desirable."

"Well, maybe *zombie* isn't what I really meant to say."

"I'm safe here," I said, meaning: So are you. So is everyone. The staff psychiatrist, a man with the lean looks and detached manner of a computer programmer, discussed "chemical maintenance," oxazepam "for anxiety" and "possible introduction of lithium as an antimanic." But I was not anxious, and I did not feel manic.

I felt determined. The hospital food was adequate, orange juice in plastic cups sealed in aluminum with a label picturing a smiling orange in a cowboy hat. There was Jell-O, lemon flavor or lime, sliced turkey or chicken in gravy. Barry said that I could have dishes of my own choice sent in, but I declined.

Two days passed, a secure, gray chapter after chapter of silence.

Rick had brought me loose-fitting athletic clothes, red sweatshirt and only slightly faded red pants. If the gray walls gave me a feeling of security, the red I was wearing seemed appropriate, too. Red was the color of life, and of danger.

I sat against one wall, feeling very much like a wrestler awaiting his opponent, perhaps that angelic wrestler, the one who contends with the soul only to bless it.

I had that worst fear, deeper than the fear of fire, deeper than the fear of a fall from a great height. I was afraid of myself.

*   *   *

There was a click, a rattle.

Out there, in the world beyond, there was a key. A key, and a lock. The padding before me shifted backward. The gray, bunched surface swung away, along neat, straight lines. A rectangle opened up, and outside air flowed in—a doorway.

Barry smelled of coffee, of the vaguest reminder of cigarette smoke, the smell of a lunchroom. "Are you enjoying the view?" he asked.

I smiled. "Splendid."

He kicked one of the walls. It sounded like someone kicking a sofa. We didn't have to go into the argument again, but his attitude was plain: You don't have to do this.

"Rick is here. He's made some phone calls. There's a really wonderful place in the East Bay. There's another place in Mendocino County . . ."

"Thank you," I said.

"Rick has a visitor. Someone I wanted you to see."

I imagined the representative of a sanitarium, with an attaché case full of pamphlets. But Barry was so winsome, standing by the door, expectant, hopeful, that I could not bring myself to disappoint him.

After two days even the expanse of a corridor was vast, and it made me feel giddy.

The furniture in this room was screwed to the floor. The chairs were those out-of-date modern scoops, the sort airports had been fond of a few years ago, except that even an airport would have forgone this sherbet-yellow upholstery. I recognized Barry's touch: a vase had been placed in the corner of the room, with a glorious eruption of irises.

There were two people in the room when I entered it. I felt fit and outdoorsy in my athletic clothes, but the people I was with were well-dressed, in the clothes one would wear to hear the reading of a will.

I knew this visitor.

Rick was nervous, whistling silently to himself. His companion was drawn into herself, a woman on a mission she would not enjoy. I let the two of them choose which yellow scoop they would sit in. They seemed to have arrived in the room just moments before I did, and we had the air of prospective jurors, waiting to be chosen, or travelers unexpectedly delayed.

The tall, handsome, gray-haired woman eyed the room as though sensing that it could swallow her. Her manner was not fearful so much as knowing and watchful. She had seen such places before and knew them well. At last, she turned and looked at me with clear gray eyes.

She did not speak. Her eyes were steady, regretful.

"Dr. Ahn drove up from Carmel," said Rick. "Barry explained that I needed her advice."

I told Dr. Ahn how good it was to see her.

Dr. Ahn had been my mother's physician during the worst of her crisis after my father's death. The truth was, that while I was pleased to see her, I sensed in her a potential adversary. I could not guess why. Perhaps I found her steady gaze cool and all-too honest.

But it was pained, too, and I realized that she was a woman of compassion. She reminded me of Nona, the way she ran a hand along the seam of her chair arm, where the thick plastic was joined. She sat easily, with a straight back, as though her figure created the room it inhabited, endowing it with color, substance.

"It's a medical matter, really," said Rick. "So I really don't have to stay."

"Stay," said Dr. Ahn.

Rick clenched his hands together, prayerful or tense. "She has a lot to say. About Mother. About both of you."

Why did I resent Rick so much at just that moment? I turned my gaze upon Dr. Ahn. "I certainly don't need the help of this distinguished doctor."

She spoke, breaking her silence. "I'm afraid you do."

"She has something very important to tell us," Rick said. "When I told her about my fears—my fears about you—she took me into her confidence."

Why did I continue to find Rick's manner just slightly offensive?

"I ran across a book of yours recently," I said, turning to Dr. Ahn. "Something about the Woman at the Well. The New Jerusalem."

"I studied hallucinations for years," said the doctor, with a strong, steady voice. "I believed that in the disorders of the mind we can see the fountainhead of religious experience and creativity."

"There's no need to establish your credentials here," I began.

"I think I was wrong," said Dr. Ahn. "William Blake said that while truth has bounds, error has none. The waywardness of the psyche can be understood, but it produces no cathedrals, writes no—or at any rate few—symphonies."

"You sound disappointed," I said, suddenly liking her very much, her thoughtfulness, the sound of her voice.

"In the end," she said, "I came to believe that our greatest discovery was not the glories of genius, or the colorful landscape of the mentally ill."

"You have me wondering," I said.

"Compassion," she said. "Not any form of vision, not any other form of understanding or any other mastery of anything. Compassion. It's our finest characteristic."

"So your studies," I said, "were not really in vain after all."

She looked at me appraisingly. "I have made mistakes as a therapist. And I have always been unorthodox. May I make an entirely personal comment?"

"Of course."

"Knowing what I know—or, at least, believing what I have heard—I expected an entirely different person."

"I disappointed you."

She did not respond to that statement. "My conversation with Dr. Valfort convinced me to come here today," she said. "Dr. Montague was persuasive, too, of course. Otherwise I would never have discussed your family with anyone. As it is, I only begin to mention any of it to save you, Stratton."

"Valfort thinks I'm dangerous," I said.

"He called me and said as much," she said. "He was very concerned. So is Dr. Montague."

I could not keep from sounding ironic. "I'm touched to be a matter of such earnest concern."

"And what do *you* think?" asked Dr. Ahn.

I could no longer sound calm. My voice was hoarse. "I agree with them."

"You don't know what you have done. You don't know what you might do."

I could hardly speak. "That's right."

"Why did you consult with Dr. Valfort?" she asked.

I cleared my throat. "I flew to Paris because Nona suggested it. Urged it."

"Do you respect her opinion?" she asked.

"Of course."

She continued, "His theories are sometimes questionable. But he is a well-established hypnotherapist and a surgeon of the best sort. He knows the human body is not a domain of chemicals and tissues."

"Look at me. Calm. Civilized. But I'm forced to wonder if I've killed people." I said this with as much cheer as I could muster.

"Valfort believes that you have killed two men," said Dr. Ahn.

She paused, waiting for me to respond, but I did not make a sound.

"You described the murders to him during hypnosis," she said. "He hesitated to tell anyone else—for example, the police—because one can never be certain whether what one hears in hypnotherapy is the literal truth, or merely what the patient wishes were true. Or really believes is true."

I remained speechless.

Rick's voice was broken. "Stratton, whatever she tells you, I want you to know that I'll help you."

I stood. I didn't want to hear any more.

Rick continued, "She has something terrible to say about Mother."

I had heard enough. "You two have plotted. You put your heads together to come up with this brutal story. Let's see how much Stratton can take. Go ahead. I'm strong. I can take it. Say anything you want. Barry is using you to convince me that I am totally mad. Maybe I am. Keep talking. Say whatever you like." I stopped myself.

I had known all along. I was guilty.

Rick was solemn, unable to meet my gaze. "She has something else to tell you. Something terrible—that I believe is true."

I fell into my choir. "What is it?" I asked.

"It's very bad," said Rick.

I turned away, knowing I did not want to hear what was about to be said.

Dr. Ahn spoke like someone reciting an old memory. "Your mother's case shook me. It was the way I handled your mother, and my failure to help her, that made me decide to retire." Dr. Ahn waited for me to prepare myself. "Your mother's mental illness predated the death of your father. For years before his death she had hallucinations," said Dr. Ahn. "She saw people who weren't there. She heard voices."

"It's hardly news that my mother was sick," I said, shifting in my chair.

"She was more than sick," said Dr. Ahn.

I prepared my next question with care. "What sort of figures did she see?"

"Beings that she felt were very powerful. Supernatural presences."

I managed a wry smile. "This kind of hallucination must be fairly common, after all."

"Not really."

"What kind of advice did these visitations give her?"

She took a moment before answering. "It's interesting that you assume that they gave her advice."

"What else would divine messengers give?" I said it with a smile, but she did not smile in return.

"She believed that your father was involved with other women. Women that were trying to woo him away from your mother. She was so afraid of losing your father. She was afraid of the scandal, the public shame at losing him."

"She is proud," I said, perhaps to forestall what I was hearing. "She taught us that to be respected is all we have. Take that away, and what are we? We have only our pride. Our good name."

"These spirits killed your father," said Dr. Ahn.

"They killed my father," I echoed, feeling dull-witted.

"So she believed," said Dr. Ahn. "These entities, these hallucinations, your mother believed, poisoned your father. Of course, your mother's own hand did the deed. She was not aware of committing any act at all."

I could not take a breath. "That's absurd!" I said, when it was possible for me to speak.

"Don't you remember how you begged us not to have an autopsy?" said Rick. "Don't you remember how you donated all that money to the blood bank in exchange for the medical examiner's quick handling of Dad's case? It would upset Mom too much, you said."

"I was right. She hated the thought of an autopsy. They're so ugly, maiming the poor corpse—"

"It's because you guessed," said Rick. "You guessed that she killed him."

I could barely whisper. "Ridiculous!"

"You knew, Stratton," said Dr. Ahn. "Or, you tried with every ounce of your spirit to forget."

"How did I know?"

"You heard Mother talking to her spirits," said Rick, his voice broken.

"No, I never did hear any such thing." But my words faded. I tried to convince myself. Never.

I had denied the truth. But it came back to me now. Or did it? I was still able to escape what was closing in on me, the heat of my own memory.

58

The process had begun in Paris, with Valfort and the candle flame.

My brother's eyes acted on me more powerfully than any hypnotic suggestion.

No, I tried to reassure myself. Surely not. You don't really remember.

I can never sleep as others can. I lie awake in the long nap, the baby brother dozing, the mother lifting her voice. The shrubbery is brambled. The trees pruned, scars the shape of closed eyes where there were branches.

It was easy to recall in that instant. She stood among the fleshy, topsy-turvy past-peak roses, and spoke to what I thought must be my father, must be—was it possible—a relative we had not yet met. Such a loving, lovely voice.

And then I saw, in my mind, a flash of what I had wanted to avoid.

Ahn's eyes were like Valfort's eyes. Something of my session with him rose up within me.

"I don't," I said brokenly, "want to remember."

My mother spoke to beings which were not there. She spoke to spirits. And I had always known this, even as a child. It had been our secret, our family's secret.

I could remember her now, how she would speak, nearly singing, standing in the back garden. Or she would be in her bedroom, holding discourse with what we all knew—and could not mention—was nothing. Nothing at all.

My father had never acknowledged it, but it was evident that this aberration on the part of my mother was acutely embarrassing to him. Was it possible? Had I actually forced myself to deny this memory of my mother's sweet voice asking, "Why have you come to see me again?" A fresh tone in her voice, a spritely tone, unlike the tone she used with anyone else. How I must have envied her spirits!

Painful. Too painful, the sound of her voice.

Everyone must have known. Friends, casual acquaintances. It must have been plain to so many.

Dr. Ahn's voice was gentle. "And now your brother wonders if the same sort of delusions are troubling you."

"She spoke to angels," I breathed. "Like the angels in the Bible. The ones that announce that a barren woman will have a child."

"Did she tell you they were angels?" asked Dr. Ahn.

I wondered. "I assumed they were," I said.

"It was a little lie you told to yourself," said Rick. "To make the truth sweeter."

How hard and ugly Rick's voice sounded.

"This is happening to you, Strater," said my brother.

"I have ghosts killing people for me, you mean?" I was shivering, the sensation in my body that of deep cold, a feverish, sick chill.

"That's what I mean," he said.

I wanted to avoid what I was about to say, but perhaps my brother's unloving voice made me respond with this recollection, perhaps as a way of hurting him, perhaps to show that my memory was, for the moment, entirely free. "I saw her in the garden. Behind the rhododendrons. I saw her there."

Words stuck.

"She was always disturbed," said Rick, plainly dismissing what I was beginning to say.

"She was talking to a man, I thought at the time. She was saying how much she loved him. I thought it was a man I must know. I was happy. Happy to hear her say such good things, because she and Father didn't really say things like that to each other, not when we could hear them. And maybe never—they were cold toward each other. And so I peeked."

I was icy. "I should not have looked. That was bad. That was very bad." I closed my eyes then. Don't, I told myself, say any more.

"She was naked," I breathed, "and she was making love. With no one."

"She was sick," he said. There was something ugly in his voice.

I gazed upon my brother. "Why are you so harsh, Rick? Maybe you don't like these memories any more than I do."

"Maybe not," he said.

I turned to Dr. Ahn. "Why didn't you tell the police when you uncovered all of this?" I asked.

"At the time of your father's death, and for a matter of two or three years afterward, I didn't know. Only in the years that followed, when we discussed her life, and searched the memories that she saved from the past, and the ones that she invented, did we begin to uncover the truth. By then, she was in the hospital your family built, ordered there by the court. I felt that it would be senseless agony to share this truth with you."

"This sort of sickness," Rick began. "This tendency. It can be inherited, right?"

"You think I hold congress with spirits? Is that what you think, Rick? None of this has anything to do with me. Come right on out and say it. Go ahead."

I stood and paced.

We are real. Don't let this woman deceive you.

I put my hands to my head.

"I don't believe you," Rick said. "I believe you are just like Mother."

"And if I am? What will you do to help me?"

"I should leave now," said Rick. "This is the sort of thing that should be done in private, doctor to patient."

"Stay here," said Dr. Ahn.

"Stratton is your patient," Rick protested.

I realized why this room had seemed so right for this conversation with Dr. Ahn. My mother's presence, her taste, the weight of her personality, was everywhere suddenly. The vase of irises—it was as though my mother had put them there herself.

"You're afraid to talk to me, aren't you, Stratton?" said Dr. Ahn.

"No," I said, truthfully. "I'm not afraid."

"What are you hiding?" she asked.

Quite a bit, I nearly said. "Do you have anything else to tell me?" I said.

"What do you have to tell *me?*"

"Someone tried to kill Nona. While she was here in the hospital. It was me, wasn't it? I tried to take her life."

Dr. Ahn looked, if anything, satisfied that I had mentioned Nona. "Valfort says that someone tried to suffocate her. She spoke about it, a gush of words Dr. Valfort couldn't quite catch. She says someone put a pillow over her head. When she was first here after the beating, when there were nurses coming and going, and she was in a twilight state."

"How could it have been me? I was in a room by myself."

"Immobilized?"

"Hardly. I could walk. I was in pretty good condition when you consider—"

Why would I try to kill Nona?

"You can get help, Stratton," said my brother.

Help. I can get help. The thought made me sit back and reconsider all that I had heard. I was shuddering, quaking inwardly, but I took a long moment to ask myself how.

How could spirits kill someone? Unless the spirits themselves were corporeal. Could spirits do harm in the world, pick things up—actual, material things of weight and texture?

Spirits need help. Spirits need a human agency. These hands. These two hands.

"Rick," I said at last. "Tell me what you knew about Mother."

59

"Nothing," he said. "I knew nothing."

He took a step back, and I followed him. A chair fell over behind us. "You didn't help her, knowing how much she hated to get her hands dirty?"

"That's a terrible thing to say, Stratton."

Rick was agitated, but he was able to hold it in. I was so close to him that I could sense the workings of his emotions, the interplay of uncertainty and confidence.

"That's why I forgot, isn't it?" I said. "Because the truth was too much to bear. You helped her."

My brother slapped me.

I was shocked at what I had said. I was shocked at his blow. My jaw did not work, and I gasped, a half-laugh, a sound of wonderment.

I rubbed the numbness on my cheek. "I wonder what that means?" I said after a long silence. "Yes. Or no."

"You can't talk to me like that, Stratton," he said, his eyes hard. "You can't get me confused with your sickness. I've helped you in ways you can't even guess. I've been a good brother to you. Stratton the man of dignity. Stratton the gentleman. I crash my car, lose my money, and people say: just like his father."

"Dad wasn't like that."

"Like me, you mean. Sure he was. You remember Dad the way you want to, practically inventing him. All he wanted was constant adoration. He played around with other women. I knew it. Everyone knew it. You're good, Stratton. Nobody in the whole family was like you. You always did belong to some other time. Not this place. Not now. You were the one who cared."

"Don't say bad things about yourself, Rick. You're a good brother." I put my arms around him. "And you hit pretty hard, too."

We laughed, with tears in our eyes.

Then, emboldened by emotional fatigue, or with my desire to be truthful, I said, "Rick is right. I hear voices. I see people who aren't there. People made of light."

Dr. Ahn looked at me like someone hearing a recitation, a poem she had heard many times before.

Go on, I told myself. You've started. Don't stop. "I am sicker than Mother ever was," I said.

The walls seemed to step back. Dr. Ahn closed her eyes, and then slowly opened them. She was not a therapist in this conversation. She was a bearer of a part of the truth, a Cassandra who was believed. And Rick was not happy, it seemed, at my sudden confession. His lips worked but he didn't say anything.

"It's true. I want to tell you everything. Shall I begin? Shall I tell you about a feather I found? A feather that could make my wishes come true?"

Rick did not know what expression to wear on his face. "Things like that don't happen."

"Maybe it's just a talent that Mother gave me, along with her feeling that the world should be a place where people can look out a window and see something beautiful. Something that makes them want to go on living."

"You're serious," he said, speaking almost entirely to himself, in a tone of discovery. He straightened his shoulders. "Whatever you want to tell me," said Rick solemnly. "I'll listen."

I felt like a comic, trailed by the spotlight, about to announce in his brisk, delightful way, the medically verified terminal illness of each member of the audience.

I told them all—the entire story, from the cold riptide to that moment we all shared, the three of us, in the chilly air-conditioned air of the hospital.

No Divine voice interrupted me. The Assembly of the Others was silent—empty.

It is not enough, at last, to confess, to share the secrets. These days that have accumulated are gone. The weight the mind feels is all the places and people who are not present. The landscape knows without knowing a thing: It is inhuman and lovely, trees and lagoons. The gardener spades, fertilizes, reseeds. We tell the story of what has happened. We think the story is true. The sky is a hole big enough for the world.

Neither of them spoke. And it might have taken a long while, or it might have been a fairly short recitation of events, of hallucinations.

I knew that as I spoke I was altering my future, because never again would I be allowed to think of myself as a normal human being. I was destined to stay in the hospital I had designed, with the person from whom I had inherited my illness.

At last I had told everything.

Dr. Ahn and Rick were diminished, stunned figures. I concluded, "All I want to know is: Did I really kill DeVere? Did I kill Blake?"

Rick was pale.

The answer was obvious. "I must have," I said.

I felt desolate, stripped of my memory of even recent events. But it was good to know the truth.

"What should I do?" I said at last. I turned to face Dr. Ahn. "Tell me what to do."

She did not want to speak. She was sorry, I felt, to have come here today. "I can't tell you. There is so much I can't understand —about your family, about the mind. I had such hopes as a young woman. I believed in myself."

I said, "If I stay here in this hospital I'll be close to Nona—"

"But you won't get well," said Rick, completing my thought. "Besides, you aren't certain that you didn't try to hurt her. It might be better to stay away from her."

My breath was gone. Rick had used a matter-of-fact tone, but his words punished me. It was impossible to think for a few moments. Then I nodded weakly. It might be better to stay away.

Rick found himself able to smile. "Have some faith. People recover from things like this."

Rick had always believed. He had always been sure. I envied him at that moment more than at any other time in my life.

"I have no special knowledge anymore. Ignorance is almost

like a blessing." Dr. Ahn was thoughtful. "I want you to go to Los Cerritos tonight. I know the staff there, and we can begin to help you."

"I'll drive him," said Rick.

Dr. Ahn did not respond. When she spoke again it was not to mention Rick driving me, and it was not to discuss any of what I had described. She said, *"Someone* killed Ty DeVere and Blake Howard."

"Perhaps they were suicides after all," said Rick.

"And it's possible," I said, before Dr. Ahn could make any further remark, "that Nona is mistaken. Maybe no one tried to take her life here in the hospital. Maybe it was a dream."

"Why not?" said Rick, as though someone had suggested a party.

"That would be the best hope," said Dr. Ahn. "That it was all a waking dream, every last blow, every drop of blood."

"You don't believe that?" I asked.

She shook her head sadly. "Valfort is sure you have done harm. I'm not."

"Then the men killed themselves—like Peterson," said Rick lightly.

She could not answer for awhile. "Maybe I have always wondered if there are such things as angels," she said.

"It would be a wonderful thing if there were," said Rick, sounding bright, tired of heavy talk, eager for some sort of action.

"Wonderful," agreed Dr. Ahn. "But frightening."

On my way to see Nona, to say good-bye, I stopped by the children's hospice. I felt athletic in my sweatpants and sweatshirt, and noted to myself the irony that I was coming not from the outdoors but from confinement.

I was eager to see Stuart. I thought that maybe I would have time to make him another one of my paper horses.

But his bed was empty, perfectly made up and abandoned. Every sign of Stuart's presence, his comic books, his posters, was gone. Stuart was no longer here.

I told myself: When I open my eyes I will look and I will see him.

He was not there.

Nurses were watching. Keep an eye on Stratton Fields, they must have been cautioned. But because my family had built so much of the hospital, they would keep their distance, hover, follow me wherever I went, surrounding me with a careful silence.

Not here.

Stuart is gone.

Rick and Barry followed me, giving me a few moments with Nona. I leaned over her bed. What could I tell her?

Don't leave her, I told myself. Stay here with her, where you belong.

I kissed her lightly so she might not stir from her sleep.

She opened her eyes. For a moment she looked fearful. Then relief flushed her features. "I'm so glad it's you," she said.

There was no way I could bring myself to tell her that we had lost Stuart. We would grieve together someday, when she was strong.

Her eyes were beautiful. I wanted to stay just as I was, gazing at her. "Who else would it be?"

Her voice was weak but distinct. "I remember my dream," she said at last.

I waited for her to speak again.

"Rick," she said. "I'm afraid of Rick."

Part Six

60

I wanted my brother at home, in the house that belonged to my family. I wanted to be in the rooms that had heard my father's voice, felt the whisper of my mother's step.

There were questions I needed to ask him, and there was something I needed to destroy.

I had lost track of time. It was night, and I was surprised at the darkness. We left the hospital, and I felt like someone recovering a land he had lost, a survivor of a one-man voyage. The parking lot was not especially remarkable, but it looked, with its red lights and carefully delineated parking spaces, like a fragment of a beautiful world.

Ask him, I told myself. Ask him why Nona is afraid.

Something about Rick. Something about Rick isn't right. Something about Rick has never been right. Has it?

"Hurry up," said Rick, but I was amazed at the sounds of the darkness. I gazed around at the buildings, the sky. A car started. Someone laughed. People were talking, their voices far away.

I reminded myself that I couldn't leave Nona here. Something bad would happen to her.

Underfoot was the solid, gritty asphalt. I would have to call Renman. I would have to tell him that his experiment had worked. No doubt he had known that I would eventually end up with the same constellation of symptoms as my mother. Renman must have figured that I would do no harm, given a chance to spin out some of my own plans. The wise, careful man had won. I could bear him no malice. I had enjoyed my hours in the light.

"We're not driving straight there," I said. "There's something I have to do." It had nothing to do with Renman, or with packing one of my bags for a long stay away from home.

"Dr. Ahn's meeting with Dr. Skeat. They'll be waiting."

"I insist."

"Absolutely not," he said, but his determination was flickering.

"It will take just a few minutes."

No response.

"A few minutes. That's all."

Rick examined the keys in his hands. He looked around at the cars, the obscure figures of passing people on the sidewalk.

"I don't like it," he said after a long moment. The stiff, distorted conical shapes of the junipers, the winking red brake lights of passing cars, all seemed to trouble him.

An older brother has a lingering, minor sort of authority. "What harm can I do?"

We both seemed to find that amusing, in a grim way. Rick gave a toss of his shoulders, as though to say: murder, suicide. Nothing much.

He started the car. "I can have clothes shipped up to you. Books, tapes. You name it."

"Home first. Please."

"It's a bad idea." There was, however, no force in his words.

I thanked him, but the way he drove troubled me, wrenching the Alfa from one lane to another, glancing into his rearview mirror. At one point I asked him to slow down, and he did not seem to hear me.

It is an ancient irony, which Milton illuminated perhaps without fully understanding it himself: in the old story Adam fell because he loved Eve, because he was enough like God to be unable to forget his heart's companion.

I found the feather in the calfskin Milton. It left an imprint on the page, and the blood left a trace of black dirt.

It was a dim object, the blood filling its shaft. I found some matches in a drawer. A feather burns quickly, with the same frizzled swiftness with which hair will be consumed. I needed a second match to reignite it, but soon even the blood, which smoldered and gave off smoke, was gone, leaving a waxy residue of ash in the ashtray, and a sultry, clinging smell.

I put the volume carefully back into its place on the shelf.

Stratton.

I am still here.

I buried my face in my hands for a moment.

I didn't want her. I knew she did not exist. She had nothing to do with reality, with the land of day and night. The flickering image was there, to one side, that figure I had begun to realize was a symptom, a lapse of consciousness rather than a presence.

She had nothing to do with me. I averted my eyes, feeling the beginning of pain in my skull. Don't talk to her. Whatever you do —don't say a word.

She spoke my name again, a sound like a page turning.

She had never existed. Grab a few shirts, I ordered myself, and get out of here. I was a man sitting in the presence of a drug that had mastered him, poised, waiting for the toxin to take its grip.

She ascended into half-focus. And stood, milk-gowned, watching me, flickering, spinning. When I looked at her directly she dimmed, and when I looked away she grew sharp and bright.

"I'm finished," I said. I had meant to say: I am finished with you.

Her voice was like wind in sails, rippling. "You have not lost us, Stratton."

It was a struggle to remain upright. I did not answer her.

"What did you want? Your name. You wanted fame. And beyond that—nothing."

I hurried through drawers. I packed this shirt, that notebook, feeling futile, my acts senseless, my shadow falling and flowing over the room. "I am a creature of my time," I said.

I bit my lip. Don't. Don't talk.

"Ask, Stratton. Ask for something great."

"Great?" I echoed the word mockingly.

Tell her to leave. Silence her. But I couldn't—that was the problem. She was proof of how sick I was.

But her words caught me. *Great.*

No, don't think, I told myself. Hurry. Leave now. My lip was raw. I whispered, "You're challenging me."

Ask, I thought.

Why not ask?

I was excited for a moment. "I would like you to do something wonderful."

"What is it you want?"

My emotion faded. "You won't be able to do it."

We are real.

I was disgusted with myself. "What are you?"

"Something beyond your grasp."

"An angel?"

The silence pulsed around me. "You'll never understand."

"The ghost of my sister—who died before she was born. Is that what you are?"

There was a laugh, like the rush of wind in a tree.

"All of the unborn, all the people who never had a chance to live, the shadow people who want a part to play in life." I stopped myself. "Am I right?"

She did not answer.

"Nothing. An absence." I took a deep breath. "You did harm."

I was answered by the sort of silence a monument casts, a promontory, immense and dumb.

"I'm beginning to see that you can do nothing for me. The death of my adversaries, the conversation with my father, were all empty theater. It was all an effect of my imagination. And perhaps I actually killed Blake. And DeVere. With these hands."

These hands. I knew it was the truth.

A whisper, from all around me. "Nona's return to life?"

I did not want to talk about Nona. "Valfort is a great physician. Besides, maybe you had her nearly killed, and kept her, until I almost took my life. As a game."

The thought-voice was beautiful. "Have you lost faith in us?"

I wanted to laugh, but I felt sick. "You don't exist."

She spoke as with the voice of a stadium, packed with voices: *You'll never understand.*

Don't listen. "I have no interest in you. It's all in my mind." I was panting. "You've been proving that to me, little by little, and now I'm convinced."

"We are what you believe us to be."

I shook with quiet laughter, but it was a furious laughter, and I ached to seize this smudge of light in my hands.

I closed my eyes. Even so I could see her radiance through my eyelids, suffused with the color of my own flesh. Was she toying with me? Or did she, in truth, have power?

Bring Stuart back, I thought. Bring him back to life and health.

But I turned away. When we mature we climb to higher ground, leaving the quicker, lower years behind. The view is greater. The tower of our own making enters the sky. We see more of the landscape around us. We press brick upon brick and stand ever taller in the countryside of our lives. And if all that happens is our flowering ignorance, what have we accomplished?

Perhaps something. Something small. Perhaps we have exchanged one sort of ignorance for another, finer kind, a fabric old and human.

"Bring Stuart back," I said.

There was no response.

The light had vanished.

61

My mother had a wonderful singing voice. It was, however, a secret voice. She sang only when she thought no one was listening, and she would sing music that I had assumed were obscure snippets of madrigals or arias, tunes that I had not yet run across in Covent Garden or the Arena di Verona.

I would never find these songs in any library, although I tried. I came to realize that these songs were her own creation. She composed them, these private fragments of opera. They were

hers, perhaps one of the gifts the spirits had given her, a corollary
to her insanity.

If only I could recall any of the lyrics to her music. Or perhaps
what had sounded like words might have been a language of her
own invention. As so many times before, I found myself wondering what it was like to be my mother. Did she feel, sometimes, as
I felt now?

The night of my good fortune was at an end. The consequence
of my contract was about to unfold. If it had all been in my mind
—as I now believed—then it was my sanity that I was about to
see lifted away from me, that caul of thought that was about to
be stripped.

What I was facing was the possibility of my madness returning,
now, tonight. My shadow slipped down the hall ahead of me.

I descended the stairs. I called my brother's name, but there
was no answer.

Each room was empty. Until I found him at last.

It was an out-of-the-way room, one I did not enter except on
rare occasions, like this, when something—or someone—was
lost. "You took so long," said Rick. He had picked up a book
somewhere and had busied himself with it, but tossed it down
with an expression of relief.

It was one of Father's favorite books, his well-thumbed Plato. I
lifted my packed bag as proof that I had been busy.

"How are you feeling?" he asked.

"How do I look?"

"You know what they say about appearances."

"So I must look all right."

I realized that Rick had found some of his old clothes somewhere in the house. He had dressed this well once during a trial
for drunk driving. He had been acquitted, the jury persuaded,
many people felt, by his appearance. He had found his way into
the pages of *Esquire* over the caption, "Sway the jury with hang
of your tie."

The heavy old Plato did not belong here. Rick stood in what
my mother would have called the sun parlor. I had redesigned
this room as a memorial to my mother's taste, the way a concert
pianist might include, in his repertoire, a Liszt or Schubert that
his family had always enjoyed but which he himself did not especially like.

The room was decorated in the manner she most admired, the style of Louis Phillippe, big vases with cherubs, and straight-legged chairs upholstered with pink, romantic figures. I dismissed this period as precious and overly pretty, but the furniture in this room was authentic and well-constructed, and there was something about this evening that made this the right room for what might be my last moments in my own house.

"You can't run away," he said.

I found a place just outside the doorway in the hall shelf for the big old volume. When I returned I said, "I wouldn't dream of it. Where would I go? Montreux?"

"You could go anywhere."

I considered his tone. "You're serious."

"You don't have to come with me tonight."

"Dr. Ahn is expecting us." The final pronoun was a deliberate choice.

He made his familiar pistol-finger gesture, meaning: You're right.

My brother and I had often engaged in fraternal combat, of the happy sort. He and I were well matched, dissimilar, similar, and my father had called us "two thorns in a pod."

I was reluctant to begin. "Tell me, Rick—why is Nona afraid of you?"

We had walked down the hall before he made any response. He turned at the front door. He gave an incredulous laugh. "She can't be."

"Forgive me for asking. My thoughts are hard to control. Perhaps I'm speaking so much word salad. Why does she think that you tried to kill her?"

His head shook, just slightly, as though he were ordering himself to say nothing. "I'm not going to talk about this sort of thing until we meet with Dr. Ahn."

"You think what I am saying is the raving of a diseased mind." This was not a question. I let the nearly classical phrasing of the remark settle between us. Our talk would be direct but formal.

But he said exactly the wrong thing. It was his flippant, unfeeling manner that stung me. "If I tried to kill someone, they'd be dead."

"Unless you were interrupted before you finished by a nurse or an aide, or maybe just changed your mind at the last moment."

Rick did not bother to respond. He tucked my leather bag into what my family had always insisted on calling the "boot" of the car, in this case a very small storage compartment.

We sat in the car, shutting doors, busying ourselves with our own thoughts.

"My son the playboy" my mother called him. The phrase smacked of smoking jackets, martinis, party girls, an obsolete set of images. My mother had stopped paying attention to the world at some point in her young adulthood.

I did not plan my words. I did not know, really, from what part of me they originated. But I spoke clearly. "You resented Father for the pain he caused. You helped Mother kill him. Was it oleander, or did you use something else? You must have quadrupled Dad's tranquilizers. Must have taken a lot of it. Or some other medicine—poison," I corrected myself. "Something one of your starlet friends took for fun. I remember belladonna being all the rage at a party or two."

I stopped myself, aghast at my words. You can't say this sort of thing. You're talking to your brother about patricide. Think what you're saying. Look at your hands now. You're shaking. Don't say another word.

There was a light mist on the windshield. We sat silently in the car, the engine idling, my brother hunched at the steering wheel, staring ahead.

Then I broke the silence. The thought of anyone hurting Nona goaded me. "Maybe you resented me, too. Maybe you wanted me to succeed and at the same time destroy myself. Maybe you hired people to attack me. Maybe it wasn't the work of DeVere's friends at all. Maybe you told your gambling associates that if I died you'd inherit what little money I had—this house, for example. Or maybe you knew enough commissions were coming in to make the calf just fat enough to suit your purposes."

He nearly spoke but stopped himself. He looked away, through the small side window of the sportscar.

He's angry, I told myself. Of course he's angry. Or maybe he's afraid. Wouldn't you be afraid of a brother who sat right next to you in a car talking about such things?

But I would not stop. "Besides, you always felt that I was the good brother, the brother destined for something great. You tried to kill Nona because you knew that I was on the edge of complete mental collapse. You wanted me hospitalized. I think you like the thought of it even now. I can tell what you must have been thinking: Strater cracks up. I look good."

Rick broke his silence. "Mom's just like that. Under that genteel surface she's all venom."

"And how about you, Rick? Under your surface, what are you?"

He wrenched the car into first, the gears whining, then pulled away from the curb. The velocity forced me back into the seat.

I let Rick drive in silence for awhile. I knew that he was one of those people who find outlet, even expression, in driving. His way of cornering, tires squealing, his way of barely slowing at a stop sign—these were all silent counterarguments.

An intersection approached. Rick sped up.

In movies there is usually a chance for a stunt driver to swerve, skid, and avoid a lumbering vehicle or two. This was like nothing so much as Russian roulette. A light turned red.

And before the cars could start up and enter the intersection we were through it.

After the event I closed my eyes for a moment. "You're going too fast," I said.

Rick forced the engine to a higher pitch. I tensed, my hand stretched out to the dash. It had taken less than a minute to go from sporty momentum to lethal speed, but now we were racing down Nineteenth Street, cars and buses a blur.

We were going the wrong way.

We should have been heading north, but we were heading south. I struggled in my seat, twisting to look one way, turning to speak to Rick. "This is wrong!"

The speed forced me back into my seat.

I steadied myself. "Maybe I've been talking about things I don't understand," I said, trying to placate him. "What I'm saying can't be true."

We were on 280, the sportscar fishtailing across the lanes of freeway traffic. We shot around a truck in the fast lane, and whipped from lane to lane, avoiding cars on the mist-dampened freeway.

We were going too fast.

I glanced at the speedometer and the needle was jammed to

the right. The cars, the lanes, the shrubbery and the overpasses, were indistinct, erased by our speed.

The highway twitched, straightened. We were on Highway 1, the reflectors in the middle of the road a steady streak. At one time I had enjoyed danger, I told myself with thin humor. My voice was steady. "Slow down, Rick. Slow down and let me out."

The car went faster.

"I want out!" I shouted. I even thought of grabbing the steering wheel, but then cringed away at the recognition of the disaster that would result. "Slow down!"

Then he spoke. The feeling his voice was not anger, and it was not fear. "You're right," he said.

As soon as he said this I knew.

My God, he's going to kill us.

The hulking shape of a gasoline truck loomed ahead, outlined by pinpricks of red.

I turned to him, sure that I had not heard him correctly. Surely not. Or maybe he's joking.

He doesn't see the truck.

62

The truck was yellow.

It had black mudguards with golden reflectors, and each rubber flap was emblazoned with the shiny silhouette of a female form. A red sign on the truck said, in tall letters: FLAMMABLE.

The Alfa shrugged to one side as Rick stepped on the brakes. The force flung us from side to side. Rick let us slide all the way behind the truck, and then he jerked the wheel, driving with one hand, the other hand supporting his head, running through his hair, his posture casual, appearing to take only slight interest in what was happening.

The Alfa slid sideways. There was the smell of rubber, and the taste of diesel in the air.

I braced myself. I could hit Rick, I thought. I reasoned it through. I could take this fist and stun him. Maybe I could grab the gearshift and—or pull on the parking brake.

Maybe it's not as bad as it looks. Rick can drive. Look at him there, looking perfectly calm. He probably drives like this all the time when he's alone. He's always surviving accidents. This is just another—I stopped my thoughts.

I was about to think: another accident.

When the course of the car was steady Rick forced it even faster, slipping from lane to lane around cars, managing to pick up speed.

As he spoke his eyes were straight ahead, watching the road. "I ran across Anna Wick in L.A. at a party. She told me that Blake and DeVere planned to keep you from winning the Pacific International prize. I knew exactly what I should do. There was never any question. You know what the real irony is? Blake was getting ready to shoot himself. I basically stayed around and made sure he did it."

I tried to tell myself I wasn't really hearing any of this.

"DeVere was not at all ready to die," said Rick. "He tried to fight back. Threw a punch or two, tough-guy punches that missed by a mile. I'm like you, Strater. I'm in shape. He never had a chance."

Another joke, I tried to think. Another one of Rick's bad jokes.

He knew what I was thinking. "Can you really blame me? I was sick of the way those small people have their way. Little, ambitious people, and the rest of us are helpless. I did it because I wanted to help you."

Just a few minutes before I had accused him of helping to murder my father. That was somehow different. That was hypothetical, so archetypal as to be beyond emotion, plausible only because of the confusion I had been feeling.

Rick couldn't kill anyone. Surely he was lying.

Tears glistened on his cheek in the light from the headlights flashing by.

But his voice was steady. "The police were about to figure it out. Childress is so afraid of doing anything at all. But he knows

by now. You were so easy to deceive. You deserved a break, but I
was afraid that once you got what you wanted you would feel that
your world was disintegrating. Because that's what happens. You
win and you lose all at the same time."

"You don't have to drive like this."

"I tried to help, but I knew what you were like. How did I
know? How did I know what it was like to be you, Strater?"

I considered wrenching the door open. My hand was on the
door handle. We had to be going well over one hundred miles
per hour, the store fronts of Pacifica past us, the restaurants of
Rockaway Beach past us, too, the distant lights of buildings multicolored streaks.

"It's in the blood," said Rick. "We're a family of mutations,
creatures that really shouldn't be allowed to live."

Okay, I thought. Okay, it looks bad, but there's a way out.
Always a way out.

The ocean was out there, surf pale in the darkness. A beach
flashed by. Then we were high above the beach. There was a blur
of guardrails. The shoulder of the road was the edge of a cliff.
We were one hundred feet above the ocean.

I decided to keep talking. "We were good people. We made
things happen. Politics. Art. People admired us," I continued,
feeling myself, in a crazy way, involved in one of our adolescent
debates. I felt lucid and giddy. Why not argue family history at a
speed like this? It made as much sense as anything.

"We were better than the other people, weren't we?" cried
Rick over the noise of the engine.

"Maybe we were."

"I'm as sick as you are," he said, his voice so low that I was
certain I had not heard him correctly.

"You're just a little mixed up," I said. "Everything is going to
be fine." I was shouting the words over the keen of the engine.
Slow down.

The car left the road from time to time, leaping from a minor
promontory, rebounding from the crest of the road. The highway
was now a two-lane. Rocky embankment scorched past us in the
dark. This section of road, called the Devil's Slide, was irregular,
constantly washed by landslides.

Rick was laughing. Weeping and laughing.

How can he see?

We were on the wrong side of the road. An outcropping of rock flashed before us. Rick avoided it, all but a feathered edge of it. The car slammed to one side, and nearly spun all the way around.

I could think only: We're going to go off.

Off the cliff.

But we didn't. Rick had the car on the road again, and back at peak speed. Against my better judgment, I jacked the door open. I sensed more than saw the streaking black asphalt. It was inches away from me. It had a smell, damp and mineral.

The highway roared. It would kill me. I slammed the door. The door bounced open again. I worked the door shut, and then wished that there was something to hang on to as the car leaped and rocked.

Rick raised his voice so I could hear. "I was tired of seeing good people suffer. I was even going to let Nona die. I was going to smother her with a pillow. Besides, everyone associated with us should be destroyed, Stratton. Everyone."

He sensed my reaction. "I changed my mind. So I didn't do it. Don't be upset."

"You didn't kill Father, either. I don't know what made me think it."

"But I did. And you must have guessed why."

I tried to say no, but my voice was soundless.

"You thought Father was a god. But he used me, Stratton. Played with me and made me play with him, for years. I hated him. Didn't you know? Couldn't you guess? Maybe your exaggerated respect for him was your way of covering it up, hiding it from yourself."

I could not stand to hear my brother suffering so.

"What are you saying?"

"Sexually, Strater. Father abused me."

There's got to be something to say. Don't sit there like this.

"It wasn't right," he said, his voice broken. "That's all I wanted, Strater. Fairness. Justice. Haven't you ever wondered how such terrible things can happen?"

Maybe I said it out loud, and maybe I nearly shrieked it in every organ of my body: *I'm going to jump out of the car even if it kills me.*

"This is the way to do it. Finish it all off. Isn't it wonderful,

Strater? You have to admit it's wonderful! Do you know something? I'm proud of what I did because we put up with so much and I showed them. I don't care what you think, Strater, I did what had to be done."

I reached for the handbrake and Rick's grip stopped me.

The car was no longer on the road. At first I believed that we had touched off of a high point in the road, but then I registered what had happened.

We were in the air.

The sportscar lofted upward for awhile, carried by its own momentum, describing an arc up into the drizzle. It swept upward for what seemed like a long time, while the sight of the dashboard ahead of me was imprinted on my consciousness.

It was blond wood, varnished, and delicately grained. In one place the varnish was flawed, leaving a little pucker, an acne scar. My hands went out to this dashboard to steady myself.

There was a tickling vibration as the engine raced, full-throttle, and the tires spun against emptiness. I felt my weight shift sickeningly. I had that unmistakable sensation: The car was turning over. There was a sound, a banshee howl that I understood, vaguely, was my own voice.

Rick was beside me, silent, both hands on the wheel.

63

We tumbled.
    There was a scribble of surf. It swung past us, and when we saw it again it was much closer. There was the deafening sound of my own cry, a sound that tore my throat. The sky was a gray blanket, and the ocean was black.

I tried to work the door handle, but my hand slipped off. I gripped hard, straining, and yet the door would not open.

*   *   *

A darkness exactly the shape of my own body filled me. It was a perfect fit. It was all of me eclipsed—all but that residue, that remembered cheater of the dark, the mind.

And the mind said: Go to sleep. Rest. You must be tired. And no wonder. Don't try. Stay still.

I climbed.

At the same time, I slipped downward. My feet stirred the pebbles of the field. It was dark. My nasal passages burned. My eyes stung. My body was heavy. My figure was bronze, clad in barnacles and coral, one of those bed-thickened relics treasure hunters find. I felt myself frozen on the posture of one of those classic deities, a figure of Mercury, crust-clad and eyeless.

There, said my mind, the tones of implacable common sense. You see how useless it is to struggle. Just go to sleep. Forget everything.

I was too heavy. I would never make it upward. Why bother trying? But I needed air.

You must take a breath of air, I told myself, lest the potsherds and mud of the landscape force me to stay where I was. "Hurry up. Be careful. Don't waste time." These messages, the urgings of the appointment book, the airline schedule, the showing times at the corner cinema, had clothed my life.

In that twilight after adulthood has begun, foreign commands clutter the desk. We have lost money, or we have not. It is not enough to have loved, not enough to have mourned. Even honesty, the prideful election of the noble path, is not enough. There is something more, something humans cannot commit, that gathers the twigs from under the ancient tree so the roots can absorb the rain, a grace the days cannot touch, and the hands cannot administer.

The actual fall—the killing fall—has happened before we know it. There is only the aftermath. My body fragmented. I gasped, speaking a name. My brother's name.

Air. Air, and the sounds of surf.

It was the surface of the ocean. I had stepped through it like someone walking through a glass door. Fragments, lights, the sensation of a new temperature on the skin.

Rick. I must find Rick. I flung my arms, my legs, disoriented.

I breathed hard, treading water. Mist fell over my face, a cold wet wool. Sky, I told myself. And, over there, the cliff. Far up a pair of headlights broke the dark. A headlight winked as a figure passed before it. Another set of headlights arrived. I called out, called upward.

Then I dived, swimming with my strongest, surest strokes. Down here, I knew, was the car. Down there with my brother.

My hands churned the sharp rocks. I kicked, searched, and then had to find the surface again. I gulped air and repeated my search.

At one point during my search for Rick, flashing red lights joined the headlights far above us, on the cliff. I called out to them, but realized that my voice would not carry over the sound of the waves.

At another point, later, after much more searching, a spotlight swept the surf, igniting it. Vapor rose from the surface. The beam swept by me, missing me, groping across the tossing darkness.

I had to dive again, and this time I knew I would find him. I felt my way through an acropolis of stones, boulders, limpet-armored berms. Once I grasped what had to be a fragment of the car. A door handle, I told myself. That had to be what it was.

I studied this bit of treasure with my fingertips, blind, until lack of oxygen forced me upward. In the half-dark I examined my find. There was no chrome glitter. There was no flash of manu-factured metal.

I held a dark implement, an accidental tool. It was a worn spool of stone, nothing more. I threw the thing away, as far as I could hurl it. And then I saw him.

He was far away.

He must have kicked off his dark suit, because now his arms and shoulders were naked. He was swimming, hard, away from the beach. Away from land. He was swimming out into the Pacific.

I told myself that my brother and I were, athletically, well matched. There was a moment in which I saw this as a contest, a grand, reckless game. But then as I swam after him, I knew what was about to happen.

I must have known this, I thought, for a long time. That night when I found the glowing feather I must have known that this would happen. Perhaps this was the price of my soul. Perhaps the Others were taking Rick, or perhaps Rick was giving himself away, exchanging his life for mine.

That was absurd, I reminded myself. This was salt water, nothing more. I was strong. I knew the waves. Rick was in decent shape for tennis or a night of dancing, but this was my kind of fight.

I was gaining on him. He turned back and I saw, in the least flicker of a spotlight, that his face was masked in scarlet, his eye a metallic glint in the flow of blood. The sight pained me, but it pleased me, too. My brother was weakened. His arms were slowing down. His kick did not cause nearly as much spray as it had just a few moments before.

Artificial light has the characteristic of illuminating what it shines upon at the cost of increasing the darkness around it, even after the light has been removed. A beam shined high over our heads, hunted the swells, finding nothing, and then, with a deliberateness that pained me, the light went out.

I could imagine someone like Childress, someone impatient to have a cup of hot coffee, someone who ached for the prose of the office and the press release. Someone who was not like my brother and myself. I had never loved or admired my brother so much as I did just then as I swam, the cold creeping into the muscles of my thighs.

But then it hit me: We were abandoned now. Civilization, that little highway of order and hope, was about to leave us. Doors were being shut even then, engines started. Rational people had determined that nothing had happened.

We were alone.

My brother's pale arms churned the water. I followed him, digging hard with my hands, pulling myself through the water, gritting my teeth. Sometimes I got so close I could hear the sound of his feet lashing the swells.

The summer afternoons flashed upon me, the *pock* of the tennis ball, the swimming lessons taught by that muscular man with white eyelashes, a former Olympian with an accent that was, I realized now, Swedish. A Swedish swimming coach, I recalled now, baffled, puzzled, as always, over my father's unusual but always exactly correct string of instructors, ex-priests, scientists, former athletes muscled with both skill and experience.

We had been raised to see ourselves as people both favored and responsible. More was given to us, and more required of us. I could hear my father's laugh. His sigh. His way of announcing that he was tired and that he had to be up at "rosy fingered dawn."

Because I was tired now, too. I was too tired to keep swimming, but I did, thrashing, churning onward. He did it, I realized. It was not a joke, not a wry pose to see how I would react.

My father: I had never really known him.

Rick and my mother killed my father. Rick killed Blake, and DeVere. I was innocent. I should have felt relief. But what I felt was an experience of being foreign to my brother, a stranger to him. I also understood what he was doing.

My brother was winning the race. He was swimming faster, now, getting better at it as he found his pace, that steady, ever-forward pace that found him out far, far beyond anything I could do.

I thought, once, that I tasted his blood in the water, but surely that was an illusion, another one of my misperceptions of the truth, as I called to him at last. Called to him, his name going nowhere, the sea air absorbing, killing my cry.

Until he was gone.

I splashed, my legs kicking to keep me in place. He had been here moments before. Hadn't he? My lungs burned. I called his name, that single syllable, as though it had power to bring him back.

But I had arrived where there were no powers—no human powers—at all. There was silence, and no sign of him.

Except, as the mist thinned, far away, a flash of pale arms still swimming, outward, where no man could take his hand.

Part Seven

64

In the weeks that followed I spent hours in the sun. Nona joined me, shading her eyes as she watched me work in the garden. I planted an herb garden of myrtle, lavender germander, and sage. I trimmed the copper beech hedge, the beet-dark leaves scattering about to be raked. And I raked, shoveled, trimmed, and turned over the soil for a wild garden of purely native plants, wild radish, wild iris, lupine, and California poppy.

Nona said that she liked watching me work. I suggested videos, books, tapes, but she laughed. "You're more entertaining," she said.

"That's wonderful," I said. "Stratton Fields, comic gardener."

"Not comic, exactly. You look strong, digging and shaking the clods off the pitchfork like that."

"Someone for the gardener decathalon?" I said.

"I was thinking something a little sexier than that."

I gazed at her, a woman in a lawn chair and a large sunhat. "I thought sick people didn't have amorous intentions."

"I'm not sick. Anyway, they do. And it's called 'sex drive,' not amorous intentions."

"I belong to some other era," I said, only half seriously. "One that never existed."

"You look so intent," she said. "You hold up that clod of dirt like its going to talk to you."

"Anything to entertain," I said.

I worked for awhile.

"You are right about angels," said Nona.

Her words startled me.

She read my expression, and added, "You said once that if an angel came to talk to someone, it would be in a place like this."

"But you didn't mean to say that there are such things?"

Nona settled back in her chair, with an expression that said: I won't talk about them anymore.

She sipped from a blue cup. I had asked Collie to bring Nona whatever she wanted, and Nona ate a selection of cakes, biscuits, meringues, and sorbets, all accompanied by a beverage of milk and honey, laced with an underflavoring of black tea.

"We could live like this forever," said Nona.

Given world enough, I wanted to say, and time. I worked hard, laboring in the garden to put Rick to rest, to lay my father even deeper into the past, where he belonged. Earthworms spasmed. Roots struggled, and gave way under the plunge of my spade.

"We'll have breakfast every day over there, under that—what is it called?"

"The camperdown elm," I said. "You can have breakfast any-where you want."

She gazed at me from under her hat, the straw brim sprinkling her face with light and shadow. "With you," she said.

The gingko tree shaded the back garden. All of its branches were full of leaf. There was something about this that continued to trouble me. The presence of this resurrected tree reminded me of something I wanted to forget.

I worked in the hothouse, too, and Nona enjoyed the smell of the place, and the new small jungle that erupted around her. I showed her how to savor a ginger blossom like honeysuckle, and there were many flowers to pick, both white and yellow ginger, because that plant, a lovely tropical weed, was as yet the most prominent in the hothouse, although the heliconia and the anthuriums were in full leaf. They promised to blossom soon.

"Does your mother know about your brother?" asked Nona one morning as I opened a new bag of potting soil.

I breathed the fragrance of the mulch. I knew that, in a gentle way, Nona was testing me. She wanted to see what I was able to talk about. "It's hard to know what she understands. I went up while you were in the hospital and told her."

Anticipating the visit had been very grim, but the actual telling, aided by Dr. Ahn, had been a peculiar experience. My mother had insisted that Rick had died years ago, in an accident on the way home from a party. I did not have to suggest to anyone that, in a sense, she was right.

Nona had prescribed medication for me, and I took it. It had a striking effect on me at first, slowing me down and making my hands tremble. Nona remained out of touch with events at the hospital, although daily she was plainly closer to going back to work. She cut pictures out of magazines, and read storybooks, marking favorite pages, anticipating her return.

One Sunday afternoon Nona called to me. I leaned on my shovel and looked back to see her pointing.

"An old friend," she said.

The white cat paused at the edge of Nona's shadow, looking across the green lawn. It was happy to stay near Nona for the moment, accepting a caress. But when it began stalking a squirrel, creeping toward the gingko tree, I laughed and told it that we had already rescued it from that very tree once before.

The tree.

It was fully alive, and wore the deep green of a tree in its prime.

The day Nona returned to work at the hospital, I was in the hothouse, rolling up the hose. The brass nozzle trailed along the gravel and the moss-edged steppingstones.

The hose was wound into circles, and hung on its frame, when I stopped moving.

The air in the hothouse is warm, but it is also thick, a world apart from the other, thin-aired diaspora. No kitchen, no desk, only shelves of plants, those remorseless stalks and leaves. Sometimes when I was in that artificial environment I would be certain that someone was approaching, and I would cock my head to listen.

The glazed windows of the place played tricks on me, I knew. But I had the sensation that I was about to have a visitor, and I prayed that it might be a human, ordinary everyday sort of messenger, and not the other kind.

65

There was a tap at the hothouse door, and a cool wind from outside. The broad leaves around me stirred, with a pattering like rain.

"It's lovely here. A world within the world," said a familiar voice.

Valfort moved a glistening leaf to one side, and it painted his cheek with water as it fell back into place.

Nona stood behind him. There was a strange expression in her eyes.

I was surprised at how happy I was to see him.

"Please accept my condolences," he said.

I nodded, clearing my throat, unable to speak for a moment. "You knew."

"You told me a great deal during our session in Paris. I did not know what was true, and what was not."

"You thought I was the killer?"

"Because you thought you were. I was wrong. And, jealous." He smiled. "I still am."

"In a way, I wish I had been. My brother would be alive."

"Instead, you are innocent."

There was something of the charming opponent about Valfort even now. "No, I'm anything but innocent. I was wrong to be so ambitious," I said.

"Ambitious! You wanted more life," Valfort said. "You were

hungry for it. You were one of those people. I've seen them before. Hungry people create the world. You were hungry."

"I'm not well."

"You know the truth, now."

I looked away. "I'm taking a maintenance dose of Molindone. I haven't, thanks to the drug, had any hallucinations for weeks."

"But you feel that you have lost something. We see the horrors of heaven and earth open wide before us and we fix it. We take a pill. We get on with our lives, aided by chemicals with gigantic names. Do you have any idea how many well-known minds cannot function without some kind of help? Americans are a practical people. A medicine for any evil."

I brushed black flecks of leaf mold from my hands. "You don't approve of drugs?"

He chuckled. " 'Approve.' What an American concept. You simplify so much into like/dislike, agree/disagree."

"We lack the famous French gift for intellectual purity."

"We could work together, Stratton. I wonder now how sick you really are."

"What did you see when you almost died?" I asked. "That event that changed your life?"

Valfort had realized that the tear that ran down his cheek was water from a nearby leaf. He brushed at the trickle and moved away from the laua'e fern. "It's not what I saw—it's what I learned."

I gestured: Go on.

"I learned that there was not good, or evil, or Heaven or Hell. There were divinities, human qualities that endure. And we make them evil—or good—by our demands on them."

The effort of translating his experience into English seemed taxing. He lifted an eyebrow and smiled knowingly: You understand me.

I did not have to answer.

"I want you to come to Paris," he said, "to speak to the conference."

"I can't."

"Nona will not be able to address the committee. She is still recovering, although doing nicely. You have no choice. She needs you. The children need you."

The air was warm and felt nearly alive, closing around me. "If I knew that my visions are all over with. If I could trust myself. But I can't."

He shook his head, a single sideways movement of his chin. "You'll reconsider."

"I don't think so."

"If you don't, you're a fool," said Valfort. From such a man the word *fool* had the ring of an epithet. "I'm giving you the chance to make history. To move men and women to joy. To clothe and shelter your fellow human beings in things of beauty. Wake up, Stratton."

"You're a good man," I began.

His voice was sharp. "What is this preoccupation with being good? Who do you think you are?"

I looked away, into the maze of plants around me.

"Do forgive me for having yet another opinion that might displease you. It is simply that Americans think so much about themselves. Their own needs, their own feelings. Perhaps it is not an American characteristic so much as a characteristic of consumerism. In psychological terms we would call it 'self-monitoring.' How much time do you spend self-monitoring? Think about it."

"You make a graceful opponent," I said. "Never out of position."

"You can help Nona. Better than anyone else alive."

"I'd like to believe you. But I can't trust myself. I'm not sure what will happen to me."

"I'm flying to Paris in—I'm late." He used the French pronunciation of that city's name as though pleased to stop speaking English if only for a single word. There was a glint of Swiss timepiece at his wrist. "I want to meet you there tomorrow. Nona has the plan. She knows who'll be there, and how important it is."

I touched a leaf, a pearl of water spilling into a trickle, falling into my hand.

"Don't think. Do. You really do need help, don't you? Not the kind of help love or medicine or money or fame can bring."

I smiled sadly. He was right.

Valfort puzzled me by not leaving. He looked at me with a

kind expression, and then he said, "Something has happened. I want to prepare you for it."

I was mystified. Nona left, and Valfort and I were alone.

"Some things you never get over," said Valfort. "Some bad things. And maybe some good things. You don't blame yourself for losing your brother, do you?"

Valfort had a way of knowing what troubled me. "No. Not really." There was a chill inside me. The Pacific had been so cold that night. "But he's gone, nonetheless."

"Exactly," said Valfort.

His casual dismissal of my grief, my own considerations, irritated me. "Make your plans without me," I said. "I can't even begin to consider—"

I stopped myself. Something was about to happen. I took a breath and parted my lips to ask what was happening, and there was a step at the door.

Nona was there in the doorway, the fresh scent of the outdoors among the plants. "Come outside, Stratton," she said.

My eyes asked the question.

"You have a visitor," she said.

Valfort's eyes, and Nona's, were alight. I brushed my hands again and found a place on the shelf for the trowel.

I was wary, and at the same time hopeful, even excited. But I told myself: Don't go.

Don't listen to them.

You don't want to see this.

66

The safe warmth of the hothouse mingled with the tide of air from the outside.

"What is it?" I said. "What's out there?"

His voice was gentle. "The world we live in does not make much sense to us," said Valfort. "But there is no reason to be afraid."

Here, surrounded by my tropical plants, I was safe—I knew what was real.

He motioned with his hand—*hurry*.

The sun outside was bright, and the air was cool.

There was a boy I did not recognize sitting on the grass, holding a large pair of shears. He was toying with them, distracted from the workings of the tool by the sound of my step.

He leaped to his feet, and ran with the shears dangling from one hand, and I could not move.

You'll hurt yourself.

Think about this, I told myself. Think hard. This is just another trick.

I turned back to see Nona, for some guidance from her. The sunlight was too bright, and I could not make her out.

He was a child perhaps seven years old wearing ordinary children's clothing, jeans, a bright green T-shirt emblazoned with an alligator, a smiling, cartoonish character.

What was happening was both clear and disjointed.

He tugged my hand. He wanted to lead me somewhere.

I said his name. He looked at me, smiling and squinting against the light.

Could I trust this? Was this happening?

He had gained weight, and he looked more three-dimensional than he had in the past, more real.

My hands, my body, belonged to someone else. Finally, I found myself able to talk once more. "I thought you were gone."

Gone. The word was a gasp, a solid door.

I couldn't believe. He was going to vanish in another heartbeat, I knew. He slipped something folded up, a piece of paper, into my hand.

Then, abruptly, as though shy, or unsure of his surroundings, "Are you still sick?"

"No," I said. "I take medicine." Then, my voice breathless, I said, "You aren't sick, either."

Stuart did not answer.

"I trim trees with those," I said. "They're very sharp." I uttered the words with a feeling of incredulity, someone experimenting in a foreign place with a strange language.

I wanted to hear his voice again. I wanted to believe it was possible.

"They're big," he said.

I saw how large and ancient this house must seem to him, and this garden, these shears.

He spoke before I could respond. "It might come back," he said.

I must have looked confused.

"My sickness," he said.

It might. That was the weight of our lives.

"He was in remission," said Nona, "that night you tried to find him. He had already begun to recover well enough to be sent home."

And then I believed it. The heft of the shears as I took them from Stuart, worried that he might cut himself, reminded me that this was happening. This was actual—the blades were gray, glazed with years of green. I let the shears fall onto the grass. I knew: This was real.

And I allowed myself joy. I put my arms around him.

Then he released himself and pried open my hand. The paper horses in my hand unfolded just a little, as though coming to life, or perhaps the tension in the paper from being folded allowed them to re-erect themselves.

"These are old," I said. "I'll make you some new ones."

He smiled, pleased at the thought, but took the old ones back, as though to protect them against harm.

"I like the old ones," he said.

I made him other horses, and frogs that jumped, and a paper airliner, one that flew, gliding in a way that delighted him, and he unfolded it carefully, and refolded it in a new way so he could keep that, too, in his pocket.

We clipped a hedge so he could see how the big shears worked, and he raked the leaves and the stems, piling the cuttings using a tool that was too long for him, and when we were done he ran to get the bicycle I mentioned was in one of the buildings bordering the garden.

It took awhile, and there must have been a moment in which I told myself that this was not happening. This was not real. You see, some voice in me must have murmured—he's gone.

He came back again steering a bicycle that cast ripples of sunlight on the grass from its bright, slowly spinning wheels.

67

Nona had insisted. We could get out of the cab and walk across the Pont-Neuf.

"I don't want you getting too tired," I said.

"Don't be silly."

So we were holding hands, gazing down at the river, figures stepping quickly past, people walking small dogs. It had stopped raining. The clouds broke into dozens of fragments, like flagstone flung down into bits.

The plane trees had grilles around their trunks, ironwork that does not constrict the tree so much as give it definition, like the lace collars in a Flemish portrait. The quays along the Seine were pocked and dimpled with fossil shells.

"Why did I bring an umbrella? It's totally unnecessary," said Nona. She wore an overcoat Anna Wick had designed, and a beret that had arrived in a box with a note from Anna herself.

The note had displayed the quick, dashed-off look of a message that has been carefully considered: "You deserve every good thing from now on." I had thought the note, in its fortune-cookie rhythm, betrayed either jealousy or a stylistic clumsiness.

Notre Dame shivered in the Seine. The city was suspended, upside down, an imperfect memory of itself. A barge, as long as a black building, approached the bridge. The coal glittered.

"Dr. Valfort doesn't think you're coming," she said.

"Why not?"

"He doesn't know you the way I do."

"He'll be surprised."

"And pleased."

We leaned on the railing of the bridge. "Are you all right?" she asked.

The feeling kept returning: *This was all about to end.*

I reassured her. No, I saw nothing, heard nothing, only Paris around us. Except—perhaps they would come for me now, at this moment of happiness. Maybe this is the hour they would select to seize me.

Seeing Stuart again had been a cause for joy, but afterward I had felt a strange combination of happiness and dread. Before Stuart's return I had begun to believe that the visions were a symptom of mental illness, that there were no Powers, no soul.

Now I was not sure of anything.

I understood, now, how little I had known about my father. I had kept myself from truths I must have known, in one part of my mind. Now I fully possessed my memories, but I had, at the same time, lost the fiction of a wise, loving father.

I could not shake the feeling that the night of my good fortune was over.

The barge passed under us, on its way south.

I insisted on taking a taxi at last. There was a disagreement. The distance was too short, said the driver, but Nona reassured him, and the man drove without further complaint. I paid him what must have been quite a bit, forgetting to even count the money, not caring. He was cheered by the amount. In English, speaking carefully, he wished us good luck.

The reception was a hive of people accustomed to power. I recognized two foreign secretaries and a number of people whose wealth was legendary. Security people circulated, mixing with the crowd.

The thought kept repeating: *all about to end.*

"You'll never be able to sell your ideas to a group like this."

I knew the voice well. I turned and a thin, tanned woman offered me her hand. "It's good to see you," I said, and I meant it. I introduced Nona to Margaret, my ex-wife.

"Stratton can do anything he wants to do," said Nona.

"Can't we all?" asked Margaret. She gave Nona a moment in which to say something barbed, but Nona held my hand and gave Margaret a pixyish smile.

I considered Margaret's words, and then said, "Margaret refined iron to an airy thinness years ago. She has a special brand of pessimism."

"Men like a hard woman," said Margaret, and gave a toss of her head, a mannerism I recognized as meaning, in this case: Who cares what men like?

"Men have always been especially fond of you, Margaret," I said. I could not help noticing how dissimilar the two women were.

"I think everything should be done to help kids. I'm interested in issues," said Margaret, her eyelids half closed. "Sick kids, dead whales. It's just—look at these people. Oil people. Politicians. A few of the politicians even have a future. My husband—you see him over there with the sunburn." She spoke with a careful lifelessness. "But Stratton—let's face it. These people are here so their wives can stock up on perfume and lingerie."

"I used to find Margaret's brand of boredom attractive," I said, turning to Nona, but then giving Margaret a smile I knew she would recognize as: *It was nice seeing you—now go away.*

Margaret acknowledged the smile with a sigh. "Stratton—I was sorry about Rick. Poor Rick. And he was always so charming. I suspected he was disturbed, of course," she added, leaning close to Nona but not lowering her voice.

Once again I was out of practice, not prepared for Margaret's breathtaking lack of feeling.

"Stratton's been good to me," said Nona. "And he misses his brother very much."

"Anyway," Margaret said after a pause, "I look forward to your speech, Nona."

"Strater's doing the talking," said Nona.

"Stratton's going to convince all these people to give away their money? This will be interesting. Good luck," said Margaret in the way that means: You don't stand a chance. She withdrew a cigarette from her handbag, and she held it in a way that seemed to indicate that she expected someone to light it for her.

Someone did, a man in a DeVere tux, snapping a DeVere platinum lighter.

"She likes you," said Nona, when we were briefly alone together.

"She doesn't 'like.' She enjoys herself, though. And we're even friends, in a distant, steel-lined sort of way."

At the edge of the crowd Margaret joined her husband. She said something to him, something about Nona and myself, I sensed from the way she nearly glanced over at us. The red-faced man laughed aloud.

Valfort shook my hand, his grip strong. "I am a little surprised," he said.

"You had no faith in me."

"I was a fool to worry."

"I'm afraid I don't like my speech, though." I had it in my pocket, blue index cards fastened with a paperclip.

"Ah," said Valfort, that single sound indicating an entire chapter of feeling, anxiety, regret, hope. I could sense how badly Valfort needed me, just then, how badly he wanted the meeting to go well.

I was embarrassed. I should not have been so frank. I had worked hard on my remarks, but I thought that Margaret might be right. I did not have a chance.

"Stratton has what it takes," said Nona. "Don't worry about him."

All about to end.

The Salle du Haut Conseil was crowded. There were worry beads and silk burnooses, there were dark-suited figures, there were security guards every few paces against the windows. Beyond was the distant view of Notre Dame, her flying buttresses keeping her in place under the dissolving clouds.

Valfort gave opening remarks in French, and then there was

polite applause as he said my name. I slipped the blue notecards from my pocket.

Useless. How could I possibly succeed? And Nona needed me. Children needed me. I felt my faith in myself, which had been weakening, crumble completely.

I stood behind the rich mahogany of the lectern. I could see curiosity—a questioning study from this distinguished crowd that was not altogether friendly. They had heard about the death of my brother to the point that they were all probably weary of hearing his name. The reputation of my family was great enough that I would have received polite attention in any event. Now, however, the attention was mixed with respect and a kind of vague pity. I was one of those common figures in public life, the survivor of a series of famous tragedies.

I slipped the paperclip into my pocket. I surveyed the words on the cards. I stacked the notecards into a neat pile and looked up again at the blur of faces. This collection of earnest platitudes about the importance of children would sound lifeless. A row of translators leaned forward at a side table, ready to translate whatever I was about to say.

Nona's eyes encouraged me from the front row. Valfort sat beside her, his hands folded, his eyes expectant.

I glanced down, ready to speak. And there, on the lectern, diagonally across the first card of notes, was a glowing blue feather.

Someone did this.

Someone playing a trick.

The room was hushed, one person fiddling with the receiver in his ear, a security guard crossing his arms at the back of the room.

There was a movement, a subtle quickening of the air. A figure entered the room from a side door. It was a woman in a flowing gown, a garment of vibrant white.

68

Not possible, I knew. Not real.

People were waiting for me to speak, and the silence was heavy, now, the self-consciousness of an audience that begins to know that things have gone awry.

She has come for you. You were right—it's all over.

Talk. Go ahead. Pretend nothing's wrong. It is, after all, what you were trained to do, something you can manage after years of habit. You should be good at it by now.

Go ahead. Begin.

The woman in white spread her arms as though to indicate: *All of these people belong to me.*

Why couldn't she have waited just a few minutes? I was sweating. I held the lectern to keep from slumping.

She took her place among them, another presence in the crowd. And then I knew.

Each of the faces around me was glowing, a source of light. I gazed about myself at the assembled people. And I saw that all of these men and women had bargained their souls. None of them were whole. All of them were missing that vital part, and in exchange for this loss had arrived where they were.

Perhaps I was mad. Perhaps not.

Did it matter?

I slipped my notes into my jacket pocket. Nona's eyes were wide. Valfort put his hands over his face.

I took a deep breath.

I prayed. *Make them understand. Make them help the children.*

I began to speak.

Our essence, I said, has already been given to the powers of life and death, the powers we cannot control, or understand. It does not matter what we are, what immortal part we manage to cadge from the confusion of life, because in the end—what are we?

The void is complete, but backlit by our temporary passions. What can be kept is not alive. Morning is coming, the days to come, when we are stone and water, but new people, our children, gather in rooms like this. What matters is how we turn to our children, and what we offer them.

Nothing else is human. Nothing else lifts the sky over our heads—the empty, meaningless sky—or makes the earth a home.

I spoke without being fully aware of the words I used. It was as though I were swimming back to a land I had thought long lost, barely conscious of what I was doing.

When I was finished there was a long silence.

I could not bear to look up. Nice try, Stratton, I told myself. You stood here for half an hour, an hour—who knows how long? And you have only the barest idea what you've been saying. Face it: You've been speaking gibberish, ruining everything.

You have let Nona down.

One person began to clap. It sounded like strained politeness. Then another person joined in, and then there was a rush of applause.

The audience was on its feet, and the sound was deafening.

Nona was smiling through tears, and I was stunned. Valfort was nodding, saying something to Nona, and she was nodding back, keeping her eyes on me.

The applause continued. The source of light on the lectern dazzled me as I gazed at it. I closed my fingers around the plume. I could know nothing. I had joined with powers I would never understand. Did I really want to do this? Couldn't I, even now, turn back?

Nona's eyes were on mine, and she was smiling, saying something to me.

Its light flowed through the fingers of my closed hand. I slipped the quill into my jacket pocket.

I could feel it there, over the beating of my heart.